The Knight Marshal

KIRALYNN EPICS

The Silk & Steel Saga

Book One: *The Steel Queen*

Book Two: *The Flame Priest*

Book Three: *The Skeleton King*

Book Four: *The Poison Priestess*

Book Five: *The Knight Marshal*

Book Six: *The Prince Deceiver*

Book Seven: *The Battle Immortal*

Additional books by Karen L Azinger

The Assassin's Tear

Power Writing: Make Your Genre Fiction Soar

THE
KNIGHT MARSHAL

BOOK FIVE OF

THE SILK & STEEL SAGA

Karen L. Azinger

KIRALYNN EPICS

Published by Kiralynn Epics L.P. 2013

Copyright © Karen L. Azinger 2013

First published in the United States of America by Kiralynn Epics 2013
Second Edition 2018

Front Cover Artwork Copyright Greg Bridges © 2013

Celtic Lettering used with permission of Alfred M Graphics Art Studio

The Author asserts the moral right to be identified as the author of this work

ISBN   978-0-9910297-0-9

Library of Congress Control Number: 2013918756

For Rick

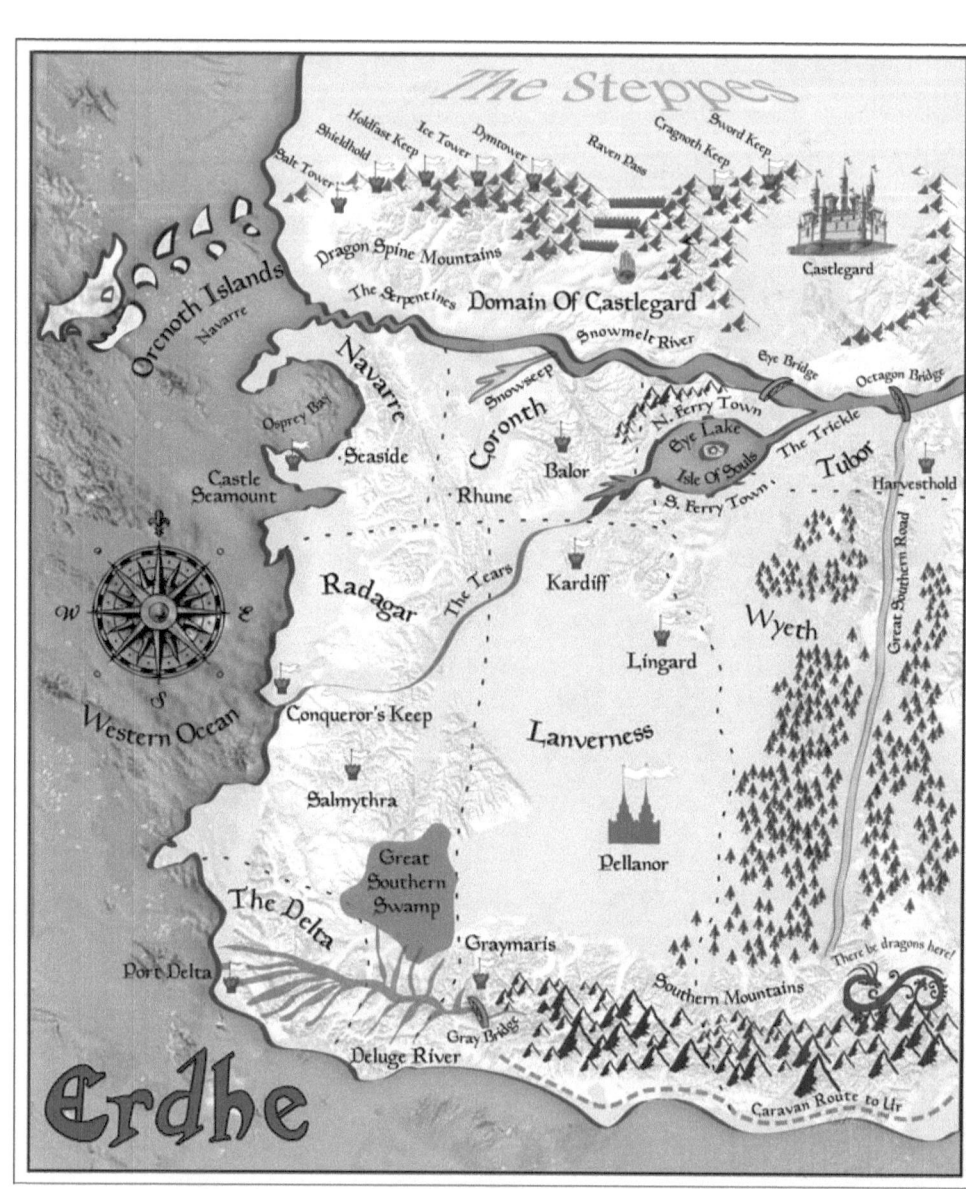

Prologue

Fear stowed aboard his ship, like an enemy waiting to strike. Lord Askal prowled the deck, noting the signs. His men scuttled away, avoiding his sharp-eyed stare, yet he saw their furtive glances and the way they fingered handmade charms to ward against evil. Fear stalked his crew till they saw ill omens in every creak of the deck, in every luff of the sail, in every screaming seagull. Offerings to Naff dangled from the prow, bits of jewelry and gold, claimed now and then by a gray wave's angry slap, but his crew's alms to the sea god were for naught. The gnawing unease festered and grew, arguments erupting over the smallest insult. Already he'd lost three men to knife fights and two to careless missteps, including one swept away by a rogue wave. Fear at sea was something a MerChanter lord rarely experienced, yet he recognized the signs, like a dry rot eating his ship's soul. Lord Askal strode to the helm, cursing his orders, knowing the only remedy was speed.

"Come two points to starboard. Keep the lines taut and the sails full. I'll not waste a breath of wind till we reach the south."

"Aye, captain." The helmsman adjusted the tiller and the *Dark Fin* surged forward like a hungry shark.

Braced upon the deck, Lord Askal took pride in his ship's brisk response. Square sails snapped overhead while a hundred-and-seventy oars plowed the foam-flecked sea. The mighty trireme cruised south, slicing through a dark ocean with all the dread of her namesake. A hull painted black as pitch, her proud sails blood-red and her bronze ram fashioned like a shark's toothy snout, she cut a fearsome figure. A coastal raider, the *Dark Fin* was built to be fast and lethal, the pride of the MerChanter fleet, yet for all her speed, his ship could not outrun the fear ripening in the captain's cabin.

It crept aboard with their passengers. By order of the Miral himself, they'd docked at the Dark Citadel, taking on a young fair-haired lord and twenty of his retainers. The lord was accorded a rare honor, given sole occupancy of the captain's cabin, while the retainers berthed among the crew. Setting sail under stormy skies, they carved a path through wintery seas, running for a port in the distant south.

At first, the stowaway went unnoticed, the fear masquerading as miasma. The young lord remained in his cabin, and his retainers kept to themselves, but all too soon the rumors began. It started with small things: a keg of wine gone sour, a side of beef spoiled, an albatross following in the ship's wake. And then the nightmares began. Evil dreams plagued his crew. Some swore they heard claws raking the ship's hull while others dreamt of a cavern weeping bloody teardrops. Exhausted and edgy, his crew turned sullen, looking for something to blame. Whispers circulated about a strange red light in the captain's cabin, an otherworldly glow, like crimson hellfire summoned by a sorcerer. Some said the hellfire would burn a hole clean through the hull, condemning the *Dark Fin* to a watery grave. Determined to quell the doubt, the lord ordered a double guard placed on his cabin, and he himself kept watch on more than one night. Rumors of the strange red light proved true, but there were no demons in the night, no claw marks on the deck, and no holes in his ship. Lord Askal kept a tight rein on his men, ordering quick discipline for any infractions, but superstition and dread were not so easily quelled. His ship sailed south with fear growing in its hold.

He moved to the railing, staring down at the wind-tossed sea. *Still too dark,* a good sailor judged his ship's reckoning by the sea's color. Waves the color of gray-green slate lapped against the hull, proving the *Dark Fin* was still in the grip of colder climes. Dark and forbidding, the ocean stretched to every horizon. They needed more speed.

A rogue wave slapped the hull, sending a salty spray across the railing. Kissed by the sea, Lord Askal licked his lips and laughed, relishing the briny taste. Born on a ship, forever at home in stormy weather or glassy calm, he reveled in the slap of wave and wind, the sway of the deck beneath his boots and the beat of canvas overhead; but for once he wished for land. He longed for a reason to put his passengers ashore. Fear mired with superstition proved hard to kill. He gripped the hilt of his cutlass, preferring a clean fight to the filthy murk of dark magic.

"Lord Captain." It was his second, Tormund, a swarthy man with plundered gold lining his teeth and an eight-armed octopus tattooed around his right eye. "Can I have a word?"

"Aye."

Tormund joined him at the railing. "It ain't right."

Lord Askal waited. Tormund was a good man but he always crabbed sideways around an argument.

"We're sea wolves, meant to be raiding the southern shores not hauling passengers to distant ports." He shook his shaggy head, gold beads clattering amongst his braids. "It ain't right, and the men know it."

"We sail under the Miral's orders." Tormund growled like a kicked dog, but the captain pressed the point. "The *Miral* himself ordered safe conduct for the passenger and his men. Not a man among us will gainsay the Miral." He held his second's gaze, but what he didn't tell him, was that the Miral's orders said the young lord was to be obeyed. *Obeyed!* Since when did a MerChanter Sea Lord *obey* a landlocked lord! The mere thought made his blood run cold as seawater. Grinding his teeth, he swallowed his anger. "Keep the sails full and the rowers at quick-time. The sooner we reach the south, the sooner we'll see the backside of our passengers, and then we'll sharpen our tridents and ransack the southern cities. Tell the crew their share of plunder will be doubled."

"Aye, captain, that'll give the lads something to crow about." Tormund tugged on his beard, "But the young lord is asking fer ya."

"For me?" He gave his second a sideways glance. "What for?"

"Damned if I know." He flashed a crooked grin gleaming of stolen gold. "But he's got landsickness. Your cabin reeks of it."

A faint hope flickered within the lord. "Perhaps he's had enough of the sea." He sent a quick prayer to Naff, offering half a year's worth of plunder if the sea god would take the strange lord off his hands. "Mind the sails and I'll see what this land-lord wants."

Lord Askal took his time, sauntering across the aft deck and down the stairs. He paused to check the trim of the sails and watched the top tier rowers for a dozen drum beats before turning to knock on the cabin door.

The door creaked open and a stunted man with a barrel chest dressed all in black peered out. A voice from behind said, "Let him pass, Dolf."

The servant bowed, opening the door wide, and the captain entered his own cabin for the first time in a fortnight. His nose rankled at the sour smell. Portholes gaped open but the nasty stench of landsickness prevailed. He glanced around his cabin, noting the changes. Chests were stacked along one wall, probably filled with flippant finery. His bunk was disheveled and his chart table littered with thick, musty tomes. The fair-haired lord sat in the only chair, swathed in a thick black robe, his blond hair straggled, his face ghost pale. Lord Askal hid a smile; the sea had a way of exacting its own vengeance. He offered the Mordant the barest of nods. The young land-lord carried a fearsome title, but his face was too young for the dread deeds ascribed to his name. Clearly he'd inherited the title from another. "The sea does not agree with you?"

The Mordant met his stare. "The sea was never my domain."

Such an odd answer, yet everything about this young land-lord struck the captain as odd. "You asked to see me?"

"I have a request."

"A request?"

The Mordant smiled, but his blue eyes remained cold as polar ice. "More of an order." The black-clad servant moved to stand behind his master. Small in stature yet he conveyed a feral threat, a baldric of nine throwing knives strung across his muscled chest.

Lord Askal kept his hand resting on his cutlass. "I'm listening."

"I have a need for certain ingredients."

"Ingredients?"

"A sea bird, whole and uninjured. And two of your men."

"Two of my men?"

"Yes, my plans have changed. An old enemy grows bold." For half a heartbeat, rage flashed across the Mordant's face, but then it was gone, hidden beneath glacial ice. "I have need of a courier. A sea bird and two of your men will suffice."

Lord Askal narrowed his gaze, outrage boiling in his voice. "I've orders to carry you south, nothing more."

The Mordant flashed a snake's smile. "You've orders to *obey*."

The words struck like a slap, yet Lord Askal remained statue-still. "Why use my men when you have plenty of your own?"

"I need their souls."

So the rumors prove true. Lord Askal retreated a step. *"Dark magic!"* He made the words a curse.

"Yes."

A sudden chill gripped the cabin, like standing in the teeth of a winter storm. "You brought fear aboard my ship."

"Superstition is a sign of weakness. It does not change my needs." The Mordant smiled like a shark certain of a meal.

Sweat broke across the lord's brow. Granting the request was unthinkable, yet the Miral charged him to obey. Caught between a rock and a wave, Lord Askal stalled, seeking another tack. "But I thought you needed to reach the south with all speed?"

"True."

"If my crew mutinies you'll never see land."

"Then you'd best keep them in hand."

"Then you'd best leave my men alone."

The servant reached for a dagger but the Mordant raised a pale hand. "No."

A cold stalemate settled across the cabin.

"Your ship is built for raiding."

Lord Askal nodded.

"It matters not where the men come from, only that they are whole and hearty." The Mordant grinned, his eyes like chips of ice. "You have till sunset tomorrow to supply my needs." His words reeked of dismissal.

Anger warred with abhorrence. The captain locked stares with the Mordant, fighting the urge to run his sword through the landsick lord and offer his body to Naff, but the law of the Miral stayed his hand. Gripping the hilt of his cutlass, he slowly backed toward the door, not daring to turn his back. Reaching the door, he fled his cabin for the clear light of day, shivering in the pale sunshine. He strode to the railing, gulping deep breaths of crisp, clean sea air, needing to clear his head and his heart. Setting his face in a stern mask, he climbed to the aft deck. "I need the sea charts."

Men leaped to obey, unrolling the chart on the helmsman's table.

Tormund joined him, a thousand questions in his stare.

Lord Askal studied the chart, noting their position. His finger traced a line to the nearest island. "Helmsman, come ten points to the larboard side and double the beat. We sail for the Orcnoth Islands."

Orders rang out and his men sprang to life. Canvas snapped overhead and timbers creaked as the ship heaved to port. The drumbeat in the hold quickened. Oars bit deep in the swirling sea and the *Dark Fin* leaped forward like a shark scenting blood.

Beside him, Tormund growled, "Why? There's not but sheep and herders on those rocks."

"Exactly." The lord gave him a sharp look, dispelling further questions. "And summon the net men to the aft deck. I want the albatross captured whole and unharmed."

"Unharmed?"

"Aye, you heard me, whole and unharmed." His anger brewed to a storm. "Now snap to, or you'll find yourself chained to an oar!"

Tormund's face paled, his eyes growing wide, but he did not argue. "Aye, sir!"

Men scuttled across the aft deck, anxious to obey. Lord Askal paced the *Dark Fin*, barking orders to trim sails and tighten sheets, pressing for speed. Prowling the deck, he studied every detail of wind and wave, sail and oar, using every scrap of seaman's lore to hasten his ship. Under his touch, the *Dark Fin* responded like an eager lover, slicing through the slate-gray sea, but he worried it was not enough. Even with a favorable wind, they'd be lucky to reach the small isles before sunset tomorrow.

All through the afternoon and into the night, he stood watch, coaxing every drop of speed from his ship. A pale moon rose and set and still they sailed. The *Dark Fin* cut the sea like a knife, cleaving a sparkle of luminescence in her wake. The captain breathed deep the salty scent, the ocean thrumming in his veins. This was what he was meant to do, to pilot a mighty ship and plunder the coast, not dabble in dark magic; yet he could not gainsay the Miral, so he sailed on, desperate to save his crew.

The sun rose red and bloody.

Bleary-eyed, the night crew sought their bunks while the day crew claimed their duties. Tormund came to relieve him but he waved him away. "Not yet."

The wind shifted, adding extra speed to his sails, as if the sea god heard his pleas. Dark oars flashed and dipped, cleaving the water with an urgent rhythm. A pair of dolphins rode the bow, an escort from Naff, but it did not dispel the tension riding his shoulders. He paced the deck, anxious for the first glimpse of land. The sun reached the noon zenith and still they sailed. Sweat beaded his brow.

"*Land ho!*" The bow lookout sang the sighting.

Lord Askal gripped the railing in relief. "We did it." Pride rushed through him, certain there was not a faster ship in all the oceans. He turned to the helmsman. "Make for the nearest rock."

"Aye, captain."

The *Dark Fin* raced towards the island. Like hungry teeth the outer Orcnoths rose from a wave-tossed ocean, white foam breaking on a jagged shore. Sharp craggy rocks and tenacious green grass, the remote islands were good for nothing but sheepherders and fisher folk.

Tormund joined him on the aft deck, his gaze full of questions. "Why the Orcnoths when there's not a speck of plunder among them?"

Lord Askal motioned his second close. "Lead the raiding party. Take what you will from the island, but bring me two men, whole and unharmed and return to the ship before sunset."

"Why?"

His temper rose to a boil. "Obey!" His voice dropped to a harsh whisper. "And perhaps this dark curse will be lifted from our ship." Turning from his second, he snapped an order at the helmsman. "Take us in."

With an impatient sweep of his dark blue cape, Lord Askal left the aft deck, pounding down the stairs to his second's cabin. Little more than a closet, yet it had the luxury of a single hammock. Aboard ship, privacy was the coin of privilege. He flung open the only porthole to admit a breath of fresh sea air and climbed into the hammock, trying to still his racing thoughts. The hammock's sway helped, like being rocked in the sea's bosom. He must have dozed, waking to a sharp knock on the door.

"It's done." Tormund stood in the doorway, backlit by the red glow of sunset.

Instantly awake, he climbed from the hammock. "You got two islanders?"

"Just as you ordered."

"Good. Take us back out to sea."

"Aye, captain."

He followed Tormund to the aft deck. His crew looked lively, turning the great trireme back out to the fathomless sea. The deck shuddered beneath his boots and canvas billowed overhead and then the *Dark Fin* leaped forward keen for the open ocean. The sun hung above the horizon, a great red orb nearly set, spilling crimson and gold onto the briny deep.

A whimpering sound came from the rear. Two captives, shackled and chained, huddled by the railing, stinking of fear. Sheepherders by the look of them, a father and son, nut-brown and filthy but they seemed whole and unharmed.

On the other side of the deck, an albatross sat trussed in nets. The great sea bird stared at him with an accusing eye. He regretted the need for the bird. The lore of the sea named it unlucky for any sailor to harm an albatross, but he'd pay any price to keep his men safe and his ship whole.

A shadow swept across the deck.

He turned to find the Mordant watching him. The pale lord was wrapped in thick dark robes, his right hand clutching an iron staff, his knife-bedecked servant hovering like a shadow at his back. "Well done."

The praise sounded slimy in his ears.

The Mordant stared toward the setting sun. "I require the use of your rear deck at dark fall."

"I steer my ship from the aft deck."

The Mordant did not seem to hear. "Once the last of the light leaves the sky, order your men below, confined to quarters until morning. I'll brook no interference this night."

"I'll not leave my ship to founder."

"Don't you trust your sea god?"

"The sea god expects a captain to look after his ship."

The Mordant nodded, a sly smile playing across his face. "Then you alone may remain," his eyes darkened, like looking into two bottomless wells, "but if you interfere, you will die, and if you watch, you will be forever changed."

"I'll take my chances."

"So be it." The Mordant turned, disappearing down the stairs, his servant following like a stunted shadow.

Lord Askal shivered as if coming out of a trance. Around the aft deck, crewmen stood frozen, staring with wide eyes. "Back to work!" The men scuttled like crabs looking for a hole.

Sails beat overhead, filling with wind. The *Dark Fin* cruised on a southerly heading, pulling away from the small island till it was just a speck on the rear horizon. Gulls followed in their wake, singing a mournful dirge. The setting sun lingered on the horizon, as if the day was reluctant to surrender to night, but the darkness was inevitable. All too soon, the first stars appeared, sending a shiver down his spine.

Tormund approached, a scowl on his swarthy face. He leaned close, his voice a whisper. "Let me stick a knife in this land-lord's back and be done with it. We'll feed him to the sea and none will be the wiser."

Lord Askal shook his head. "Would that we could, but the Miral has bound our hands. Best play along and hasten the journey to its end."

"I don't like it."

"Nor do I, but we sail the sea despite the storm."

"Aye, that we do."

"Then I'm trusting you to keep the men below deck while I see to the ship."

"As you command, but keep your cutlass close."

Lord Askal nodded. "Aye, I will." He strode to the heart of the aft deck and roared a string of commands. "Strike the sails and ship the oars! All oarsmen to stand down. All crew confined below deck till morning light."

Crewmen scurried to obey. In short order the sails were furled, the sheets secured, the oars shipped, and then the men disappeared below deck. The pulse of his ship slowed, the drumbeat in the hold silenced. A strange stillness settled over the great trireme, like the calm before a terrible storm. Without sails, their speed bled away. The *Dark Fin* slowed to a drift, rocked to a slow lull by the waves' caress. The lord captain stood alone on the aft deck, his hands on the tiller, as if he sailed a ghost ship on a midnight sea.

Footsteps on the stairs.

The Mordant appeared, a strange red light glowing from the tip of his staff.

Dark magic, Lord Askal sketched the sign of the sea god, sending a fervent prayer to Naff.

The Mordant loomed close, his face pale in the red light. "Know this, no matter what you see, no matter what you hear, your ship will not be harmed."

Lord Askal nodded.

"Do nothing, say nothing, if you wish to live."

The servant appeared carrying a large stoppered flask. The Mordant took the flask, throwing the stopper into the sea. Moving to the center of the aft deck, he stood with his head bowed, muttering a sibilant chant.

Lord Askal stood gripping the helm, every sense alert. The Mordant's gibberish washed across him, slapping him like a drowning wave, but he understood nothing. Meaningless words dripping with evil, the Mordant summoned the Dark. The night grew thick and heavy, wrapping around his ship with ill-intent. Even the stars disappeared, shrouded by Darkness. Lord Askal shivered, resisting the urge to flee.

The *Dark Fin* swayed, floundering like a ghost ship lost at sea. Time seemed to drag...and then the chant stopped. Lord Askal dared to look.

The Mordant raised the flask to the heavens and then poured a libation onto the deck, but this was no mere flagon of ale. The liquid glowed red, like molten lava, and where it struck the deck, it hissed, raising the stink of burnt wood.

"*No!*" Lord Askal reached for his cutlass, but the small man pounced, holding a knife pressed to his jugular. "Interfere and you die." Lord Askal froze, a trickle of blood at his throat. His hand released his cutlass and the knife disappeared. Like a malevolent shadow, the Mordant's servant retreated, melting into the darkness; but the captain could feel his stare. Keeping his hands on the helm, Lord Askal's gaze slid back to the Mordant. What he saw made his blood run cold.

A red pentacle glowed on the *Dark Fin's* deck, the mark of the Dark Lord.

The Mordant lifted his hands, as if invoking the gods. And then he began to dance, circling the pentacle, pounding a strange rhythm into the deck. Round and around, he danced a frenzy. Like a priest of the netherworld, the Mordant screamed a chant, a strange hissing sound, like no language the captain had ever heard. Leaping and shouting, he raised his staff to the heavens.

Overhead, the clouds began to roil. A funnel cloud appeared, churning above his ship, a promise of death on the high seas.

"*Sion tarmath!*" The Mordant hurled a command skyward, stabbing his staff toward the swirling cloud.

Lightning answered.

A bolt of red lightning crashed down, striking the staff.

The power of the strike hurled Lord Askal to the deck. Cringing backwards, he shielded his face. All around him, the air hissed and crackled, the sulphurous stink of brimstone choking his throat, as if the gates of hell were thrown wide open. Fearing for his ship, he dared to look.

The Mordant stood in the center of the pentacle and he *glowed*. A nimbus of red light surrounded him, as if he'd swallowed the lightning bolt. "*Bring them!*" The voice that roared out of the Mordant held the power of a god.

Lord Askal clutched the tiller, his heart thundering. This was no mere man he'd brought aboard his ship; this was a demon, a devil incarnate.

The dark-clad servant moved to the prisoners. Shredding their clothes with flicks of his dagger, he cut their bonds. Naked and cowering, the sheepherders clung to the deck, fingernails scraping against wood, begging for mercy. "Spare us!" The stink of urine filled the air, but the Mordant's servant was relentless. Dragging the naked men towards the pentacle, he hurled them across the glowing lines.

Red light flared as the prisoners crossed the glowing boundary. Something gripped the two men, like a hand claiming a sacrifice, holding them upright within the glowing pentacle. The two sheepherders writhed in pain, their backs arching, their mouths stretched wide in horror. Lifted a hand span above the deck, their bare feet flailed the air. Screams erupted from the two men, as if their very souls caught fire. The Mordant waved his hand and the screaming stopped. Released, the prisoners crumpled to the deck as if their bones were turned to water. Pale as worms, they stared up at the Mordant, making strange mewing sounds.

The albatross was next. The great seabird squawked and fought till it was thrust inside the pentacle and then it flopped to the deck like a sack of feathers, its great wings all askew.

The Mordant stood in the pentacle's heart, glowing like a fiery fiend. Pointing his staff at each of the victims, he bound them with lines of red light, and then he began to chant, a strange discordant song. Twisted and wrong, the ancient words roared out of him like vomiting darkness.

Lord Askal closed his eyes. Clinging to the tiller, he bit his lip. Focusing on the pain, on the taste of blood, he tried to distract his mind, but he could not stop his ears.

An unearthly howl rose from the prisoners, like nothing he'd ever heard. Human voices clawed the night, ripping at his soul, but Lord Askal refused to look. His skin prickled and the hairs rose on the back of his neck. Shrieks and howls beat against him, the torment of the damned, yet he kept his eyes closed. Drenched in sweat, he clung to the tiller, like a man afraid of being sucked into a whirlpool. Lightning flashed across the deck and heat seared his face, but he never once opened his eyes, keeping his teeth clamped tight against a scream.

And then it was over.

A heart-pounding silence claimed his ship, like slamming the door to hell.

He dared to look, and what he saw would forever haunt his mind. The Mordant no longer glowed, his magic spent, but the albatross was changed. Lord Askal shook his head, bile rising like a flood to his mouth. Unable to look away, he watched as the albatross bowed to the Mordant. No longer just a bird, *it was a living horror, a ghoul-bird with the eyes and mouth of a man!*

The Mordant bent over his creation, whispering words in a strange tongue and then he raised his staff to the heavens. *"Fly! And let my will be done!"*

The ghoul-bird raised its human face, great white wings beating against the deck, and then it rose into the sky, flying toward the east.

The Mordant slumped to the deck, but his servant caught him. Without a word, he carried his master down the steps.

Lord Askal watched them leave. Unable to move, he knelt on the aft deck, clinging to the tiller, clinging to his sanity. His stomach convulsed, and his dinner roared out of him, but he could not purge his mind. Exhausted, he lay sprawled on the deck.

Tormund found him there the next morning, but the captain was not alone. Two *things*, naked and pale, lay crumpled within the charred outline of the pentacle. One had no mouth and the other no eyes, pale flesh sprouting where the openings should have been. They lay on the deck, soiled in their own filth, like worms without any will. Whatever spark made them men was missing, drained and sucked out, leaving mere husks of flesh.

Tormund helped his captain stand. "What in the Nine Hells are those...*things*?"

"Sheepherders turned sacrifice." His voice sounded hoarse in his ears. "Kill them and dump them overboard before the crew lays eyes on them." He gripped the railing, fighting to suppress a shudder. A second wave of bile rose to his mouth as he stared at the pentacle branded on his deck. "And get the shipwright up here. I want that cursed symbol erased from the deck."

Tormund was quick to obey. His dirk slashed the throats of the two worm-men, rolling their bodies over the side, horrors consigned to the sea. Dark fins churned the water, following his ship; Naff's hounds come to claim the corrupted flesh.

The crew emerged from the lower decks and his ship slowly came to life, but everything had changed. His men stared at the pentacle branded into the aft deck, horror etching their faces. Muttering charms against evil, they whispered of demons haunting the night. Fear had finally claimed his ship, yet his men obeyed.

Reeking of sweat and brimstone, Lord Askal clung to the tiller. "Speed, we need speed." Over and over, he repeated the words like a chant. "Give me speed!" A fresh wind blew out of the north, filling the sails. The oars ran out, answering the beat of the drum. The *Dark Fin* leaped forward but the captain took no joy in his ship. He haunted the aft deck, worrying every detail, desperate to reach a port in the distant south. Speed might save his crew, might save his ship, but nothing could save his soul.

In the North

1

Katherine

Kath woke with a harsh gasp. Sodden with sweat, she fled her nightmares...only to realize they were true. *Duncan!* She keened his name, remembering the horror of the bloody cavern. Tears threatened but Kath refused to let them flow. She'd tried to save him, but silver daggers riddled his flesh, biting deep, a hundred gaping wounds. Breaking the chains, they'd rescued him from the foul darkness, carrying him up into the dawn's bitter light but the victory proved hollow. So short the time she had with him, she would have held him forever, clutching him close beneath the gulls' mournful cries, but the others intruded, insisting he was dead. They buried him out on the steppes, in clean earth untainted by darkness, the vast blue sky arching overhead. The Painted People raised a warrior's mound over his grave, an earthen cairn of captured weapons and battle banners, a hero's tribute. She'd watched as if she wore someone else's body, unable to believe he was gone. Her heart ached beyond the telling, yet she'd promised to live. Words so easily spoken, yet so hard to keep.

Hollow with hurt, she abandoned her bed, belting her sword to her side, the crystal dagger secure in its sheath. Twirling her maroon cloak around her shoulders, she shrugged on her throwing axes. Night lurked beyond the lead-paned windows, as cold and bleak as her soul. Bleary-eyed, she wandered the Mordant's palace. Every room screamed of decadence, marble columns, golden doors, and gilded braziers. The gaudy display bludgeoned the senses with tasteless wealth, a monument to Darkness. The palace repulsed her, yet night after night Kath roamed the labyrinth hallways as if seeking something lost. Retreating to her memories, she pulled her maroon cloak close. *Duncan,* his name throbbed in her heart. She gripped his silver warrior ring, her fingers tracing the aspen leaves, willing herself to remember his face, his touch, his voice.

Something intruded. She felt watched. Her hand gripped the crystal dagger. Kath woke from a trance and found herself surrounded by nightmares.

Demons leered down at her. Devils, harpies, and orcs carved in stone, so real their talons seemed to reach for her, stone hungering for flesh. She lurched backward, remembering the gargoyle gates, but the carved stone remained fixed to the wall, a frozen frieze. *A hallway of monsters,* the riddle drew her forward. Beneath the show of wealth, the Mordant's palace hid nightmares but this was blatant, unlike anything she'd seen. A pantheon of monsters capered along the walls and across the ceiling, a seamless horror carved in gray stone, *but why?* Duncan's dying words whispered in her mind, *"Find the demon hallway and press the devil's horn."* And then she remembered. *"Eye of varg and claw of balrog, tongue of ghoul and skull of lich."* Like a code writ in stone, she searched for the first clue. A grinning devil winked at her as if he kept a secret. Setting her thumb against his left horn, she pushed. The horn slid into the wall, a soft grinding noise. Intrigued by the stone riddle, yet Kath slowed, warning herself that this was the *Mordant's* secret. Caution was advisable. Keeping a grip on the crystal dagger, she followed the clues. Hidden amongst the details, she found the pressure points cunningly wrought, secrets sculpted into stone.

She pressed the last clue.

A secret door ground open.

Kath crouched, sword in hand, expecting shadowy demons to belch from the doorway...but the hallway remained still as night. She crept forward and peered inside.

A lich-king glared from the darkness, ruby eyes glinting in the torchlight.

Her heart lurched, but it was just another carving, a horror etched in stone. Beyond the carving, spiral stairs wound down to absolute darkness. She shuddered, remembering the red cavern but Duncan's dying words urged her on. Wresting the nearest torch from its bracket, she dared the stairs. Cobwebs hissed in the flames, a reminder that this way was secret. Down and around, the torchlight played against dark stone, a cold musty smell riding the air, like entering a tomb. She reached the bottom and light reflected back at her. Gold glittered from every corner, a treasure trove of coins strewn across the floor. She lowered the torch, discovering jeweled crowns and gilded armor lying scattered amongst the coins, wealth beyond imagining. So this was the Mordant's treasure vault, but Kath cared little for gold. Raising the torch, she explored the hoard, coins clinking at her feet. Silver gleamed in the darkness, catching her gaze. *A winged throne,* her breath caught. Sculpted into silver wings, the throne glowed like captured starlight. Elegant yet powerful, the throne called to her, like something long lost yet somehow dear and familiar. Letting the torch fall, she crossed the chamber. Yellow diamonds glittered along the tall seat, fashioned in an eight-pointed star. *"The Star Knights!"* Her fingers caressed the silver armrests, needing to know it was real. Memories of the ruined tower lost in Wyeth crowded her mind, the very place where she'd found the crystal dagger. A certainty shivered through her, this throne did not belong here, a prisoner chained in Darkness.

Pulling her maroon cloak close, Kath bowed low, wondering if she dared. Gripped by curiosity mixed with a hungry need, she sat upon the throne.

At first nothing happened, but then chimes filled the air like windblown music, defying the stillness of the crypt. The throne flared to life, glowing like unchained starlight. Light blazed from the silver wings, filling the chamber with radiant beams.

And then she saw him, hovering at the Light's edge, his body whole and unbroken, his mismatched gaze full of love. *Duncan!*

She froze, afraid to hope, her words a whisper. "Am I dreaming?"

"Perhaps we're both dreaming." He gave her a smile that filled her with warmth. *"You must not lose heart, for the Light is as real as the Dark."*

She wanted to touch him, to wrap her arms around him and hold him close...but she feared he would disappear, nothing more than a delusion. "I miss you."

"And I you."

"Will you stay?"

"You know I cannot. Yet I will wait for you in the Light." His smile softened. *"Do not lose hope, do not lose heart, both are needed to defeat the Dark."*

The throne began to dim. "No! *Stay with me!*" She gripped the silver armrests, willing the sculpted wings to stay bright, but the glow faded to darkness.

"Duncan!" She screamed his name but he was gone, disappearing with the light. She willed him to return, willed the throne to blaze bright...but the winged silver remained dormant. Darkness encroached, the torch sputtering among the coins. Battered by emptiness, her dam of tears burst. Kath sobbed, wracked by loneliness and loss, a river drenching her leathers.

An eternity later, her tears ran dry.

Gasping for breath, she struggled for composure, grateful no one had seen her weakness.

Darkness crowded close. The torch was nearly extinguished, nothing but a faint glimmer.

She refused to succumb. "Darkness is real but so is the Light." She'd married Duncan under the starlight and nothing would ever change that. Binding her grief with memories, she reached for the torch. At the stairs she paused, her gaze drawn to the silver throne. Among the Mordant's gold, she'd found a single treasure. She did not know if her vision of Duncan was real or imagined, but she clung to the memory like an elixir meant to last through an endless drought. Gripping her sword, she climbed the stairs back to duty.

2

The Knight Marshal

A cold wind howled out of the north, a bitter herald of death and destruction, but the knight marshal refused to be cowed. Like an old oak with roots gnarled deep in the soil, he stood unbowed, keeping vigil by a fresh-laid cairn of rocks, the tomb of his king. The world had changed and not for the better. Raven Pass was broken, the Octagon Knights scattered, their king felled by deceit, but honor and courage had to count for something. He tightened his grip on his great sword, watching as the dawn's first light crested the Dragon Spine Mountains, bringing an end to his vigil...but he did not want to be released. "I never thought to outlive you." His heartfelt words went unanswered. Sorrow battered his soul like an enemy sword yet duty claimed him. "For Honor and the Octagon."

Stiff from standing, he bowed to his king one last time and then sheathed his sword and made his way down the hill to the others. He found them clustered around the wagon, three knights, a squire, and the brown-robed healer. Their weary stares speared him with a single question but he had no answer. "The king is dead. I'll lead the Octagon till another is found."

His gruff words quelled their question...at least for a time.

Sir Abrax spoke for the others. "What now?"

"I gave orders for the Octagon to scatter and regroup. We'll meet at Stonehand. Sir Lothar will be named as knight marshal if I fall."

Sir Abrax flashed a feral grin. "Then we fight?"

Sir Blaze and Sir Rannock fingered their weapons, a deadly edge to their faces. The marshal was not alone in wanting vengeance for the king. He gave them a slow nod. "We lost the first battle but not the war. We'll bleed the dark horde for the king." Approval lit their faces, their courage undaunted. The marshal drew strength from their conviction. "We'd best be gone, we have a war to fight." He strode to the wagon and took up the king's blue steel sword, Honor's Edge, and thrust it into the bedroll affixed to his saddle. At least his lord's sword was safe.

Mordbane lay shattered on the battlefield, the prince's blue sword broken by the black, but before the fight the king had entrusted his own sword to his squire's care, a legacy for his heir. "Baldwin, you did well to protect the king's sword." The young man burned bright red under the compliment. "But duty calls us in other directions." His gaze turned to the healer, "Quintus, you'd best unhitch the horses and empty the wagon. From now on we'll need to be stealthy." The pudgy healer moved to the traces, the king's squire leaping to lend a hand. "Baldwin, to me. I've a more important task for you." Surprise flashed across the squire's freckled face, but he was quick to obey.

"This way." The marshal led the lad into the woods. In the dim morning light he scoured the ground, using his sword to hack at the brambles.

"Sir, what do we seek?"

"The blade that killed the king." He heard the squire's sharp intake of breath. "I think I threw it in this direction." They split up, searching the thicket.

"It's here."

"Don't touch it." He scrambled to the squire's side. The great sword lay among the brambles like a slash of Darkness. Despite the dark color, it was well crafted with dragons coiled around the hilt in an intriguing design. Dark and deadly, the sword was made for a champion's hand, so tempting to claim it, like a siren's promise of power. He found himself reaching for it till the monk's warning blazed in his mind, *not meant for the hand of man.* Snatching back his hand, he gave the squire a stern look. "The blade's said to be cursed. Never touch it." As an afterthought, he added, "Go fetch a blanket from the wagon and a length of rope."

As Baldwin sped away, the marshal used his sword to lever the dark weapon from the thorns. It fell to the ground at his feet, deadly black against the snow. Crouching, he studied the blade, careful not to touch it. Steel so black it seemed to drink light, but it was the pommel that snared his attention. *"By Valin, it cannot be!"* The sword held the shape of a legend, an octagon pommel with a pair of coiled dragons gracing the crossguard. Beneath the guard the blade held the final damning detail, the maker's mark, an octagon surrounding the initials *OS. Orrin Surehammer,* the first smith to forge a blue steel blade. He staggered backwards, stunned by a legend twisted to a curse.

Baldwin returned clutching a bloodied blanket and a length of rope. "What's wrong?"

"A legend twisted to an abomination! This sword was forged for Boric."

Awe flooded the lad's face, *"The first blue steel blade!"*

"Just so,"

"But why is it dark?"

"It's been corrupted, perverted by evil." A shiver of foreboding raced down the marshal's back. It was said that blue steel blades held their shape forever, never dulling, never melting, refusing to be reforged, but somehow the Mordant had corrupted the very metal of the sword, turning the sapphire-blue steel to darkest black. He wondered at the power required to corrupt the very nature of steel. "Somehow the Mordant tainted the sword with evil. An octagon-forged blade turned black, sent against us like a curse."

"But Boric's blade was lost long ago."

The lad saw the truth of it. "Lost centuries ago, yet the Mordant saved it for our time. Saved it to slay a king." The weapon screamed of power and planning and foul intent. A legend-forged blade yet it lay at his feet as if cast aside by a demon, waiting for a knight to take it up. The marshal looked away, refusing to be tempted. "The monks have the truth of it. This blade was not meant to be wielded by men." He used the blanket to wrap the sword. Even through the thick wool, he could feel the blade's keening cold, like a malevolent force trying to suck the life from him. Shuddering, he bound the blanket-wrapped blade with rope, fashioning a strap for carrying across the back. Finished, he turned to the squire. "I have a task for you, a final service to your king."

"Anything."

Seeing the eagerness in the lad's face, the marshal hesitated, but he had no knights to spare. "Take the sword to Eye Lake. Get one of the fisher folk to row you out and hurl it into the deep. Perhaps the lake can cleanse the blade of taint, or at least keep it hidden, locked away in the watery depths."

Baldwin saluted. "As you command."

For the first time he noticed the hint of red stubble on the lad's chin, nearly a man grown. King Ursus had talked of raising his squire to a knight. "You served the king well. This is a man's task that I ask of you." He settled the rope strap across the young man's shoulders, the blanket-wrapped sword riding high across his back. "Ride swift and hard and cast the gods-cursed blade deep into the lake. Let no one interfere with your mission. And when you return, you'll be raised to a knight. The octagon has need of every sword."

Baldwin's eyes blazed bright. "It will be done."

They returned to the others and the marshal saw the squire mounted on the swiftest horse. Saluting with his fist to his chest,

Baldwin set spurs to his warhorse and rode for the south, soon swallowed by the trees.

A hushed stillness settled on the forest. The marshal turned to the others. "Mount up. The sooner we get to Stonehand, the sooner we wet our blades against the enemy." They swung into their saddles; the healer perched bareback on one of the dray horses. Swords held at the ready, they rode through the winter-bare woods following the ridge till they reached a snowy knoll overlooking the valley. The marshal dismounted, Sir Abrax at his side. The two crept forward till they gained a view of the valley. A grim sight awaited them. The enemy army choked Raven Pass like a black pestilence, but instead of a slavering horde, they marched in disciplined ranks.

Beside him, Sir Abrax grunted. "I'd not have believed it."

The marshal knew what he meant. "More proof the Mordant rules with an iron gauntlet."

"It will make the horde harder to defeat."

A hundred thousand boot prints marred the valley below, churning the snow to mud. Finding the view too grim for words, the marshal had no reply.

Sir Abrax scowled. "Looks like they've claimed the wall. Little good the Whore will do them."

But the marshal saw their strategy. "The Whore will help them hold the pass while their foragers ransack the other walls. They'll be feasting on our winter stores whilst we go hungry." His stomach chose that moment to rumble, reminding him that he hadn't eaten in over a day. "We need to find the others."

They edged backwards, keeping their heads low. Remounting, they followed the ridge south, always keeping well within the trees, the horses forging a path through the lightly crusted snow. Single file, they rode throughout the day, hunger gnawing at them like a second enemy. By twilight they ran out of ridge, descending a steep trail to the flatlands.

A low growl echoed through the woods. Instead of retreating, the marshal turned his horse toward the sound. They emerged from a stand of white-barked aspen to find a pack of wolves feasting on a fresh-felled stag. A dozen wolves snapped and snarled over the kill. Sir Abrax drew his great sword, "Looks like we've found dinner."

The marshal gave him a stern look. "Careful. Voices carry."

Sir Abrax nodded, lowering his visor.

Silent as snow, the three knights charged the wolves, their armor gleaming in the fading light, their swords raised high. A great gray wolf whirled to meet the charge. Fangs bared, he stood his ground, menacing a deep-throated growl, but fangs were no match for Castlegard steel. Sir Abrax took his head with a single sword stroke while Sir Rannock rode amongst the others, his morning star carving a deadly whirl. The wolves broke and ran. Sir Abrax pulled his warhorse to a halt. "Knights against wolves, how the mighty have fallen, but at least we've gained a meal." He peered down at the bloody carcass. "Does anyone know how to dress a deer?"

Silence reigned; they were knights not huntsmen.

The healer caught up to them, bouncing on the back of his horse. "I'll do it." Quintus slid from the horse, pulling a packet of leather-wrapped surgeon's knives from one of his many pockets. "Skin and muscle are much the same, though some are tougher than others." The knights stood guard while the healer carved the stag. Beyond the hill, the wolves howled a mixture of frustration and anger. One shaggy-maned wolf stood sentinel, a gray shadow on the hilltop.

Quintus finished his work, blood up to his elbows. "I've salvaged as much as I can, but the meat will need to be well cooked." He knelt, scrubbing snow on his forearms. "A pity we don't have salt."

"There's many things we don't have." The marshal threw the healer a spare blanket. "Wrap the meat in this; we need to be off." They remounted and the marshal led them deeper into the flatlands. Behind them, the wolves yipped and howled, reclaiming the carcass.

They rode for the better part of an hour. Coming across a clump of boulders, the marshal called a halt. "This is as good a shelter as we're likely to get. We'll rest here and dare a small fire. Carve the venison into strips and cook all of it. From now on every fire will be a risk."

They picketed the horses and scrounged for firewood while the healer cut the meat into strips. In the lee of the boulders they coaxed a small flame to life, setting the venison to cook on sticks. Sir Rannock filled his helm with snow and set it near the coals. Sitting in a circle, they watched the meat like starving wolves. Too hungry to wait, they burned their fingers on half-cooked venison, the juices staining their beards. The marshal was just as impatient as the others, cramming his mouth with venison. The sizzling strips proved tough and stringy but they filled his empty stomach. Reaching for the helm, he quenched his thirst on snowmelt. No one spoke. His hunger finally sated, the marshal watched his men, three champions of the maroon reduced to skulking like brigands, eating meat stolen from wolves...but at least they lived, surviving to fight another day.

Sir Abrax noticed his stare. "So we'll camp here tonight?"

"We dare not tarry. We need the dark to slip past the enemy. We'll sleep once we reach Stonehand."

"A long ride."

"Then we'd best get started."

Dousing the fire with snow, they filled their empty saddlebags with cooked venison and mounted their weary horses. By the light of the moon, the marshal led them east, sneaking across the mouth of the pass, hooves crunching on snow. Twice they paused, hearing the clink of armor, but no challenge came their way. In the small hours of the morning they reached the forest on the far side, the trees offering the promise of cover against the dawn.

Weary from the long night, the marshal let his horse pick a path up into the snow-dusted foothills. He struggled to stay alert but his mind kept wandering, hammered by fatigue. So much had changed in so short a time. Only two days ago he'd fought atop crenellated battlements, holding the Mordant's hordes at bay till the gates were sundered, shattered by foul magic. Two days for his world to be upended; the Octagon defeated by trickery and gods-cursed magic. Now his men were kingless, scattered in retreat, riding through the night like brigands. Somehow he had to find a way to restore the maroon to glory. Honor and courage had to count for something. "By Valin, I'll not let the Octagon fail!" But the oath sounded hollow in the night. He stared at the stars, so cold and distant, wondering if the gods cared.

3

Katherine

Kath startled awake, her hand reaching for her sword. *Give it to us*...the spectral voice slithered through her mind, a memory and a threat. *"No!"* The shout rose unbidden to her lips. Unsheathing her sword, she stared at the shadows. A feral fear clung to her, planting a deep seeded dread. Like so many nights before, she woke plagued by nightmares...but this felt different, this was a memory. Her heart pounding, she clutched her gargoyle, relieved to find it on the leather thong around her neck. Duncan's warrior ring was there as well, but what of the other? Grabbing her clothes puddled on the floor, she ransacked the pockets, turning them inside out, *nothing!*

Perhaps it had fallen out.

She clung to the slender hope. In the dim light, she knelt, frantically running her hands across the cold marble floor, praying to find it. *Nothing!* Worse yet, she could not feel it.

Closing her eyes, she took deep calming breaths, straining to sense the magical bond...but her efforts were for naught, as if the link was severed. The stink of her own fear filled her nostrils. Quelling her panic, Kath tried to remember the last time she'd held it. She remembered sheathing her sword and reaching for the amber pyramid...*in the cavern of nightmares!* Fear spiked through her. She couldn't have lost it there! Memories of the demons' grasping hands shredded her denial. A chilling thought seized her. Zith had warned her countless times that the Quickner could not fall into the hands of Darkness...and now she'd lost it...in the worst possible place. Her dread fought a tug-of-war with a desperate hope. Perhaps she could get it back. Shoving her stockinged feet into her boots, she hastily dressed. Grabbing her throwing axes, she crossed the marble hallway to bang on the nearest door. "Wake up! I need you!" Her fist beat against the door.

Bear was quick to answer. Clad in fighting leathers, weapons studded his belt. "Svala?"

Sometimes she wondered if he slept with his sword. "Wake Boar and get Blaine."

A moment later, Boar emerged, his great axe in his hand. Nodding towards her, he jogged down the hallway to the Mordant's opulent chambers. When they'd first explored the palace, Kath had shunned the Mordant's chambers, repulsed by the thought of sleeping in the enemy's bed, but Blaine had leaped at the chance. The knight claimed the honor, reveling in the obscene decadence. He'd fought like a hero so she could not gainsay him the indulgence, but she did not want it for herself.

"Svala?" Bear waited patiently at her side. "What do you need?"

"To return to the bloody cavern."

Bear raised a bushy eyebrow in shock, or perhaps protest, but he said nothing.

The other two men came jogging down the hallway, a jangle of weapons and chainmail. Blaine looked sleep-fogged, cracking a large yawn. "What's so urgent?"

"I can't find the Quickner."

He stared at her. "But the monk said..."

Dismay rode her voice. "I know."

"Where?"

"It has to be in the bloody cavern...or on the steps to below."

Blaine gave her a chilling look. "You really want to go back down there?"

"No...but I need to find it. I need to get it back."

He gave her a grim nod. "Lead the way."

Kath turned and led the three men toward the outer doors of the palace. Braziers lit the hallways. A painted warrior stood guard in the cavernous entranceway, leaning on a spear. At a nod from Kath, the guard put his shoulder to the great gold-clad door and shoved. Cold seeped inside, a deadly chill.

Kath slipped through the narrow opening, stepping from warmth into winter. A bitter wind howled out of the north, cold enough to freeze bone. Hugging her maroon cloak close, she ran across the great rune-carved courtyard, her long blond hair whipping behind like a battle banner. She dreaded returning to below, but she needed to reclaim the Quickner. A sickle moon hung low in the night sky, grinning among the stars as if mocking her loss. Ahead, the great dark monolith thrust up from the heart of the courtyard like a monstrous tombstone. A cleft in the stone gave entrance to the netherworld. Muttering a quick prayer to Valin, Kath darted through the cleft and then skidded to a sudden halt, teetering on the top step. *Darkness* gaped below, pitch black and impenetrable.

The torches had gone out...and no one dared relight them.

Retreating a step, Kath bumped into Blaine. "The torches are out." It seemed like an ill-omen...or a threat. The darkness felt alive, a brooding menace lurking below. "We can't go down there without light."

Bear said, "I'll get a torch."

They waited on the top step, caught between darkness and a killing cold. The wind howled outside like a beast denied.

Bear returned, torchlight dancing across the dark stone.

Kath wrested an unlit torch from the nearest bracket, holding it to Bear's till hers ignited. The torch sizzled and hissed as if protesting the blaze, but the fire took hold. Blaine and Boar both did the same, multiplying the light. The four torches carved a slender niche from the ominous dark.

Poised on the top step, Kath stared down the dark gullet, assaulted by painful memories. *Duncan!* Pushing her nightmares aside, she strained to feel the Quickner...but felt nothing. Resigned, she started down the long stairs, torchlight shimmering behind her. Crouched low, Kath checked every step. Sweeping her torch back and forth, she prayed to find it, prayed to be spared the horror below. A chilling darkness choked around her, as if it might snuff all hope. The rough-carved stairs spiraled down, descending into the depths of hell. A cold sweat sheened her face, yet she refused to turn back. Down and around, they descended a thousand steps into the gaping darkness. No one spoke, nothing but the clink of arms and armor.

A horrible stench rose from below, the putrid smell of death.

"It must be the guards." Kath kept her voice to a hushed whisper.

They reached the bottom, a rock-hewn antechamber dominated by the great copper door. Two guards lay crumpled on the floor, both bloated with rot, the source of the stench. Kath fixed her gaze on the door. Green with age and covered in runes, the great round door stood open like a portal gaping to hell. Beyond the doorway, the cavern was utterly dark.

Behind her, Boar whispered, "It's a trap."

"Perhaps, but we have to find the Quickner." Murmuring a fervent prayer to Valin, Kath stepped across the threshold. The air smelled foul, brimstone mingled with a rotting stench. Her torch flickered feeble against the devouring darkness. Every sense screamed at Kath to flee, but she refused to retreat. Sweeping the torch low to the ground, she crept forward, straining to feel the amber focus. Darkness swallowed the light, a malevolent weight pressing down. The hairs prickled on the back of her neck. Sensing a threat, she whirled right and then left, straining to see. Her boot struck something, making a loud clatter. She winced at the sound. Broken stalactites littered the floor, the stone javelins of an angry god.

"Who dares the Darkness?"

Kath's heartbeat raced at the spectral voice.

The chamber awoke.

Five braziers erupted in red flames, sparks shooting towards the ceiling. Shadows slithered overhead, weaving amongst the blood-red stalactites. Smoke billowed from the braziers, mingling with the shadows, giving them substance.

Impaled by nightmares, Kath froze.

Behind her, Bear whispered. "Svala!"

Kath drew her sword, needing the feel of cold steel. Averting her gaze from the menacing shadows, she crept forward, desperate to find the Quickner. Keeping her torch low, she threaded a path around the shattered stalactites, her doeskin boots whispering against the cold marble. A golden pentacle gleamed at the chamber's cruel heart...and embedded in the floor, the shattered chains that had held Duncan. *Duncan!* Blood encrusted the chains. *His* blood. Pierced by the memory of his pain, Kath bit her lip, struggling to force the grim thoughts away. Clutching her sword, she stretched her senses, determined to find the small amber focus.

Dark forms slithered overhead.

"Who dares the Darkness?"

Kath's gaze was drawn aloft.

Smoke and shadow coalesced. From the swirling darkness, details appeared taking the form of a horned demon. Hooked claws, curled teeth...and glowing red eyes that pulsed with a malevolent hatred, a massive demon reared overhead.

Kath gripped her sword, her heart thundering. The demon seemed real...much more real than last time, as if the shadows had grown stronger. A forked tail lashed towards her. Kath leaped aside. Puzzled by the demon's solid substance, she stared at it, trying to pierce the riddle of its strength...and then she felt the Quickner! The realization stunned her like the fatal jab of a spear.

The demon flashed a fang-filled mouth. *"Knight of the Octagon...we see you...we curse you...we mark your soul as ours!"*

Blaine unsheathed his great blue sword. "Go to hell!" Striding forward, he struck a killing blow at the demon's heart...but the fiend split itself in half. Seeping away from the blue blade, it dissolved back into smoke. The dark cloud billowed, retreating deeper into the cavern. Clawed hands and glowing red eyes reappeared. The shadow-demon reformed into a taunting menace. *"Your steel can no longer harm me!"*

Kath stretched her hand aloft, straining to summon the Quickner...but it no longer answered her call. "Cut its right hand off!"

Blue steel lashed out, slicing through the demon's right wrist. Arm and hand dissolved into inky smoke, flinching away from the sapphire blade...but somehow the demon kept the Quickner! The focus hovered overhead, captured by shadow. Kath could feel it but she could not reach it.

Mocking laughter rippled through the cavern. *"Body and soul, you shall be ours, a knight of Darkness, bound for all eternity!"*

"Never!" Blaine advanced, swinging his sword in a deadly arc...but Kath sensed it was futile. Swords alone would not slay the demon, not as long as it held the Quickner...yet the fiend toyed with them, tempting them deeper into the cavern, as if it had some purpose. Understanding struck. She threw a harried glance backwards and saw the great copper door begin to swing shut.

"The door!"

Boar was closest. He hurled his battle axe and it lodged in the frame, holding the door ajar.

"Retreat!" Kath sprinted for the door.

Boar reached it first, his muscles straining to hold it open.

"No!" The demon's voice roared through the cavern. *"You shall not leave!"* The cavern floor began to heave and shake.

Kath tripped and fell hard, tasting blood in her mouth. Bear grabbed her arm. Yanking her to her feet, he pushed her towards the door. She cast a glance backwards, watching as Blaine struck at the demon. *"Blaine, run!"* She yelled for the knight, but Bear forced her forward. "Get out, Svala!"

Stalactites speared down, shattering into deadly shards.

Kath dodged a stone spear, running for the door. A stone chip struck her cheek drawing blood. The floor lurched beneath her boots, trying to trip her. She staggered left, leaping over a fallen stalactite. Reaching the door, she turned and saw Blaine retreating in front of the demon, holding the fiend at bay. *"Run!"* She ducked beneath Boar's straining arms and tumbled into the antechamber. Bear squeezed through behind her. Turning, he stood between her and the door, a sword in one hand, a torch in the other. Kath reclaimed her dropped torch and stood beside him, her heartbeat hammering. *"Hurry!"*

The ground quaked, as if the earth yearned to swallow them.

Blaine appeared, squeezing through the narrow opening, his sword and torch clattering to the stone floor. For half a heartbeat he was stuck, half in, half out. Fear spasmed across his face...and then something yanked him back.

"*Blaine!*"

A single gauntleted hand gripped the door frame.

Bear's sword and torch clattered to the floor. Grabbing the knight, he strained to pull him into the antechamber.

Boar bellowed. "*Hurry!*"

With a mighty heave, Bear pulled the knight through the narrow opening. Both men clattered onto the cold hard floor.

Boar released the door. Yanking on his battle axe, he leaped away. The great axe came loose...and the copper door snapped shut.

The companions stared at each other, relief warring with a primal fear, but then the ground shook with renewed violence, rock dust falling from above.

"*Run!*" Kath leaped for the stairs, taking them two at a time. The others came behind, torchlight darting across dark stone. Beneath her boots, the stairs shuddered and shook like an angry dragon. Twice Kath fell to her knees, landing hard. Ignoring the pain, she continued to climb...and then her torch went out, as if snuffed by Darkness. She flung it aside. Placing one hand on the rough-hewn wall as a guide, she raced up the stairs. Two more torches snuffed to smoke, she felt the Darkness reaching for them. Kath quickened her pace. Ignoring the pain daggering her side, she scurried up the winding stairs. Fear breathed at her back. A single torch against the malevolent darkness, she felt the menace closing around them...and then a biting cold stung her face. Winter-cold air poured through the cleft, a breath of fresh air. Kath reached the top and stumbled out into the biting wind. Dawn broke across the sky, a single crack of light banishing the darkness.

Exhausted, Kath fell to her knees.

The others stumbled from the monolith. Sagging to the courtyard, Blaine stared at her. "I never want to do that again."

"Never." Kath agreed, but the loss of the Quickner bit deep. "I want that stairway sealed, choked with rock from the Pit, the demon forever buried in the depths. Alone in the dark, it can choke on the Quickner." The courtyard quaked beneath her, as if the demon railed in anger. Kath stood, coated in rock dust and sweat. She'd risked the others for a bitter answer. She'd failed to save Duncan, and now she'd lost the Quickner. Doom seemed to dog her since coming to the Mordant's Citadel. Kath prayed it wasn't an omen of things to come.

4

Blaine

The Mordant's palace overflowed with riches beyond Blaine's wildest dreams. Bright tapestries, golden doors, marble statuary, the entire palace dripped with wealth, a decadent monument to Darkness. As the son of a pig farmer, such unbound luxury made him feel both diminished and elated. Refusing to be intimidated, he was more than willing to partake of the bounty, a conqueror's due. His boots rang on the marble hallways, gilded braziers glowing with heat. He reached the great golden doors and pushed them open, entering a massive bedchamber. Kath shunned the larger bedrooms, leaving Blaine the pick of the palace. The choice was easy. He grinned, liking the irony of an Octagon Knight sleeping in the Mordant's bed. To the victors go the spoils. He'd never dreamt of such rich spoils.

Tapestries filled the walls, vibrant with color, but all of them showed victories of the Dark. Blaine scowled, tempted to rip them down and order them burnt, but they looked fine enough to fetch a duke's ransom, so he did his best to ignore the details. Shrugging his sword harness from his shoulders, he tossed it onto a velvet divan. His maroon cloak and chainmail followed, leaving a trail of armor and clothes strewn across the marble floor. Naked, he padded to the marble water closet. A golden tub filled the far wall, the sound of water trickling down an elaborate fountain, probably from a rain cistern on the roof. Splashing brazier-heated water on his face, he made his toilet and returned to the bedchamber, marveling at the royal luxuries.

Scented candles lit the room with a soft glow. An enormous bed dominated the chamber. Large enough to sleep six, the enticing mound of silken pillows and supple furs beckoned. Weary from the long day, Blaine fell into bed, sighing as he sank into the goose down mattress, like floating on a cloud. He rolled amongst the silken sheets, so many luxuries he'd never tasted. Sprawling across the middle, he reveled in the downy comfort. Pulling a fur coverlet across his chest, he let sleep take him.

"My Lord?"

Blaine swam from a dream to find three scantily clad women peering down at him, a blonde, a brunette and a redhead. All three were breathtakingly beautiful. Bemused, he hugged the coverlet close. "Am I dreaming?"

The women tittered, their faces lovely as angels, but the curves beneath their silken sheaths would shame a harlot.

"My Lord, may we join you?"

"*Join me?*" He was very confused, except for his manhood, which was standing stiff as a knight's salute. "Who are you?"

"We served the Mordant."

The blonde smiled. "And now we wish to serve you, the hero of the citadel."

"We only wish to please." The brunette gave him a pretty pout.

Hero, he liked the sound of that. "But you're free. You don't need to do this."

"But we wish to serve."

"Won't you let us pleasure a hero?"

"Won't you let us please you?"

It was like talking to a three-headed hydra, a very lovely hydra. And they used that word again, *hero*. Blaine sat up, his mind at odds with his manhood. He'd never been called a hero, except in derision, and never by such beautiful women. Perhaps he'd finally earned the title. He'd be a fool to turn them away. Throwing back the covers, he revealed his eagerness. "Join me."

They smiled, shrugging silken sheaths from their shoulders, revealing luscious curves. Naked, they climbed into his bed. Blaine could not believe his good fortune. Lying back amongst the pillows, he opened his arms wide, smothered by naked beauty. His hand found a ripe breast while tender lips found his manhood. He gasped at the intimate touch, straining to keep control. Some of the things they did seemed strange at first, but he soon succumbed to their tender pleasures. It was like nothing he'd ever experienced. Every touch was exquisite, every part of him licked and fondled. He groaned with ecstasy, shivering on the brink. He'd done it before, but the town whores always made short work of it. This was different, so very different. The women found ways to make it last, an eternity of pleasure, a night of dalliance. Blonde, brunette, and redhead, he sampled a bouquet of delights. They took turns riding him like a stallion and then he took them like a bull in heat, bellowing his delight. Three times he reached ecstasy, finally collapsing in a stupor of pleasure. Sated with sex, he slept entwined with beauty, like a hero feted in paradise.

Tap...tap, tap, a noise intruded on his sleep. Blaine tried to push it away, reluctant to leave dreams of endless pleasure, but the sound persisted. Tap...tap, tap. He swam awake. The women snuggled close around him, oblivious to the disturbance. Groggy from sex, his gaze circled the chamber. Night darkened the room, most of the candles melted to stubs, but nothing seemed amiss.

Tap...tap, tap.

The sound came from the far doors, but he could have sworn there was nothing out there but a balcony, a sheer drop overlooking the tiered city.

Tap...tap, tap.

Freeing himself from the feminine tangle, Blaine struggled from bed. The blonde sighed but none of them woke. Blaine grinned, perhaps he'd given as good as he got. He reached for a candle, a small circle of light against the dark, and padded naked toward the double doors.

Tap...tap, tap.

Annoyed at the intrusion, he yanked the doors open. A cold wind gusted in, snuffing his candle. He blinked against the dark, but then he saw it. A giant albatross fluttered to the railing. Pale as death, the great bird stared back at him, its head at eye level, but instead of a bird, it was a monster. *Eyes and mouth of a man!* The winged beast was an abomination, a fiend sprung from hell!

"The Mordant sees you, Knight of the Octagon."

Stunned, Blaine staggered back a step.

Its voice was a dry rasp. *"The Mordant marks your soul for you dared to breach his Citadel."*

Blaine reached for his sword, shocked to realize he stood naked before the fiend.

"Pain will be your future, and forever will be your service, for he shall twist flesh and meld souls crafting you into one of the damned." The great wings flapped as the creature hovered above the railing. *"Look at me to foresee your fate, to foresee your doom."*

"No!" Blaine threw the candle, a feeble weapon.

The fiend laughed. *"You will be a man no more!"*

Blaine whirled, desperate for his sword. Tripping over the trail of clothing, he finally reached the divan. Sweeping the blue sword from its scabbard, he charged the balcony, but the fiend was already gone, great wings beating toward the moon-drenched clouds. Naked, Blaine stood on the balcony, his sword raised to the heavens, his shout chasing the monstrosity south. "I'll kill him! *I'll kill him first!*"

A winter wind beat against him, snatching at his words. Shivering against the bitter cold, he slammed the doors shut and set the bar. Shaking, he returned to bed to find the three women watching him, the fur covers clutched close.

"Did you see?"

Pale faces stared back at him. The redhead gave a grim nod.

Blaine's voice was a low growl. "What was that thing?"

"A gorelabe, a messenger of the Mordant." Her voice dropped to a whisper. "It means our master still lives."

"Your *master!*" Her answer infuriated him. He yanked the covers from the bed, revealing their nakedness. "Get out! All of you out!" He brandished his sword and they fled before him, scampering from the bedchamber with a piteous squeal.

The door slammed shut and he was alone.

Scaring naked women, Blaine shook his head, ashamed of himself, yet he could not let them see his shaking hands. He climbed into the massive bed, pulling the warm furs close, clutching his sword. The luxuries of the palace were forgotten, poisoned by nightmares. His gaze haunted the balcony doors. *An albatross melded with a man,* he shuddered at the horror. How could such a twisted creature ever come into being? How could swords defeat such fell magic? The monster's threat echoed through his mind, *"Forever will be your service."* Blaine made the hand sign against evil. "I'll kill him first." He clutched his sword, his words full of defiance, but in his mind a ravening fear took hold.

5

Katherine

Torchlight played across the frieze of demons, shifting shadows granting the illusion of life. While the palace slept, Kath escaped the bonds of duty, fleeing to the demon-carved hallway. Like a restless spirit she returned desperate for succor. Stone-carved demons leered down at her, as if they sensed her weakness, but Kath did not care. With urgent fingers, she sought the hidden key. Eye of varg and claw of balrog, her fingers pressed the riddle wrought in stone. Tongue of ghoul and skull of lich, she longed to see him. Tooth of snarg and scale of dragon, she pressed the last stone praying for her heart's desire.

The hidden door whispered open. She sped past the lich king and down the spiral stairs, torchlight playing across dark stone. The treasury crypt remained just as she'd found it, gold coins spewed across the floor, cedar chests stacked along the far wall, a trove of incalculable wealth, but Kath cared for naught save the winged throne. Silver sculpted into wings, the elegant throne drew her like a lodestone. Whispering a prayer to Valin, Kath dared to sit in the regal seat. Her maroon cloak wrapped close, she held her breath, hoping, praying...but the throne remained dormant. Gripping the armrests, she willed the throne to life...but the shadows held sway. The darkness mocked her. Kath slumped against the throne, her hope dwindling to a whisper. "Come back to me!" but her plea went unanswered.

For five nights she returned to the crypt, sitting in the silver throne till her torch sputtered to embers, all to no avail. On the sixth night, she brought the monk.

"What is it you want me to see?"

"Best if I just show you."

"Must we do this in the dead of night?"

Kath shrugged, taking a torch from the wall bracket. "The less eyes the better."

He gave her an odd look, but said nothing more, following her through the marble labyrinth. Zith gasped when he saw the demon-carved hallway, his voice changing from annoyance to a wary interest. "What is this place?"

"The Mordant's secret." She pressed the stone riddle and the hidden door whispered open. "This way. Mind the stairs are steep." She went first, holding the torch behind her so the monk could see. He lurched down the steep stairs, still awkward from his missing hand, lost in their first battle with the gore hounds. Reaching the bottom, Kath stepped aside, torchlight glittering on gold.

Zith gasped. *"By the gods!"* He stepped amongst the coins, turning in all directions, his face full of wonder. "How did you find this?"

"Duncan told me." She watched the monk's face. "Bryce told him."

His gaze snapped to hers. "My son?"

She gave him a solemn nod. "I told you, Bryce still lives. Somehow in that hellish cavern, he spoke to Duncan, whispering the Mordant's secrets."

"Then he still serves the Light." Pride leavened with fierce resolve flooded the monk's face. "We'd best make use of it."

"Tell me about the throne." Kath crossed the crypt to the silver wings. Her fingertips stroked the sculpted metal, so cool to the touch, but there was no answering light. Hearing the monk gasp, she turned to see the wonder in his stare.

"The Throne of the Star Knights!"

"So you know of it?"

"Only by myth and legend. Lost a thousand years ago, during the War of Wizards," Zith shook his head. "We thought it destroyed, melted down for silver."

"Do you know what it does?"

"Does?"

"What magic it holds?"

"There are none who know. Its secrets are lost to the ages." Zith's gaze narrowed. "Have you woken the throne?"

Kath shrugged. "I'm drawn to it."

"Have you dared to sit in it?"

She gave the smallest of nods.

"Show me."

Hoping to see Duncan's face again, she wedged the torch between two chests and then sat on the throne...but nothing happened. Kath smothered her dismay.

Zith shrugged. "A relic from another time, a forgotten trophy from a battle long lost." He turned away, his gaze ensnared by the wonders crowding the chamber.

Kath swallowed her disappointment, watching as the monk circled the crypt, sending coins scattering across the floor like a rich man's chime. He paused to sniff the air. "I smell oil. Bring your torch."

Kath crossed the chamber, handing the torch to the monk. With his one remaining hand, Zith held the torch to the wall, dipping it into a runnel. Light flared along the runnel, illuminating the four walls and spilling into basins. Like magic, the crypt glowed bright. The light multiplied the treasure. Gold glittered from every corner, coins and scepters and bejeweled crowns, the wealth of countless kingdoms spilled careless across the floor. The crypt's corners held martial splendors. Golden helms and scabbarded swords, imprisoned in gossamer cloaks spun by spiders, they awaited a hero's hand. Lances leaned against the wall. Rune-forged weapons wrapped in moldering battle banners whispered of ancient glory. Kath's interest quickened. Zith plucked an uncut ruby the size of his fist from the floor. "Wealth undreamt of," he let the ruby fall, "a treasure of the ages, but the Mordant does not seek gold...he craves *power!*"

Kath saw the chamber with fresh eyes. The glowing walls made new details clear. An empty armor stand snagged her attention. *Empty*, a sense of foreboding gripped her, she wondered what other treasures were missing, lost to time...or taken in service to the Mordant. Islands of bare stone sat amongst the strewn coins, showing where cedar chests had once stood, an ominous sign.

"Look here." Zith called her to the far side. Dust on a tabletop showed the outline of a two-handed great sword.

Kath's eyes flared wide.

"Did you take it?"

"No, I took nothing!"

"Then the Mordant must have it. I'll wager he took the most powerful items with him." Zith turned, studying the chamber. "But he intended to return. Look how much he left behind." He opened a cedar chest, revealing a trove of scrolls. "Every chest, every item will have to be examined. Who knows what magic lies hidden amongst the gold."

"Magic?" Her hand crept to her mage-stone gargoyle, clasping it close.

"Magic is power." Zith gestured to the four walls, his voice brimming with excitement. "Look at this chamber, a priceless hoard of knowledge, wealth, and ancient magic! Just think what we might discover!" His gaze caressed the cedar chests crowding the crypt. "Who knows what lies within? Perhaps the perfect weapon to defeat the Mordant." He circled the crypt, his gaze bouncing across the glittering trove. "We'll have to test every item, the crowns, the jewelry, the armor, anything could be a focus." He snatched a jeweled dagger from a pile of coins. "Here, try this."

"Try it?"

"See if you can sense any magic."

"I can't."

"Just try." He pressed the dagger on her, flashing a reassuring smile. "With the Quickner you should be able to sense other magic, perhaps even wakening other focuses and wielding them. The gods granted you a powerful gift when your hand found the Quickner."

Kath took a step backwards, the taste of ashes rising to her mouth. "No."

He proffered the dagger, his voice insistent. "Just try."

Kath shook her head. "I can't."

His gaze narrowed. "What do you mean, you *can't*?"

She felt nauseous but the truth needed to be told. "I lost it."

"You *lost* it?"

"It was stolen."

"*Stolen?*" His face paled. "By whom?"

"By the demons in the bloody cavern."

Zith's face turned pale as ice, the jeweled dagger falling from his fingers. He stared at her as if an executioner's axe hung above his head. "Tell me."

Kath began to pace, the words flooding out of her. "I'm certain I had the Quickner when I descended the long stairs to the bloody cavern. I remember holding it in my hand." She fisted her hand as if it still held the amber pyramid. "I killed the guards and then the rune-covered door shuddered opened of its own accord...almost as if it wanted me to enter." She flashed him a wary look, but he did not argue. "I ran inside and found Duncan." Kath shuddered against a tide of bitter memories. "I tried to free him...but the shadows came alive. Shaped like demons, they reached for me. And I swear they said, *Give us the Quickner!*"

Zith sank to the ground as if he had no bones. "They knew...or they sensed it."

Kath nodded. "And then the Mordant spoke and the shadow demons attacked. It was only later...much later, that I realized it was gone."

Silence blanketed the crypt like a tomb, but there was more she needed to say. "I went back."

Zith raised his stare, skewering her. "And?"

"I took Bear and Boar and Blaine and we went back down there." Kath shuddered at the memory of the demon's strength. "A shadow demon has it." She dared a look at his face, scorched by the desolation in his gaze. "The demons are stronger. Much stronger. Our swords could not harm them."

"So you ordered the cavern sealed with rock." His voice sounded as if it came from a grave.

"Yes." Kath sank to the floor, idly running her fingers through gold coins. "I've failed you. I've failed you all."

For the longest time, he said nothing, but then he stirred. "No." His grim tone belied his word.

Kath looked away, daring to whisper her secret fear. "If the demons have the Quickner, will it serve the Mordant?"

Zith gasped. "I hope not. I *pray* not."

"Prayers don't seem to matter anymore."

The monk rallied. "The loss of the Quickner is a grievous blow, but you've gained a great victory by taking the Mordant's citadel."

Bitterness rode her voice. "You don't understand. We've taken the Mordant's city, but the viper's lair is empty, the monster fled south. And now we're trapped here, trapped by winter. Yes, I have an army, an army that's tasted victory, but none of them can ride, and even if they did, there's only enough mounts for a hundred or so. Winter is cruel in the north. I dare not lead them into the frozen steppes, or sure as hell, winter will kill them all." She glared at him. "The Painted People deserve better. I'll not use them so."

His gaze softened. "True enough. But there must be a way."

She felt the weight of duty crushing her shoulders. "Then the gods will have to provide, for I do not see it."

They settled into a grim silence.

"I made a mistake coming here." Her voice sounded small in the chamber. "Instead of victory, it feels like a trap. It feels like a tomb."

"You must not give up hope."

"Hope?" She shook her head in disbelief. "I do not see it, for we've lost so much! Duncan is gone, Danya is locked in a magical trance, you lost your hand...and now the Quickner is stolen...such a steep price. It does not seem like we won anything."

"There is always a price, yet much was achieved with this victory. An entire city is freed from the grip of Darkness. You saw the horrors of the Pit. You cannot regret your victory. And you've given the Painted People a better future, released from the Mordant's shadow." He gestured to the crypt. "And you've gained all this. The Mordant has been dealt a grievous blow, though I doubt he'll learn from it."

His words intrigued her, slipping past her misery. Kath sat cross-legged, her maroon cloak gathered close. "Learn from it, what do you mean?"

"After a thousand years of victory, I doubt he'll learn from his mistake."

Kath stared at him, weighing his words.

"Just look at this chamber," Zith picked up a fist of coins, letting them fall in a shower of gold. "The Mordant *never* gives up power. He never intended to lose this hoard or his citadel. The Mordant never anticipated your victory, he never anticipated *you*." The monk grinned. "Don't you see? You've proven he's not infallible, that he can be defeated...that he does not see you."

Kath thought back to the cavern of weeping rock, how Duncan told her to hide, how the Mordant spoke to Blaine. A shiver passed through her. "You're right. He does not see me."

Zith nodded. "He overlooks the blade bearer."

Her hand went to her belt, to the hilt of the crystal dagger.

"The gods grant a strange power to those who are overlooked, the power to do the unexpected." His eyes blazed. "Do the unexpected. Defeat the Mordant."

Kath nodded, her voice solemn. "I promised Duncan." Her stare roved the crypt. "Somehow I have to find a way south...but in the meantime, we must wrest an advantage from this victory."

"The scrolls might hold a clue, a manifest to the plundered trove. Perhaps we'll learn what magics the Mordant has hoarded...or what he's taken with him."

More magic, a shudder raced down Kath's spine recalling the Mordant's power in the bloody cavern. "Down in the cavern, the Mordant spoke through Duncan. Even from a great distance, he wields a terrible power."

Zith nodded. "The Mordant is a formidable foe, his power magnified by dark magic. For centuries, he's hoarded focuses, seeking to rival the power of the ancient wizards. This crypt is proof of it."

Kath shivered. "We need to know what we face...and we need an advantage."

"Perhaps the Mordant's hoard will betray him."

Kath prayed for it to be so. She offered the monk a hand. "Let's see what secrets the Mordant left behind." They spent the long night sorting through treasure, searching for a glimmer of hope.

6

The Knight Marshal

Stars glittered overhead like the souls of fallen heroes, but the knight marshal took no comfort in the heavens. The gods had forsaken the maroon, their only hope residing in cold hard steel. As if in rebuke, the west wind battered his face, crusting snowflakes in his bearded stubble. Chilled to the bone, the marshal pulled his maroon cloak close, urging his horse up the steep trail. The healer and three knights followed close behind, their saddlebags bulging with venison stolen from wolves. The marshal grimaced at the thought, feeling more like a hounded brigand than a leader of knights.

At least they'd found the right trail. An army of hoof prints dinted the snow, more proof that winter was a second foe. He'd have to figure a way to foil the snow prints, or better yet, turn the tracks to an advantage, another worry to nag at his mind. Little wonder most sane commanders avoided winter wars.

A pair of maroon-cloaked knights stepped from the trees. Both held spears while the taller one carried the curved horn of a sentry slung on a baldric. Grim-faced and hollow-eyed, they nodded as he rode past but not a word was spoken.

The marshal nudged his horse up the trail, his stallion blowing plumes of mist into the chill morning air. Softly falling snow muffled every sound yet he heard the jangle of arms and armor before he saw them. The trees fell away revealing a balding mountaintop, the white snow bloodied with the remnants of an army. Men huddled around meager camp fires, while others slept wrapped in their maroon cloaks, their swords close by their sides. More than a few bore wounds, blood seeping through make-shift bandages. The brave sat side-by-side with the battle-shattered; the first honing their weapons while the latter sat empty-handed, staring with vacant eyes. Defeat was such a bitter thing, something he'd never thought to taste. Looking at the bloodied army, he realized defeat was a disease, leaching the heart from the men. Victory was the only cure and it fell to him to find it. Taking a deep breath, the marshal squared his shoulders and rode among his men, nodding to friends and comrades-in-arms, sharing words of encouragement. His appearance caused a stir, a ripple of murmurs spread in hushed tones. He knew what they sought. All too keen he felt the absence of the king.

The healer dismounted to tend the wounded, but the other three stayed at his back. "Come, we need to find the captains." Holding his mount to a walk, the marshal picked a path among the maroon, seeking the officers. He found them at the summit, ringed around a campfire, sitting in the shadow of the great mage-stone hand. *Stonehand,* the massive statue captured his gaze, thrice the height of a tall man. Unweathered by wind or snow, the ancient mage-stone sat boldly at the mountain's crest, a relic from another age. For half a heartbeat, the great hand seemed to glow. Startled, the marshal reined backwards, but then he realized it was just a trick of the light, the dawn's first rays rearing over the mountaintops. Chagrined, he glared at the statue, its meaning lost to the ages, nothing more than a rallying spot for a routed army.

A campfire illumed the statue's base, snapping and crackling with the promise of warmth. The officers stood at his approach. A squire leaped to hold the marshal's horse as he swung down from the saddle. Lothar was first to greet him. Gripping him close, the leather-faced captain whispered a harsh question. "Is it done?"

"Yes." The single word was laden with sorrow. Lothar looked away, smitten with grief, but the others still held a wild hope in their questioning gazes. One by one, the marshal greeted the knight-captains. Sir Dalt of Ice Tower, Sir Gravis of Sword Keep, Sir Varlin of Dymtower and Sir Krismir of Shieldhold, but two of them were missing. The marshal turned to Lothar. "Sir Boris?"

"Dead from an arrow at the Shieldbreaker. Saw him topple off the wall myself."

"And Sir Kilgar?"

"Took a nasty sword cut in the retreat from the Whore. I sent him with the wounded back to Castlegard. I expect he'll lose the arm." His voice dropped to a husk. "We'll be needing to make some promotions."

"Too many, I fear." Every man lost was a blow to the maroon, especially the officers. Reminded of the king, his gaze went to the squire holding his horse. Caught listening, the young squire blanched pale and then began to lead the horse away, but the marshal stayed him with a word. "Wait." Rounding the far side of the stallion, the marshal tugged the king's sword from his bedroll. *Honor's Edge* gleamed sapphire blue in the morning light, the monk's crystal set in the pommel.

The marshal felt the weight of their stares. More than any crown, this sword symbolized the king of the Octagon. With both hands, he held the great sword aloft, a last tribute to his king. A solemn hush smothered the mountaintop, for the masterless sword told its own tale. One by one, the knights stood in homage, a bitter groan swirling through their ranks.

Sir Gravis was the first to speak, his voice rough with chained emotion. "So it's true. We all hoped..."

The marshal shook his head. "The king took a grievous wound, a sword thrust to the lungs." Their faces turned gray, knowing it was a killing stroke. "We raised a cairn for him on the far side of Raven Pass." He waved the squire away with the horses but kept his three companions close. Cradling the king's sword, he took a seat at the fire. "There's more you should know." His one-eyed stare swept the officers, holding them to silence. "Our king was felled by treachery." Anger leaped through his brother knights, their hands closing on their sword hilts. "I got a good look at the Skeleton King before I slew him. Twin scars marred his face, the brand marks of a broken octagon." Anger rippled around the fire. "It was not the Mordant who slew our king, but one of our own."

"An unmade knight!" Sir Dalt shook his head in disbelief.

"*Raymond!*" Sir Lothar spat the name like a curse. "King Ursus should have executed the slimy bastard rather than exile him."

Sir Gravis said, "But how? Only a champion could best the king and Raymond was never a champion."

The marshal scowled. "It was never a fair fight. Raymond's hand dealt the blow, but the sword was cursed, bespelled with dark magic. You saw how the black blade shattered the blue. Only a cursed sword could do that."

Sir Abrax and Sir Rannock seconded him. "The blue blade shrieked in pain whenever it struck the black. The king waged a mighty fight till the prince's sword failed him. *Mordbane* shattered like it was made of crystal. Dark magic slew our king."

More than one captain made the hand sign against evil. "Never trust the pentacle!"

"The gods curse them all!"

"Damn their black souls to the deepest hell!"

The marshal let them rail, waiting for their anger to simmer. When silence returned, it was Krismir, the youngest among them, that asked the question. "So what do we do now?"

The marshal did not hesitate. "We fight, as the Octagon always does. Harry the enemy at every turn and give them no quarter. Hound them till they retreat to the north or die beneath our swords."

"And claim vengeance for our king." Sir Gravis's voice was as cold as a winter storm.

"Just so." The marshal's words carried the weight of an oath.

Sir Lothar said, "So it'll be a winter war."

The marshal nodded. "The back end of winter for a backhanded war, like none we've ever fought." He tried to keep the worry from his voice, "We'll need supplies. And more men."

Lothar replied, "Already done. I've sent riders to every castle and keep along the Spines. The old veterans can hold Castlegard but I've given orders to empty the others. No sense guarding the wall when the gate's already breached. And if needs be, we'll have Castlegard to fall back on."

"True enough." A grim thought, but the marshal could not fault the logic. "And what of the enemy?"

"They've set up camp at the Whore, securing the entrance to the pass, almost as if the bastards are waiting for something."

Waiting for what? But the marshal left the question unsaid. Instead, he focused on the needs at hand. "We'll set rings of pickets and scouts so we'll have plenty of warning if the enemy comes hunting. And we need to find a way to keep the snow from betraying our every movement, or better yet, use the prints to our advantage."

Lothar gave him a wolfish grin. "I've got an idea about that."

The captains huddled around the crackling fire, discussing tactics and battle strategies. Most were accustomed to fighting behind stout walls. The marshal soon learned that old ways died hard. Working with Lothar, he prodded their thoughts towards fresh paths. Outnumbered and forced from their walls, they'd have to fight like brigands, striking where they were least expected and then disappearing into the forest. The biggest problem was the snow's betrayal. When the final plans were laid and all the details discussed, one thing remained unspoken. To a man, the captains turned their stares toward the marshal, their gazes dropping to the masterless sword of a dead king. Lothar broached the unspoken question. "Will you wield it?"

A lethal silence settled around the fire. Now that the question was finally upon him, the marshal felt a strange sense of relief. "I'm not worthy."

His words sparked an outrage, "Who's more worthy than the marshal?"

"Surely the king named a successor!"

"One of us should take up the sword!"

Sir Rannock said, "The maroon needs a king...and all the Anvril sons are dead!"

The harsh truth doused their words like water to a flame. Sir Gravis, ever the king's man, repeated the question baiting every tongue. "Did the king name a successor?"

The marshal took a deep breath, as if girding for a fight. "He spoke of his children."

"But all the sons are dead!"

The marshal met their stares. "There is another."

Puzzlement scrawled their faces. "What, a bastard prince?"

Lothar was the first to remember. "Not the Imp!"

"A *daughter!*"

"Only a scamp of a girl!"

The marshal parried their protests. "She's the king's one true heir."

"But a daughter can't lead."

Sir Varlin gave a wolfish-grin. "But she can *breed!* Wed her to a captain and we'll get a true heir for the Octagon."

"Aye, she'll need a strong sword in the night!"

Their talk angered the marshal, their faces transformed from sworn knights to wolves stalking a hen house. Surging to his feet, he thrust the king's sword into the ground. *"Enough!"* The sapphire blade quivered upright, the crystal gleaming like a baleful eye. "There'll be no talk of wedding or bedding. We've a battle to fight and a war to win." He stared at them till shame colored their faces. "For now, *I* will lead the Octagon. And no man will wield the king's sword till a true heir is acclaimed." Dissension smoldered in some of their faces, yet none dared to protest, at least not openly. "Let the war prove the worth of the king's successor." That got them thinking. "*Honor's Edge* will be sent to Castlegard to await the hand of the heir. In the meantime, we have a war to fight, a war to win."

A murmur rippled through the men, talk of kingship and swords, but the ugliness had been averted.

The marshal raised his voice above the murmur. "You've all got your orders and there is much to be done. Weapons need to be honed and men selected for each sortie. We attack at twilight."

"Twilight!" Sir Dalt's voice rang with protest. "But the men have barely recovered from Raven Pass."

The marshal met his stare. "I'll not let them dwell on defeat. They need a victory and the enemy needs to bleed for the king." His voice hardened to steel. "You have your orders. See to them or I'll appoint another captain in your stead."

Their stares crossed like swords, but Sir Dalt was the first to concede. With a stiff salute, he stalked away. The others followed till only Lothar was left. His friend sidled close, joining him in the shadow of the great hand. "Do you think that was wise?"

"What? Challenging Dalt? The chain of command must be obeyed." Weary to the bone, the marshal leaned on the king's sword.

"No. You not claiming the sword, leaving them without a king."

"We have no king."

"But they won't wait for a mere slip of a girl."

"It's not about the girl; it's about the monks."

"What?" Lothar shied away as if madness was a contagion, but the marshal pulled him back with a sharp look. "There's much you don't know. When I stood vigil on the king's cairn, a frost owl flew out of the night to join me. When it landed, it changed into a monk."

"A *shifter!*" Lothar hissed making the hand sign against evil.

"You've met him before. We both have. The same monk who brought warning to the king, the day we learned a demon possessed a prince." A vision of glowing red eyes filled his mind, like looking into the very pits of hell. The marshal suppressed a shiver. "For the sake of the Light, the monk asked me not to name an heir."

"So now we're taking counsel from monks? And a shifter no less?"

"Yes, but the monks have been right before. They held the truth about the demon-prince. Their counsel bears considering."

Lothar chewed the edge of his mustache. "So they expect us to wait for a mere girl?"

"They expect us to fight, to play our part in the battle to come."

"Our *part?*"

"There's more you should know."

Lothar waited, his face braced for battle.

"After the death of the king, I took a good look at the black blade that slew him. The pommel was shaped like an octagon with a pair of coiled dragons gracing the crossguard. Beneath the guard, the maker's mark was clear, an octagon surrounding the initials *OS.*".

"*Orrin Surehammer,*" Lothar's face paled. "The lost blade!"

The marshal nodded. "Boric's sword, the first blue steel blade, but instead of sapphire blue, the sword was dark as pitch, corrupted and cursed. With my own hands I pulled the sword from the king's chest. Even through my gauntlets, I felt the cold dread of it. That sword radiates Darkness," his voice dropped to a whisper, "and it called to me...with a promise of power."

Lothar's hand crept to his sword hilt. "What did you do?"

"I hurled it into the woods." The marshal shrugged as if trying to dislodge a great weight. "Later, after we'd raised a cairn to the king, I went in search of it. I wrapped it in a blanket and charged Baldwin to throw it in Eye Lake. Perhaps the lake's depths can chain the evil." He hesitated to speak the rest, yet he needed to tell someone, "At night, the blade haunts my dreams...and taunts me with the promise of victory."

Lothar made the hand sign against evil. "More sorcery. Better to send it to a watery grave."

"True enough." He gave Lothar a wary look. "But it tells us much about our foe. The Mordant pits our own legends against us."

"A cursed sword sent to slay a king, makes you wonder what else we're fighting."

"Darkness, we're fighting Darkness itself." The marshal pulled the king's sword from the cold, hard ground. "Heaven help us if we fail."

7

Blaine

Blaine's sword sliced the air with a vicious whisper. Haunted by nightmares of the winged fiend, he slashed left and then right, a whirl of steel, but his foe slipped away. Pivoting left, he loosed a head-high cleave. Kath ducked beneath his swing and lunged forward. Anger flashed across her face as she loosed a whirlwind of strikes. Blaine retreated, parrying her assault, steel clanging against steel. He'd never seen the girl fight with such venom. She lunged forward, the flat of her sword striking his chainmail with a resounding ring.

"What's wrong with you?" She glared up at him. "You're sparring like a wounded bear."

"And you're fighting like a demon possessed." Blaine snarled and stepped back, breathing plumes of mist into the cold morning air. "Enough." He rammed the training sword into the sheath as if it would quench his anger. Taking up his blue steel sword, he shrugged the harness across his shoulders and began to turn away.

Kath grabbed his arm. "What troubles you?

Anger spiked through him. He turned on her. "*What troubles me?*" Rage rode his voice, yet the girl did not flinch. Fists clenched, he glared at her, but he could not speak of the whores in his bed or the winged monster pecking at his window, shame and fear and lust all tied together in a terrible knot. Instead, his anger lashed in a different direction. "That *voice* in the bloody cavern."

Kath nodded.

"It said that the Octagon is fallen. That the king is dead."

Her face paled but she did not look away.

"The voice lied, right? That was just an evil lie?"

Her voice choked to a whisper. "No."

"*No!*"

"Duncan said it happened."

He reeled at the answer, unwilling to believe the Octagon was defeated. "And you believe it?"

Kath gave a grim nod. "I believe Duncan." Her gaze slid away. "Other things he said have proved true."

His rage exploded. "Then why do we sit here, doing nothing?"

"What would you have us do?"

"Take the horses and ride south! Find the Octagon and add our swords to the maroon!"

"In the dead of winter? Across the steppes? How far do you think we'd get?" She glared at him. "And what of Danya and Zith? They'll not survive the ride...and I'll not leave them."

"So you'll sit here and rot?"

Her head snapped back as if slapped.

Anger snarled his voice. "I want the Mordant's head."

"No." Kath's face turned ghost-pale. "He must die by the crystal dagger or it will be no true death."

He glared at her. "The king gave me a hero's sword. I mean to use it."

"No." She gripped his sword arm. "It's not about heroes. We *must* put an end to the Mordant. His evil has grown too great."

"Or maybe you want the glory for yourself." Blaine pulled away. Beneath his feet, the rune-carved courtyard quaked.

"Do you feel that?" Kath glared at him. "Evil is real. We fought evil in the cavern and won a victory for the Light."

"Did we win? It does not feel like a victory!"

She looked away. "I know."

Beneath his boots, the tremor slowed to a stop. Blaine turned away, watching the line of captured soldiers pass rocks into the gullet of the bloody cavern, sealing the demon in the depths. "The Citadel is ours, but the Mordant's long gone, marched south with his vast legions. For all we know, he could be ravaging the southern kingdoms while we sit here, idly waiting." He glared at her. "Instead of a victory, this feels like a trap."

"We're not idle."

"Aren't we?" He choked on a bitter laugh. "Zith wanders the halls searching for scrolls and magical trinkets while the rest of us sit around, sharpening our swords. I call that idle."

"We'll find a way south." Her gaze slipped away. "The gods will help."

"Really?" Sarcasm leavened with bitterness rose like bile in his throat. "And what of the Octagon? Did the gods help the maroon?"

"Will two more swords make a difference?"

"I'd like to think so."

She gave him a crooked smile. "I'd like to think so too, but we're charged to slay the Mordant."

"And how will we do that from here?"

"We'll find advantages...and we'll find a way south."

He heard despair in her voice, despair laden with frustration, yet he could not quell his own anger. "The bloody monks said we need to slay the Mordant ere the red comet set." He jabbed a finger toward the west, toward the red comet hovering above the dark waters. "The bloody comet is getting low in the sky."

"I know."

Her voice sounded so small it galled him. He wanted to help her, he wanted to shake some sense into her and ride south, he wanted to find the Mordant and slay him with his blue steel sword, but he could do none of it. Instead, he reached for his maroon cloak and swirled it around his shoulders. "My sword is yours." Blaine stalked away, anger in his stride, wondering how victory could taste so empty.

8

Katherine

Awolf's howl shivered through the marble corridors, piercing her gloom. Kath smiled to hear such a glorious wildness set loose in the Mordant's palace. She imagined how it would enrage the former ruler to find wolf droppings in his gilded hallways. Her smile broke into a feral grin, a petty revenge. Kath followed the mountain wolf's howls, Bear and Boar padding silent as shadows at her back.

A pair of wolf-faced warriors stood guard at the doorway, nodding at her approach. "Svala."

"How is she today?"

Balthus, the taller of the two answered, "The same, Svala. She will wake when the gods will it."

Always the same answer, always said with the same complete confidence. "Let's hope the gods will it to be soon." Balthus nodded and Kath passed through the doorway. They'd claimed a corner chamber, the outer doors flung wide, opening onto a crenellated turret, but instead of frigid cold it was cozy as a wolf's den. Rich wool tapestries draped the turret like tents, thick wool carpets strewn across the floor. Ruby reds, sapphire blues, and bright golds, the vibrant colors hung at every angle, an odd jumble of embroidered faces peering from the ceiling like a complex painting. The effect was dazzling.

Bryx yipped a greeting. The mountain wolf lay sprawled beside a pallet heaped with furs. Danya slept beneath the furs, her long brown hair combed out, her face pale but serene, as if she dreamt a good dream. Kath stared at her friend, willing her to wake.

"Come and sit, Svala." Neven shifted amongst the pillows without releasing Danya's hand.

Kath sat cross-legged beside the wolf-faced warrior. "How is she?"

"The same, always drinking the broth drizzled on her lips, but otherwise she does not stir." He bent his head, brushing a kiss across Danya's hand, the open affection so effortless it sent a pang through Kath's heart.

"What is it, Svala?"

Kath closed her face, lest it betray her, unable to speak of Duncan and their marriage in the shield forest...and how much she yearned for his touch. "It is good that she has you to care for her."

The wolf-faced warrior flashed a warm smile. "She's captured my heart. We will wed when the war is finished, and she will take the full tattoos of our den."

"Danya's found her true place among you. She never really belonged in the south."

Bryx chuffed as if in agreement, licking Danya's face.

"And you, Svala?"

"What?" His words caught her off guard.

"Where do you belong?"

The question opened a chasm in her heart. Duncan was gone, her father dead, the knights of the Octagon defeated...she reeled at so much loss. "I...don't know."

Behind her, Bear's deep voice rumbled, "The Svala belongs with us."

Neven's gaze quickened. "Is it true, Svala? Will you return with us when the war is ended?"

Kath did not answer, for somehow it did not feel true. "We have another war to win before I can go home." They looked at her, but she did not say where that home would be. In truth, she had no answer, just a gaping hollowness inside. Tugging on Duncan's warrior ring, she looked away, hiding her own uncertainty. "I just came to see how Danya is faring." She stood to go.

"Svala?"

Neven stopped her with a question.

"Yes?"

"When you go south, you must take us," he gestured to Danya and Bryx and the other wolf warriors sitting in the shadows, "all of us with you."

"When Danya wakes, she can decide for herself."

"No, Svala."

His voice held such certainty that she stared at him.

"The Ancestor said that the Beastspeaker must go south with the War Helm...and Danya agreed. She made us swear before we marched on the Citadel."

More prophecy, Kath shivered, but she did not want to risk another friend. "Danya's already done so much...she deserves the peace of the north."

"There will be no peace unless we win."

The words hit her like a hammer blow, the weight of the world falling on her shoulders.

"Will you swear, Svala?"

"Yes," for she could give no other answer.

"Good." Neven settled back amongst the pillows, never releasing Danya's hand. "When the time is right, we will be ready."

Bryx yipped as if in agreement.

Kath took her leave, stepping from the tented sanctuary. Lost in thought, she roamed the marble hallways, shaken by the exchange. Her friend lay locked in a healing coma, yet she'd found her heart's desire...while Kath's heart felt like ashes. Somehow she had to find a way south and she had to win...but she felt so empty. Frustration warred with sorrow, she felt so hopeless, so lost. Kath gripped the crystal dagger, feeling like a pawn of prophecy.

9

Juliana

"*C*aptain!*" A harsh knock on the door startled Juliana from sleep. *"Captain, I need to see you!"* Nestled beneath a warm quilt, she stirred, placing a hand against the hull to feel her ship. The gentle creak and sway spoke of a smooth sea and the faint thrumming of the hull bespoke a full sail. Reassured, she smiled knowing the *Sea Sprite* sped homeward at steady clip. Rising, she peered through the salt-encrusted porthole. Dawn cracked the horizon, a glimmer of golden light reflected on calm seas. *Smooth waters, no enemy in sight, and no footsteps drumming overhead,* the apparent calm belied the urgency in her first mate's voice. "A moment!" Juliana took the time to pull on her boots and belt a long dagger to her waist. Tucking a wayward strand of copper-bright hair behind her ear, she opened the cabin door to find her first mate hovering outside, an anxious look on his suntanned face.

Marcus stabbed her with a daggered glare. "Wren found this tied to the crow's nest. He swears it was not there yesterday."

Her gaze flicked to his hands, shocked by what he held. "Come in." She stepped aside, locking the door behind him.

Marcus filled her cabin. A big burly man with dark wavy hair tied at his nape, a gilded seashell dangling from his left ear for luck, he smelled of leather and salt. Setting the pouch on her chart table, he stepped back as if it held a coiled cobra.

A red and blue checkered shield surmounted by a white osprey with wings spread wide emblazoned the pouch, marking it as a royal dispatch. Juliana's fingers traced the embroidery, but instead of tanned leather, the pouch was made of sealskin...as if it was meant to weather a storm.

"Never seen one like that."

"Nor I."

"Never found one tied to a crow's nest either."

And that was the riddle. Messenger pouches usually waited for her in ports of call or were passed from ship to ship. They didn't just appear while under sail betwixt a long sea crossing.

"I've sworn Wren to silence." His deep voice was a low growl. "Can't let rumors of magic fester."

"Just so." As a Royal J, Juliana was acquainted with magic, enough to value its uses without stirring irrational fears, but her seamen were a superstitious lot and ill omens could scuttle a voyage. "You did well, but there's no one in Navarre who could magic a message pouch halfway across the Western Ocean."

"Yet it's here."

She gave him a slanted look. "And the watch noticed nothing unusual?"

"Nothing reported."

"Then we'd best learn the meaning behind the riddle." She untied the elaborate knot, more proof the dispatch came from Castle Seamount. Inside she found two scrolls. One bore the seal of her father, the king of Navarre, and the other bore the seal of her sister. *Jordan!* Her swordish sister was meant to be Wayfaring with the Kiralynn monks deep in the Southern Mountains, a long way for a scroll to travel, a riddle of another sort. At the bottom of the pouch, she found a wooden disk with a message coil. The message coil gave her pause for they were only used in dire times.

Marcus hissed when he saw it. "An ill-omen."

"Perhaps." She reached for her sister's scroll first. Cramped handwriting crowded the page. The familiar scrawl told a tale of ambush in the monastery, of a long journey across Erdhe, of strange visions and a wedding in a ruined keep...and then it spoke of death. Juliana issued a strangled cry. "Death at Castle Seamount!"

"Navarre's been attacked?"

"Assaulted by treachery." Juliana sank onto her bunk, feeling gut-punched.

"Treachery?"

"The Curse of the Vowels."

Marcus gasped making the hand sign against evil. "The king?"

"Survives, but many Royal Is are dead, my aunts, my uncles, felled by poison." Juliana struggled to hold back tears. "How could this happen?"

Marcus had no answer. "Perhaps the other scroll?"

Taking a steadying breath, she broke the second seal, her gaze scanning her father's bold hand. *"Impossible!"* The vellum slipped from her fingers.

Marcus stared at her. "New orders?"

"A death sentence." She nudged the scroll towards him.

He scooped it up, holding the vellum to the light, his lips silently forming the words. *"By the gods!"* He glared at her. "This must be a lie!"

"Yet the seals and the knot work name it true, though I cannot believe the king would issue such orders."

"But you cannot sail the fleet *there,* 'tis madness."

"Poison and prophecies," she shook her head. "Perhaps we live in mad times." Her gaze sought the message coil. "Or perhaps the answer lies within."

He hovered beside her, his fists clenched.

"Best if you wait outside."

Marcus gave her a grave nod. "I'll be waiting."

She saw him to the door and locked it behind him. For half a heartbeat she leaned against the sturdy door, absorbing the sounds of her ship. Taking a deep breath, she stared at the wooden disc spooled with parchment as if it carried a venomous adder. Message coils always accompanied the most dire dispatches. Bearing only a few words, the coils either verified or negated the scrolls they accompanied. She'd heard tell of coils that read 'ignore', or 'do the opposite', or simply 'obey'. Juliana prayed for the first and feared the latter. Whatever the message, she was charged to follow the will of her king. "Only one way to be sure." Snatching the wooden coil from the table, she carefully removed the long thin strip of parchment. A swirl of red ink marked one end, followed by a long list of words. On its own, the list was gibberish, but every ship's captain carried a means to decode the message. Setting the parchment aside, she unlocked her sea chest, fishing through charts and spare clothing till she found the leather satchel. Opening the satchel, she revealed four wooden rods imprinted with the crest of Navarre. Ranging in thickness from a skinny chicken bone to a cook's rolling pin, each two foot rod bore a colored dot and a nail in one end. Matching the red swirl to the blue rod, she pierced the parchment with the nail and began wrapping it around the rod, overlapping the parchment in such a fashion that only the first letter of each line remained visible. When the winding was complete, she took a steadying breath before reading the message. Writ along the length of the rod in clear script, the message read, *"Believe and obey with all haste"*.

"No!" The cry shivered out of her. Sinking to her bunk, she read it again, but the words remained the same. A cold foreboding claimed her. She shook her head in disbelief. They were asking her to risk her

entire ship, nay the entire fleet, for the sake of prophecies and visions. It was madness, an insane folly, a cruel jest of some sort. Desperate to disregard the message, she reached for her sister's scroll and read it again, clutching at details. So many phrases sounded like Jordan, yet the message spoke of god-given visions and death. Her swordish sister had always been so steady and sure, as dependable as steel, and now she claimed a seer's powers? It was damn near impossible to believe...but duty mattered to Jordan...as much as it did to Juliana...and the message was properly sealed and confirmed.

A fist hammered the door. "*Captain!*"

Delay would not change the message. Carefully unwrapping the parchment coil, Juliana returned the rods to her sea chest. Taking a steadying breath, she unlocked the door.

Marcus gaped when he saw her face. "So it's true!"

She gave him a grim nod. "Raise the pennant flag for captains' parley. The fleet has new orders."

His face paled. "You won't do it. It's a death mission."

She steeled her voice. "You have your orders."

He stepped back as if slapped. "Yes, captain." He turned to do her bidding.

She closed and locked her door. *Death and duty,* the thoughts chased her mind. Leaning against the sturdy wood, she worried that Marcus was right.

10

Blaine

Something darted behind the statue. The sneaky movement snagged Blaine's gaze, yet he never slowed the speed of his sword. Blue steel cleaved the cold morning air as he worked through the classical forms of the sword, but his gaze remained fixed on the statue. This early in the morning, the great rune-carved courtyard was usually deserted, yet something skulked behind the statue, he was sure of it.

Flowing from *slash of the snake* to *strike of the eagle*, Blaine whirled, deliberately turning his back on the statue. Poised on the balls of his feet, his blue sword gripped in both gauntleted hands, he listened for an attack, yet none came. Six heartbeats later, he pivoted just in time to spy a small dark-haired lad scurry up the palace steps, disappearing between the golden doors. Skinny and short and clad in a filthy tunic, the lad looked like a street urchin...yet he carried a short sword. *A short sword*...mischief or malevolence, Blaine decided to follow.

Taking the stairs two at a time, Blaine slipped between the golden doors just as the lad turned down the left hand hallway. Blaine followed, stepping lightly across the marble floor. Braziers glowed the length of the hall, striping the walls with light and shadow. The boy moved like a thief, scurrying from one shadow to the next. Carefully peering around each corner, he flinched at any sound. Clearly the boy was afraid, yet he pressed deeper into the palace, the sword clutched awkwardly in his two hands.

Intrigued, Blaine followed, keeping just enough distance to remain unheard. The palace was a labyrinth of luxury: marble hallways, gilded braziers and rich tapestries; yet the urchin seemed to know his way, compounding the riddle. Blaine turned the corner...and the lad was gone. He scanned the hallway, but found nowhere for the lad to hide. Swearing silently, Blaine peered around the far corner, but saw no sign of the urchin. Puzzled, he retraced his steps. A strange, bitter smell rankled his nostrils. Breathing deep, he traced the smoky scent to a tapestry. *A tapestry!* Twitching the tapestry aside, he discovered stairs leading down, a bracketed torch glittering at the bottom. The god-cursed palace was a tangled labyrinth, worse than he'd ever thought.

Sword at the ready, Blaine descended the stairs. Instead of dark marble, the walls were dull granite, gray and unadorned. Perhaps he'd stumbled onto the servants' quarters...or something worse. The smoky smell grew stronger, scratching at his throat. Bitter and irritating, the noxious scent was vaguely familiar. He'd smelled it before, in other parts of the palace, but never this strong.

Peering around the corner, he spied the urchin-lad standing in front of a closed door, the short sword raised in his both hands. Gripping the sword, the lad glared at the door as if summoning his courage.

If the lad truly needed the sword, he wouldn't stand a chance. It was time to end this charade. Blaine stepped into the hallway, torchlight glittering on his silver surcoat, but the boy never turned. Instead, he opened the door and plunged inside.

Angry shouts erupted from the chamber.

Blaine leaped forward, barreling through the doorway. Bitter smoke stung his nostrils, a blue haze clouding his vision, but then he saw them, dark-robed *priests!* With long bright knives, they slashed at the boy. Blaine grabbed the lad by his tunic, and hurled him backwards. Stepping between the boy and the priests, Blaine snarled, "Fight me!" He slashed left and right. The tip of his sword caught a priest's throat, opening a bright red slash. Blood sprayed the others, a flailing corpse falling to the floor.

By all rights, the priests should have fled...but instead, they leaped to a frenzied attack. Knives slashed towards his face. Hands clawed at his legs. They fought like rabid dogs, biting and kicking. Blaine struck left and right, cleaving a path through flesh and bone. Screams filled the chamber and blood spattered the walls bright red yet the priests pressed the attacked. Stumbling over fresh corpses, they clung to Blaine's arms and legs, trying to pull him down, trying to bite through chainmail and leather. And then he saw their faces, their mouths stained dark blue, their eyes filmed white like wet maggots. Horror and revulsion gripped him in equal measure. Flinching from their touch, he swung his blue blade, severing limbs and heads. A berserker's madness took him. Laughing, he hacked and cut, his sword cleaving flesh till nothing moved save twitching corpses.

Blaine staggered to a stop, blood dripping from his sword. His nostrils stung from the blue smoke. Spying a wine flagon, he dumped it on the brazier, quenching the flames. A billow of noxious blue smoke laced with wine belched to the ceiling. Peering through the smoky haze, Blaine saw pallets pushed along the wall, mounds of clothing and hoarded food stacked between them, as if the thrice-damned priests had nested in the chamber. "*Priests!*" He made the word a curse.

"Not priests."

He whirled, his sword raised...but it was just the boy.

"Not priests...acolytes."

"How can you tell?"

"By their robes, poor quality wool, too scratchy for full-sworn priests."

Blaine reached for a robe, feeling the scratchy weave. "You've a good eye for cloth." He used the robe to wipe the blood from his sword.

The boy stepped close, staring down at the dead. "And besides, priests would never be chained to Vetra."

"Vetra?"

"A plant they grow in their secret gardens."

"Why?"

"To chew or smoke in their braziers. It's supposed to cause visions, to let them hear the Dark God's voice, but too much makes them crazy. Chained to the smoke, they become rabid like animals, craving it always, willing to kill for it...till it turns their eyes white as blind mice. Once their eyes turn, it kills them." He kicked a dead foot as if daring the corpse to rise.

"Smoke that turns men into monsters." Blaine scowled, backing away from the brazier. The Citadel held a legion of horrors. "How do you know so much?"

"My brother was chosen as an acolyte."

Things began to make sense. "And you came looking for him?"

The boy nodded.

"To kill him or to rescue him?"

The boy gave him a dead-eyed stare. "Depends on his eyes."

Blaine looked at the lad with a measure of respect. "You see him here?"

The boy took his time, making his way through the tangled corpses. His face paled at the carnage but he did not puke. Returning to Blaine, he gave the smallest of nods. "No."

"You think there's more nests like this?"

"Yes."

"Priests as well as acolytes?" Blaine shepherded the boy from the room, wanting to get away from the foul smoke.

"Yes."

"I've a mind to hunt some priests."

The boy gave him a fierce look. "I can help."

"I thought you might." Blaine sheathed his sword. "What's your name?"

"Dermit."

He led the boy back up the stairs and through the tapestry curtain. "When'd you last have a good meal, Dermit?"

The boy looked away. "Can't remember."

"My name's Sir Blaine and all this fighting has made me hungry." He steered the boy back towards the royal kitchens. "Come on, let's find something to eat. And then we'll talk about hunting priests."

11

General Haith

General Haith stood atop the battlement of Raven Pass, savoring the victory. As the Mordant's battle commander, he'd ordered all memory of the maroon to be struck down and destroyed. Soldiers in black prowled the battlements, checking the bodies, dumping slain knights from the ramparts. A few still lived, screaming as they toppled from the walls. Bodies piled below, scavenged by the victors. Octagon shields were defiled before being shattered. Maroon battle banners were severed from their poles, cut loose to ride the wind like flotsam. A single banner fluttered southward like a frightened eel, homeless, despoiled, vanquished, an omen of things to come. A smile rode the general's face; he'd waited a lifetime for this victory, the beginning of a great conquest.

Smoke rose in dark pillars from the central yard. The dead burned upon a massive pyre, a fitting sacrifice to the Dark Lord. Battle clerics in dark robes supervised the fire, often despoiling the corpses before consigning them to the flames. The general despised the priests but they had their uses. Turning his back on the greasy stench, he continued his progress along the wall.

The knights had built well. Twin battlements spanned the chasm, blocking the way south. Strong and tall and crenellated, the battlements were impressive yet they'd proved no match for the Mordant's magic. In one mighty blast, the Wizard's Fist had smashed the gates to oblivion, turning the siege into a rout. Magic was a dread weapon, something the knights forgot at their peril.

The general reached the central barbican and found a massive catapult crouched upon the turret like a wood-carved dragon. Snapping his fingers, he captured the attention of a centurion. "Disassemble the catapult and reposition it at the southern mouth of the pass. We'll turn the enemy's own weapons against him." Soldiers leaped to obey, black cloaks swarming the mighty catapult like a plague of ants. Numbers always mattered in battle. His army had vastly superior numbers *and* magic, an invincible pairing. The general stared down the gullet of Raven Pass, a narrow gash sundering the Dragon Spine Mountains, the keyhole to the southern kingdoms. His troops swarmed the pass, a formidable mixture of taals, duegars and men, a hundred thousand strong, an invincible army keen to wreck havoc upon the south.

"General Haith!"

He turned to find Trantor, his personal snargon of the duegars waddling toward him. Squat and barrel-chested, the duegar's height barely reached the general's belt buckle, yet his teeth were filed to points, displaying a ferocity that belied his size.

"My lord, we finished the sweep."

The general waited, "And?"

"We've sniffed out the chambers of both walls and found no hint of magic save our own." The duegar grinned, "The knights left in a hurry. Their storerooms are stocked with weapons and food but there's no magic."

"Are you certain? You know our lord craves magic."

The snargon bristled. "I know my craft."

"Then sniff out the king's quarters again, just to be sure. Do it yourself, don't leave it for one of your minions. I'll be sleeping in the king's bed tonight and I don't want any surprises."

"As you command." The snargon gave him a sloppy salute and then turned to waddle away.

The general bit back a rebuke. Duegars were surly little bastards, a spawn of the Pit, but they had their uses. Having witnessed more magic than he cared to remember, the general made it a habit to always keep a snargon close, a protection from enemies both within and without. One did not gain gray hairs in the service of the Mordant without a certain amount of precaution.

A cold wind snatched at his fur-lined cloak. Winter's bite was milder in the south, yet he found himself looking forward to a warm bed protected by stout stone walls, a *king's* bed, a fitting start to the conquest.

The general finished traversing the battlement. The sheer granite walls of Raven Pass towered overhead. His gaze climbed the lichen-stained granite, patches of bright yellow forming the crude figure of rearing horse. A noble talisman, yet it had brought no luck to the knights.

He reached the end and found his aide, Major Ruggar, waiting for him. Tall and blond with a pock-marked face, Ruggar had a weasel's cunning leavened with a strong sense of survival, the very traits the general sought in his aides. The major snapped a smart salute, "I've seen to the horses. The stables are impressive, spacious and clean and well stocked with hay, but the knights did not leave a single nag within the stalls."

The general smothered his disappointment; horses were crucial to his plans. "Post double guards on the stables and keep the taals well away." The taals were fierce fighters but they viewed horses as easy meat, a mistake he could not afford. The general gave his aide a piercing glare. "You dare not lose a single mount." Responsibility laced with threat, such was the way of the north. The general watched as Ruggar gave a terse nod, "Yes, sir."

"And order the cooks to prepare a feast for the officers, the best the octagon has to offer. We'll dine on a king's fare tonight. To the victors go the spoils."

Ruggar flashed a knowing grin. "Yes, sir."

"Now tell me about the treasure."

Ruggar braced as if for a storm. "So far we've only found only one chest of coins, mostly silver."

The general scowled, his words laced with suspicion. "A meager trove for a king. There must be a hidden storeroom somewhere."

Sweat beaded Ruggar's face. "We'll keep searching."

"Do that. And be sure to take my share before the priests claim their tithe."

"Already done."

"Good. And what of their maps?"

A chilling howl erupted from the far end of the courtyard, a savage sound to set men's souls on edge. A second howl chased the first, till the yard rang with the blood-lust of a hunting pack. General Haith swore, "By the Nine Hells, those beasts had best be well chained."

"Voltran has the hounds in hand."

The general gave his aide a sharp look. "You're a fool if you believe him. No one cows a gore hound save the Mordant." The major had the good sense not to answer. The general grimaced at the twisted howls. He would never have brought the gore hounds south save for the Mordant's orders. "Those beasts pose as much a threat to our own army as to the enemy. Tell Voltran to feed them some dead knights. It might quell their bloodlust and give them a taste for the enemy."

"The priests will protest."

Anger snarled through the general. "The priests serve at my sufferance."

Ruggar stiffened, "As you command." He snapped a salute and started to turn away but the general forestalled him. "And Ruggar, when you are done with Voltran, see to it that my personal effects are placed in the king's chamber. Do what you can to make them more befitting a battle commander."

"As you say, my lord," Ruggar sped for the stairs.

The tortured howls intensified, grating against the general's mind, unearthing visions of gruesome rituals in the Mordant's bloody cavern. Some memories were better left buried. Deciding to quit the battlement, the general followed his aide down the stairs, the thick oak door mercifully muting the howls.

A single turn of the stairs brought him to the knights' quarters. Earlier in the day, he'd taken a cursory tour of the honeycombed rooms, walking the hallways till he found the king's chambers. He'd expected opulence, dismayed to discover size was the only true difference. Cold and austere, the royal chambers showed no adornment save for a wall of ancient swords and battered shields. Grim quarters for a king, proving the octagon knights knew how to fight but not how to live. Service to the Mordant was so very different. Those who served well, lived well, but the struggle to reach the higher tiers was slippery and fraught with danger. Having gained the pinnacle, the general fully intended to enjoy the luxury owed to his power.

A young centurion approached. "My lord, General Marris is asking for you."

"Lead the way." The centurion led him to a small dining room. Black-cloaked officers crowded around an oak table, an iron candelabra hanging overhead. Spare and plain, the room was heated by a roaring hearth, a pair of windows shuttered against the cold.

"Attention!"

The officers flung irritated glances toward the door and then snapped to attention once they saw him. General Marris was the first to speak. "My lord, we found the maps you were hoping for."

His interest piqued, he strode to the table. Scrolled maps were spread across the tabletop, mountains and rivers and castles inked onto parchment. His gaze drank in the details. Mapmaking was a military art and these were exquisite. "Show me what you've found."

General Marris unrolled a parchment depicting the Dragon Spine Mountains. "This shows all the Octagon's strongholds. It seems they've cut more trails through the western Spines than we ever guessed."

The general grinned. "Maps are the perfect traitors. They let you see the land through the enemy's eyes." He studied the detail, squinting at some of the markings. "It shows more than just strongholds. I'll wager these horseshoes denote stables for fresh mounts, most likely for messengers." His gaze circled the officers, choosing two captains. "Lyndon and Crowley, take a pair of cohorts and raid the two nearest stations north and south of the pass. Kill the knights and capture the horses. Bring the mounts back unharmed." His voice stabbed like a knife. "I want those mounts. Horses are key to the Mordant's plans."

The two captains snapped brisk salutes.

"Go at once. Take whatever men you need but take no taals and no mounts."

Crowley stammered. "Go afoot? Even the officers?"

"Yes. All mounts are to be held in reserve for a special mission. Anyone who dares use a horse without my express permission will be fed to the gore hounds."

A grim silence fell on the chamber.

The general snarled, "You're wasting time."

Saluting, the captains beat a hasty retreat.

The general's gaze sought the maps. "What else have you found?" A wave of dizziness ambushed him. Perhaps it was the blazing fire, or the closeness of the room, for he found himself slick with sweat, leaning against the table. "Open those shutters."

A major leaped to obey.

A cold breeze blew in, banishing his dizziness. The general moved closer to the window, thankful the gore hounds had fallen silent. "Have you found any maps of the southern kingdoms?"

An aide unrolled a map painted bright with color. Castlegard was proudly embellished with gold, the great castle protecting a saddle-shaped valley at the start of the Southern Road. The general's gaze followed the ancient road south to the foothills of the Southern Mountains. Beyond the foothills all details disappeared, swallowed by a vast toothy maw of snowcapped mountains. So the Octagon knights were ignorant of the Kiralynn Monastery, or at least their maps said so. He stared at the inked mountains as if will alone could unearth their secrets.

"General Haith!"

The croaking cry came from beyond the open window.

"General Haith you are summoned!"

Recognizing the demonic nature of the voice, fear gripped the general's neck. "This is for me. The rest of you wait here." His hand on his sword hilt, he strode from the council chamber making straight for the stairs. Climbing the spiral, he stepped out onto the battle ramparts. A brisk wind caught at his gray hair, his black cape flaring behind him.

"General Haith you are summoned!" A gorelabe circled overhead, a demonic malformed-creature with the body of an albatross and the

eyes and mouth of a man. Of all his lord's creations, gorelabes were the most hideous and the most feared, fashioned to be the eyes and the voice of the Mordant.

Soldiers in black fell prostrate to the battlement in a clatter of arms and armor. Covering their heads with their arms, they lay prostrate, displaying a mixture of terror and submission. The general did not blame them for their fear. Refusing to cower, he strode across the battlement, throwing his voice at the gorelabe. "I am General Haith."

Great wings flapped overhead, spiraling down till the gorelabe settled upon a nearby merlon. Odd how it retained a seabird's graceful flight while everything else reeked of corruption. The general forced himself to meet the creature's gaze, suppressing a shudder. Eyes that were too-knowing stared back at him, a man's soul captured within the body of a bird turned demon. Rumors ran legion about the gorelabes. Some whispered the Mordant could peer directly through the creature's unnatural eyes, spying on his subjects. The general wondered at the rumor's truth, but either way, the demon was dangerous, a messenger who must be obeyed. He bowed towards the misshapen fiend. "I serve the Mordant."

"*Give my creature proof. You know what I seek.*" The voice had an unnatural rasp, as if it came from the pits of hell.

The general knew the required proof. Unlacing the bindings of his surcoat, he pulled the garment down and to the side, revealing the dark rune etched above his heart, the mark of the Dark Lord. The gorelabe leaned forward. For a moment, he feared the beast would strike but then it settled back on its perch. "*Your proof is accepted. The plan is changed. The octagon knights are to be ground into oblivion. There will be no major battles, no fodder for bards, just a slow, inglorious bloodletting, till the maroon is no more. Grind them into dust. Make them suffer till they perish for they've earned my wrath. Do you understand?*"

"Yes, my lord," but in the back of his mind he wondered what the knights had done to so alter the battle plan. "So you want me to attack Castlegard?"

"*No!*"

The general flinched at the anger riding the demon's voice.

"*That castle is a deathtrap best left alone. Make Raven Pass your stronghold. Ransack the farmsteads of the domain, pillage their food and torture the farmers. Make the knights fight you here. Slay them in the snow and the muck, till their honor and their memory are both ground into oblivion. Destroy the knights and do not look to the north for reinforcements.*"

The last sentence ambushed him, but he kept his questions to himself. "Yes, my lord."

"*Now feed my gorelabe, for it has many leagues to fly.*"

He dared not hesitate, nor take the time to fetch a prisoner. "Remove your helms!" Men obeyed with shaking hands, keeping their faces averted. The general's gaze roved among them, finally settling on a soldier of low rank with graying hair, someone who had served but never achieved. The general unsheathed his sword, stepping towards his choice. "Know that your death serves the Mordant." Raising his sword in two hands, he severed the head from the body in one deft stroke. Eyes wide in horror, the head rolled toward his boot, fresh blood pooling on the stone rampart. "Your feast is laid."

The gorelabe flew to the blood. Soldiers scuttled backwards, moving like frightened crabs. Folding its great wings, the gorelabe crouched by the severed neck, its pink tongue lapping at the fresh spilt blood.

The general watched, keeping the revulsion from his face.

When the creature had finally drunk its fill, it struggled to hop to the nearest merlon, a seabird floundering on land. Having gained its perch, the gorelabe stared back at him, blood dripping from its mouth like a blasphemy. "*Serve well and live well!*" And then it laughed, a hollow, mocking sound. Licking its bloody lips, the creature spread its wings wide and caught a gust of wind. With a grace that belied its true nature, it soared south to serve its master.

General Haith stood statue-still, watching till the gorelabe flew from sight, its parting words scratched in his mind. He'd heard the saying a thousand times, *serve well and live well*, a promise and a threat, but coming from the gorelabe's bloody mouth it seemed an ominous lie.

12

Baldwin

Baldwin glanced over his shoulder, scanning the forest as he rode. For the hundredth time he saw nothing. *His eyes lied*; he knew it in his gut. Something followed him. A warning pricked the back of his neck, like a hare sensing a starving wolf. He'd felt it ever since he'd gained the flatlands. Setting spurs to his mount, the king's squire asked for a faster gallop. He threaded a path through the winter-bare trees, a cursed sword strapped to his back. His horse began to tire, lathered and blowing hard, but Baldwin refused to slow, lashing his mount as if the hounds of hell gave chase.

Wrapped in a blanket and bound with rope, the great sword thumped a rhythm against his back, keeping time to the galloping hoof beats. *Boric's blade, the first blue steel sword,* the words thrummed through his mind like a bard's rhyme. Stories of the sword were legion. Every squire knew the legend, how Orrin Surehammer was more than just a smith, a wizard of old, forging luck and strength and courage into the first blue steel blade, creating an invincible sword for an uncertain time. And now it was strapped to his back, but the sapphire-blue blade was corrupted, turned black as sin, a cursed sword returned from history, the slayer of a king. Baldwin shivered, still finding it hard to believe that King Ursus was dead, felled by treachery. At least he had a mission, a way to serve the Octagon, but he couldn't shake the feeling of being followed. Leaning low in the saddle, he urged his horse to speed. "Faster, we need to go faster."

Using the pale winter sun as his guide, he rode on a southerly course, making straight for the Snowmelt. In the untamed lands of the Domain, the Snowmelt River was one of the few sure markers, better than any map. He planned to ride to the Snowmelt and follow the raging tumult east, crossing the bridge to reach Eye Lake...but something followed him. Whatever it was, Baldwin sensed it wanted the black sword. He knew it in his gut, sure as death and sunrise. When he reached the lake he'd be rid of the cursed sword and whatever chased him. His horse couldn't gallop fast enough.

Twilight ambushed him, falling too soon for his liking. Baldwin slowed his horse to a trot, looking for a place to camp. An uprooted fir tree proved the only shelter, the giant's exposed roots forming a tangled shield wall at his back. Dismounting, he quickly unsaddled his horse and rubbed the stallion down before collecting wood. A fire was probably unwise, a beacon to the enemy, but the feeling of being followed overrode caution. He built a raging bonfire and then sat with his back to the root wall, munching on a hard biscuit. His gaze kept sliding to the blanket-wrapped sword. He'd never really gotten a good look at it. Boric had named it *Dragonsteel,* the name alone enough to inspire legends. Forever keen and imbued with magic, Baldwin wondered what it would be like to wield such a sword, a weapon forged for heroes.

A wolf howled in the night...but just a wolf. Baldwin unsheathed his short sword and kept it close, straining to see past the firelight. Sleep stalked him but he struggled against it, certain whatever followed him would come at night. Gripping his sword hilt, he stared into the darkness...but it was so hard to stay awake. Leaning against the tangled roots, he stared at the dark till weariness ambushed him.

Baldwin jerked awake, alerted by a nervous whinny. His fire had died to embers, the first streaks of dawn lighting the eastern sky, and then he heard it. A shrieking yowl pierced the forest, the call of a saber-toothed cat. The sound shivered down his spine, setting his teeth on edge, the kind of primal sound that loosed men's bowels and made them run for shelter...and it was close, too close. He snatched up his short sword and scrambled to his feet. His horse nickered and squealed, multiplying his fear. Movement snared his gaze, a pair of tawny mountain lions prowling the snow-dusted forest, but these were big, unnaturally big, and they padded straight towards him. He tightened his grip on his sword and backed towards the root wall. The cats drew close, undaunted by naked steel or glowing embers. Staring at him, they yawned, displaying saber-sharp teeth. Baldwin shivered, too many teeth, rows and rows of them, an unnatural bristle of death. And then he noticed their claws, like the talons of eagles, wicked and keen. One of them issued a low growl. Baldwin locked stares with the beast...but there was something wrong with its eyes, something knowing, something hateful. A chill shivered through him. These things were monsters, twisted abominations, minions of the Dark Lord loosed on the south.

His horse squealed, breaking the spell. The stallion had the truth of it, better to flee than fight. Baldwin kicked at the embers, scattering hot coals towards the saber cats. Snatching up the blanket-wrapped sword, he tugged the reins loose and vaulted onto the stallion's back. The horse leaped to a gallop, panic giving wings to its hooves. Baldwin clutched the stallion's mane, riding bareback, struggling to keep his seat. White-eyed and stinking of fear, the horse tore a path through the forest, running at a blind gallop. Baldwin risked a glance behind. The two saber cats followed at a ground eating lope, but they did not close the distance, almost as if they were toying with him.

His horse lurched to the right. Nearly flung from his seat, Baldwin turned to find a branch snapping across his face. The branch hit hard, sending him sprawling. Snow padded his fall. Dazed, he watched his horse gallop away.

A snarl brought him back to his senses. He sprang to his feet and unsheathed his short sword. The saber cats circled, displaying their teeth. Fear pushed him backwards. Baldwin scurried towards the nearest tree, putting his back to the trunk. The cats tightened their circle, undaunted by his sword. Baldwin nearly wept, a short sword against such monsters, he didn't have a prayer in hell. Hurling his sword at the nearest cat, he reached for Boric's blade. Even through the wrappings, he could feel the cold steel scalding his skin, but he paid it no heed. Tearing away the bindings, he loosed the great dark sword. A thing of deadly beauty, he held it aloft, a pair of dragons entwined on the hilt. Gripping the sword with both hands, he felt a jolt of power. Strength and courage and something else flowed into him, like an elixir searing his veins. He felt powerful. He felt invincible. He felt destiny calling. Brandishing the sword, he reveled in his new-found strength, feeling like a hero of old. "This is what you want! Come and get it!" Flush with confidence, he barked a laugh. Testing the sword, he slashed left and right. Perfectly balanced, it sliced the air, so keen and light and deadly. The black blade seemed alive, hungry for blood. Infused with courage, Baldwin snarled a challenge. "Attack if you dare."

The first cat sprang, revealing a snarl of saber-sharp teeth. The thing was fast, but the dark sword was faster. A quick downward slash and the dark blade cleaved flesh and bone. Beheading the first in a single stroke, Baldwin whirled to meet the second. Tawny fur flashed towards him, talons outstretched. Sidestepping the charge, he struck out with the sword. The dark blade struck quick as lightning, severing a talon-tipped paw. The cat shrieked in pain, but it did not die and it did not retreat. Blood spewed across the snow, steaming in the cold.

Hobbling on three legs, it snarled, spitting at him, its golden eyes glowing with hate.

Any other animal would retreat, but this *thing* stood its ground. Baldwin kept his sword tip raised. "What are you?"

The beast attacked. The sword moved with frightening speed. The black blade struck true, going straight to the heart. Impaled, the beast stared at him, making a strange guttural sound. Baldwin thought he heard laughter, and then he caught two words amongst the low growl, "*I'm...you.*"

"No!" Baldwin released the sword. Staggering backwards, he slipped on a patch of bloody snow. Panic seized him. He ran into the woods, fleeing the monster impaled on the black sword, fleeing the nightmares...but he did not go far. Hiding amongst the trees, he crouched behind a cedar, his hands shaking, blood staining his tunic. He stank of blood. He stank of fear. He smelled like a coward. Baldwin hated being scared. In the back of his mind he remembered what it felt like to wield the sword, the feeling of invincibility, the feeling of a god-given destiny. The memory gnawed at his mind till it consumed him. At twilight he returned. The sword was still impaled in the beast, the hilt standing upright as if awaiting his hand. He did not hesitate. Grasping the sword, he pulled it from the beast's heart. Elation rushed through him. He felt like a hero of old. Baldwin raised the sword to the heavens and then he started marching north. He had a destiny to fulfill.

13

Katherine

So cold the northern winters, cold enough to freeze tears, Kath sat perched on the topmost rampart, her maroon cloak a thin shield against the bitter wind. Below her, the city fortress curled around the great monolith like a sundered seashell, icicles studding the dark walls. The Mordant chose a grim place for his capital. To the west, an angry ocean pounded a line of dark cliffs, while the snowbound steppes stretched east as far as the eye could see, as if the fortress straddled two halves of infinity, one white, the other dark, both bleak and cold and unforgiving. Her gaze sought the only horizon that mattered, a burial mound on the cliffs' edge, a sadder form of infinity. *Duncan.* Seagulls circled overhead, their mournful cries echoing in her soul.

A tremor shook the city, the quaking of an angry beast chained beneath bedrock. Kath shuddered, remembering the demon's cold smile. She'd lost the amber pyramid, but perhaps she could entomb its power. Her gaze turned to the prisoners. A human chain toiled up the tiers, winding all the way from the Pit, to the city gates, to the dark monolith. She'd ordered rock brought from the Pit, enough to choke the bloody cavern. Vanquished soldiers carried the rock across the rune-carved courtyard and down the gullet of evil. Quakes shook the city, as if the demon protested, but the work never ceased. She'd pour an avalanche of rock into the cavern till it spewed from the stairs, sealing it for all time. If only evil was so easily stoppered.

"My lady?" A blond-haired girl approached, skinny enough to be a waif or a beggar. Her face was empty of tattoos, proving she was one of the newly freed.

Wrapped in her own misery, Kath ignored the girl.

"My lady." The girl drew close, pecking like a magpie.

Kath sighed. "Take your troubles to Zith," she gestured to the far side of the great circular courtyard, "the one-armed monk in blue robes, you can't miss him."

The girl did not move. "My lady, they say his name was Duncan."

Kath gasped, her gaze fastening on the girl.

The waif flinched as if scalded, but she stood her ground, a straggle of long blond hair framing a half-starved face.

"You knew him?"

The girl nodded. "In the Pit, I helped him escape from the iron mine...though I did not know his name."

"You helped him..." tears threatened Kath's eyes, but she blinked them back. "Tell me," her voice scraped raw with hurt, "tell me everything."

"My name is Mara, and I was a slave of the Pit." In simple words, the girl told her tale, explaining how a life of cruelty and rape changed when she discovered a cat-eyed stranger prowling the mine's upper corridors. "You need to know he was a hero, especially to me." She spoke of crossbows and ambush and vengeance, of taking a knife to those who had raped her. In measured tones, she told how Duncan released the captives, bringing hope to the mine. Rebellion spread through the carved tunnels like a whirlwind, only to be stopped by betrayal. Her voice dropped to a hush, the tale of triumph turning to pain. The girl told how Duncan and the other heroes were hung on the standing stones at the heart of the Pit, tortured by the weight of their own bodies.

Kath felt the words flay her soul. *So much pain,* she bit her lip, a trickle of blood running down the side of her mouth.

"They all died, save him, as if he had something more to live for."

The words pierced Kath's heart.

"And then the Mordant's own guard came into the Pit. They took him down from the standing stone and bore him away. It was only later that I learned his name...and his fate." Mara worried her hands into knots. "I'm sorry for your loss."

Kath forced herself to breathe, one breath at a time, lest she shatter into a thousand pieces.

The girl waited, her gaze downcast.

A hundred heartbeats passed before Kath could bring herself to speak. "You have my thanks...for aiding him, for telling me. I didn't know about the Pit," her voice cracked with raw emotion, but she reined it in. "I treasure every memory." She fumbled to find the words, "Do you need gold or food or..."

"There's more." Mara raised her head. An angry fierceness glowed in her eyes, transforming the magpie into a hawk. "Yesterday I saw the traitor, the one who betrayed him."

Kath sprang from the rampart, naked steel whispering to her hand. "Where?"

"He's claimed a house in the third tier. His name is Bruce."

"Show me."

With a slight bow, the girl turned, cutting a straight path across the circular courtyard. Kath followed like an avenging wraith, her naked sword gleaming in her fist, her maroon cloak billowing in the wind, oblivious to everything except the magpie turned hawk, loosed from her fist to hunt a traitor.

They crossed the rune-carved courtyard, an unlikely pair, the waif leading the warrior. A part of her knew that Bear and Boar followed, faithful companions guarding her back, but Kath did not spare them a glance. Zith hailed her, but she did not stop. A handful of painted warriors approached, but once they glimpsed Kath's face they shied away. The girl led her to the top tier's shattered gates, torn asunder by battering rams. Passing beneath the ruined gates, they took the spiral road down into the tiered city.

People stopped and stared. A few bowed. Others called out, "*Svala!*" The human chain of moving stones slowed at her passing till whips cracked, the captives hefting their burdens with renewed vigor. Kath ignored them all, her gaze intent on the magpie turned hawk. A crowd followed in her wake, but nothing mattered save the traitor.

The girl never slowed, leading Kath to a well-appointed house in the third tier. The door was locked. Gripping her gargoyle, Kath reached through the stone to unlatch the door. She kicked it open, the bang heralding her entrance. A hallway tiled in mosaics led to a large room heated by braziers. A big blond-haired man leaped to his feet, a dark-haired woman lying naked upon the divan. The woman screeched, clutching a blanket to cover her breasts, while the man hastily laced his pants. "What's the meaning of this?" Naked from the waist up, he yanked a metal poker from the brazier, the tip glowing red hot. "Who dares break into my house?" He brandished the poker like a sword. "Get out! Get out or I'll break your bones!"

Kath studied him through hooded eyes. A tall man with the advantage of reach and plenty of muscles earned by hard labor, but he held the poker like a thug instead of a soldier. And then she saw his boots, gray lizard-skin boots. Her heart lurched and her blood ran cold. "Your name?"

His gaze narrowed. "What of it?"

Others crowded behind her, but Kath kept her gaze on the traitor.

Mara hissed, "He's the one."

Kath took a step forward, her sword arm hanging loose by her side. "Your name?"

"Bruce Tragger. I fought in the Pit and then in the city." Sweat beaded his forehead, his eyes darting to the crowd behind. "I've earned this house," he feigned a grin, "to the victors go the spoils."

"And those boots?"

Confusion clouded his face. "Boots?" He shrugged, "a gift."

"Payment for betrayal."

Truth flashed in the depths of his eyes, quickly smothered by bluster. "Get out."

Behind her, Bear growled a warning.

"Do you remember him? The one who led the rebellion?"

The big man flinched backwards, the glowing poker held like a sword.

"His name was Duncan." Kath glided forward, her voice as cold as night. "Take off those boots." She read his eyes, the way his gaze weighed her and found her wanting.

"Get out!" Anger sparked across his face, so predictable. He leaped forward, the glowing poker arcing toward her head, enough power to crush her skull.

Kath exploded in movement. Her sword clanged against the poker, knocking it from his grasp. Swift as thought, she swept the blade down in a classic form known as Slash of the Dragon. Steel cut flesh, slicing through his abdomen, careful to cut just deep enough. *For Duncan!*

A scream rent the chamber. The big man crumpled to the floor, struggling to hold his guts in place. Writhing in pain, a pool of blood seeped across the mosaic, a fatal stain, as ugly as betrayal.

Kath wiped the gore from her sword. "A mortal wound but your death will be slow and painful, as befits a traitor." She flicked a glance back toward Bear and Boar. "I want his boots."

The two painted warriors sheathed their weapons, and then knelt, yanking the boots from the writhing corpse.

Zith pushed his way through the crowd. "What have you done?" His gaze swept the chamber, his face going pale. "At least kill him and be done with it."

Kath pulled a dagger from her belt and dropped it at the monk's feet. "If you want him dead, kill him yourself."

Zith gaped at her, disappointment in his gaze, but Kath did not care.

Bear handed Duncan's boots to her. She hugged them to her breast, seeking better memories. The traitor's screams grew feeble behind her, the smell of shit fouling the chamber.

Zith followed her. Plucking at her sleeve, his voice dropped to a whisper. "Revenge is a bitter road."

"Revenge?" Kath shook her head. "I call it justice." She moved towards the hallway. The crowd parted, opening a path to the door, but Kath barely noticed. She walked with her head down, Duncan's boots clutched close to her heart. "There's too little justice in Erdhe."

14

Baldwin

A roar ripped though his mind, the roar of an angry dragon hungry for blood, the roar of his sword. The sound drove him to a killing frenzy. Baldwin slashed and spun, the black sword cutting a deadly arc. Nothing could stop him, not swords, not battleaxes, not chainmail. Like a whirlwind he tore through the enemy, fueled by the insatiable roar filling his mind.

And then the roaring ceased.

Silence, blessed silence, Baldwin staggered to a stop. He bent double, gasping for breath, blowing plumes of mist into the crisp mountain air. And then he noticed the blood. Blood everywhere, sprayed on his surcoat, splashed on the snow, crimson against white. He'd done it again. *"Gods!"* Exhausted, he sank to his knees, closing his eyes against the gore. Half afraid to look, he shook his head in denial, but he needed to know the truth. Through hooded eyes, he dared a glance. Relief shuddered through him. At least this time, all the dead wore black.

A patrol of sixty or more, not just dead, but hacked to pieces, slaughtered, butchered to a man. The dead rebuked him, staring with lifeless eyes. How could one man defeat so many? But in his heart, Baldwin knew the truth. It wasn't him, it was the sword. A cursed blade, so dark it seemed to drink the light, starving for blood, starving for death. The dark steel seemed to vibrate beneath his hands, as if it yearned for more. Baldwin shuddered to hold it, a strange mixture of fear and lust. A weapon of legend, it made him more than just a man. It made him fearless. It made him invincible. It made him...*evil!* Something snapped inside of him. "No more!" With a roar of defiance, he stood and hurled the blade into the forest.

Suddenly empty, he crumpled to his knees. Like a fighter who'd taken one too many punches, he flopped back onto the snow. His hands shook with a terrible palsy and sweat poured out of him, a mere mortal once more. As soon as the blade had left his hands, he'd felt drained, diminished...but he also felt cleansed. For the longest time, he lay statue-still, staring at the sky, remembering what it was like to be merely Baldwin, the king's squire, a candidate for the maroon. Such a small ambition, a part of him wondered that it had ever satisfied him.

Dark wings circled overhead. The crows began to arrive, dropping out of the sky to feast on corpses. One landed near his boots, pecking at a dead man's face. Appalled, Baldwin flapped his arms to scare it away, but the dark bird was relentless. Fluttering its wings, it hopped away, seeking another corpse, intent on the grizzly feast. Disgusted, Baldwin climbed to his feet. Yelling like a madman, he ran in circles till he tripped over a severed head. Snow stung his face like a cold slap. The crows cawed in victory, claiming their meal. Beaten by their numbers, Baldwin let them eat. After all, *he* was the killer, the provider of the feast, while the crows merely sought to survive.

Survival, his own hunger came roaring to the fore. Ravenous, he ransacked the dead. Finding half loaves of bread and dried meat and even a pouch of raisins, he stuffed the food in his mouth, taking swigs from a half-empty wineskin. It seemed of late he could never get enough, especially meat, he craved meat. Always hungry, he searched for more. Wine dribbled down his chin, he wiped it away with the back of his hand, surprised to find the red peach-fuzz on his face had grown into a prickly beard. Manhood at last, but it also meant his boots had begun to pinch and his chainmail tugged at his shoulders.

A pair of crows cawed, squabbling over a string of intestines. Annoyed, he sent the birds a glare. "There's plenty for all," and then his own words sank in: so many dead, so many boots to choose from. At first he hesitated, but then he told himself it was no different from taking food. He scavenged a shiny pair of knee-high boots from an officer, supple and black with plenty of room for his toes, and then took a chainmail shirt from another. Spying an especially fine pair of gauntlets chased with silver and lined with wolf fur, he took them as well, a good fit, with just a hint of blood on the fur. Another corpse yielded a dagger worked with a snarling gargoyle on the hilt. And then he found a shoulder harness embossed with garnets, a fitting scabbard for the black sword. *The sword,* he shuddered at the thought. Could he really leave the sword?

He turned to look upon the dead, but this time he really saw them. The devil was in the details, chainmail sliced like leather, heads severed from bodies, shields shattered, helms smashed, ordinary swords sheared in half. More than a slaughter, it was an unbelievable victory. *One against sixty,* it was the stuff of legends. The black sword was a fearsome weapon, a blade forged from legend, one that could do far more than just win battles...one that could turn the very tide of war. The realization hit him like a hammer blow. If the Octagon Knights came upon him now, standing here amongst the slain, they'd hail him as a hero. No one need ever know about the others he'd killed, the ones who wore maroon cloaks. Memories of the slaughtered knights lit a spark of guilt in his mind, but he doused it with cold logic. This was his chance to change everything. By taking up the black blade, he could lead the maroon to victory. He turned toward the woods, hunting for the sword. As if it called to him, he found it gleaming in fresh snow, a black gash against the white. Such a beautiful weapon, black dragons coiled around the hilt, a weapon meant for a hero...meant for a king.

He took up the blade, a perfect fit for his gauntleted hands. Strength flowed through him, strength and determination and a roaring ambition. *Lead the Octagon to victory,* the thought pierced his mind. Startled, he chewed on the thought. It felt right; it felt like destiny, a calling to become the true heir of the king. He'd wield the dark blade to victory and then claim the octagon throne for his own. *King Baldwin,* the thought whispered through him till it became a roar. He knew what he had to do. Behind him, the crows took wing, filling the dawn with their raucous caws. Like heralds they flew before him, dark wings riding a tide of death.

15

Katherine

Kath hugged Duncan's boots close, slowly climbing the cobbled street. The magpie's tale filled her mind, a tale of courage, betrayal and death. *A hero to the people of the Pit,* Duncan had lived a hero's life, yet the gods let him die, pierced by a hundred dark-cursed knives. Kath railed against the cruelty of fate, against heaven's cold indifference. At least she'd avenged him, dealing justice with a swipe of her sword. *Justice*...yet it felt so hollow.

A girl shouted, "Look out!"

Someone shoved her from behind.

Kath staggered forward, her sword leaping from the scabbard.

A rock shattered the cobbles where she'd stood, *a rock thrice the size of her head*. A captured soldier raced towards her, his empty hands outstretched, madness glazing his eyes. *"Witch!"*

Kath raised her sword, but before she could strike, a blade erupted from the soldier's stomach. Skewered from behind, the attacker died, spitted on Bear's blade. Putting his boot on the dead man's back, Bear shoved the corpse from his sword. He turned to glare at the captured soldiers, all of them bearing rocks intended for the bloody cavern. "Anyone else?"

The prisoners looked away, hastily passing rocks from one pair of hands to the next.

Their guards snarled, cracking whips, laying bloody stripes across the prisoners. Rocks moved with renewed vigor, passed from hand to hand, toiling up the human chain.

Behind her, Boar hissed, "They should all be killed."

Kath turned, her voice sharp with rebuke. "Then we'd be no better than Darkness."

Boar scowled. "They'll never change. Soldiers of the pentacle are weaned on cruelty."

"He's right." The words came from the magpie. She stood a hand span away from the thrown rock, her face chalk-pale. At Kath's stare she retreated a half step.

"So you think they won't change?"

The blond-haired girl looked from Kath to the line of soldiers and back again. "The ones taken from the Pit or the poorest tiers might...but not those born to serve the Pentacle." Mara gestured towards Boar. "The painted warrior has the truth of it. Those born to the Pentacle truly are weaned on malice and cruelty."

Kath considered her words. "Can you tell the difference?"

"Of course," the magpie brightened, "by the tattoos on their arms."

Kath knew those who served the Pentacle bore tattoos but she'd never known the meaning behind the marks. "How can you tell?"

The magpie rolled up her left sleeve. Extending her arm, she revealed a rune tattooed in black ink. "We're all tattooed at birth." Her face flushed red. "This is the rune for the Pit, the lowest of the low."

Kath studied the rune. "And those born to be soldiers bear a different rune?"

"Yes." Mara pulled down her sleeve, covering the mark, as if ashamed of it.

Kath crouched by the dead attacker. Drawing a dagger, she slit his left sleeve. Peeling back the dark wool revealed a single rune tattooed on his forearm, different from the one Mara bore. "And this rune?"

Mara craned over her shoulder. "It's the rune for the fifth tier, the tier of soldiers."

"So if a man is born in the Pit but is trained as a soldier?"

"Then he'd bear his birth-rune, the rune of the Pit, as well as the rune for the fifth tier, giving him the privileges of a soldier."

Kath had seen the disparity between surviving the Pit and thriving in the top tiers. "That's quite a promotion."

Mara gave her a solemn nod. "Enough to tempt a man who knows better into doing things he shouldn't."

Kath stood, considering the dead soldier. "Can you help my warriors sort the fanatics from those who might change if given a chance?"

"I can help sort the runes, yes, but some might still be fanatics, tainted by the priests."

"Good enough." Kath sheathed her dagger. "Walk with me."

Mara fell into step beside her, Bear and Boar shadowing behind.

Kath cast sideways glances at the girl. Her long blond hair was clean but tangled, her tunic worn to a drab brown, but carefully sewn and patched. On her feet she wore black leather boots laced to her knees, obviously too big for her, probably taken from a dead soldier. Her face was young and girlish, but beneath the shabby tunic she had a woman's budding curves. She walked with a slouch, as if trying to hide the truth of her age, a riddle wrapped in rags.

"My boots are stolen."

"What?"

The girl flushed red. "I saw you looking at my boots."

"So?"

"I got them from a dead soldier."

Kath shrugged. "More use to you than the dead."

"In the Pit, boots are a sign of wealth...and betrayal."

Talking with this girl was like unraveling an endless riddle. "Why betrayal?"

"Because they're a sign of favor," her voice was laced with venom, "a sure sign you serve *them.*"

Curiosity got the better of Kath. "What did you do in the Pit?"

"I was a serving girl, and later a seller of dung patties...and at night, I served..." her voice choked to silence, her face twisting in hate. "Beauty was a curse in the Pit."

The Citadel was like a cesspool...filled with endless layers of evil. "And now that you're free of the Pit, what will you do?"

The girl gave her a sheepish look. "I...don't know."

"There must be something you've always longed to do?"

Mara stopped, her head tilted back to stare at the afternoon sky. "Born in the Pit, I longed for a glimpse of the true sky." Wonder touched her face. "I heard it was the color blue. And at night, it's full of stars!" She looked at Kath and flashed a warm smile. "You gave me blue!"

The honest joy in the girl's face staggered Kath. She could not imagine a life deprived of the stars and the sky. "So now that you can choose, what will you do?"

Mara stared at her. "I've never had a choice. How does one choose?"

Kath slowed to a stop. "Are the people from the Pit all like you? Unaccustomed to choices?"

Mara flushed. "We are born to our station. We live to serve. We work to eat. And we obey or die."

Such a harsh life, the soul-numbing yoke of pure Darkness, Kath shivered, making the hand sign against evil. "You still have to work to eat...but now you have a choice. A choice of what you do and how hard you work."

Mara stared at her. "Yes, but how does one choose?"

Kath could not imagine a life with *no* choices. Defeating evil was not just about swords. "Look around you. It takes many crafts, many trades to run a city. People need food, and boots, and candles, and clothing. You could be a healer, or a baker, or a candlestick maker."

"Or a warrior?"

Kath gave her a slow nod. "Or a warrior, but it takes many long years of training if you don't want to be a *dead* warrior."

"And how do you gain these skills?"

"In the south, we have apprenticeships. Master craftsmen take on apprentices who work for food and lodging while learning the skills of the trade. After an agreed upon number of years, the apprentice becomes their own master. Then their success depends on how well they learned the trade and how hard they work."

"And this could happen here?"

"Yes, of course. The upper tiers are full of skilled masters, from blacksmiths and weapon makers, to chandlers, cobblers, weavers, herbalists, seamstresses and scribes."

Mara looked thoughtful, her brow furrowed.

"Come, I'll take you to Zith. After you show my warriors how to separate the prisoners by their rune markings, perhaps you can help the people of the Pit gain apprenticeships?"

Mara gave her a slow smile. "I would like that."

The girl was both clever and brave...all she needed was a chance...and a choice. Kath gripped her sword hilt, shuddering at the foul evilness of the Pit. All her life she'd fought for a chance and a choice...and now she'd help bring both to the north. It felt better than justice...or perhaps it was a different kind of justice. Staring up at the blue of the sky, Kath swore she'd find a way to defeat the Mordant.

16

The Knight Marshal

S now blanketed the forest, so silent, so cold, so deadly. The marshal surveyed the hillside, checking for telltale signs. Winter made for tricky warfare, the thrice-damned snow betraying every movement. Nested ambushes proved their best weapon, a deadly game of cat and mouse.

He led a troop of thirty mounted knights behind a copse of cedars, a screen of dark evergreen obscuring the path below. Weapons bared, they listened for the signal. Horses stamped and armor jangled, every noise sounding like a shout to the marshal's ears. Throwing a stern glare at the others, he settled his horse and gripped his sword, the borrowed weapon of a dead knight. For the thousandth time, the marshal pondered his impulse to claim the great sword from the ashes of a funeral pyre. Always a saber man, he'd come to appreciate the added heft and extended reach of the great sword, yet he wondered if the blade had last served a hero or a traitor. He scowled at the futility of his musings. Sir Tyrone was long gone, nothing but ashes blown on the wind. Only the gods knew the truth of it.

Sir Abrax gave him a warning glance, and then he heard it, the muffled tramp of an enemy patrol, but there was no sound of hooves and harness. The invaders rarely risked their horses, one of the few advantages left to the maroon. Lowering his visor, the marshal nodded to the others, poised for the signal.

Bowstrings twanged, answered by the first scream. A warning horn blared from below, cut short in mid-note. *"Damn!"* the marshal swore. Urging his horse to a gallop, he led his men around the cedars. Silent as death, they fell on the invaders, thirty mounted knights against fifty foot soldiers.

His warhorse slammed into the nearest enemy, bowling him backwards. The marshal dropped the reins, guiding his horse with just his knees. Wielding the great sword with two hands, he lay into the enemy, cleaving heads from bodies with a single stroke. The battle lust took him, his breath sounding harsh in his helmet. His one-eyed gaze reduced to a narrow visor-slit, he turned left and right, searching for foes. A spear stabbed towards his face, but he hacked it away. Swords clanged around him, blood spattering the freshly fallen snow. An enemy attacked on his blindside, landing a solid blow to the chest. He swayed in the saddle, gripping with his knees, thanking the gods his armor held. Beating the sword away, he regained his balance and found himself deep within the enemy's ranks. Hands grabbed at his legs, determined to pull him from the saddle. He swung his sword like a scythe, desperate to gain some space. Trained for battle, his horse reared, hooves lashing at the enemy. Screams died beneath those iron-shod hooves yet the enemy pressed close. A soldier clawed at his stallion's bridle till the marshal slew him with a single stroke. Another grabbed at his boot, but he kicked him away. Striking left and right, he fought to win clear.

"To the marshal!" Sir Abrax led the charge, his great blue sword cleaving a swath through the enemy. The others thundered around him, a spearhead of maroon pushing back the black.

The enemy broke and ran.

Discipline held within the maroon. The knights slowed their mounts, refusing to give chase. Breathing hard, the marshal lifted his visor to better survey his men. Sir Brock was bent over his horse, his armor rent showing a nasty wound in his side. Sir Keifer was blanched pale, his left arm dangling at an unnatural angle. If any of the others were wounded, he could not tell, yet the trampled snow ran red with blood. More than thirty of the enemy sprawled along the trail. Thirty for two, it seemed a fair trade, till he considered the size of the enemy horde.

"Sir Zakery and Sir Tradon, see the wounded back to the main camp."

The two knights saluted, escorting the wounded up the steep mountain trail.

A handful of archers ghosted out of the forest, maroon octagons sewn on their leather jerkins. Saluting the marshal, they set about pilfering the dead. A deplorable practice but such was the necessity of a winter war. The maroon needed supplies, especially food and arrows. Anything scavenged was a welcome addition to their meager stores.

Benford, the lead archer approached. "We'll take what we can and then head for the ridge."

The marshal nodded. "Choose your trail wisely. The last time they brought their cursed hellhounds."

A flicker of fear kindled in the man's face but it was quickly smothered. "We'll follow the streambed before turning north."

"See that you do. Archers are scarcer than arrows and we're not like to get more."

"Yes, m'lord." Benford saluted, melting back into the snow-dusted trees.

The marshal turned his horse away, picking a path through the dead. "Come, we've got more battles to fight." The others fell in behind, Sir Abrax riding on his blindside.

With the battle over, the pain intruded. The marshal pressed a fist to his breastplate, plagued by the ache beneath. His armor had held but his chest felt bruised, making every breath painful. Other hurts vied for his attention. His right arm began to stiffen and his left knee ached from the infernal cold. He was getting too old for the battlefront, but the maroon needed every sword and the men looked to him to set an example. Swallowing his pain, he kept his horse to a walk, giving the men and their mounts a chance to recover. At least there was no need to rush. The enemy would follow, of that he was certain, but they'd come afoot, howling for vengeance. The key was to pick the next spot, an ambush nested within an ambush, Lothar's solution to thwarting the traitorous snow.

More flakes began to fall, veiling the mountains. The trail snaked up and around a rocky outcrop and then plunged back down into a narrow saddle-shaped valley, the perfect spot for the second ambush. The marshal let his horse pick a path across the snow-crusted valley. A sixth sense warned he was being watched, but the marshal quelled his unease, knowing the rest of his archers hid in the wooded hillside, awaiting the second ambush. He scanned the hillside but saw no telltale signs, just winter-green blanketed in white. Snow continued to fall, bringing a hushed peace to the valley but it was an illusion, an added trap for the enemy.

The valley narrowed to a funnel, the woods dense on either side. Smoke from campfires drifted toward him, a dead giveaway. Emerging from the pinch point, he found Lothar and three hundred knights encamped in a meadow, all of them armed and armored, awaiting the next battle. Sentries saluted as he passed, snow crusting their maroon cloaks. The marshal swung down from the saddle and turned to find Lothar striding towards him, relief scrawled across his face. "I gather the ambush went well?" The leather-faced captain offered him a steaming mug.

The marshal tugged off his gauntlets and wrapped his bare hands around the mug, savoring the warmth. "Brock and Keifer were both wounded. We traded two knights for thirty of their foot. The others broke and ran."

"Will they come?"

"They'll come." He sipped the soup and nearly spat it out. "Bloody hell, it tastes like old saddle!"

Lothar chuckled, "We had to throw something in the pot! Besides, it's hot."

The marshal glared but then took another sip, knowing he'd get nothing else. "You'll need to put those fires out; I smelled the wood smoke halfway up the valley."

"The men have orders to douse them on your arrival."

He looked around and saw that it was true. Despite the cold, discipline held. Lothar steered him towards one of the snow-doused fires. The other knights saluted and then withdrew, giving their commanders a respectful distance. The marshal eased down on the felled log nearest the glowing embers, grateful for the residual warmth.

"You're limping again."

The marshal shot his friend a piercing stare. "Damn knee doesn't like the cold."

"And I trust you kept Sir Abrax on your blindside."

The marshal scowled. "I've been fighting with one eye for longer than Abrax has fought with two."

"More reason you shouldn't be leading the sorties."

Anger spiked the marshal's retort. "The men don't have a king. They need victories and they need an example."

"You've given them both. Let the captains take the risk."

"The king always led from the front."

Lothar glared, "You said yourself that this is a different sort of war, a game of hounds and foxes. The maroon can't afford to lose you."

The marshal's chest still ached from the battering, but he was damned if he'd admit it. "We'll need to change tactics anyway."

"What do you mean?"

"This is the fourth double ambush. They're bound to learn."

"So you think they won't come?"

"No, they'll come."

"Why?"

"Because of Raven Pass." Lothar raised a bushy eyebrow but the marshal forestalled his question. "That battle's been scratching at my mind like a splinter. Think about it. The Mordant sent his hordes against our walls, but he sent them without cavalry, without catapults, without siege engines of any sort. He let the hordes hurl themselves against unbreakable walls for nigh on a week before he ever loosed his foul magic against our gates."

Lothar's gaze widened. "Fodder. He uses men like fodder."

The marshal nodded. "He's got the numbers but he does not care how he spends them...but that makes no sense unless..." his voiced dropped to a deadly whisper, "unless this war is just a feint." The idea had been festering in his mind like an open sore. Troubled, the marshal stared at his friend.

"What do you mean, a *feint?*"

The marshal shrugged. "I'm not sure, just a nagging suspicion."

"A vast horde just a feint? It makes no sense."

"Unless it's one part of a larger battle plan."

Lothar gaped. "You mean another horde? *One* horde is more than we can handle."

"No, something else."

"Then what?"

"That's what plagues me. I'll be damned if I know."

Lothar fingered his battleaxe, his face troubled. "How do we defeat such a foe?"

The marshal had no easy answer. "We do what we can."

Lothar scowled, stirring the ashes. "A war of attrition...except we're the ones getting nibbled to death."

They sat in silence, hunched over the dying embers, the snow falling around them like a curtain. Other knights approached, taking seats around the dead fire. They all knew the battle plan so there was no need to speak of it. Instead, they traded words about small things, remembering better meals and warmer beds. The marshal listened, heartened by the camaraderie. Hungry, cold, and badly out-numbered, yet the maroon remained unbowed, determined to fight. Warmed by pride, the marshal took a whetstone to his great sword, taking comfort from the steady rasp of steel against stone. A mere hour passed before a scout came running. *"They're coming!"*

The marshal looked up. "So soon?"

Breathless, the scout nodded.

"How many?"

"Jansen reckons six hundred and they're all afoot."

"By the nine hells!" Lothar swore, "How'd they assemble so many so quickly?"

The marshal gave his friend a warning glare. "Their tactics are changing."

The scout blurted the rest. "They've brought their hellhounds."

A cold silence blanketed the men.

Sir Abrax said, "So do we run or fight?"

A circle of stares as thick as spears surrounded the marshal. The odds were bad, but better than facing the horde. "This battleground is of our choosing. We stand and fight." The marshal raised his sword. "For the king."

"For the king!" The men saluted and then scattered to their horses, making adjustments to girths and armor. The marshal pulled on his gauntlets and swung into the saddle. Lothar rode on his right, Sir Abrax with his blue sword on his blindside. The maroon formed a column behind, five knights across and over sixty deep. They carried no banners and blew no horns. The pomp of war had died in Raven Pass. Like iron forged to steel, the knights rode as pure warriors, intent on killing.

Spurring his horse to a trot, the marshal led them to the pinch point, to the narrow throat of the valley, and then he reined his horse to a stop. Unsheathing his great sword, he stared across the valley floor.

At first there was nothing but white.

Snow drifted into the valley like gently blowing veils. Evergreens darkened the steep hillsides, a counterpoint to the white. So peaceful, so deceptive, but then he heard it. A deadly howl knifed the valley. Eerie and chilling, it sent a primal shiver down his spine. His warhorse shied, but he settled it with his knees. And then he saw them, dark shapes erupting from the snow. Like hounds loosed from hell, they tore across the valley floor. Tongues lolling, teeth bared, spiked collars around their necks, the shaggy beasts slavered as they ran, howling for the kill. Larger and more vicious than wolves, they reeked of evil, deadly demons fashioned into fur.

"Steady!" The marshal watched them come, keeping a tight rein on his horse.

Howling like the damned, the hellhounds ran at a ground-eating lope. Halfway across, the archers loosed the first volley. Growls of pain erupted from the pack but none fell. More arrows rained down, a deluge of feathered shafts. The marshal expected carnage, but it took multiple arrows to fell a single hellhound. The pack thinned to half. The remaining beasts kept coming, slavering for the kill.

"Better to meet them at a gallop." The marshal raised his sword. "For the king!"

"For the king!" the war cry echoed through the maroon.

The marshal spurred his horse. The bay stallion leaped forward, churning the snow to a gallop. Behind him, the maroon knights surged, thundering to a charge. Spreading wide like armored wings, they swept across the valley floor. *"For the king!"* Visors snapped closed and lances lowered, a solid wall of armored knights galloped to meet teeth and claws. The marshal picked a foe, a massive hellhound with a single arrow protruding from its shoulder. Leaning forward, he aimed a blow for its head, but the beast swerved at the last moment, avoiding the blade. Shocked, the marshal nearly lost his seat. A second hellhound charged. Claws scrabbled against his saddle. The beast lunged, dagger-sharp teeth snapping for his face. Too close to bring his sword to bear, the marshal punched its snarling snout. His mailed fist hit a solid blow. Squealing, the brute dropped to the ground, slithering under his stallion's belly. His horse reared, hooves lashing. The marshal sought to control his mount while frantically searching for the hellhound. It lurked behind, hunched for a rear attack. The marshal whipped his sword around. The beast's own leap impaled it on the blade, spitting it through the mouth. Teeth snapped shut, gnawing on the sword. So close the marshal could smell its fetid breath, he locked stares with the beast, shocked to find a knowing hatred in its gaze. "By the gods!" The marshal yanked his sword from the toothy maw, kicking the cursed carcass away.

Lifting his visor, he took stock of the battlefield. Chaos swirled around him, a primal battle of steel against claw. Hellhounds howled and horses screamed, thickening the air with fear. Nearby, a hound pulled a knight from the saddle. Clawing the helmet open, it savaged the knight's face. The marshal spurred his horse to a charge, his great sword descending in a reaping blow. The blade struck deep, severing the beast's spine. Yelping, the brute collapsed, but the knight was already lost, his face nothing but a bloody maul.

The marshal reined his mount to a halt, searching for another foe, but all the howls were silenced, replaced by squealing horses. A dozen writhed in agony, iron-shod hooves churning in pain. Half as many knights lay savaged, but the cursed hellhounds were vanquished, their blood darkening the snow.

"They're coming!"

The marshal snapped his gaze to the far end of the valley. A swarm of black-cloaked soldiers poured down the mountain trail. Howling vengeance, they came at a run.

The battle of beasts was done; it was time to slay men.

17

Katherine

Kath tossed and turned, besieged by the need to escape the north. Twisting beneath the wool blanket, she found no answers and she found no peace. Her glance speared the lead-paned window but it remained stubbornly dark, proof it was too early to rise.

A fist pounded on her door.

Startled, she reached for her sword, steel slithering from leather.

The pounding continued, hard and incessant.

"Coming!" Kath cracked the door and cast a wary glance into the hallway.

Blaine grinned back at her. Clad in chainmail beneath his surcoat, his great sword rearing over his shoulder, he looked ready for battle. "I've heard rumors of another a nest."

His words made no sense. "A nest?"

"A nest of acolytes and priests, they're infesting the palace."

Kath rubbed the last remnants of sleep from her eyes. "And we need to do this now?"

His grin widened. "Catch the bastards while they're sleeping."

She might as well fight priests as wrestle blankets. "One moment." Ducking back into her chamber, Kath hastily finished dressing. Swirling her maroon cloak around her shoulders, she strapped on her throwing axes, belted her sword to her waist and made sure the crystal dagger was secure in its sheath. Touching her mage-stone gargoyle for luck, she stepped from her sleeping chamber.

Bear and Boar waited in the hallway with Blaine. Both painted warriors wore mismatched armor, most of it black and gold, scavenged from the enemy. In defiance of their scavenged colors, they wore tattered strips of maroon cloth tied like proud talismans to their right biceps, the symbol of her personal guard. Hands on weapons, they nodded to her. "Svala."

Kath shrugged. "It seems were hunting priests and acolytes before the morning meal."

The two warriors flashed feral grins as if they preferred blood to bread.

Swayed by their enthusiasm, Kath gave them an answering grin. Tossing a quizzical look to Blaine, she said, "Where?"

"The throne room." He turned and strode down the marble hall, setting a brisk pace.

The throne room, Kath shivered, making the hand sign against evil. Disgusted by the oppressive palace, she'd made a conscious decision to avoid the Mordant's throne room, yet somehow Zith knew. The monk nagged her to see it, arguing she needed to understand her opponent, yet Kath found endless excuses to delay. Perhaps this was fate's way of getting her to confront her true enemy. Her hand on her sword hilt, she marched through the shadow-choked corridors, following Blaine to the throne room. All too soon, they reached the great bronze doors.

Thrice the height of a tall man, the double doors bore a massive pentacle inlaid in gold, the symbol of the Mordant. Gripping her sword hilt, Kath nodded and Bear put his shoulders to the cold bronze. The great doors slowly swung silently open. Blaine took a torch from the wall and stepped inside.

Kath gasped, daunted by the sight, like nothing she'd ever seen.

Built of mitered stone, the cold immensity of the basilica seemed impossible. A vast domed ceiling vaulted overhead, but instead of airiness it held a brooding darkness. Pierced by the first faint rays of morning light, the sunbeams died before ever reaching the marbled floor, strangled by darkness. Twisted pillars upheld the dome, everything built of dusky-colored stone. Dark and dominating, the scale was brutal, the heavy gloom hammering down, crushing mortal souls into submission. Kath's footsteps faltered, slowing to a stop. Vast and dark and brutal, the basilica felt soul-numbing.

"Coming?" Blaine strode down the central aisle, using his flaming torch to light candles on either side. Even the candles were massive, six-foot pillars, twisted and deformed. Screaming faces pressed through the pale wax as if souls of the damned writhed within, striving to break free. Remembering the gargoyles gates, Kath wondered if the twisted candles were soul traps. Shuddering, she made the hand sign against evil.

Blaine continued down the aisle, seemingly indifferent to the nightmares sculpted into wax and stone.

Candlelight illumed the path forward. Built of cloistered stone, the basilica was cold as a tomb. Pulling her maroon cloak close, Kath followed the knight into the gloom. Even her footsteps were diminished, swallowed by the cavernous space. Everywhere she looked, Kath saw opulence cunningly contrived to oppress mortal supplicants. And then she noticed the marble floor. Names were written upon the basilica's floor. Most were unfamiliar...but then she recognized a few. Names of battlefields lost, castles betrayed, and cities plundered, forever cast in stone beneath the Mordant's boot heels. The names inscribed the length of the basilica, a litany of pain and loss and suffering. Bile rose in the back of her throat. So this was the Mordant's plan for Erdhe, to be forever trod beneath his boot heels, subject to his dark rule.

"Come, Svala."

Bear's voice pulled her deeper into the basilica. Gold gleamed in the distance, torchlight illuming the details. Hammered gold clad the stairs rising to the Ebony Throne, enough wealth to feed a kingdom for a year, used for nothing more than adornment beneath the Mordant's boots. Kath shuddered at the cruel hubris of dark power.

Blaine prowled along the back wall, his torchlight beating back the gloom, searching for hidden doorways...but Kath was drawn towards the throne.

Unable to avoid the countless names inscribed upon the marble floor, she reached the dais and stared up at the throne. In the Mordant's treasury crypt, she'd longed to sit upon the winged throne, but this was different, very different. The Ebony Throne repulsed her.

Sit upon the throne, the thought shivered through her mind like a command. Kath shuddered at the words, yet she found herself climbing the dais stairs. Drawing closer, she realized the massive seat was carved from a single block of wood. Jet-black with rich swirls of emerald green in the ebony grain, the throne must have been carved from the heartwood of a great-grandfather tree. Duncan would have hated this throne, nature twisted to the service of Darkness. Sickened by the abomination, she made the hand sign against evil.

Kath stood before the throne, dwarfed by its scale, wondering what secret powers it harbored. With a single finger, she dared to touch the throne.

Nothing happened.

The ebony wood was smooth and cool beneath her touch.

She cast a sideways glance at Bear and Boar. They waited at the foot of the dais, stalwart and stoic, their torches casting islands of light.

Taking a deep breath, Kath dared to sit upon the Ebony Throne. Expecting magic, she cringed, hugging her maroon cloak close.

Nothing happened, the throne remained dormant...but then the very stones began to groan.

The great basilica shuddered and shook, another tremor from the depths, as if the demons raged at her sacrilege, but the throne remained dormant. The tremors slowed to a stop, a sprinkle of dust falling from the domed ceiling. Bear coughed, the sound swallowed by the return of the basilica's brooding silence.

Seated upon the throne, Kath drew a deep breath and stared out at the basilica. *So this is the Mordant's throne.* Exalted above the great space, she took in the whole of it, from the vast vaulting darkness looming overhead, to the wealth of gold beaten into the dais, to the river of names carved the length of the marble floor. *Invincible power wrought into stone*...the Mordant's chilling challenge hammered against her with the force of a battering ram...but within the details she found the monk's potent message whispering through her mind. How many deaths in the river of names? How many souls lost to Darkness? How much pain and suffering for the glory of the Mordant? *This* is what he would make of Erdhe, a vile temple to Darkness built on suffering. Kath realized she'd embarked on a struggle that was far more than an ancient prophecy, far more than justice for Duncan; it was about the brutal enslavement of all of Erdhe. It was the Battle Immortal, the struggle of Light against the Dark. Shivering with desperate resolve, she gripped the crystal dagger and bowed her head, praying to Valin for the strength to prevail.

Something snicked in the darkness.

Something metal slammed into the throne where her head would have been.

Kath glanced up to find a dart embedded in the ebony wood.

"*Svala!*" Bear and Boar dropped their torches. Weapons unsheathed, they sprang up the dais, standing in front of her. "*Assassin!*"

Bear's warning jolted her to action. Leaping from the throne, Kath drew a throwing axe. She peered into the gloom, searching for the enemy. Something clad in black scuttled down a massive column, clinging to the marble like a cockroach. "*There!*" Her axe whirled, metal striking marble with a harmless clang. The assassin dropped to the floor, landing in a crouch. Elbows and knees bent, he looked like a giant spider, death lurking in the shadows.

Somewhere in the back of the basilica, she heard Blaine's shout and the clash of steel.

Bear and Boar attacked. Bellowing a war cry, they charged the assassin, weapons raised for the kill.

The assassin remained crouched. Lifting a slender tube to his blackened face, his cheeks puffed.

"No!" Kath hurled her last axe.

Snick, time seemed to slow.

Her axe whirled, end over end, gleaming in the torchlight.

Unsheathing her sword, she raced to follow her axe.

Something struck near her heart.

Snick, the assassin blew again, and then he lurched away, but he'd waited too long. Her axe took him in the chest, releasing a spray of blood across the dusky marble. Bear reached the fallen assassin, his sword pressed to the enemy's throat.

Boar uttered a strangled cry and crumpled to the ground.

"No!" Kath veered away, racing to Boar. "Not you too!" Falling to her knees, she cradled his head, horrified to find a dart embedded in his throat. Yanking the dart free, she flung it into the gloom. Such a small wound, a pinprick of blood, yet the big man shuddered and shook, his skin turning clammy. "We need Zith!"

"Too...late." Boar struggled for breath.

"No." Kath shook her head in denial, but she knew he spoke the truth.

Slick with sweat, he gazed at her, gentle brown eyes in a face tattooed with a fierce boar, a warrior who'd become her friend. A single tear fell on his cheek. Boar struggled to speak, his gaze turning cloudy. "For the Svala..." Life fled from his body. She shook him, willing him to live, but it made no difference. Kath closed his eyes, and settled him on the cold marble floor.

"He's gone, Bear." Her voice cracked with sorrow.

"Svala, this one still lives."

Kath stood. Her sword in her hand, she strode toward the assassin.

Clad all in black, a baldric of nine throwing knives slung across his chest, the assassin lay sprawled on the dark marble. Arms and legs askew, he looked stunted and broken, her axe buried in his chest. Blood frothed from the axe wound, and from the side of his mouth, yet his gaze was razor keen, locked on hers. *"Just...a...girl,"* his voice wheezed with blood.

"Why did you kill him?"

"A girl...defiling...master's...throne" His gaze hardened, his face flushed with pain. *"You...will die...screaming."*

Anger thrummed through her. "Not today." Her sword flashed down. "For Boar." With a single stroke, she severed his throat. Blood spurted from the wound, staining the dark marble.

And then she heard the clash of steel. *"Blaine!"* Tugging her axe from the assassin's chest, Kath raced toward the sound. In the rear wall of the basilica, a door stood open, torchlight glowing from within. The doorway led to a narrow corridor, a corpse slumped at the far end, black robes suggesting a priest. Beyond the corridor, steel clashed against steel. Kath followed the sound, her sword in her right hand, her throwing axe in her left, her deerskin boots silent on the marble floor. A bitter stench clogged the hallway, rankling her nose. Reaching the far doorway, she peered inside.

Blaine fought two dark-robed priests, his blue sword beating against two gleaming sickles. His back to the doorway, he attacked the far priest, landing a killing blow. The priest howled in pain, yet he clutched the blue blade with blood-slick hands, keeping it embedded deep in his stomach. While Blaine's sword was entangled, the second priest lunged from behind, wielding a vicious swing of the sickle.

"*No!*" Kath leaped forward, her sword meeting the sickle.

Steel clanged against steel.

Startled, the priest whirled, slashing at her. Kath stepped close, loosing a downward slash. Her sword struck flesh, severing the priest's hand. The silver sickle clattered to the floor but the priest never slowed. Shrieking like a banshee, he shoved his bloody stump into her face. Clawing at her eyes with his remaining hand, he tried bite her face, his lips blackened, his teeth snapping close enough to bite, his eyes glazed like a ghoul.

Horrified, Kath lurched backwards, struggling to bring her weapons to bear.

The rabid priest clutched at her, teeth snapping, his breath horrid on her face.

Kath squirmed away.

Suddenly the priest was jerked backwards. Blaine hurled the rabid fiend across the chamber. Slamming against the far wall, he crumpled to the floor, knocking over a lit brazier. Before the priest could rise, Bear was on him. One blow of his sword took the head from the body.

Kath gasped, wiping the blood from her face. "What was that...*thing*?" She shuddered, staring down at the severed head.

Blaine answered while stomping on coals spilled from the brazier. "A priest chained to Vetra."

Dead priests littered the floor, all of them with blackened lips and sunken eyes. She nudged one with her boot, making sure it was dead. "Vetra?"

"A sacred herb they use for trances." Blaine poked a corpse with his sword. "Too much holy herb and they turn into ravening ghouls. Eat enough of it and it kills them."

"It's not killing them fast enough." Kath coughed, choking on the bitter smoke clouding the chamber. "How do you know this?"

Blaine gave her a hard look. "I've been hunting priests."

Kath heard the rebuke in his voice.

"Did you enjoy sitting on the throne?"

She gaped at the anger in his voice.

Bear answered. "An assassin attacked us."

Blaine raised an eyebrow. "An assassin?"

Bear nodded. "Clad in black, he moved like a spider."

"Boar is dead. Slain by the assassin." Kath's voice sounded flat and lifeless. "He will be sorely missed."

Bear gave her a solemn nod. "He died an honorable death, protecting the Svala. The Ancestor will long sing his name." Bear stared at her, an odd look on his tattooed face. Crossing the room, he reached out, plucking a dart from Kath's chest. Lodged in the leather harness of her axes, the dart had missed her heart by a finger's width.

Kath shuddered, feeling the nearness of death.

Bear held the dart towards Blaine. "The assassin fought like a coward, using poisoned darts." Giving Kath a fierce look, he hurled the dart into the gloom. "Not today."

She gave him a slow nod. "Not today." Sheathing her sword, she surveyed the chamber. Runes covered the walls, polished onyx inlaid in gray granite. The chamber appeared to be a small chapel converted to a hiding hole for the priests. Bedrolls and bulging sacks were shoved along one wall, but it was the altar that caught Kath's gaze. A black stone altar dominated the far wall, and on that altar sat a small ornate box, gold bejeweled with dark diamonds. "What's that?"

Blaine shrugged. "Their hiding holes are full of trinkets and treasures." Climbing the dais, he flipped open the lid. "Well look at this!" Surprise rode his voice. Reaching into the box, he removed a pale shard of crystal the length of a small dagger.

Kath gaped to see it. Climbing the dais, she unsheathed the crystal dagger and held it next to the shard. One was a sharpened dagger with a small cross-hilt, the other a rough shard of pale quartz, a tooth plucked from the depths of the earth. Both looked to be made of the same crystal.

"Is it?"

Kath nodded. "What the monks use to test for harlequins."

"What's it doing here?" Blaine gestured to the bejeweled box. "And why treat it like a holy relic?"

Understanding struck. "Because the Mordant subverts the weapons of Light to Darkness. Somehow the Mordant used this crystal to his advantage. He turns our own strengths against us." Kath shuddered to hear her own words, like a portent of doom, but the answer felt right, leaving a bitter taste in her mouth. "We need to show this to Zith."

They searched the chapel, but found nothing else of significance. Returning to the throne room, Kath knelt by Boar's body. Whispering a prayer to Valin, she bid him farewell. Taking a deep breath, she gathered herself and surveyed the throne room one last time. "I want Boar buried next to Duncan. And I want the gold stripped from the dais and put to a better use. And I want the throne burned, released from its terrible service."

Beneath her boots, the basilica shuddered and shook.

Bear gave her a solemn nod. "It will be as you command, Svala."

"And I will never come here again." Kath turned and strode from the basilica, fingering the crystalline shard. *Weapons of Light turned to Darkness,* she shivered, making the hand sign against evil.

18

The Knight Marshal

The marshal stood in the stirrups, watching the enemy pour down the mountain trail. He judged the odds to be three to one against, yet he refused to sound the retreat. *"Form the line!"*

Maroon knights answered his call, presenting an armored line across the bloodstained valley.

The marshal raised his sword, *"For Honor and the Octagon!"* Putting spurs to his mount, he led the charge. Hooves churned the bloody snow as arrows sang from the forest. The maroon struck at a gallop, hitting the enemy like a massive battering ram. Swords rang against axes and men died beneath iron-shod hooves. At first it was a rout, the maroon's heavy horses plowing into the enemy, the speed of the gallop making scythes of their swords, but then the charge slowed and the swarm brought their numbers to bear. The line crumbled into individual battles, small knots of maroon surrounded by churning black, a chaotic swirl of kill or be killed. The marshal fought side-by-side with Sir Abrax, two great swords carving a circle of death, but the press of the enemy never slowed. Stroke and parry, he struggled to keep his seat. Sweat stung his eye and his sword arm ached, yet he endured. *Fight or die,* he steered his horse with his knees, swinging his great sword at the nearest foe.

A shout rose from the enemy and the ferocity of the fight trebled. The black tide surged around him, threatening to devour the maroon. The marshal stood in the stirrups, trying to make sense of the battle.

"They've got an ogre!" Sir Abrax pointed and the marshal saw it was true. Towering head and shoulders above mere men, the ogre waded into battle, wielding death with each swing of its massive war club. As the marshal watched, it crushed the skull of a horse with a single blow and then aimed a back-handed slap at the rider, hurling the knight from the saddle. Black-cloaked soldiers swarmed the fallen knight like roaches to a feeding frenzy.

The battle tide was turning, slipping away from the maroon. Standing in the stirrups, the marshal yelled, *"Kill the ogre!"*

Sir Abrax lifted his blue sword in acknowledgment and began cutting a path to the ogre. The marshal angled his horse to approach the beast from its left side, fighting his way through a tangle of foot soldiers.

At the heart of the field, Sir Abrax reached the ogre, his sapphire sword gleaming like a beacon in the afternoon light. The ogre bellowed, swinging its studded war club in a deadly arc. A fearsome sight, the hulking ogre dwarfed the knight. Bulging with muscles, it had freakishly long arms and a giant's crushing strength. Clad in furs, it seemed more beast than man.

The marshal urged his horse forward, refusing to let Sir Abrax fight alone. Hacking his way through the press, he carved a path to the center. *"Knights to me! To me!"*

Mounds of bodies surrounded the ogre, a grizzly rampart of the dead and dying. The marshal asked his horse to a gallop, leaping the carnage. At the height of the jump, he gained a clear view of the ogre, watching in horror as Sir Abrax went down, his horse felled by the ogre's punch. *"Fight me!"* Spurring his horse, the marshal closed the distance. He bellowed a war cry as his stallion barreled into the ogre.

Hit in the chest, the ogre stumbled backward, a startled look in piggish eyes, but it did not fall. *It did not fall.* So close, the marshal could see the stubble on the ogre's lantern jaw, its cruel teeth filed to points. Snarling, the ogre lashed out with a ham-handed fist, punching the marshal in the chest. The fist struck like a battering ram. Pain exploded in the marshal's chest. Starved for air, he felt crushed. Something struck him from behind. Stunned, he realized he'd hit the ground. Floundering in the snow, he gasped for breath while trying to avoid his horse's plunging hooves. A spiked war-club struck the ground, narrowly missing his head. The marshal rolled away. His great sword glittered in the snow. He lunged for it. Grabbing the sword, he staggered to his feet. The massive war club swung in his direction. The marshal raised his sword, braced to parry. Wood struck steel, a mighty blow that nearly forced him to his knees. His sword bit deep, embedded in the club. The marshal tugged, but his sword was stuck fast. The ogre twisted the club, wrenching the sword from his hands.

Cruel laughter rumbled from the ogre, a terrible mocking sound. *"Now you die!"*

The marshal stood his ground, unsheathing his dagger.

The ogre hefted his war club for the killing blow.

Sir Abrax sprang from the mound of corpses like a knight resurrected from the dead. His blue sword flashed, severing the ogre's descending fist, cleaving the hand from the arm. The ogre roared in pain, droplets of blood spattering like red rain. One-handed, the ogre flailed its club, smashing circles of death, heedless of friend or foe.

The marshal staggered backwards. Avoiding a vicious swing, he tripped over a corpse. The dead man held a spear. *A spear!* Dropping his dagger, he took up the spear and rushed the ogre. Somehow he got inside the club's fearsome swing. With a roar, he thrust for the ogre's abdomen. The leaf-shaped blade bit deep. Eight-inches of cold steel embedded in the beast's belly. The ogre bellowed in pain but it did not die. *It did not die!* The marshal clung to the blood-slicked shaft, twisting the spear to disembowel the beast. A horrible stench filled the air. Beside him, Sir Abrax rained blows on the ogre's thick hide. Just when it seemed the beast would never die, the ogre made a gurgling noise and toppled backwards, felled like tree.

Releasing the spear, the marshal staggered backwards, flicking a grateful glance at Sir Abrax. "What happened to you? I thought you dead."

The knight planted a booted foot on the ogre's war club. "The ogre punched my horse. With one blow, it killed my mount and then the poor horse fell on me. Took me a while to get loose." Yanking the trapped sword from the club's fierce bite, he tossed it to the marshal. "If you hadn't come, the ogre would have ground my bones to dust. *Behind you!*"

The marshal whirled, raising his sword to block an axe blow. The battle resumed in a rush. Ignoring his exhaustion, he fought for his life. Stroke and parry, the fighting seemed to drag on to forever, but then he heard the horn, three short blasts followed by one long note. The marshal grinned, knowing it had to be Gravis. He risked a glance toward the far side of the valley, relieved to see maroon knights galloping down the mountain trail. Two hundred knights attacked with lances lowered. Panic claimed the enemy. Instead of fighting, they began to run. The battle became a rout.

The fighting swept past him. Desperate to catch his breath, the marshal leaned on his sword, watching as younger knights finished the battle. The falling snow trickled to a stop and the air seemed warmer, or perhaps it was just his body heat rising like steam from beneath his armor. Exhausted and aching, he surveyed the field. Snow ran red with blood, the valley littered with the dead and dying. He found himself standing near the ogre's corpse. Sir Abrax kicked its booted foot. "How many of these do you think they have?"

The marshal raised his visor, relishing the cold against his face. "Whatever the number it's too many."

Sir Gravis approached at a trot, his sword dripping red with blood, his warhorse slick with sweat. "The field is ours."

The marshal nodded. "What took you?"

Sir Gravis scowled. "They set a rear guard. We had to fight our way through."

The answer made sense but it felt like a sword blow to the marshal's gut. "They're changing tactics. They expected an attack from the rear." He wondered what other surprises the enemy had in store, but he was too weary to think. "Tend to the wounded, count the dead, and loot the enemy, we need to be gone from here."

Sir Gravis saluted and wheeled his horse away.

The marshal glanced at Sir Abrax. "We'd best find mounts." He searched the field till he found his stallion cropping grass from an opening pawed in the snow. Relieved to find his horse alive, he approached with soft words. "You did well, my friend. You deserve an apple." Feeling a rumble in the pit of his stomach, the marshal added, "We both deserve apples. Pity we have none." It hurt just to swing into the saddle. Every part of his body ached, his chest worst of all. He thanked Valin his armor hadn't crumpled beneath the ogre's blow.

"Water. Give me water."

The marshal heard the weak plea and traced it to a mound of bodies. Dismounting, he found a maroon knight lying amongst the enemy, blood drenching his surcoat.

"Water?"

He knelt, gently removing the man's battered helm. *"Devlan!"* Recognition hit like a hammer-blow. The squire was newly raised to a knight, barely old enough to shave and now he'd seen his last battle. Sick at heart, the marshal held a flask to the lad's lips, wishing it was brandy instead of water. "Drink, for you fought well."

"My Lord Marshal!" The lad gulped the ice-cold water but his gaze was full of questions. "Victory?"

"Yes, victory. And judging from the dead around you, you've brought honor to the maroon." A crooked smile graced the lad's face. The marshal held him close while his gaze searched the lad's wound. A foul smell told the tale, a fearful cut through the bowels, but judging from the lad's pallor the pain was almost over. The marshal sat with him, cradling his head till his eyes glazed over. Death came without a sound. Straightening the body, the marshal found a sword and placed it in his hands. He bowed his head and sent a prayer to Valin, "A worthy squire and a promising knight, you should have seen more than one victory." Laden with bitterness, the marshal swung back into the saddle. He felt old, so old, yet there was no one else to lead the Octagon.

He rode back through the carnage, offering words of encouragement to the wounded while counting the living. Too many knights lay dead, perhaps a third of his force, yet the battle was won. It seemed a hollow victory.

Someone hailed his name. He turned to find Lothar cantering towards him, but instead of a roan stallion he rode a bay mare. Seeing his friend, the marshal struggled to keep the relief from his voice. "I see you've found a new horse."

Lothar offered him a lopsided grin. "Glad to see you too. Guess we're both too tough to kill."

"The young are always the first to fall." The marshal winced at the bitterness lacing his voice. "What happened to your horse?"

"Savaged by one of those damn hellhounds. I found myself afoot and lost you in the fray."

"And the mare?"

Lothar grimaced. "Belonged to Sparlin. He won't be needing a horse no more."

Another young one struck down, the marshal spared a moment to remember the young blond-haired knight with the ready smile.

Lothar nudged him out of his grim thoughts. "At least the ambush worked."

"This time, but they're changing their tactics. And that damn ogre nearly had us."

"But a victory none the less."

"True, but the cost was high." The marshal watched as his men worked with quiet efficiency, loading the wounded onto travois, looting the dead and butchering felled horses for their much-needed meat. "At least we'll eat meat tonight."

A column of maroon formed up behind him. Lothar took his position on the marshal's right with Sir Abrax on his left. Giving a last glance at the dead, the marshal nudged his horse to a walk, leading his men up out of the valley. They rode in silence, their armor jangling, the snow crunching beneath iron-shod hooves. The trail snaked upwards, probing deeper into the Dragon Spine Mountains, a fortress of another sort.

Horses and men both hung their heads, breathing plumes of frost into the crisp mountain air, exhausted from the battle. They reached the crest and followed the narrow trail to a broad alpine meadow, but instead of pristine white, the snow was bloody with corpses.

A flock of ravens took wing at their approach. The marshal reined his stallion to a halt, shocked by the butchery. Body parts lay strewn across the blood-drenched snow. All the dead had been hacked to pieces, mutilated and defiled. The marshal was accustomed to the gore of battlefields but this carnage was appalling. Not a single body remained whole. Blood and entrails smeared the snow. A severed head lay close, as if flung across the field in warning. The marshal prodded his horse forward, staring down at the ruined face.

Dead eyes stared wide in horror above a protruding lantern-jaw, *an ogre*. The marshal studied the field with fresh eyes. Amongst the gore, details leaped out at him, fur cloaks and cudgels and spiked war clubs, black and gold, the colors of the Mordant. "An ambush. They planned to ambush us with ogres."

Nothing moved in the killing field, not even the dark wings of carrion birds. A faint wind moaned through the trees like the lament of souls. Instead of a battle, this was a slaughter. The marshal reckoned sixty or more lay dead upon the field, most of them ogres. A single ogre had nearly turned the tide of the last battle...two score would decimate the maroon, yet here they lay, their bodies hacked to pieces as if struck down by a mad god. The marshal surveyed the field, uncertain if he should be pleased...or frightened.

Lothar reined his horse beside the marshal. "They're turning our own tricks against us, using ambushes nested within ambushes, but who did this? It's as if the gods struck them all dead and then tore them asunder."

"A vengeful god drunk on blood," Sir Abrax made the hand sign against evil. "Something's wrong here, we should not tarry."

The marshal gave the knight a stern look. "It's a riddle, nothing more. We need to know why so many ogres died. Search the field and see if we can find a survivor."

As if in answer something stirred at the far end of the meadow. Arising from a pile of corpses, a lone figure waited. Clad in a hodge-podge of maroon and black armor, he looked like a scavenger...or warrior who could not make up his mind which side to serve. Tall with broad shoulders, the hilt of great sword reared over his left shoulder.

Lothar whispered, "Friend or foe?"

The marshal had no answer, but a warning shivered down his spine. He swung down from the saddle, his hand itching for his sword. "Let's find out."

19

Blaine

Blaine did not trust the palace. Ever since that monstrous *thing* came calling at his bedroom window in the dead of night he'd been plagued by nightmares. He'd banished the women from his bed and slept with his great sword by his side, but it did not help, so he spent his time hunting shadows.

Unlike the others, he knew the citadel could be conquered but not tamed. Kath seemed content to brood while Zith spent his time hunting for scrolls and magical trinkets, but Blaine kept his sword sharp. He formed a hunting party, four painted warriors and a guide, a street urchin from the fourth tier. Together they prowled the citadel hunting priests and assassins.

"This way, m'lord." Dermit was a quick lad, small for his age, but he had an eye for detail and he knew the citadel's back ways like a rat knows the sewers.

The Dark Citadel was as much a city as a fortress, a monstrous beehive of stone riddled with crannies and back alleyways. Blaine had learned that each tier had a distinct purpose, slaves and serfs on the bottom, the ruling tiers near the top, the starving poor forced to serve the pampered rich. Nearly everything about the citadel sickened Blaine, but the hell-spawned tiers helped to narrow the search. Reserved for priests and their acolytes and families, the second tier proved a perfect hunting ground for malevolent shadows.

Dermit led them to the main seminary. A soaring temple of dark marble crowned by a pentacle, it might have been impressive if not for the battered doors and the heads rotting on spikes. Empty eye sockets glared down at them, the putrid flesh sagging with rot, distorting the faces into gruesome nightmares. Blaine pushed his way through the broken doors. Tingold and Ruthgar followed carrying torches. Corwin and Tomkin came last, their swords drawn. Torchlight danced across the cavernous hallway, revealing a scene straight from hell. Headless bodies in priests' robes sprawled across the floor. A few were young, little more than boys. Steps led to a great altar smeared with excrement and stripped of anything valuable. The stench was appalling. Something skittered in the corners. Blaine drew his great sword and crouched for battle. Red eyes glowed in the corners, but they were nothing but rats emboldened by the feast.

Blaine smothered his nose against the horrid stench. "This is useless. The crowd's already wrought their vengeance."

"No, m'lord, you'll see." Dermit picked a path through the dead. Along the far wall, another battered door gaped open like a startled mouth. They passed through the door, making their way through a warren of narrow hallways and sleeping cells. More dead littered the hallways, but the somehow the stench was not nearly as bad. Perhaps the bodies weren't as ripe. Towards the back, the rooms grew more opulent. Bright mosaics decorated the floors, gilded braziers stood in the corners, the shadow of pilfered tapestries on the walls, but everywhere Blaine saw signs of death and looting. "We're wasting time. This place has been thoroughly ransacked."

"No, lord, we're nearly there."

And then they found the chapel. Sunlight filtered through stained glass windows, illuminating the chapel with an eerie red light. A gilded mosaic soared along the back wall, the image of a man in dark robes wielding a glowing staff, a nimbus of red light surrounding him. *"The Mordant!"* Blaine stared up at the looming figure but the face was shadowed and obscured, as if the mosaic kept a secret, yet the image screamed of menace and frightening power, a formidable foe etched in history and obscured by legend.

Beside him, Corwin hissed. *"The altar!"*

And then he saw it. Instead of gold and other precious offerings, the dark altar was laden with food, great rounds of bread and lidded pots that smelled of stew. Tugging off a gauntlet, Blaine touched one. "Still warm."

The others gripped their weapons, suddenly alert.

Blaine looked to the boy. "Someone brings food?"

"For the priests that hide. Follow the food and you'll find the skulkers."

"But why do they bring it?"

"Out of fear...or seeking favor."

Blaine felt betrayed. "But I thought the priests were hated?"

"And so they are." Dermit gave him a cautious look. "But some think the priests will rule again...when you leave."

Tingold swore. "By the nine hells, the priests will never rule." The wolf-faced scout flashed a crooked grin. "Especially when they're all dead."

Blaine nodded. "Just so. But we have to find them to kill them."

They searched the chapel. Someone had made an effort to wipe the gore from the marble floor. Bloodstains showed where corpses had been dragged to the outer room. Blaine supposed those in hiding did not want to eat with their dead. Tingold knelt by the far wall. "Look here!"

Blaine crossed the room to crouch by the scout. Tingold held a torch near the floor, illuminating a bloody boot print half severed by the marble wall, as if someone had walked through the stone. "A secret passage!"

Tingold nodded.

Blaine put his shoulder against the wall and pushed, but it remained firm. "Must be a trigger somewhere." He turned to the boy. "Do you know about this?"

Dermit shrugged. "The priests are full of secrets, most of them nasty."

He heard the warning in the boy's voice. "Find the trigger." Blaine climbed the dais to the altar. A pair of onyx gargoyles supported the altar stone, twisted monsters with misshapen heads, eagles mixed with lions and dragons. He ran his hand across the carved stone, prying and pushing. The head *turned*. Stone grated against stone, and the far wall swung open releasing a breath of musty air.

Blaine whirled, his blue sword held at the ready, but there was nothing but darkness lurking beyond. Steps led down, every other one marked by a bloody boot print. The trail disappeared into the depths. "Let's find the bloody bastards."

Tingold went first, a sword in one hand, a torch in the other. Dermit started to follow, but Blaine stopped him. "You wait here."

The lad shook his head, a stubborn look on his face. "A squire would never leave his knight."

"Stop badgering me, boy. You're too small, you're too scrawny, and a squire's position must be *earned*."

"But you *need* me!" Hope and pleading warred across the lad's face. "None of you know the citadel the way I do."

Blaine gave in. "Fine, but stay out of the way."

Dermit flashed a rogue's grin. "Yes, m'lord."

Blaine went second, followed by Dermit. Ruthgar and Corwin and Tomkin brought up the rear. The air held a musty stale smell. After the rotten carnage of the upper halls, the stale smell was a welcome relief.

The two torches cast circles of light, revealing rough cut stone instead of dressed marble. Blaine wondered if the stairs led to a dungeon, or maybe a storage chamber turned hiding hole. The stairs leveled off and they came to a large vaulted room cluttered with treasure. Rolled tapestries, gold candlesticks, silver incense burners, cedar chests, an inlaid screen, an ebony chair, religious icons, all of it haphazardly stacked against the far wall as if it had been hastily snatched from the chambers above. Taking a deep breath, Blaine caught the bitter scent of Vetra, the toxic smoke the priests used for their rituals. "Smell that?" He took another breath to be sure. "They've been here. And not too long ago."

Tingold circled the chamber, spilling torchlight across the treasure. "Look at this loot. The thrice-cursed priests pilfered their own halls."

Blaine opened a small silver box. Jewels winked inside, sapphires, emeralds, garnets and topaz, a duke's ransom in cut gems. "Why is evil always awash in riches?"

"It's their nature," Corwin answered, "the bastards are better at stealing, especially the god-cursed priests."

"No reason they should have all the reward." Blaine emptied the gems into his belt pouch. He flipped a large sapphire to Dermit. "For your help."

The dark-haired lad flashed a grin, tucking the gem into his pocket.

Surveying the stacked treasure, Blaine spied a long narrow chest of carved wood, a curious shape for a box, just the right size for a great sword. He pried the lid open, disappointed by the find. A silver staff topped by a pentacle sat nestled in dark velvet. It looked like something Zith would take an interest in.

Dermit hissed. "Don't touch it, lord!"

Blaine stayed his hand. "Why?"

"Priestly stuff can have strange powers."

"What kind of powers?"

Dermit backed away. "Scary and hurtful."

Blaine shut the lid. "We'll leave it for Zith."

Corwin growled, "We've found their loot, now let's find the bloody bugg..." his words ended in a strangled scream. Dropping his sword, he clutched his throat, pulling a bloody dart from his neck. He held it towards Blaine, foam flecking his mouth, his eyes already dead.

Something *snicked* through the air. Blaine whirled, catching a glimpse of moving darkness. A heavy weight thudded onto his back, a thin wire looping over his head. The wire cut into his throat, drawing blood while threatening to strangle him. Blaine dropped his sword, clutching at the wire, struggling to breathe. Desperate for release, he flung himself backward, crashing his assailant onto the floor. The wire loosened. Blaine tore it away, turning to grapple with the enemy. Clad all in black, his assailant was small in stature but he had a barrel chest and a blacksmith's strength. Gloved hands closed around Blaine's throat in a death grip. Blaine bucked against the deadly choke, one hand reaching for the dagger sheathed at his belt. His assailant rolled on top. Fingers closed like iron bands around Blaine's throat. The enemy straddled him, flashing a malicious grin...that suddenly went slack. The assailant slumped forward, blood blooming on the back of his head. Blaine flung the limp form away. Pulling a dagger from his belt, he pounced on the assassin. His dagger plunged down. Once, twice, thrice, his dagger bit deep, making sure the attacker was dead. Gasping for breath, Blaine looked up to find Dermit standing over him with a golden candlestick in his fists.

The lad looked pale as death.

"You saved me." Blaine's voice sounded hoarse.

Dermit nodded, dropping the candlestick. "An assassin," the lad pointed to the dead assailant, "an assassin of the ninth rank."

Blaine flicked a glance to the others. Corwin and Tomkin were both dead, felled by poisoned darts, a coward's weapon. Ruthgar was tying a cloth around a bloody gash on his arm while Tingold cleaned his sword, a dead assassin at his feet. "Took two of us to kill the bastard."

Blaine retrieved his blue sword. Sheathing it, he cleaned his dagger, pausing to take a good look at the dead assassin. Small in stature and clad in supple black, he wore a baldric of nine throwing knives across his chest. "How many assassins are in the citadel?"

Dermit shrugged. "No one knows...but they only serve the most high."

"The most high what?"

"Priests."

A shiver raced down Blaine's back.

Ruthgar said, "We could use a few more swords."

Blaine shook his head. "If we leave, they'll bolt." He nodded towards the far door. "Let's see what's ahead." Blaine sheathed his dagger and drew his blue steel sword.

To his credit, Dermit did not balk. The lad picked up Corwin's torch, and followed Blaine through the far doorway. Tingold and Ruthgar came behind, their swords drawn. The narrow passage twisted left and then right, torchlight glinting off of rough stone. Twice Blaine caught the faint scent of Vetra, but the chambers were empty. They passed several sleeping cells, nothing in them but bedrolls...and then the passage seemed to darken. Blaine edged forward, his sword held at the ready. So dark, the inky blackness seemed to repel the torchlight. Blaine strained to see, yet saw nothing. Hairs prickled at the back of his neck.

A voice from the darkness whispered, "*Imbolith flamous an!*"

Flames erupted on Blaine's hands. Fierce heat bit through his gauntlets, scorching his hands with unbearable pain. Screaming, he dropped his sword. Slamming his hands together, he tried to beat out the flames, but instead of dying, the fire grew. Flames raced up his arms, engulfing his face. His hair ignited, becoming a glowing nimbus. Maddened by pain, Blaine beat at his face, shrieking in agony. Heat engulfed him, a terrible blistering heat. Blaine felt like he was melting, roasted within his chainmail. Blackened and burned, he felt the skin peel from his face. Howling, he fell to his knees writhing in agony, surrounded by fire.

A figure approached, a man in dark robes. "I will make a dark sacrifice of you, knight of the Octagon!"

Blaine fought against the agony. In the back of his mind, a voice whispered, *Remember the Mist! See the truth!* Blaine fought the pain, struggling to understand. *See the truth!* He looked at his arms, looked through the flames and saw fire engulfing his hands yet nothing burned! Nothing was charred, nothing was melted, and nothing was singed. *Lies wrapped in sorcery!* He knew the truth, yet pain shuddered through him.

The dark priest approached, a silver staff gripped in one hand, a sharp sickle in the other. "Kneel before me, for I will have your life's blood!"

His blue sword lay abandoned on the floor. A searing agony roared through Blaine, yet he made himself move, lunging for the sword. His hand felt charred and ruined, yet he gripped the hilt, swinging the blade upwards. The point took the priest in the throat. He rammed the blade deep, bright blood spraying wide. The priest gaped, a startled look on his bearded face. The staff and sickle fell from lifeless hands, clattering on the stone floor.

The flames disappeared...and so did the pain.

Shuddering, Blaine crumpled to the cold stone floor. For the longest time, he lay twitching next to the bloody corpse, gasping for breath, tortured by the memory of mind-numbing pain. Strength slowly returned. He checked his hands and his face, but nothing was blackened, nothing was burned, only a terrible memory. Relief washed through him.

Blaine struggled to stand. The terrible darkness was banished. He could see the two torches sputtering against the stone floor. The others looked stunned, yet they seemed unharmed, twitching like fish dumped fresh-caught onto dry land. "Are you hurt?"

Tingold gasped. "I thought I was on fire!" His hands patted his face as if to be sure it was still there. "What in the nine hells was that?"

"Sorcery, foul sorcery." Blaine kicked the staff, a clatter of silver on stone.

"But how did you know..."

"...the fire wasn't real?" Blaine shrugged. "I've seen its like before, at a monastery deep in the south. I didn't know it then, but it was a warning of sorts." He shivered, remembering the Guardian in the Mist, silently thanking the old bastard for the painful lesson. He stared down at the dead priest, no different than any other corpse. "The priest tortured us with lies, sorcerous lies."

Ruthgar swore, "By the all the gods, how do we fight magic like that?"

Blaine gripped his blue steel sword, "With heart and steel and determination...and truth." He nudged the corpse, "Their foul sorcery is the very reason we dare not lose this war."

The others stood, reclaiming their torches and swords.

Blaine cleaned his sword on the priest's robes.

Dermit edged forward, his voice a hiss. "I've seen this one!" His eyes widening, the boy took a sudden step backwards as if the corpse might bite. "That's the high priest, Gavis! You've killed the high priest!"

Blaine took a closer look. The dead priest's face was sallow, his dark beard unkempt, but his robes were of the finest make, plush black velvet with golden runes embroidered on the collar and sleeves. And his staff and sickle were both clad in silver, gleaming wicked in the torchlight. "The high priest, eh?" Blaine hefted his blue sword, striking the head from the body. Lifting the grisly trophy by the long dark hair, he handed it to Dermit. "Go and spike this above the outer doorway. If the people see the high priest is well and truly dead then maybe they'll believe the priesthood is finished."

The lad took the dripping head, holding it well away from his body. "Yes, m'lord."

"And then run to the palace and find Zith and Fanggold. Tell them to bring more swords so we can clean out this rat's nest."

"Yes, m'lord."

The boy started to turn away, but Blaine said, "And Dermit."

"Yes, lord?"

"You did well, showing courage befitting a squire of the Octagon."

The lad flashed a blazing smile, "Yes, m'lord!" and then he sped down the long hall.

Blaine turned to the others. "Shall we see where this leads?" The two painted warriors growled their assent, keen for vengeance. Hefting their swords, they prowled down the corridor, their boots whispering across dark stone. Blaine tightened his grip on his blue steel sword, remembering the pain of the priest's fire. Invoking Valin, he silently swore to slay every dark-damned priest lurking in the citadel...and then he'd find a way south and kill the Mordant.

20

The Knight Marshal

Alone raven circled the slaughter field. Cawing twice, it swooped low over the feast of corpses but it did not land. Dark wings beat skyward, shunning the dead as if they were tainted. The marshal scowled, telling himself that he did not believe in ill-omens.

Beside him, Lothar muttered, "Perhaps ogres aren't to its liking."

"Perhaps."

An orange sun sank in the west, loosing twilight upon the mountains. Dismounting, the marshal tossed his reins to a waiting knight. "Lothar, Sir Abrax with me. Perhaps the survivor knows the riddle of the dead." His gaze flicked to Sir Dalt and the host of knights riding at his back. "The rest of you keep a sharp lookout. The enemy has shown a penchant for tricks this day." Sir Dalt gave a grim nod, sending riders along the column with fresh orders.

A lone survivor stood amongst the carnage. He wore an odd mishmash of armor, silver mixed with black and gold, but a knight's maroon cloak hung from his shoulders. The clash of colors suggested a mercenary, or a scavenger...or worse, a turncloak. Too weary to sort through the riddle, the marshal strode towards the stranger. "Come, let's hear his tale."

Sir Abrax took his blindside, while Lothar stayed on his right. Snow crunched beneath their boots as they crossed the blood-soaked field. Bodies lay hacked to pieces, entrails and heads strewn in a gross display of butchery, as if killing alone was not enough. A terrible stench clogged the air, the awful stink of butchery, bad enough to make a veteran gag. The marshal had trod many a battlefield but this one reeked of evil.

The stranger waited at the heart of the field. Tall with broad shoulders, he stood with boots spread wide, his gauntleted hands hooked in his belt, a sheathed great sword rearing over his left shoulder like a threat. If the stranger bore any wounds, he showed no signs of it. A knight's maroon cloak hung from his shoulders, but the marshal did not recognize his face, wondering if the thick, ruddy beard obscured a traitor's brand.

Stopping two sword lengths away, the marshal spoke first, thrusting straight for the heart of the matter. "Who are you, stranger, and how did you survive this slaughter?"

The stranger remained mute as stone, his dark gaze glowering beneath his helm.

Sir Abrax growled, "Answer the Lord Marshal."

The stranger cocked his head as if considering. "*Survive* this?" He spread his arms wide, encompassing the dead. "You stand upon a field of great victory. *I* ambushed these ogres. *I* slew the enemy. I've come to save the Octagon."

Sir Abrax gaped, "*One man?* You've taken too many blows to the head!"

The stranger's voice turned cold. "I don't lie, Sir Abrax."

Shock riddled the knight's voice. "You know my name?"

The stranger merely nodded.

The marshal had a bad feeling about this.

Sir Abrax scoffed, his voice dripping with scorn, "One man, fighting alone, and you claim to have slayed a whole troop of ogres? You lie!"

"*I speak the truth!*" With liquid grace the stranger unsheathed the sword strapped to his back and held the blade aloft. Black as sin, the sword seemed to drink the light, metal-forged dragons curled around the hilt. "Behold Boric's blade, the sword of legend returned to the Octagon!"

The marshal staggered backwards, "*The cursed sword!*" His gaze was drawn to the dark blade, feeling its power, feeling its pull. Tearing his gaze from the sword, he studied the wielder's face. The survivor had Baldwin's voice, and the squire's ruddy coloring, but somehow he'd gained a man's growth in merely a moon-turn. No longer a lad, he sported a thick beard and broad shoulders and stood a head taller than the marshal. "*By all the gods, this cannot be!*" Something was very wrong here, as if the Dark God himself came stalking the Octagon. "Baldwin."

It was a statement, not a question.

Baldwin smirked as if pleased to be recognized.

"I gave you orders."

Baldwin sneered. "Discard this weapon? I think not."

"That sword slew the king!" Anger rode the marshal's voice, hiding his fear. "That blade is cursed! I ordered you to throw it in Eye Lake."

"Cursed!" Outrage rode Baldwin's voice. "I say it is *blessed!* Look around you! With this sword a single knight slew an entire troop of ogres! Who among you can match such a feat?" He lowered the dark sword, holding the tip level with Sir Abrax's heart, a challenge and a threat. "You wield a hero's blue steel sword, yet how many ogres have you killed? One? Two?" Baldwin spread his arms wide, "Or *sixty?*"

Lothar hissed, "He's right! This sword could decide the war!"

Sir Abrax growled, "It's a trick, a trap set by the enemy. I don't believe it."

"Believe it!" Baldwin's roar echoed against the mountains. "Use your eyes...and then use your knees."

A cold fist gripped the marshal's heart. "What?"

"You heard me." A sneer claimed Baldwin's face. "With this sword I have the power to save the Octagon. Against Boric's blade no foe can stand. By right of conquest, I claim the king's crown. Kneel to me!"

The marshal voice turned deadly cold. "Surrender that blade."

"Surrender!" Baldwin's face contorted in rage. "I bring you victory and you sneer at it!" Quick as a snake, he swung the black sword toward the marshal. "Kneel to your king."

The marshal's voice seethed. "You are *not* my king."

Sir Abrax attacked. Sapphire-blue steel descended in a mighty killing arc...but the black blade met the stroke. The two swords clashed with a tortured shriek. Sparks flew between the blades, the combatants locked in a fearsome blur. As champion of the sword, Sir Abrax had few peers, yet Baldwin parried every blow, the black sword moving with uncanny speed. Stroke and parry, the two swords fairly flew at each other, sparks dancing along the edge. With every clash, the blue sword screamed as if in agony. Sir Abrax attacked with lightning speed but Baldwin countered like a demon possessed. They fought like champions; they fought like mortal enemies, trading mighty blows. Baldwin attacked with an overhead swing. Blue steel blocked the black, the two swords meeting in a ferocious clash. And then the impossible happened. Screaming in mortal pain, the blue blade *shattered!*

The marshal gasped, *"No!"*

Unhindered, the black blade sped downwards, sundering the knight's armor, cleaving deep into his chest, his heart's blood fountaining across the snow.

Shocked, the marshal gaped as Sir Abrax fell.

Baldwin wrenched the black sword loose with a scream. *"You should have knelt!"* His face contorting in hate, he attacked the knight's body, hacking at limbs and head, making a bloody mockery of the dead.

"*No!*" Without thought, the marshal unsheathed his great sword. Leaping forward, he braced to parry the black, protecting his friend's body. The dark sword never slowed, descending in a mighty blow. The two swords met with a hideous clang. Ordinary steel parried the black with a deafening screech. Pain shuddered down the marshal's arms, nearly hammering him to his knees. His sword bucked in his hands, but it did not shatter. Across the blades, he locked stares with Baldwin. "Drop your sword!"

Baldwin's face twisted in hate, so contorted he seemed more fiend than man. "*Kneel!*"

"*Never!*"

Baldwin attacked, raining blows with frightening speed. The marshal retreated under the onslaught, desperate to keep his sword raised. Instead of a squire, he fought a demon. Other knights joined the battle, rushing to his aid, but somehow the demon held them at bay, parrying every blow while focusing his rage on the marshal. Baldwin fought like a whirlwind, the black sword relentless in his hands. Outmatched, the marshal could only dodge and parry, struggling to stay alive. Every blow hammered his arms, pain shuddering through his whole body. His chest ached from the beating, his sword vibrating in his hands. He feared his blade would shatter but all he could do was fight. Sweat poured out of him. His breath grew ragged and his legs turned to lead. Parry and retreat, he struggled to keep his footing, his strength bleeding away with every blow. Death stalked him, chased by a cursed sword, but then an otherworldly voice whispered through the marshal's mind, *For honor and the Octagon!* A second strength flowed from the sword into his arms. Shocked, the marshal nearly dropped the blade but a warrior's instinct kept his hands locked on the hilt. Death whistled close. Parrying the blow, the marshal scrambled backwards, tightening his grip on the sword. Flushed with renewed vigor, the marshal attacked. Beating back the dark sword, he looked for an opening. Baldwin sneered, loosing a fearful blow at his head. The marshal ducked low and saw his chance. Lunging upwards, he aimed for a chink in the armor. His blade struck true, driving into Baldwin's armpit. With all his might, he rammed the great sword heart-deep.

Baldwin stared wide-eyed, a gurgle of blood at his mouth. "*How?*" He crumpled to the ground, the black blade falling from his hands. The marshal kicked the cursed sword aside and then yanked his own free. Holding the tip to the squire's throat, he said, "Yield."

Other swords surrounded Baldwin, forming a thicket of death.

"*Yield!*"

The battle-madness bled from Baldwin's gaze and his features seemed to soften, revealing the lad hidden beneath a man's tangled beard. "My Lord Marshal...how?" Bewilderment filled his gaze, followed by pain.

The marshal knelt. "Why did you do it?"

"To...save...the Octagon."

Relenting, the marshal removed the lad's helm and cradled his head. "You served the king well."

A tear trickled down Baldwin's face. "Failed...you."

"No." The marshal held him close. "The fault was mine. Your service to the maroon will be remembered."

"*Remembered...*" Baldwin gasped in pain and then his life fled, soaking into the blood-trampled ground.

A bitter wind whistled through the naked trees, a lament to the dead.

The marshal closed the lad's eyes, whispering a fervent prayer to Valin

A jangle of arms and armor surrounded him. The marshal looked up to find a circle of maroon knights standing guard, their weapons bared, their faces grim with questions. More than a few bore fresh wounds.

Lothar was the first to lower his weapon. "Corbin and Tancil are both dead, slain by this fiend."

Two more knights dead, yet the battle had taken only mere moments, as if Baldwin had possessed the strength of ten demons. The marshal knew he was lucky to be alive. Standing, he surveyed the field. *Sixty dead ogres*, they were *all* lucky to be alive.

Sir Dalt gestured to the slain squire. "What happened? He fought like a demon."

The marshal stood, swaying from exhaustion. "The black sword is cursed. We dare not wield it." He glanced down at Baldwin. "This was my mistake. All those who died here today will be accorded full honors." He cleaned the blood from his sword. "Check the dead, for we dare not tarry."

Sir Dalt gave him a questioning look but the marshal stopped him with a glare. Saluting, the knights moved to obey.

Leaving the dead to the others, the marshal stepped towards the black sword. It gleamed dark and deadly, lying in a bloody patch of snow. Lothar crouched beside it, peering at the blade. "Baldwin spoke true. The blade bears the mark of Orin Surehammer and the coiled dragons fit the legends."

The marshal shivered, fearing the awe in his friend's voice. "The blade is cursed, Lothar. It cannot be wielded."

"Yet a mere squire single-handedly slayed sixty ogres. It begs to be wielded."

The marshal nodded. "Yet we dare not."

"But we cannot leave it for the enemy."

"No." And there-in lay the trap, for the cursed blade truly was a two-edged sword. "Go and get two cloaks from the dead. Two *black* cloaks, I'll not soil the maroon with this curse."

Nodding, Lothar moved among the dead while the marshal stood guard over the sword. Even without touching it, he could feel its allure, like a siren singing his blood to a battle lust. Shuddering, he gripped his borrowed sword of plain Castlegard steel, resisting the pull.

Lothar returned with two bloodstained cloaks and a wolf pelt.

"Spread them on the snow."

Lothar spread the wolf pelt fur down, and then the two black cloaks, one on top of the other. The marshal kicked the black sword with his boot, levering the blade onto the cloaks. Kneeling, he rolled the sword into a bundle. Even through the wad of cloth and fur, he could feel its power.

Lothar stared at the bundle. "What now?"

"We guard it. We resist it. And we keep fighting."

Lothar gave him a measured look but he did not argue.

A knight brought their horses. Strapping the bundle to his cantle, the marshal pulled himself into the saddle. "Mount up! We still have a long way to ride." The knights formed a column behind him, maroon cloaks fluttering in the wind. The marshal nudged his stallion to a walk, picking a path through the carnage, but his gaze kept returning to the black sword bundled in fur and tied to his saddle. Such a weapon could truly turn the tide of war, but at what cost? A shiver raced down his spine. The marshal sent a silent prayer to Valin, begging the Warrior God for the strength to prevail.

In the South

21

Bryce

The great ship sped south under a cloud of fear. Rows of oars struck the water with a relentless beat, but the slate-gray sea stretched to forever. Locked within the Mordant, Bryce watched through his spy hole, noting the terror etched on the crew's faces as they fingered their sea charms. Even the captain averted his gaze, avoiding the stare of the dark-robed passenger. Sailors were a superstitious lot, but in this case they did right to fear.

Five times the Mordant took possession of the trireme's rear deck. In the dead of night the oldest harlequin stood upon the open deck and called on the power of Darkness. And every time, Darkness answered. Red lightning speared down, striking the Mordant's upraised hands, surrounding him with a nimbus of power. Cowering within his prison, Bryce watched and hid and watched again, awed and frightened by the fearsome display. Steeped in the powers of Hell, the Mordant performed ghastly rituals, twisting souls and flesh into monstrous forms, creating foul abominations. Captured albatrosses and a hapless sea eagle were melded with sacrificed men. Part man, part bird, the twisted abominations arose from the ship's deck, taking wing toward Erdhe to work their master's will. But for each unholy melding, the Mordant paid a steep price. Collapsing in a magical stupor, his stunted attendants, assassins cloaked as servants, carried the Mordant to the captain's cabin and saw to his needs.

While the Mordant languished abed, swathed in misery imposed by spent magic and the sea's rocking motion, Bryce took his chance. After each summoning, the bonds of his prison seemed to weaken, as if the workings bled away the Mordant's power. Careful to avoid detection, Bryce pushed at his prison walls, seeking to reclaim his body. He battered at the void, desperate to escape, all to no avail. Locked in his prison, he railed at the gods, till failure made him seek a subtler way. Yearning for movement, craving a single touch, he strained to remember that one time in the Mordant's treasury crypt when he'd slipped his bonds and felt his body. Stilling his mind, Bryce imagined his hand lying upon the blanket, the feel of rough wool beneath his fingertips, the caress of a breeze across the hairs on his hand. He imagined his fingers moving...and then he *felt* the coarse wool. He *felt* it! Elation thrummed through him...till a devastating suspicion struck like a cold sword. Fearing a trap, a trick of the Mordant, Bryce retreated into his prison, curling into a ball, waiting for retribution...but none came. Emboldened, he dared to plan his escape.

Grown attuned to his captor's misery, Bryce waited for the perfect moment. The Mordant's twisted rituals took the heaviest toll. Sundered by magic and wracked by seasickness, the Mordant fell into a death-like torpor. While his jailor lay insensate, Bryce took his chance. Like a thief in the night, he reached beyond his prison, nothing more than a thin wisp of thought. Small and unobtrusive, he avoided anything significant, merely seeking control of the left hand. Memories strengthened the link. Like donning a living glove, he took possession of skin, and blood, and sinew. *Wood beneath his hand*, he nearly swooned from the touch. A sea breeze caressed the hairs on the back of his hand, as gentle as a lover. Bryce shivered with longing, swamped by the sensation of touch. So many senses so long denied, a flood of emotion swept through him, but Bryce fought for control, refusing to be distracted. Straining with effort, he willed the hand to move.

Nothing happened.

Stiff as rusted armor, the hand refused to obey. Bryce raged in his prison, refusing to let the opportunity be nothing more than a god-cursed tease. Focusing all his effort, he willed the smallest finger to move. Still nothing. He strained like a man trying to shift a mountain...and then it happened. The smallest finger twitched.

And then the Mordant groaned.

Bryce pulled back, retreating to his prison. He made himself small, a lost soul hiding from his jailor's wrath, but no punishment came. Elation flooded through him, he'd taken the first step toward defeating the Mordant.

But one victory did not win the war. Bryce bided his time, practicing control. He started with the smallest finger, and then two, and then the entire fist. When the hand clenched tight, triumph flowed through him like a bonfire.

The days passed. Sometimes the Mordant slept in his cabin, while other days the assassins carried him aloft, creating a padded bed on the rear deck. As the assassins kept vigil, the Mordant slept curled on his side, like a cat warmed by the sun. Peering from his spy hole, Bryce watched the restless sea change from slate gray to turquoise blue. As the days passed his control grew and so did his plan. The Mordant hated the sea. Plagued by seasickness, it was as if the sea rejected him, rejected his Darkness. Perhaps the sea would be his downfall.

Storms claimed the ship for nigh on a week. The Mordant's seasickness worsened, a prime opportunity, yet he remained in his cabin, confined by illness and foul weather. Bryce thought he might go mad with waiting, but then the storms cleared and the assassins carried the Mordant aloft.

Swathed in a nest of blankets, they settled the Mordant near the ship's railing, a clear view of the sea between the carved railings. Bryce waited, timing the swell of the waves and the attention of the assassins. When the sailors brought the mid-day meal, Bryce took his chance. Focusing his will on the left hand, he reached toward the railing. The hand moved, flopping on the deck, but not far enough. Bryce struggled for control, like pushing thoughts through molasses. He focused his will and the hand crept across the deck. Fingers grasped the railing, the feel of salt-stained wood beneath his touch. Like a drowned man Bryce clung to the railing, struggling to regain his strength. So close but yet so far. One strong pull and he'd roll the Mordant between the railings, dumping the enemy into the foam-crowned waves. Bryce stared at the sea, at the rolling waves, like a promise of freedom, a promise of release. He wondered what it would be like to drown. He wondered if he'd even feel it. Death held the promise of release, to kill a monstrous evil while ending a hellish imprisonment, yet his conscience plagued him. In his heart of hearts, Bryce knew he should wait for the crystal dagger, but he yearned for release. The sea offered him a chance that would not come again. Desperate for release, he tugged the Mordant towards the railing. The waves helped, rocking the deck, adding speed to the roll.

The Mordant groaned.

Bryce panicked, feeling the Mordant rise from his torpor. He tugged on the railing with all of his strength.

"My Lord, are you well?" The assassin was there, rolling the Mordant well away from the edge.

Inside his prison, Bryce howled in frustration

"*Land ho!*" The cry rang from the mast tops. The crew cheered, swarming the deck. Sails snapped in the wind as the ship hove towards shore.

Bryce watched as the ship sped towards land, towards a great crescent-shaped harbor surmounted by a gray castle. *The end of the voyage, the end of hope.* Despair crashed down like a castle portcullis sealing his doom. He'd lost his secret alliance with the sea, his best chance to slay the fiend...and the cursed Mordant reached the southern kingdoms unopposed. Already he could feel his jailor regaining his power, regaining control. Consumed by misery, Bryce curled in a ball, a prisoner once more.

22

The Priestess

Another sleepless night. Restless with the need to know, the Priestess climbed the stairs to Silverspire's tallest tower. Moonlight glowed through the open window, silvery and bright, but it was Darkness she sought. Lighting a single candle, she shuttered the windows, snuffing the moon's pale glow. The single candle guttered, a frail circle of light surrounded by a rich velvety Darkness. She'd made the tower chamber her private haven, tapestries lining the walls, silken pillows strewn across the floor, her chapel to the Dark. The silver scrying bowl waited in the center, already filled with spring water. The Priestess knelt among the cushions. Reaching within her tight-fitting bodice, she removed the great moonstone. Cradling the oval gem in her hands, she breathed upon the milk-white stone. It wakened with her breath, glowing with an otherworldly light. A legend of darker times, the Eye of the Oracle throbbed like a heartbeat within her hands. Power thrummed through her, a luxurious delight. As the Oracle Priestess, it was her right to wield the moonstone, her right to use the Eye to spy on the servants of the Dark. The Priestess reveled in the power.

She lowered the moonstone into the scrying bowl. The water hissed and spat like a boiling cauldron. It was always this way, a clash of competing powers. The Priestess held her breath, but Darkness held sway. The waters calmed, turning midnight black, a perfect mirror for Dark deeds. The Priestess knelt, her raven-dark hair forming a silky curtain surrounding the scrying bowl. Gathering her power, she breathed upon the water. "Show me the servants of the Dark Lord."

Mirror-dark waters rippled with images, giving the Priestess a bird's eye view. Her gaze sought Navarre, waves crashing against Castle Seamount, the dark castle thrust up from the ocean like a defiant fist. Jealousy and rage spiked through her. By right of blood and conquest, the crown of Navarre should have been hers if not for her meddling niece. A snarl curled her lips, wishing vengeance upon her kin. But all was not lost. She'd left death in her wake, the royal family decimated by poison. While her kin mourned their loss, her revenge lingered, a coiled serpent hidden within the royal household, a dagger poised at the kingdom's heart. Laughter rippled out of her, plots within plots. She'd always known that schemes were better than swords, the true reason women were meant to rule, but she kept that secret to herself.

Her thoughts roved elsewhere. Images flowed across the water, following her thoughts. She found him sprawled in a large bed, two raven-haired beauties naked by his side, more proof he yearned for her. "Oh Steffan, how your pride blinds you, yet the truth is writ upon your face." A throaty laugh escaped her, "Desire is the greatest poison." No matter how many women he took to his bed, Steffan would never find her equal. She'd watched from her scrying bowl as he squandered his army in Pellanor, letting a crown slip through his fingers, yet the Dark Lord spared him for the great Dark Dance. Handsome and arrogant even in sleep, she studied his face, the white streak in his hair dyed black, proof of his shame and his failure. Plots within plots, if the Dark Lord had a use for Steffan then perhaps she did too, something to consider for when he came calling.

Turning from pleasures to threats, the Priestess leaned low, breathing upon the waters. The scene changed, this time moving north to Raven Pass. A vast horde threatened the southern kingdoms, but it was their master, the Mordant, that worried her far more than all their ravening swords. For the thousandth time, she searched among them for the darkest soul, for the oldest harlequin, but she found no trace of him. Fear spiked through her. She liked it not that he remained hidden. She scoured Erdhe, searching everywhere, yet she'd found no trace of his dark powers. His absence felt like a doom waiting to descend. It gnawed at her mind, preying on her imagination, scaring her more than she cared to admit.

Suddenly weary, the Priestess pulled back from the scrying bowl. The Eye dimmed to a dull white gem, its power drained, nothing more than a large moonstone lying fallow beneath clear waters. So many images, so much Darkness afoot in Erdhe, the Priestess had much to consider. The kingdoms of Erdhe were changing, like a battlefield trampled by the gods, yet few mortals understood the rules. Dire change brought great opportunity but only to those bold enough to risk everything. Schemes and plots tumbled through her mind. Erdhe was sundered by war, yet the greatest hammer stroke had yet to fall. The Mordant remained hidden, yet she sensed his handiwork beneath the Dark weave. With the oldest harlequin embedded in the game, chaos and strife were sure to follow. The Priestess shivered at the threat...beguiled by the risk...enthralled by the reward. She dared to play the Dark Dance, but first she needed to fortify her strength.

Sheathing the great moonstone in a black velvet bag, she unlocked her rosewood chest, careful to turn the skeleton key to the left instead of the right. Avoiding the poisoned needle, she opened the chest, releasing familiar scents of dried herbs and dark ingredients, her hoard of deathly delights. She hid the Eye in a secret compartment beneath the poisons, a single treasure among a thousand deaths. Locking the chest, she raised her voice to be heard beyond the thick oak door. "Come."

The door creaked open. General Tarmin stood guard, his hand on his sword hilt. His gaze sought hers, his eyes glazed like a man enthralled.

"Come and worship my Darkness."

The door closed behind him. His sword belt thumped to the thick carpet. He shed his armor to stand naked and rampant before her. "My priestess...my queen!"

A large hairy bear-of-a-man, she took him among the scented pillows. He plowed her hard and deep, a primal coupling full of earthy lustiness. With every stroke, she drew on his vitality, stealing moonturns from his natural lifespan. Power flowed through her, renewing her prowess. Her scent, her touch, her magic enthralled him, multiplying his stamina. Clutching him tight, she rode him hard, giving him waves of pleasure. Surfeit with power, she released him. Bellowing his triumph, he arched his back, his face a snarl of ecstasy. Sated with sex and oblivious to his loss, he collapsed beside her, succumbing to sleep. Soft snores echoed through the chamber. Rolling free from his embrace, she wrote her true name in the sweat of his chest, deepening her hold on him, another conquest on her path to power.

23

Megan

Megan, Queen of Navarre, dreaded the night. Avoiding the royal bedchamber, she haunted the castle ramparts, evading sleep, yet sleep could not be escaped. Exhaustion and the king's loving arms conspired against her, pulling her back to the royal bedchamber. Night after night, she struggled to remain awake, but sleep always claimed her. Ever since the poisoned feast she'd been plagued by ill-omened dreams. No matter how much wine she drank, the nightmares hounded her. Sleep became a bitter enemy, a battlefield of wills. Memories of the poisoned feast tortured her mind, forcing her to re-live that fateful evening. In her mind's eye, she watched as Igraine crumpled dead upon the floor while Ian clawed his throat bloody, choking on poison. The Curse of the Vowels was real, a nightmare come calling, plaguing her family. Megan shuddered against the memories, hearing the witch laugh as she held the promised antidote aloft. Like a marionette, she watched herself cross the great hall to kneel before Iris, swearing fealty to the witch in the hopes of saving her husband and his kin. *I, Megan of Navarre, acknowledge Iris as the rightwise queen of Navarre and pledge...and pledge my loyalty to you.* The foul pledge seared her soul. Locked in the nightmare, she tossed and turned upon silken sheets, desperate to escape.

Laughter rippled through her mind, cruel and mocking. *You said the words, you swore the oath, and now you must obey.*

No, you're long gone, banished from the castle. You're nothing but a nightmare, a wicked illusion.

Gone but not forgotten. The words stabbed her mind, full of malice. *You swore to serve me. Reach for the dagger hidden beneath the pillow and use it!*

There is no dagger and I will never serve you.

The dagger awaits, hidden by your own hand.

No, you lie!

Serve me, or you will never sleep again. Now reach for the dagger and do my bidding!

The queen struggled to refuse, but the invading voice was relentless, a cold-blooded witch harping commands. *Reach for the dagger and slay your husband. Kill the king as he sleeps. Seal your vow of fealty with his blood.*

No, never! Megan thrashed against the command, but her traitorous hand slowly crept beneath the pillow. She reached for the dagger...but found nothing! *There was nothing there!* Relief flooded through her...chased by cruel laughter.

You reached for the dagger! Triumph laced her sister-in-law's voice, a menace invading her mind. *Next time, the dagger will await your hand!*

No, I'll never do it! She thrashed against sodden sheets, desperate to wake.

You swore an oath. You serve me now! It is only a matter of when!

No! The queen screamed in denial but the words clogged in her throat.

"Megan, wake up."

Strong arms held her. Megan startled awake.

Ivor was there, holding her close. "You were moaning in your sleep. Another bad dream?"

She wanted to warn him, to tell him the truth, but the words would not come, as if the witch had placed a geas upon her tongue. "Yes...a nightmare."

He pulled her close, tucking her in the crook of his arm. "You're safe here with me."

But are you safe with me? The question froze her heart. The witch had said it was only a matter of time. Huddled next to her husband, Megan shivered, praying to be released from the foul spell. The Curse of the Vowels had exacted a terrible toll, reaving the royal Is. By all the gods, the witch would not have her husband too.

24

Liandra

Silk became her so much more than steel. Queen Liandra shed her armor, but she wielded pomp and ceremony like a sword. Ordering formal receptions, she heaped praise and honors on the heroes of the Flame War. Loyalty was rewarded, courage feted, promotions flowed, and the people's morale was bolstered, but in the privacy of her solar the queen girded for another war.

Flanked by her son, Crown Prince Stewart, by Lord Dane, second in command of the Rose Army, and her shadowmaster, Lord Highgate, the queen met with emissaries of the Deep Green. A page opened the outer door and a breath of wilderness swept into her court. Tall and broad-shouldered, the three men wore huntsman's leathers, striding into her solar with an insular pride. Smelling of woodsmoke and cedar and pine, they stood before her throne offering the barest of nods.

The queen supposed a nod was all their stiff-necked pride would allow, and though she found it irksome, she offered a gracious smile. "You are welcome in our court."

Lord Cenric wore his cloak of peacock feathers, half a hundred turquoise eyes shimmering in the firelight, a magnificent dash of exotic elegance mixed with feral wildness. The feathered cloak was striking, but it was the men's eyes that made the greatest difference. Golden cat-eyes set in a man's face, their eyes gleamed unnaturally bright in the firelight. Like demon eyes come to life, their golden eyes were startling, evoking a primal fear, the stuff of childhood nightmares, but their actions proclaimed them allies, and the queen was desperately short of allies.

Liandra inclined her head. "We have received you in our formal audience hall, proclaiming you Friends of Lanverness before our court, but we wish to do more. We owe you and your people a debt of thanks for turning the tide of battle. We wish to make you forever welcome within our kingdom." She gestured and Prince Stewart offered Cenric a scroll festooned with wax seals and emerald ribbons. "This royal writ is a deed to two tracts of land. The nearest is Crown Hill, a royal hunting preserve just north of Pellanor. The second tract is much larger, Onet Forest, a large stand of old growth forest nestled against the Southern Mountains and our border with Wyeth. The crown deeds them both to you, hoping that your people will settle the forest, forever adding your strength and friendship to the kingdom of Lanverness."

Cenric's nostrils flared as if scenting the air. "We do not think of the forest as something *owned*."

Hearing the distaste in his voice, the queen hastened to smooth his ruffled feathers. "Then think of it as a stewardship, a grant for your people to live within the forest."

"And the trees? Will this *parchment* spare them from axe and fire?"

"If that is your wish."

Cenric stood stock-still, his nostril's flared wide. For several heartbeats nothing was said, but then he flashed a smile, offering the queen an unexpected bow. "The Rose Queen is both wise and wily."

"So you accept?"

"Gladly. Long have my people sought a welcome within the southern kingdoms. We will protect Onet Forest, dwelling beneath leaf and bough, far enough away to let your people grow accustomed to our eyes. And at Crown Hill we will keep a smaller clan near to your court. By our presence, the trees will be kept safe." He hefted the scroll. "We will accept this charge with the honesty with which it is given. My people will settle the forest and keep your laws while always following the wisdom of the Treespeaker."

The Treespeaker again, they brandished the name like a monarch...or a sorceress. "We would meet with your Treespeaker to hear her wisdom for ourselves."

"Then you must travel to the Deep Green, for she will never leave it."

More mystery wrapped in riddles. "Monarchs rarely leave their domain, so instead we wish for more time to talk with you. We would make you a member of our court, Lord Cenric. We wish to talk with you and hear tales of your home in the Deep Green."

"As you wish." With a swirl of his peacock cloak, Cenric and his clansmen took their leave with the barest of nods.

The door clicked shut and the feral wildness was gone.

Behind her, Stewart released a long held breath. "Deftly done, mother."

She gave him a wry smile. "Not so deft. Lord Cenric knows we need his bows, but the best deals are those in which both sides prosper."

Her shadowmaster said, "Let us hope there is enough prosperity to go around."

"We must do better than hope. By wits, by golds, and by swords, we must ensure it." The queen's gaze turned to Prince Stewart and Lord Dane. "What plans for the war in the north?"

Lord Dane spread a map across the table. "By all reports, the Mordant's army remains here, in Raven Pass. The Octagon Knights have been defeated, but we suspect they're mounting some type of rear action."

The queen studied the map. "A war in winter," the mere words carried a deadly chill.

Prince Stewart's face was grim. "A terrible war to fight. And if the rumors of the Mordant's numbers are even half true..." he shook his head, "may the gods aid them."

"We can't leave it to the gods. If the Octagon still fights, then we must help them."

"How?" Prince Stewart stared at her. "By the time we march north the Octagon will be defeated or holed up in one of their castles."

"Swords are not the only way to lend aid." She reached across the map, tapping a bejeweled finger on the great eight-sided castle drawn in bold ink. "If the knights wage a winter war then Castlegard will know of it. They'll sorely need food and horses and other supplies. Our gold can buy them that. We'll send to Harvesthold, purchasing food and horses, ordering the farmers of Tubor to deliver them north to Castlegard." Her voice turned thoughtful. "If nothing else, it will buy us time."

"Time?" The prince quirked an eyebrow.

"The most precious of commodities. The longer the knights fight, the more time we shall have to prepare." She leaned back against the carved throne, fingering her necklace of royal rubies. "After the Flame War, we sorely need more time to recover from the damage." Her gaze turned to the prince. "What of your plans for the army?"

"Numbers rule in warfare. Given the size of the Mordant's horde, we dare not meet them in a pitched battle. Instead, we'll fight another war of attrition, nibbling away at their flanks, taking small bites, trying to whittle them down to a fightable size, much the same as we did with the Flame. But it will take much more map, a lot more map." His finger traced a path from Pellanor north. "We'll march fast, trying to reach the Snowmelt before they cross."

The queen nodded. "Better to fight the length of Coronth than Lanverness."

"Just so." His face turned grim. "But war will eventually come to Lanverness."

The words sounded like a doom. "We know." The queen took a steadying breath. "We shall have to be prepared. When will you leave?"

"We'll march within a fortnight."

"Then the wedding will be a rushed affair, for we'll want an heir seeded before you leave."

The prince gaped. "Mother..."

The queen forestalled him with a raised hand. "King Ivor consents to the marriage and so does Princess Jemma, so bend a knee and ask her. While you woo the maiden, we'll make the official arrangements. This alliance with Navarre is important and you will not find a better wife for your future queen."

"Mother, I..."

Lord Dane interrupted. "Perhaps I can take my leave? There's much to be done before the army is ready to march."

A strange look passed between her son and Lord Dane. The queen offered her ringed hand. "See to the army, for so much depends on it."

The young lord kissed her ring and then beat a hasty retreat.

"Lord Dane seems eager."

The prince muttered, "I cannot blame him." Taking a deep breath, he gripped the hilt of his blue steel sword and raised his stare to the queen. "Mother, we must speak of my marriage. I cannot marry Princess Jemma..."

She cut him off. "More of your romantic falderal. Love may come in due time, but for now we need this alliance and we need more heirs. It is your duty as crown prince and it is all arranged."

"I can not..."

"Of course you can!"

Looking exasperated, the prince fairly shouted the words. "I'm already married."

The queen gasped. "*What?*"

"I'm married." The prince stood sword-straight, his back to the roaring fire, the saber scar prominent on his face. "I married Princess Jordan at the Crimson Keep." His voice softened. "So you have your alliance with Navarre, and in time, the gods willing, you'll have your heirs."

The queen felt like a ship without sails. "Where? When?"

"After I escaped the brigands and before we attacked Lingard." A smile burst across his face, as bright as sunrise. "Jordan saved me. It was if the gods brought us together. So I had to marry her, I couldn't wait."

"Where did this happen?"

"At Crimson Keep, an ancient ruin just south of Lingard."

"Married in a ruin? As if that's not an ill-omen."

"Mother!"

The queen sifted through the scant details seeking an escape. "And who married you?"

"One of the Kiralynn monks said the words. We wed beneath the stars and all the gods." He gave her a shrewd look. "And there were witnesses, mother, Ronald Rognald, and the monks and some of my royal guard. And by now the King of Navarre will have heard the news from Jordan." His voice turned hard. "This marriage of my heart shall not be put aside."

"And where is your...wife?"

"In Navarre, we both know the importance of duty."

"You speak of duty, but what of your children, my heirs?"

"Gods, mother! Give us time."

"But what if she can't?"

"What?"

The truth needed to be said, an ugly suspicion she'd harbored since word came from the monastery. "What if she isn't capable?"

The prince paled, clearly ambushed. "What do you mean?"

"Princess Jordan was attacked in the monk's monastery, dealt a terrible wound to the abdomen. The monks healed her...but what if she is no longer fertile?"

The prince sank to the nearest chair, his face ashen. "I saw the scar, a terrible wound...but she is healed, whole and well."

"Is she?" The queen slumped in the throne, sundered by the turn of events. "You are our only living child, our only heir. Without grandchildren, our line ends."

"There will be children. The gods can not be that cruel." Forced confidence filled his voice but his face remained pale.

"Never count on the gods. We've found them to be a fickle lot."

Lord Highgate said, "The royal line of Navarre is unusually fecund."

The prince sent a grateful look towards the shadowmaster. Rising, he stood with his hand gripping his blue steel sword. "I've married for love, to a princess royal, sealing the alliance between Navarre and Lanverness. We are wedded and bedded and in time there will be children."

"May it be so."

"Be happy for us, mother."

She ceded him a mother's smile. "We wish you joy in your marriage, we truly do. But we also wish you children." Worry laced her voice. "War comes, and we need more heirs."

"Give us time and I will place a grandchild in your arms." Bowing, the prince took his leave.

For the longest time, the queen stared into the fire, the golden flames crackling around pine logs. Her son's marriage had ambushed her, shocked her, even stunned her, casting doubt on her own choices. She'd succeeded as a queen, guiding and preserving her kingdom...but perhaps she'd failed as a woman, dooming the Tandroth line to extinction.

Her shadowmaster broke her gaze by stepping in front of the fire. "He will make a fine king."

"How do you know?"

He gave her a warm smile. "He married for love. And he dared defy the strongest queen I know."

"There is that."

"You worry too much."

"There is much to worry about." She gazed at him, sorrow in her heart. "If only our daughter had lived. A daughter to love...and a second heir to secure the Tandroth bloodline."

Concern flashed across his face. "You still think it was poison?"

"We know it." Her words lashed with rebuke. "The babe was alive and well." The queen laced her hands across her empty womb. "We felt her kick. We felt her grow...and then she was murdered. Killed before she took her first breath."

"I should have been here. I should have protected you."

The queen shook her head. "We were at war. You were needed elsewhere, but Robert, now that you're here, you must find this murderer. We fear an enemy lurks within our castle. You must find this killer of babes and gain justice for our daughter."

He knelt before her. "I will scour the shadows for her murderer."

"Find the killer, for we cannot rest until it is done."

He kissed her ring. "As you command," and took his leave, softly closing the door behind him.

Alone, the queen sat in front of the fireplace. Light and shadow danced across her solar. In her heart, Liandra knew a murderer lurked within her court, yet the killer left no clues and no witnesses. How does one catch a murderer when he leaves no trace, disappearing like mist in the dawn's first light? At least Robert believed her, but she'd set her shadowmaster a difficult task. She craved justice for her unborn daughter...and she needed to feel safe in her own castle. Her hands locked across her empty womb, feeling bereft, feeling threatened. Staring into the fire, Liandra shivered, despite the heat. In the depths of her soul, she felt Darkness draw near...and she knew she was not ready.

25

Megan

Queen Megan craved sleep, yet she dared not close her eyes lest the nightmares claim her. She'd tried strong wine, drinking herself into a stupor, yet the witch was waiting for her, lurking in her wine-besotted dreams, whispering foul commands. Sleep was no longer safe. A terrible weariness dogged the queen. She needed something stronger, something to block the witch and give her peace.

A knock sounded on the door to her solar.

"Come."

"Majesty, your horse is saddled and waiting." Sir Leon nodded towards her, his silver mustache drooping past his stubbled chin, his face as sad and lined as a hound dog's, belying his sunny nature. She gave the old dear a smile. His sword arm was no longer steady or sure, but he still served, a knight and a loyal friend, her favorite escort on market day.

Swirling a plain brown shawl around her shoulders, she followed him down the spiral stairs and out into the courtyard. Saddled and bridled, Buttercup was waiting, straining to munch on an errant weed. The queen stroked the pony's silky muzzle, offering her a winter apple, surprised by the gray hairs sprouting among the silver. "Never mind, dear, we both have gray in our hair." Megan had never been much of a rider, but she made an exception for the silver mare. A gift from the king, Buttercup had a sweet disposition and an easy fluid gait that took the terror out of riding.

Sir Leon gave her a leg up and then swung onto his eighteen-hand warhorse.

The queen felt like a child riding beside the knight. She gave her pony a reassuring pat. "Size isn't everything."

Guards opened the castle gates and the salty breath of sea air blew into the courtyard. Like magic, the causeway was exposed, stretching from the castle gates to the shore. The queen clucked Buttercup to a trot, although there was no need. The little pony knew the routine, following the warhorse down the ramp and across the causeway.

The weekday market was held in the tournament field overlooking the harbor. Merchants sold everything from fresh-caught fish, steamed mussels and abalone, herbs and vegetables, to exotic silks and curious trinkets. Seaside's market was famous for exotic goods brought from distant ports, but the merchant fleet had been absent for nigh on four moonturns. Anything exotic was long since sold, but the people searched anyway, enthralled by the thrill of the hunt.

Sir Leon secured their mounts and then followed her through the market, a wicker basket on his arm. "It's good to see you out and about again, majesty."

In her younger days, the queen had enjoyed the market, hunting for unexpected treasures, gifts to give her children and her husband...but those days seemed a lifetime ago. "Yes, it is good to be out." She turned her face away, lest her eyes betray the lie.

The queen meandered the market, looking but not seeing. She tasted some buttery mussels swimming in a garlic sauce and then made her way to a weaver's stall, stopping to finger half a dozen wools before deciding on thick blanket dyed a brilliant sea-blue. "Yes, I'll have this one."

Sir Leon paid the price, carefully folding the bright wool into the basket.

The queen laid a hand on his arm. "Would you be a dear and wait by the horses?" Leaning close, she whispered, "I need to see a wise woman about a female remedy."

The knight blazed bright red. "Of course, my lady."

It always amazed her how big brave men wilted at the mere mention of 'female remedies'. He gave her a firm nod and then marched stoically back to the horses. Quit of the knight, the queen pulled her shawl up around her head to better hide her face, and then made her way to the back of the market. Beyond the market, a honeycomb of narrow cobble streets climbed the hillside. It had been a long time, but her feet knew the way. She found the door painted a bright red, incised with subtle runes, and rang the dangling bell cord, praying Matilda was home.

The old crone answered the door, wisps of silver hair escaping a tightly bound bun. Amidst a wrinkled face creased with nearly a century of laugh lines, the old woman's blue eyes twinkled bright and keen. "Majesty! Come in! It's been such a long time."

The queen entered the small shop that also served as the wise woman's home. Bundles of herbs hung in one corner, releasing comforting scents of basil, marjoram and thyme. Shelves filled with ceramic jars and exotic bottles lined the far wall. In the center of the room, a small round table draped with a fringed shawl sat beneath a star-shaped lantern.

The old woman ushered her to a seat at the round table and began lighting candles. "You look troubled, my lady, how can I help?"

She'd known Matilda for nearly all her life. A wise woman, an herbalist, a midwife, and a fortuneteller, the old woman was ever perceptive...and discrete. Staring at her friend's wise eyes, the queen longed to unburden her troubles, to explain about the nightmares, to confess her oath and the witch's evil commands...but the words died on her tongue. Frustrated, she blurted, "I can't sleep."

"Chamomile tea will calm the nerves and soothe the stomach, but then again valerian is even better, gives a deeper sleep, although the taste is quite bitter, best taken with a dollop of honey."

"I need more than tea! Last night I emptied my husband's best brandy and still the nightmares came!"

Matilda peered at her, as if reading the lines on her face. "It's all those funerals, isn't it? So many deaths at the castle, little wonder you're plagued by nightmares."

"It's worse than that."

Matilda gave her a squinty-eyed look. "The Curse of the Vowels?"

The queen could only nod.

"Such a dreadful curse...with such long tentacles, but there's no lore I know that can break it."

"I know." The queen's voice sounded small in her ears. "Yet I need help. I need answers...and sleep."

"Then you've come to cast the runes."

It was a statement, not a question, yet the queen answered. "Yes."

"Then together we'll invoke the higher powers." It was mid-day outside, bright with sunlight, yet Matilda circled the chamber lighting candles and lanterns as if to dispel every shadow. Opening a cedar chest, she removed a red velvet drawstring bag and a folded linen cloth. Returning to the table, the wise woman spread the linen cloth across the tabletop, revealing a twenty-pointed star painted in gold. Her wrinkled hands smoothed the white linen, following each point of the painted star to the table's edge, as if invoking the gods' blessings from every direction. Folding her hands across the star's heart, Matilda used the words of ritual. "Now the petitioner invokes the blessings of her god."

Most Navarrens worshiped the sea god, but Megan was from Harvesthold. Closing her eyes, the queen beseeched Magery the

Mother, Queen of the Harvest, benevolent protector of mothers and children. *Help me, Mother, help me defeat the witch.* Opening her eyes, she found the wise woman staring at her.

Matilda held the velvet bag high above the painted star. "The petitioner extracts seven runes."

Without looking, the queen delved her hand into the velvet bag. She swirled the rune markers, cool against her fingertips. Selecting seven, she removed her fist from the bag.

"Now the petitioner asks the question, casting the runes upon the many-pointed star."

"Show me the way." Silently posing her question, the queen cast the runes upon the star. Small tiles of colored glass, worn smooth by time and many hands, scattered across the tabletop. Runes painted in bright gold shone from four of the tiles. Three others landed face-down, hiding their runes and inverting their meaning. Red, green, amethyst and gold, the glass tiles glinted colorful in the candlelight. The queen glanced at the runic pattern but it made little sense. Instead, she fixed her gaze on the wise woman, startled by the fear etched on the crone's face.

"This cannot be." Matilda reached for the runes, as if to gather them up, but the queen stayed her hand, her voice laden with sepulchral tones. "Tell me."

The crone's voice quavered. "Sometimes the runes respond to a higher question, a force or a predicament that overshadows the petitioner." Her wrinkled hand gestured to the spread of runes. "This pattern must refer to the Curse of the Vowels."

The queen's mouth turned desert dry, yet she needed to know. "Why?"

"I see Wunjo, the rune of happiness lying face down, happiness turned to sorrow; and this is Thurisaz, the demon rune lying in a position of strong influence; and here, Naudiz, the rune of need lying close to the heart. But the worst is this rune." With a shaking hand, the crone reached for the rune marker lying at the star's very center. Face-down, the glass was dark purple, so dark it was nearly black. The crone turned the rune, revealing the bright gold symbol. "This is Kauno, the Torch, rune of light and life inverted to darkness..."

"...and death."

The crone gave a grim nod.

"*No,* death cannot be the answer!" Fear laced the queen's voice.

"Majesty, remember what I said. Oft times the runes describe the influence, *not* the answer. This spread surely refers to the Curse of the Vowels, to the death and sorrow visited upon Navarre's royal house."

She gazed at the queen, her voice full of entreaty. "Cast the runes again and seek a fresh answer."

The queen shivered, feeling the gods' hands at work. "No. I want no more foretellings." She smothered the quaver in her voice. "I need help of a more practical sort, a bottle of your best sleeping draught. I seek a dreamless sleep, not to wake till sunrise."

"Then you'll be wanting Valerian tea..."

The queen leaned across the table, gripping the old woman's hands, the wrinkled skin as dry as parchment. "Matilda, if ever you loved me, like the daughter you never had, then you'll give me your strongest sleeping draught, for none else will serve."

Foreboding flickered in the old woman's eyes. "Given the rune pattern, I fear it."

"Why?"

"Because the best sleeping draughts are also deadly poisons. The difference is in the dosage. Sometimes that difference is slender."

Poison, the weapon of the witch, a shiver raced down the queen's spine, yet she refused to be defeated. Perhaps with the crone's help, she'd turn the witch's best weapon against her. "Show me."

Matilda went to the shelves, returning with a small stoppered bottle, dark blue in color. Clutching the bottle close, the crone gave the queen a hesitant look. "Tincture of Belladonna, the queen of all sleeping draughts, best taken with wine. Two drops brings a feeling of euphoria followed by dreamless sleep. But take care with the dosage lest you sleep forever. Two drops for sleep...four drops to kill, a slender difference between slumber and death."

"Two drops for sleep...four for death, I'll remember." The queen slid a small purse of gold coins onto the table and then extended her hand.

"Are you sure, Majesty?"

"Yes."

The crone set the bottle in her hand. The queen held it tight, the answer to her most dire need. "Blessings of the Mother be upon you," she took her leave of the crone. Clutching the bottle in her deepest pocket, the queen returned to the bustling market. *Sleep, a dreamless sleep,* tonight she'd foil the witch, beating Iris at her own game.

26

The Mordant

Silent and forbidding, the dark hull sliced through night-darkened waters, ghosting into the harbor. With three tiers of oars and a bronze ram fashioned like a toothy snout, the coastal raider loomed over the fishing vessels like a shark among minnows yet there was no hue and cry. Smooth as a sheathing sword, the MerChanter ship slipped into a berth near the harbor mouth. The Mordant watched from the prow. Wrapped in dark robes, he shivered with sickness, leaning on a pair of assassins posing as servants. Sagging against their strength, he studied the town, comparing memories to the present. So much had changed. In a past life this same harbor had been nothing more than a cove for smugglers. Now a formidable castle brooded above a burgeoning town, a martial warning mixed with a merchant's welcome, the perfect place to begin.

Lines were slung from the ship with nary a command. An eerie silence smothered the trireme, the top deck empty save for the captain and a pair of mates, but the Mordant felt the others. Cowering below, the crew hid, swathed in terror. Fear clouded the ship like a fine perfume, teasing a smile to the Mordant's face. How little they knew what they carried.

The boarding plank thunked against the dock with a sharp finality. The two assassins eased the Mordant toward the ramp. He passed the captain without speaking, the man's haunted eyes saying more than enough.

Wracked by seasickness, the Mordant leaned heavy on his servants. How he hated the sea, a bitter enemy leaching at his powers, yet he'd dared the voyage to leap ahead of his army. Once again, his will prevailed, all part of a master plan.

A fat harbormaster scuttled towards them. His servants intercepted the man. A thick purse changed hands and nothing more was said. The Mordant hid his smile. Of all the southern kingdoms, Radagar was ever the whore, and whores he knew very well.

They reached the end of the dock and the Mordant hissed a command. "Wait." His servants froze, holding him erect. The Mordant stepped from the dock, planting his boots on firm land. For a moment, the sea held sway, a terrible dizziness rocking him, but then he felt it. Darkness rushed to fill him, a surging power rising from his boots. Like a banished curse, the torpor of the sea-god fled. His powers returned, yet his hands still shook with a pitiful palsy, his body weak from the long sea passage. Disgusted, he hid his hands within his robe. There was always a price, but this time the goal was more than worth the temporary indignity. "Get me to an inn."

Men in dark cloaks glided from an alleyway. Swords in hand, they circled the Mordant like an honor guard. Their leader, a swarthy man with a thick beard sketched a deep bow. "My Lord, we've awaited your coming. All is in order."

The Mordant nodded. "Lead the way."

His escort led him through dim-lit alleys to the back steps of an inn. The Mordant soon found himself ensconced in a sumptuous chamber, a four-poster bed draped in gold velvet, a fire crackling in the hearth, all the luxuries of a palace suite. Satisfied with the accommodations, he sat before the hearth soaking up the fire's warmth, yet the smell of the sea still lingered. His clothes repulsed him, stinking of salt and sickness. "Undress me." His assassins disrobed him and then washed him in rose-scented water. Finally cleansed, he sank into the feather bed, a welcome haven from the sway of the sea.

For three days he nested in the inn. While his body recovered, his mind craved news of the southern kingdoms, fodder for his plots. He summoned Bishop Borgan while supping on garlic roast lamb and the inn's best wines. The portly prelate had been sent ahead to prepare the way.

Clad in merchant's robes of sumptuous silk, the bishop bowed low before the Mordant. "Everything has been prepared, just as you ordered."

"Good." The Mordant sat before the blazing hearth, sipping a fine brandy. "What news of the south?"

"Much has happened while you sailed south. The Cobra crown has changed hands. Cyrus is dead, killed by poison. Razzur has claimed the crown.

"And what of this Razzur?"

"They say he wants to return Radagar to the old ways, to restore pride and honor to the desert-descendants."

"*Honor*," the Mordant spat the word with contempt. "What do mercenaries know of honor?" Such a change did not favor his plans. "Honor is a rank stupidity that reeks of the Light. I like it not. Dispatch an assassin to Salmythra. Holdor has the skills. One assassin of the ninth rank should be sufficient for the Cobra crown to change hands once more."

"Will you favor another contender?"

"I favor chaos. Let the princes fight for the crown."

Borgan bowed. "As you command."

"And tell our brokers in Radagar they may begin selling Vetra."

The bishop paled, "But my lord, Radagar has ever been a secret ally to the north!"

The Mordant flashed a chilling smile. "Erdhe is changing. Those who think of themselves as allies will soon learn they are mere vassals. They live to serve. Pass the word that Vetra is to be sold in the marketplaces, but only in Radagar. The MerChanters will bring a steady supply to the usual smuggling ports." The Mordant's smile deepened to a predatory grin. "Let the rot begin."

The bishop bowed low. "As you command."

"Now tell me of the other kingdoms, especially Lanverness." The Mordant sipped brandy while he listened. The news did not disappoint. Neither did his youthful body, for he soon regained his vigor. Standing before the blazing hearth, the Mordant flexed his muscles. The resiliency of youth was such a potent gift, yet so fleeting, even for an immortal. Smiling, he reveled in his stolen youth. Summoning his servants, he dressed in dark leathers, practical and nondescript, perfect for traveling.

In the dead of the night, the Mordant slipped from Radagar's coastal city. He led his men east, putting the sea's salty stink at his back. Sixty mounted men formed his guard, mostly assassins and magic-sniffing duegar, a hand-picked cadre of killers sent south from the Dark Citadel. Laden with weapons, they dressed in dark leathers and carried no banners, their cloaks empty of emblems. Save for four leather chests strapped to a string of packhorses, they traveled lean, just a shadowy band of menace slipping through Radagar's countryside.

The Mordant set a blistering pace, carving a serpentine path across the mercenary kingdom. Riding at night, they avoided cities and stayed in towns only long enough to resupply. Anyone that stood in their way was quickly cut down. Horses died under the lash, ridden to death, a casualty of speed. When a duegar was thrown from his horse and his leg badly mangled from the fall, the Mordant had him put down like a dog. He drove his men hard and the horses harder, brooking no delay. The great game was in motion, the pieces moving across the board towards a great Dark Destiny. Time was of the essence.

27

Liandra

A false gaiety pervaded the queen's court. Her lords and ladies danced till midnight, celebrating a narrow victory over the Flame, but beneath their gaiety the queen felt an edge of desperation, a frenzied need to deny that something worse lurked ahead. Liandra danced with the rest, maintaining her royal image, but she did not celebrate. Unlike the others, the queen could ill-afford to ignore the encroaching doom. Her shadowmen had returned bearing their latest crop of secrets, none of it good. The Mordant's hordes threatened in the north, holding Raven Pass, the gateway to the south. *The Mordant,* the name alone conjured nightmares. Wrapped in so many frightful legends it was hard to separate truth from myth. How did one prepare for a myth-cloaked evil? Meanwhile her kingdom reeled from a terrible holy war. Pellanor nearly captured, Lingard in ruins, her army diminished, her peasants and farmers scattered in fear. She needed to strengthen her defenses, needed to get her farmers back on the land before the spring planting, and she needed commerce to resume flow. So many problems, so little time. Little wonder she was plagued with headaches.

The queen made the obligatory dances, making sure to change partners often so her royal favors were equally distributed. Three times she danced with Lord Cenric, dashingly handsome in his cloak of peacock feathers despite his strange yellow eyes. Laughing in his arms, the queen sent her court a clear signal that he and his men held her royal favor. Liandra suspected feathered cloaks would soon become the new fashion in Pellanor. She made a note to invest in a supplier of feathers.

Satisfied that duty was done, the queen retreated to her solar. Divested of finery, she sat swathed in a warm velvet robe, sitting before the fire, sipping a red wine while contemplating the chessboard. Her shadowmaster, Lord Robert Highgate, appeared and took his place on the other side. They sat in companionable silence, chess pieces clashing across the checkered board. Pawns and knights and monks, Liandra's mind kept skittering to armies and farmers and defensive walls, a thousand problems begging to be solved.

Moving his castle across the board, Robert captured her beleaguered queen, a rare coup. "Where are you?" He reached across the chessboard to caress her hand. "You're not concentrating on the game." The tone of his voice changed from playful to serious, "Or are you?"

So shrewd, he was the one man in her court she trusted, the one man with the intelligence to see the whole game, her spymaster, her confidant, her lover. "Yes, the bigger game, the chessboard of Erdhe." She met his stare. "So many problems, we feel time strangling us like a noose."

"You are not alone. Which problem plagues you this evening?"

She gave a false laugh. "Too many to count." Reaching for the fallen chess pieces, Liandra lined them up like an army of worries as she recounted her kingdom's legion of problems. "Famine threatens if the farmers do not return to the land. Lingard must be rebuilt. The defenses of Pellanor need strengthening. And then there is the army. How can the Rose Army stop what the Octagon Knights could not? And what is the Mordant's intent, his true game? And who is he anyway? Is he a man or is he a legend steeped in nightmares? It is hard to play chess against such a shadowy opponent."

"Yet you will find a way." He reset the chessboard, positioning the white pieces like a flanking army, a row of pawns in the vanguard. "You count your worries but not your assets. You have the love of the people, your treasury is full, your shadowmen are unparalleled spies, you have staunch allies in Navarre, the cat-eyed archers have entered the game, and the Kiralynn monks have already proven their worth." He positioned the white queen in the center, surrounded by knights and monks, "And *none* play the game of chess like the Queen of Lanverness."

His confidence was like a balm to her soul. "Flatterer."

He gave her a wolfish grin. "How else to woo a queen?"

"Is that what you do? Woo a queen?" The game moved to a different level, a welcome distraction. She felt herself aroused.

"Woo her, yes." He flashed a rakish smile. "When I'm not making love to her." His voice was deep with suggestion.

So tempting to let him sweep her off to bed, to let the heat of his lovemaking drive the worries from her mind, to indulge the woman instead of the queen, but a crown was not so easily ignored.

His gaze smoldered. "Together we might make another child."

Her breath caught, her bejeweled hands threading across her empty womb, missing the daughter that might have been. She'd so wanted the child, despite all the complications to her crown. An unwed queen, an unnamed father, a risk to her image, a threat to her power...yet her arms felt achingly empty and Lanverness desperately needed a second heir, especially given Stewart's marriage. She reached for a chess piece, fingering a black knight. "Have you found the murderer?"

"You know I have not. You've sent me chasing shadows."

"We've sent a shadowmaster to catch a shadow, you must have learned something?"

He leaned back in his chair, fingering the dagger at his belt. "I've talked to your women, your ladies-in-waiting, and I believe they are loyal."

She gave him a measured nod, relieved that his opinion bolstered her own conviction.

"And your healer, Crandor, seems above reproach."

"Crandor is an old dear. He's served the Tandroths all his life." She leaned forward. "You must suspect someone?"

He gave her a level stare. "Have you considered that there are two unsolved murders in your court?"

She nodded, remembering. "The monk, Fintan."

"Brutally beheaded. A murder designed to instill fear."

"An emissary of the monks slain within our own castle." She recalled the odd details of the monk's chamber. "A murder full of riddles and warnings, but no witnesses and no clues."

"Perhaps the riddles and warnings *are* the clues."

Hearing the truth in his words, her skin prickled in warning. "We like how you think, though we fear the implications." She stared at the chessboard. "No witnesses and no clues, so you think the two murders are linked, the monk and the babe?"

"A monk and a royal heir."

Liandra shivered, chastising herself for thinking like a mother instead of a queen. "Just so." She stared across the chessboard. "Someone plays a larger game."

He gave her a grim nod.

"But who stalks the monks *and* a royal heir?"

"That is the question."

"It seems an unlikely pairing."

"Yet it is the only clue we have."

She sat in silence, staring at the chessboard. Fingering the black knight, Liandra considered the scant clues. Slaying a babe in the womb was such a fiendish tactic. The act implied a ruthless enemy who took a long view of the game...a very long view. And this enemy was also an enemy of the monks. Liandra shivered at the implications, her concern doubling. She felt stalked, as if someone made her a pawn within a greater game. A queen should never be used as a pawn. Her ringed hands tightened into fists.

"You think too much."

"Thinking may be our best weapon to defeat this foe."

"Agreed, but sometimes you need warmth to chase away the shadows." He pulled her to her feet and kissed her softly. "Perhaps between us, we could make another heir?"

She kissed him back, needing his solid strength, longing for another child. "You make duty such a pleasure."

He lifted her into his arms. "If only I could make all your duties pleasurable." The train of her robe swept across the chessboard, scattering pieces in every direction, but she no longer cared. The heat of his body proved a bonfire to her need. He carried her to the royal bed, a massive canopied affair of pillows and velvet. Nestled among the quilts, he lay next to her, his fingers skillfully rousing her. She reached for his buckles, too many fasteners, hastily stripping away his leathers until it was just skin against skin. Liandra reveled in the strength of his arms, in the deftness of his touch. He rolled on top, moving with deliberate strokes, making the ecstasy last. She moaned with unbridled pleasure, indulging the woman beneath the crown.

Later, much later, her head nestled upon his shoulder, she asked the question lodged deep in her heart. "Do you ever want the subterfuge to end?"

"Subterfuge?" He gave a low chuckle. "My lady, I am your shadowmaster, and you are the queen of spiders. Between us subterfuge is by far our best weapon."

"No, not the court game." She feared to broach the subject, yet it needed to be said. "The late nights, the secret passageways, the subtle subterfuge, surely we both deserve more?"

His breath stilled, waiting.

She forced her thought to words. "We have the nights but come the dawn's first light my bed is always empty."

"It is a royal bed," his voice was husky with unplumbed depths, "and I know you will never have a king."

"No, not a king," she dared to say it, "but perhaps a prince consort."

He reared up, surprise on his face. Propped on one elbow, he gazed down at her. "My queen, you honor me, but your court will never abide it. Royalty does not flow in my veins."

"Who in our court has earned it more?" Outrage mixed with bitterness. "And how dare they gainsay the queen."

"Image has always been your best armor."

He knew her too well. "But perhaps I want more. This bed is so cold and lonely in the mornings."

He smiled. "Now you're thinking like a woman instead of a queen."

"We like to think we can do both."

He laughed a light chuckle that warmed her heart. Taking her hand, he kissed her palm. "My lady, you do both exceedingly well."

"Yet you avoid our question."

"A shadowmaster paired with a spider queen makes for a formidable combination, but only if we maintain the advantage of secrecy. You said it yourself. A second storm approaches, one that may prove far more deadly than the first. And if our suspicions about the two murders prove correct, then we play against a devious and ruthless foe. Now is not the time to lay down our best weapons. Let us keep our subterfuge till the storm passes. I can serve you best from the shadows."

How rare to find a man who did not grasp at her power. Liandra loved him all the more for it. "But what of my lonely bed?"

"We still have the nights."

The worries of her crown intruded, making her wonder how many nights they truly had before the next storm broke.

"You're thinking again." He smothered her mouth with a kiss, long and deep, tenderness turning to ardor. "Now about that child." He rolled on top, and the worries of the gathering storm were soon forgotten.

28

Megan

Night fell and for once Queen Megan did not fear it. Hidden deep within her pocket, she fondled the crone's blue bottle, the answer to her prayers. To sleep without dreams, she longed for it. By the grace of belladonna, she'd sleep tonight, foiling the witch's foul commands.

Servants fluttered around the royal solar, clearing the remnants of a late-night supper. Savory aromas of sea bass sizzled in garlic butter lingered in the chamber, the king's favorite. King Ivor leaned across the table, offering the queen the last flakey bite.

Megan savored the morsel.

The king gave her a contented look. "These intimate suppers have been lovely...but the king and his queen must be seen in the great hall."

After the poisoned feast, she'd shunned the great hall, haunted by the lingering horror. "It's too soon."

He captured her hand, pulling it to his lips for a gentle kiss. "Darling, if we change our ways, then Iris wins." Iron determination flashed across his face. "I'll not let her win."

"No, she mustn't win."

"Then you'll join me for dinner in the great hall?"

"Not yet." She needed a victory in the bedchamber ere she set foot in the great hall. "The nightmares are still too raw."

"When?"

"Give me two more nights?"

He sighed. "As you wish," kissing her hand, as if to seal the bargain. "Come to bed."

"A glass of brandy first. Will you join me?"

"Of course." He flashed a warm smile, for a small glass of brandy was often a prelude to their lovemaking.

Extracting her hand, she stood and turned towards the sideboard. Keeping her back to her husband, she filled two crystal goblets with a thumb's worth of brandy. Reaching for the bottle hidden within her pocket, the queen whispered a silent prayer. *By the Maid, by the Mother, by the Crone, I'll not be an instrument of your hate.* Unstoppering the bottle, she carefully poured two drops into the nearest goblet, *two drops for a dreamless sleep.*

*You swore an oath! Serve me!** The witch's command spiked through her mind.

No! The queen fought the command, shocked to feel tentacles of the witch's will coiling around her, taking possession of her body.

*You sought to use poison against me! Poison is my domain. Now you'll serve!**

The queen's hand shook above the goblet, a battle of wills.

Megan watched horrified as her hand upended the bottle, emptying the poison into the goblet, turning the brandy into a potion of death. Lifting both goblets, she turned towards the king.

I'll not do it! The queen strove to bring the deathly brew to her own lips, but instead, she watched in horror as her hand offered it to the king.

"Thank you, my dear." He took the goblet of death, raising it in salute towards her.

Screaming in her mind, the queen watched as he raised it to his lips.

No! Terror lent her strength. Something snapped in her mind, banishing the witch. Leaping forward, she struck the goblet from the king's hand. Glass shattered against stone, the deadly poison dripping down the wall.

Startled, the king stared at her. "Why?"

"*Poison!*"

"What poison? You poured it yourself!"

Bound by the geas, she could not answer. Trembling, she said, "Hold me?"

He folded her into his arms, holding her close. "Is it the nightmares? Do you still dream of the feast?"

"Yes." She clung to him, her face buried in his chest.

He lifted her into his arms, carrying her to their bed. "This fear must end."

"Yes, it has to end." She snuggled close to him, warmed by his body, but sleep would not come. In the back of her mind a cruel voice whispered, *You serve me now. It's only a matter of time.**

29

Jordan

Death and funerals and royal mourning, it was not the homecoming Jordan imagined. She climbed the stairs to the castle's topmost tower, a breath of cold sea air blowing through the arrow-slit windows. *Castle Seamount,* the only home she'd ever known but the great castle chafed at her like a sea creature that had long outgrown its shell. Each morning she sought the tower tops, needing a view of the restless ocean, as if the roiling waves mirrored her soul. The castle felt small and confining, yet she remained at the king's request, but everything had changed. The seaside kingdom was plunged into deepest mourning. The Curse of the Vowels had come calling, spewing death and betrayal. Warned by the gods, she'd ridden halfway across Erdhe, desperate to save her family and capture her aunt, but she'd failed at both. So many deaths, but at least the rightful king still ruled Navarre. She consoled herself with the thought but it seemed a cold comfort.

Jordan reached the tower top and unlatched the heavy door, stepping out onto the windswept battlement. A stiff westerly snatched at her short sandy-blond hair, her checkered cloak streaming behind like a velvet wing. She paced the winter-cold ramparts, consumed with worry. The dreams that had driven her across Erdhe had stopped with an abruptness that took her breath away. No more visions from the gods, as if they no longer had a use for her, or perhaps she'd failed them. Gripping her sword hilt, she pushed that grim thought away. For the longest time, she'd wished the visions away, feeling burdened with a freakish curse. But now that they'd fled, Jordan felt strangely adrift, like a ship without a rudder, abandoned by the gods to wander uncharted seas. Hugging her checkered cloak close, her thoughts turned to Stewart. Their marriage in the Crimson Tower almost seemed a dream, a fairytale come true. The mere thought warmed her heart...but she hadn't yet told her royal parents. With all the death and sorrow of the poisoned feast, she'd not found the right moment. Such news deserved a celebration not the crepe of mourning.

Seagulls cawed, circling the tower. Jordan leaned out to watch them dance the wind. Swooping and turning with a carefree grace, they dove towards the frothing ocean, fishing for minnows. Jordan laughed, delighting in their freedom, but then she spied a banner of white on Osprey Tower. White cloth rippling against the slate-gray sky, it looked like a signal of surrender...or distress. Jordan leaned out for a better view. A woman in a silken shift tottered onto the crenellated rampart, the wind whipping her auburn-gray hair.

"Mother!" The wind snatched at Jordan's startled cry. A chill gripped her throat, a premonition of dread. Her heart thundering, she raced for the doorway and plunged down the steps, taking them two at a time. Reaching the bottom, she burst through the door into the main hallway, startling the servants and guards. *"Get the king! Bring him to Osprey Tower!"* Servants scattered to do her bidding, but Jordan never slowed. She reached the tower entrance and raced up the stairs. The topmost door gaped open. Praying for time, Jordan burst through the doorway and skidded to a sudden stop. Her mother stood barefoot atop the battlement, the wind billowing her silken shift like a shroud, one step away from death. *"Mother, no!"*

Her mother turned, teetering on the edge, her long hair wild and disheveled, her face haggard, her eyes glazed, looking like a mad banshee.

Jordan gaped, shocked by her mother's appearance. "Mother *don't!"*

Madness glared from her mother's eyes. "Get away from me!" The queen howled a piercing shriek. "Get out of my mind! I won't do it, you hear, I won't do your bidding."

Jordan took a single step, her hand extended. "Mother, it's me, come down from there."

"I swore an oath to you, but I won't do it. I'll take my own life first."

And then Jordan saw the dagger clutched in her mother's fist. "Please mother, it's only me, your daughter, Jordan, come down from there." She crept forward, her voice soft and cajoling.

"Jordan?" The queen uttered her daughter's name like a talisman. For a heartbeat, the madness fled her gaze. "My daughter of the sword, I've missed you so." Something in her voice shifted, gaining a touch of iron resolve. "It's fitting that you're here. Of all my children, you'll understand the best." The queen stared down at the long drop, at the waves pounding the tower's base. "Yes, I finally understand."

"Understand what, mother?"

Her mother danced barefoot along the edge, a brilliant smile flashing on her careworn face. "Here, standing on the knife-edge between life and death, I'm finally free of her geas."

"Mother, come down from there."

"No, you must listen." Her voice dropped to a conspirator's whisper. "The Curse of the Vowels is not done." Her mother shook her head, anger in her voice. "The witch plagues my dreams, always whispering, demanding allegiance. I try to refuse, but it's so hard." She looked down at her hand, hefting the dagger like a poisonous snake. "I woke this morning, clutching this. A dagger meant for the king's heart, hid beneath my very pillow. She orders me to kill my own dear husband, to slay him in our bed." The queen flung the dagger into the sea, a bright glitter of steel. "Last evening...I nearly *poisoned* him!" She shuddered at the words, horror etched across her face. "But now I understand the runes. The gods spoke the truth." Steel entered her mother's voice. "I've never wielded a sword, but I can fight. I won't let her win."

Jordan crept forward, gauging the distance. "Come down from there, mother. All of Navarre will protect you."

A gust of wind snatched at her mother's shift, a billow of white silk, so fleeting and insubstantial. Jordan reached for it, but her mother flitted away, dancing along the edge.

"Don't!" Her mother's voice turned hard. "I swore an oath and now she haunts me. She's a witch, a sorceress, a black-hearted bitch. You can't protect me from my dreams. You can't protect me from *her*."

"Protect you from whom?"

"*Iris!*" Her mother spat the name, making it a curse. "She's a bitch, a witch, trying to poison us all. Now she poisons my mind, poisons my very dreams, but I won't do her bidding, not now, not ever." Her mother swayed on the parapet, buffeted by the wind. "I'll spoil her plans. I'll have the final victory. The sea will absolve me from all oaths. You'll see, you'll understand. I do this for love." Her mother smiled, a blinding smile full of triumph. And then she fell backwards, her arms spread wide like a sacrifice.

"*No!*" Jordan lunged, her fingers snagging a whisper of silk but the white cloth slipped through her grasp. Her mother tumbled backward without a cry, a streak of white plummeting silent to the sea. But it was not a clean fall, her head thudding against the castle walls. "*No!*" Jordan screamed in denial, but it made no difference. A pinwheel of white, the fall seemed to last forever, like a nightmare etched in her mind. Her mother's body landed hard amongst the rocks, bright blood blossoming on her white shift, her limbs bent to impossible angles like a rag doll tossed from the tower top.

"What is it?" The king raced to her side, peering to the sea below.

Jordan choked on the words, her voice thick with grief. "It's mother!"

The king loosed a keening wail. *"Megan! My Megan!"*

Jordan crumpled to her knees, dissolving into tears. "She said it was the Curse of the Vowels. The curse claimed her and I never saw it coming!" Without the visions, she'd had no warning, no foresight. Jordan shuddered, a sob escaping her. "We've lost so much...and now mother!"

30

Liandra

Candles burned to stubs and still she had no answers. Liandra plucked another scroll from the pile, squinting at the spidery script, one of a hundred she'd read that day. Scrolls overflowed her desk, spilling onto side tables while hundreds more sat stacked in baskets along the wall. Liandra was drowning in parchment, yet her gaze kept returning to the ancient scrolls, histories penned by forgotten scholars, some so old the ink had nearly faded.

A knock from the inner door, Liandra smiled, welcoming the distraction.

The secret door swung silently open and the Master Archivist stepped into her solar. "Still reading?"

"Still?" she rubbed her tired eyes, "more like always."

Tall in dark robes, he moved across her solar like a fluid shadow. "What is it tonight? Urgent requests from Lingard? Complaints from the carpenters' guild? Ledgers from the treasury? Or dispatches from the army?"

"All and none. You'd think we'd be content with rebuilding our kingdom but…"

"You've started a new inquiry."

Her spymaster never missed a trick. "So you've heard."

"The archivists stir like bees carrying parchments to the queen's chamber. I'd have to be blind not to notice." He stood behind her, his hands kneading the stress from her shoulders. "You're tense with worry."

Liandra closed her eyes, melting in the momentary bliss. The fire snapped and crackled, and for a while she knew nothing but the balm of his hands.

"What do you seek?" His question brought her back to the riddle at hand.

"The Mordant."

For half a heartbeat his hands stilled, and then continued. "What have you learned?"

"His name stretches back through antiquity...or versions of it."

"As a man or a myth?"

"Perhaps both." She gestured to the basket of scrolls lining the walls. "One scroll speaks of the Lord Mordranth, another of the Lord Morganth, there's one reference to a Sir Mordred and several tell of a Prince Mordrith. Are they misspellings or coincidences? Are they same man, the same soul, or merely names that sound the same?"

"Coincidences are often history's harshest lessons."

She rubbed her weary eyes. "Lessons repeated until we learn them?"

"Just so." The fire snapped and crackled. His hands slowed. "I always thought the Mordant referred to a title rather than a man...until Lord Turner."

Liandra shivered. "A parboiled corpse dancing in the cauldron, its red eyes glowing with the light of hell," she made the hand sign against evil. "Who could forget? Our nightmares are not so easily shed."

"Just so." His hands resumed their comforting work. "So what have you learned?"

"Little enough. History taunts us. The Mordant's name looms across time like an omnipresent threat, the eternal bane of Erdhe, causing so much death and destruction, yet so many details are maddeningly absent." She plucked at the scroll in her lap. "This scroll speaks of the War of Wizards, hinting at a counselor named Mordranth. The scribe's handwriting is atrocious, but if you puzzle through the ancient script, it reads like the aftermath of a tidal wave, detailing terrible devastation yet there is little to describe the inciting incident. Not a scrap of evidence to provide any insight to his motives or methods. We need to know the why of it." The queen considered what she'd read. "And then there are the quiet times, where the Mordant's influence seems to disappear, like a tidal wave subsumed back into the sea." She stared at the mountain of scrolls. "The Mordant is like a re-occurring plague...or an eternal riddle, casting a pall across Erdhe." Frustration laced her voice. "We need to understand the man within the myth. We need to know what he wants."

"The motive is obvious, conquest and destruction."

"Yes, but it is the methods we seek."

"To know your enemy."

"Precisely."

His hands withdrew and he moved around her desk, taking a seat on a stool in front of the roaring fire. Sitting sword-straight, he stared at her, his dark eyes as keen as a hawk's, his face lined with thought. Liandra knew she had his full attention and the weight of his considerable intellect...but she missed the comfort of his hands.

"It seems obvious enough. His army has taken Raven Pass and defeated the Octagon Knights. His legions are poised to conquer the southern kingdoms." He gave her a shrewd look, "Yet you expect something else, something worse?"

Liandra nodded. "His army is the most immediate threat...but it seems too *obvious*."

To his credit, he took her seriously. "You've read half a hundred scrolls, you must have discerned something?"

There was a fleeting feeling she got from reading the histories, but it seemed little more than a woman's intuition. She hesitated to voice it.

"Tell me."

She tried to explain. "The Mordant seems...slippery."

"How so?"

"It is not what is in the scrolls, but rather what is missing. As if his methods are so devious and convoluted they defy description." She had another thought. "Or perhaps they defy notice, ambushing their victims."

"Explain."

"War has always existed, a waste of lives and a swath of destruction, but it is almost as if the Mordant brings something more terrible, something subtler than war. The oldest scrolls hint at something deeper, something ominous. Almost as if," she fingered a scroll, reluctant to give voice to the thought.

"Tell me."

Drawing strength from his stare, she gave breath to her fear, "In the Mordant's shadow, civilization is unraveled, forced back into darkness, as if mankind as a whole is lessened, diminished, becoming more beast than man. Where he reigns, truth and justice have no meaning. Civilizations are destroyed, trampled to rubble, and then he disappears, leaving mankind to wallow in the chaos."

A chill descended on her chambers.

"And the Mordant has been dormant for a long time."

She nodded.

"I begin to understand your inquiry." He gave her a leveling stare. "There must be more in the histories. Most victors like to brag."

"And therein lies the problem!" She plucked a scroll from her lap. "Our histories were written by the few that survived! Most did not know the storm approached till it consumed them. The survivors wrote of the aftermath, the destruction, the suffering, but never of the strategies that brewed the storm."

"And you're searching for the man beneath the myth?"

"Or the monster." Their stares locked.

His face etched in thought, her shadowmaster reached for a chess piece, the black king. "But if the Mordant doesn't stay to rule what he's conquered, then what's the point?"

His question chilled her. "Perhaps the destruction is the point."

He gave her a hollow-eyed stare.

"Or perhaps he takes a longer view...a much longer view."

"Like Lord Turner."

The queen nodded. "More life."

"He gains more life by destroying civilizations?"

"Just so." The shadows in the room seemed to lengthen. The queen shivered.

"But how do we defeat such a foe?"

Her voice was grim. "I don't know, but somehow we must find a way."

"The Kiralynn monks must know more."

"Yet they did nothing when it came to Lord Turner."

"True, they came late to Lanverness, but since then, their help has made a difference. There's no telling what they know."

"True enough." She considered the monks. "But of late they've been scarce from our court, ever since the death of Fintan."

"The *murder* of Fintan," he scowled.

"Have you made any progress?"

He shook his head no.

"Perhaps it is all part of a greater threat." Liandra could feel the tension building in her shoulders.

"I like it not." He took a troubled breath. "So how do we prepare?"

"Remain vigilant. Expect something devious and twisted. Expect deception."

He gave her a flinty smile, "Life as usual in the Rose Court." His smile faded. "And in the meantime, we solve the problems we can."

She nodded. "Rebuild Lingard, strengthen the army, get the farmers back on the land and the merchants back on the road. Commerce must flow and the grain must be sowed else we will not survive another war." Always the same litany of problems, Liandra grew weary just thinking about it.

He must have sensed her distress. "One step at a time. What news from the crown prince?"

"The Rose Army marches north through Coronth. So far they've met little resistance. It seems the Flame has burnt itself out. Chaos rules Coronth, leaving the countryside parched of hope and food."

"And Balor?"

"If any of the cursed Flame priests survive, they'll be entrenched in Balor. We've advised Stewart to avoid the city, leaving that hornet's nest for another time."

He gave her a measured look. "A people parched of hope might welcome the steady rulership of a queen."

She'd thought of that, a chance to double her holdings. "But first we have a war to win. With the fall of the Flame, Lanverness has lost a buffer to the north. If our army fails, the Mordant's legions will sweep through Coronth like a scythe."

"It could be worse. The Flame might have allied with the Mordant."

"So true." Liandra shuddered at the thought. She gave him a hooded stare. "Your shadowmen bring rumors of a new queen in Rhune."

He nodded. "A queen named Selene. She styles herself as the monarch of the moon, a most pretentious title, another riddle that needs to be plumbed."

"We need allies, not enemies."

"And what of Navarre?"

She winced at the question, like poking an open wound. "We've sent word to King Ivor. We await his answer, wondering if he accepts the marriage."

"And you do not?"

She'd railed at Stewart when he'd spoke of his unauthorized marriage, unleashing a torrent of anger, but the deed was done, the marriage blessed and consummated, albeit in some ruined tower without the queen's consent. "At least she is a princess of Navarre, though not the one of our choosing. We console ourselves with the alliance."

"My lady, I know you better than that." His words were soft. "You cannot deny the prince what you do not deny the queen."

She looked away, feeling her cheeks color with heat. "There is that."

"The crown prince will find strength in love...as we do."

His voice was rough and full of meaning. She fought for composure. "When do you leave?"

"On the morrow."

Her breath caught. "So soon?"

"The sooner to get back to you." He looked away, twirling a gold ring on his finger, her love token to him. "I'll ride hard to the north, to secure the borders. Then to Lingard to ensure the crown's golds are well spent. The fortress must rise from the ashes as a symbol of strength, a stout defense against the Mordant's hordes. Then your web of shadowmen must be rebuilt and there is none but the queen's shadowmaster to see it done."

The queen knew the necessity of the trip, but the woman bitterly mourned the parting. "We shall miss you." A spark leaped between them. "Let's not waste the night."

He crossed the distance in three strides, closing his mouth on hers. Urgency sparked between them. Liandra drank him in, reveling in his strength, his smell, his touch. Silk ripped away as he carried her to the bed. "Hurry!" She clung to him, her fingers loosening his bindings. The last bindings broke as he tumbled on top. For a while, all the duties of the crown were forgotten.

31

Jordan

Grief annealed to a dull numbness that eventually smoldered into rage. Her mother's funeral was a fortnight past yet the pain was fresh as a sword stroke. Jordan paced the chamber, railing at the gods. She'd answered the gods' call, riding to Castle Seamount with all haste. After chasing her wicked aunt from the castle ramparts, she'd returned to the great hall to witness her family's desperation. The survivors knelt, lapping at the antidote puddled on the floor, the meager remnant from the shattered flask. The king and queen both survived the poison...but it was a lie. Hounded by nightmares, her beloved mother paid the death-price for the family curse. Jordan gripped her sword hilt longing for vengeance. Evil was real but she never imagined it could strike with such a long arm. The gods had much to answer for.

The doors opened and a page dressed in the checkered livery of Navarre bowed toward her. "The king will see you now."

Jordan smoothed her leather jerkin, tucked her sandy-blond hair behind her ears, and followed the page down the hall to the throne room. A pair of guards opened the doors and then snapped to attention.

Waves of soft blue-green light lapped the small round chamber. Sunlight streamed through the domed windows, the stained glass depicting a rolling ocean, layers of blue and turquoise and sea green. The shifting sea colors proved enticing, beckoning her forward. As a child, she'd been entranced by the throne room, like walking into an underwater enchantment. The breathtaking beauty was still there, though much of the wonder was gone. Jordan crossed the lapis floor engraved with sea charts to stand before the Seaside Throne. She bowed low to her father, the king. Bedecked in robes of blue velvet, King Ivor sat upon a throne carved of driftwood adorned with polished seashells. The royal council stood on either side of the dais, their numbers greatly diminished by murder, so many of her aunts and uncles slain by the Curse of the Vowels.

Jordan waited in silence, sundered by the strain evident in her father's face. Gray dominated his hair and grief-worn tracks engraved his face, as if he'd aged two decades in two weeks.

"Daughter," the king gave her a wan smile. "Age has caught me." A protest sprang to her lips but he stilled her with a raised hand. "The Royal Is have passed their time. Iris struck at our strength and our heart. Our loss is too great to be borne, yet our tasks are multiplied. It is time to pass the crown."

"No, it's too soon!"

The king raised a hand, quelling her protest. "There is much you do not know. While we have grown weak, evil has grown stronger. Dire news comes from the north. The Octagon has fallen. The Mordant marches south."

Jordan gaped. "How? When?" The news struck like an arrow to her chest.

"Raven Pass is broken and the knights are scattered. A horde of Darkness claims the way south. War is nearly upon us."

The Octagon Knights defeated, the news staggered her. "But I never saw this! The gods gave me no visions of the knights."

"Perhaps they did."

Jordan struggled to understand.

"We listened to your council and ordered the merchant fleet to sail north. Perhaps the gods gave you warning of our need, sending the fleet to seek allies in the far north."

"The gods are too cryptic by half." The weight of so much loss beat against her. "Isador, Igraine, Ian, Mary...and now *mother,*" her voice broke with pain, "all died because I came too late!"

"Ivy, Garth, and your king *lived* because you came in time." King Ivor gave her a piercing stare. "And perhaps the kingdom will be saved because we sent the fleet north."

"But I came too late!"

The king's voice overrode hers. "You *came,* you heeded the voice of the gods and you made a great difference." His voice softened. "My daughter of the sword, we must put grief aside and deal with the threats arrayed against us."

Jordan took a deep breath, struggling to turn her mind to the problem. "War comes from the north...Lanverness will fight."

The king nodded. "An army already exhausted by war, but yes, Lanverness will fight. Even as we speak, the Rose Army marches north, but we are here to talk of Navarre. It is time to pass the crown."

A chill gripped her. "But our Wayfarings are not yet done."

"War changes everything. Navarre needs a strong leader to battle the Dark tides. The council has deliberated and a decision has been made. In times of war a warrior is called to the throne." King Ivor gestured toward his only remaining sibling. Ivy stepped forward bearing the Sea Crown upon a velvet pillow. Sculpted of silver, the curling waves formed an elegant crown studded with sapphires and rubies. Beneath the dome's blue-green light the crown seemed to glow with the colors of the sea. "Jordan, heir of Navarre, will you accept the Sea Crown?"

The king's words seemed otherworldly. Jordan stared at the crown, an honor and a duty. She'd dreamt of it as a child, but so much had changed. Her mind groped for another solution. "If the crown calls a warrior then why not Jared? He chose Castlegard for his Wayfaring, surely Jared would be best?" Her words faltered as her father's face paled to ghost-white. "What is it? What's wrong?"

"Jared is dead."

"*Dead?*" Her handsome brother was *dead*? Jordan staggered backwards, wondering how much more pain she could bear. "When? How?"

"He never reached Castlegard, ambushed by brigands on the road to his Wayfaring. We believe it was thugs serving the Flame."

Ambushed, murdered, the words beat against her. "Why didn't you tell us?"

"There was nothing you could do. Your mother and I thought it best to let you finish your Wayfaring without the shadow of death staining your life." The king's voice turned bitter. "But death hunts our house like hounds loosed from Hell. Navarre needs a warrior and you have always chosen the sword." His voice turned hard as steel. "I will ask again, daughter of the sword, will you wear the Sea Crown?"

Her mouth tasted of ashes. "I can not."

"You *can not?*"

A murmur of outrage rippled through the council.

Jordan cursed her own silence, another mistake. "I can not because I am married to Prince Stewart of Lanverness."

"*Married!*"

"*Without the king's consent!*" Outrage ripped through the council.

The king gave her a hollow-eyed stare. "But Jemma is betrothed to the prince."

It was worse than she thought. "Betrothed by the machinations of the Spider Queen, but *I* was always his love. I married Stewart less than two moonturns ago. A wartime wedding witnessed by monks of the Kiralynn Order and consummated in the ruins of the Crimson Tower. We are wedded and bedded and my future lies with Lanverness." Her voice faded to a whisper. "I know it's wrong to wed without the king's consent, but this is war, and I thought I'd lost him." She steadied her voice. "I'm sorry, father. I meant to tell you, but with all the death and betrayals, there never seemed a moment for happiness."

The king sank into the throne as if diminished. *"Married."* The whispered word carried a tone of desperation.

The council closed around her, peppering her with questions, but she ignored them, her gaze fixed on the king.

"Be gone." The king gave his council a feeble wave. "Leave us."

"But majesty?"

A flicker of iron filled the king's voice. "Leave us!"

The council retreated, closing the doors behind them. Alone with the king, Jordan sank to her knees. "Forgive me, father?"

He gave her a weary smile. "You were always headstrong." His gaze held hers. "Do you love him?"

"Very much."

"Love is not supposed to influence royal marriages...but how can it not?" He gave her a knowing smile and then took her hand, becoming the father instead of the king. "My dearest daughter, I cannot gainsay you for following your heart, for I did the same."

For the first time, Jordan noticed how her father's hands shook, his skin spotted with age. Gripping his hand, she stilled her face, smothering shock mixed with grief.

"From the moment I first saw your mother, I loved her. I loved her so very much; I can't believe she's gone." Grief claimed him. Jordan clung to his hand, trying to share her strength. Her father stifled his tears. Taking a long shuddering breath, his face stilled. He looked like a man girding for a last battle. Releasing her, he leaned back in the throne, the king once more. "You've gained a husband, and a royal marriage, and Navarre is bound closer to Lanverness, but you've set me a fine nettle, daughter. War comes yet we are caught without a wartime leader. First Jared is taken from us, then Isador, and now you. Evil stalks us, stealing our strength. I fear for Navarre."

"I cannot wear the crown but you've not lost my sword."

He looked at her, a well of questions in his gaze.

"You said that Lanverness would fight."

He nodded.

"Stewart will lead the Rose Army and I will lead the archers of Navarre. Together we will hold the Dark tide at bay."

"So you'll do what the Octagon Knights could not?"

She quailed at the thought. "We'll do our best."

"And the Sea Crown?"

"Offer it to Jemma. She's learned much from the Spider Queen. She'll make a fine ruler. Evil strikes at Navarre in more ways than just swords. If anyone can weave a defense against the long tentacles of Darkness, it is Jemma." Thinking of her petite sister, Jordan added. "Jemma's always wanted the crown, as does Juliana."

"So it comes down to my petite beauty and the sea captain," the king steepled his hands, lost in thought. For the longest time, he said nothing. Jordan sank to the lapis floor, sitting cross-legged by the throne, keeping vigil. Eventually the king roused himself. "Nothing is as I expected. So many dreams turned to dust, yet the realm must be protected." He looked down at her. "Navarre needs your sword, daughter. You will be given command of the army and I will meet with the council to decide the fate of the throne. Together we must steer a course through this tempest of evil. But this time I wonder if any safe harbor can be found." He gestured toward the closed doors. "Call the council, for we have much to discuss."

She bowed to him and then crossed the lapis floor to summon the council, but she could not get the image of his shaking hands from her mind. Grief had aged the king far beyond his years. So much death, so much loss, Jordan wondered if evil had struck a mortal blow to Navarre.

32

Steffan

Pellanor, the very name stuck in Steffan's throat like a bone. He'd lost everything, his army, his power, his priests, nothing left but the clothes on his back and a piebald mare for a mount. Rage thundered through him. He should have ruled the richest kingdom in Erdhe, should have worn a gold crown upon his brow, but somehow everything had gone terribly wrong. His army routed, the city lost, victory snatched from his hands, tricked by a mere woman. Yet the Dark Lord had spared him; that had to count for something.

Nameless and alone, he rode west, fleeing the Rose Army. At first his saddlebags hung empty, but thanks to the Dark Lord's gift, they soon filled. Steffan plied the dice in villages and hamlets, making sure to lose just enough not to be challenged. The gift of dice might have seemed a minor power to some, but Steffan leveraged his winning ways into a small fortune, an endless purse of gold. Even in war-ravaged Lanverness, he found men willing to gamble and women willing to bed him. His rakish good looks and his luck of the dice served him well. Wealth flowed his way, his purse bulging with golds, his saddlebags full of silken finery.

Steffan's circumstances improved, yet the scars of war were everywhere, from the refugees clogging the roads to the abandoned farmlands and the hasty graveyards. Stares followed him as he rode through the countryside. Uneasy with the attention, he dyed his white forelock to match his black hair and put off his raven cloak, hiding it in his saddlebags lest someone recognize him. Seeking richer pickings, he turned his mare towards cities untouched by the war. In the great city-fortress of Kardiff, he traded his piebald mare for a gleaming black stallion, a mount befitting his true aspirations. Lingering for several moonturns, he plied the dice, leaching luxuries from the queen's loyal subjects, but the pleasures soon grew stale. Even his many mistresses could not please him, unable to compete with his dreams. He missed the Priestess in his bed. He missed the thrum of power in his hands. He missed the great Dark Dance.

Ambition goaded him to action. Steffan turned his ear toward gossip, collecting scraps of hearsay and innuendo. Sifting through the many-colored threads, he wove a fresh picture of Erdhe. Everything was changing. Lanverness reeled from war, while Coronth lay stricken from the Flame's collapse. From the coast he heard strange whispers of a poisoned feast, Navarre's royal family decimated by an ancient curse. And from the distant north, he heard rumors of the Mordant. Darkness swept across Erdhe like an implacable tide, yet Steffan's own power waned, slipping through his fingers like sand through an hourglass. His position might have seemed hopeless to some, but Steffan knew chaos oft provided the best opportunities. And then he heard a rumor that piqued his interest. A new queen had arisen claiming a corner of Coronth and whispers said she was a raven-haired beauty. Steffan packed his saddlebags and rode north.

Spring lit the trees with the first hint of green. Peasants emerged to work the fields while merchants and traders reclaimed the roads. A nervous peace prevailed, yet beneath it all the pall of war lingered. Bands of soldiers straggled north, deserters mixed with the wounded and the vanquished. Clogging the roads, they hid their Flame-colors beneath peasant's cloaks of brown or dun. Their halberds were gone, abandoned or surrendered, but Steffan spied swords beneath their cloaks and desperation on their faces. *Defeated but still dangerous*, he spurred his stallion to a gallop, keeping his distance, hiding his purse as well as his name.

Rolling farm fields gave way to small villages. The boundaries of kingdoms were not writ upon the land, but Steffan knew when he crossed into Coronth. Signs of the Flame were legion, but instead of thriving temples he found only blackened shells. The Flame Army's defeat had sounded the death knell of belief. The religion of the Flame collapsed, becoming a casualty of war. Betrayed by promises of victory, the people's anger sparked to a fearsome rage. As he rode north, Steffan found temples reduced to charred timbers, priests murdered or fled, whole villages turned secretive and wary. The war had ripple effects he'd never expected. The collapse of the Flame galled him. Perhaps he should have stayed in Coronth and plied the powers of religion instead of turning to war, but that coin was already spent. Better to look to the future than live mired in the past.

Steffan pressed northward, lingering just long enough to collect gossip and golds. Always he asked about the raven-haired queen. A tankard of ale bought a fistful of rumors. Villagers bragged of the new queen's intoxicating beauty and the way she ruled with a firm hand. Some even spoke with affection, as if they preferred a queen to the Flame. Such talk singed his pride, but Steffan swallowed his anger. If only the villagers knew whom they spoke to, but in truth he was glad the Lord Raven went unnoticed. He didn't fancy being caged and broiled alive like the priests, so he took what he needed and rode north, keeping his name to himself.

Most villages were sparse with food but rich with rumors. All the rumors led to Rhune, an ancient holdfast in the southwest corner of Coronth. Famous for its hot springs, Rhune was the ancient seat of winter palaces, a retreat for royals through the ages. He'd visited in his vagabond years, drawn by flocks of wealthy widows, but that was long before the war. Curious to see the changes, Steffan timed his arrival for mid-morning. Riding down the main street, he caught the smell of fresh-baked bread wafting from the bakery while the ring of hammers came from the forge, proof the town still flourished. The main street was paved with cobbles and the three inns were large and spacious. Even the smaller homes and shops were built of dressed stone, bedecked with prancing lions carved into lintels and keystones, the proud symbols of a bygone royalty. Wealth clung to the ancient city like a comforting blanket, just the type of place the Priestess would favor. *So she'd come to Coronth to be a queen*, bitterness rose like bile in Steffan's throat. Rhune should have been his, just a small portion of a larger kingdom, but he'd risked it all on war. Steffan swallowed the thought, knowing he'd come for a gamble of a different sort.

He took a room at the best inn, ordered a soaking tub, a girl to wash his back, and a bottle of their best brandy. Come evening he dressed in his finest black leathers, twirling a cape of sleek otter fur around his shoulders, black as midnight and rich as sin. Glancing in a mirror, he approved of his dark attire, a perfect complement to his dashing good looks. Tucking a sapphire ring in his belt pouch, he left the inn and mounted his stallion.

He followed the road out of town, cantering through blossoming cherry orchards. White petals fell like soft snow, strewn before him like a conqueror's tribute, as if the very land mocked his return. Anger snarled through Steffan. He spurred his horse to a gallop, churning the petals to dust.

The landscape changed from rural to royal. Sculpted gardens and statuary heralded the keep. Most of the statues were headless, marble monarchs felled by religion. Steffan wondered if the palace had fared any better. Topping a hill, his gaze was captured by Silverspire. Tall and elegant, the slender keep was clad in white marble, glittering like its namesake in the rising moonlight. Part palace, part military stronghold, Silverspire reeked of ancient wealth, the winter home of pampered royals, the perfect setting for the Priestess.

Putting spurs to his mount, Steffan rode to the great iron gates, struck by the color of the guards' tabards. Gone was the blue of bygone royals or the red of the Flame. Instead all the soldiers wore dusky purple, the changing faces of the moon emblazoned in a golden circle on their tabards. Another color, another emblem, the woman was as changeable as quicksilver, but for all her airs, Steffan expected her to be the same between the bed sheets. *That* woman he knew very well.

A pair of guards moved to block his way, hands on their sword hilts.

Steffan pulled his mount to a halt. "I'm here to see the lady of the keep."

"You mean the queen."

So her guards were protective. "As you say."

A bearded captain emerged from the gate. "And who are you to be asking for an audience?"

An audience, the woman was definitely putting on airs, but Steffan could play the game with the best of them. "Lord Steffan of Darkmoor."

One of the guards grumbled, "*Darkmoor,* ain't never heard of no Darkmoor, but I think I've seen this one before."

Steffan swallowed his unease, keeping his gaze fixed on the captain. "Your queen expects me."

Their stares locked. The captain looked skeptical but he clearly wasn't willing to brave the wrath of his mistress. "I'll send a runner. Meanwhile you wait here."

Told to wait outside the gates, Steffan hid his ire. The guards shared a jest around a brazier, while Steffan sat stoic on his horse, warmed by thoughts of the coming night. Just thinking about her made him hard. More stars emerged and the night sky deepened to indigo. He was beginning to wonder just how long the bloody woman would keep him waiting when a page came running. "The Lady will see you now."

Iron gates clanged open and he rode through thick walls into a cobbled courtyard. The sweet sounds of a fountain greeted him, a pride of marble lions spouting water into a central basin. Whole and undefiled, the lions had fared better than their royal masters. Perhaps the keep remained intact. A page scrambled to claim his horse while a pair of guards gave him an appraising stare. "Your weapons."

Steffan gave them an amiable smile. "Is this really necessary? The lady awaits."

"Your weapons."

He relinquished the sword from its scabbard and the knife from his belt sheath, but that left him with the dirk hidden in his right boot and another tucked at the back of his belt. The guards never checked, waving him through. Steffan hid a smile, *vigilant but not thorough.* He climbed the steps to the inner keep, to massive doors studded with silver, another sign of flaunted wealth. Steffan appreciated their elegant beauty, surprised the silver had survived the rise and fall of the Flame.

A young page-boy liveried in dusky purple opened the doors. "This way, m'lord."

At least the page showed some deference. Steffan followed the lad into the depths of the keep, a pair of guards keeping pace at his back. Colorful tapestries lined the hallways while his boots rang on polished marble. The keep lived up to its reputation, a sumptuous palace fit for royalty, proving the lady kept her taste for luxury. Steffan approved her choice, anticipating the luxuries to come. He wondered where she'd choose to meet him, perhaps a moonlit garden, or better yet, a well-appointed bedroom. Spurred by desire, he quickened his pace. The lad led him to a pair of tall doors fashioned like butterfly wings. Sparkling with stained glass and semi-precious stones, the butterfly doors screamed of royal wealth and whimsical excess...but they also dashed his hopes. *So it was not to be a garden or a bedroom...but a formal audience hall.* Guards rushed to open the butterfly doors, revealing an elegant throne room. Vaulted ceilings of white marble arched overhead while moonlight poured through mullioned windows, silvering the chamber. Steffan hesitated, *brought like a suppliant to her audience chamber.* Anger blazed through him. He crossed the marble expanse, his gaze seeking the seductress of his dreams. A vision in dusky silks, she sat alone on a silver throne, a minstrel strumming a lute at her feet. Every curvaceous detail exceeded his memories. Desire took hold. Like a moth drawn to a dark flame, he strode across the moonlit marble to stand before her throne. His gaze drank her in. Lush curves swathed in shimmering silk, her mouth ripe and full, her dark hair cascading past her shoulders, but it was her eyes that caught and held him, so full of wicked promise.

"So the Priestess of the Isle has become the Lady of the Moon," he gave her a sweeping bow. "Beauty to rival my dreams, I've crossed kingdoms to find you." His voice oozed charm but silence was his only answer. "I did not come empty handed." The ring flashed in his hands, a cornflower-blue sapphire the size of his thumb surrounded by diamonds, a queenly gift guaranteed to make a woman swoon.

The Priestess gestured to the minstrel. "Mario."

The motley-colored dandy leaped up, his hand extended for the ring. Steffan glared, but the minstrel waited and the Priestess watched. He relinquished the ring, fuming as the fop knelt to slip it on her finger. Like a well-trained pet, the minstrel retreated down the dais to reclaim his lute. The Priestess held her hand aloft, the sapphire jewel sparkling in the moonlight. "Yes, a pretty bauble, no doubt won at dice."

She was going to make him work for it, Steffan swallowed a scowl. "You've done well for yourself."

"Better than most."

Her smugness pushed him to anger. "Queen Selene, the Lady of the Moon. Another name change?"

"Actually the same, Selene Cereus, a rare night-blooming flower. Appropriate, don't you think?"

Steffan shrugged, "Another name, another kingdom," his voice turned surly, "but this time you took something of *mine.*"

She raised an eyebrow, "Was it yours or was it lost? And who are you to complain, Lord Steffan of *Darkmoor?*"

The false title struck like a slap. Steffan narrowed his gaze. "You've changed your colors."

"Purple becomes us, a fitting color for my queendom."

He barked a laugh. "*Queendom?* That isn't even a word."

"Why is it any less of a word than kingdom?"

This wasn't going the way he'd planned. Instead of lovers reunited they were bickering like an old married couple. He sought a different tack. "And now you're the lady of Rhune. But why the moon?"

"A fitting symbol. Men are like the sun, strong and glaring and always in your face, while women are more subtle, like the night, dark and mysterious and always changing." She gave him a look more intimate than touch.

This was the woman he longed for. Encouraged, Steffan flicked his gaze to the minstrel. "We don't need an audience."

She gave a negligent wave. "Mario, leave us."

The minstrel kissed the hem of her gown and then bowed his way from the chamber.

The simpering fop raised Steffan's ire. "I'm surprised the palace survived the Flame."

"It was infested with bishops, and bishops like their luxuries." She flashed a triumphant smile. "When they saw the size of my army they dropped their robes and fled."

Anger flamed within him. "So you trampled my religion."

"No, merely swept aside the ashes. Defeat killed your religion, the defeat of the Pontifax, the defeat of your army, and the harsh yoke of your priests. When a fanatical religion falls, it falls hard, leaving a gaping emptiness. My army merely filled the void."

Her words rankled but he knew she spoke the truth. "Much has changed."

"Yes, I've used my army while you lost yours."

"Your army used to be *mine*."

"We had an agreement, I held up my end, or did the mercenaries of Radagar not turn and serve you?"

More barbs, he decided to sling some of his own. "I thought you sought the crown of Navarre?"

Her eyes flashed in warning. "I took my revenge and then I claimed Rhune." She leaned back in the throne, a pose designed to expose her cleavage to best advantage, a dark jewel amongst the glittering silver. "The palace becomes me."

He grew tired of slinging arguments. "Rumors say the Mordant comes south."

For a long time, silence hung between them. "I know." Her words fell like dirt into a grave.

"We should be allies, working together, scheming to profit from the chaos to come."

She gave a throaty laugh. "You think he brings profit in his wake? Then you know him not."

"Chaos always brings opportunity," he leaned toward her, "especially to those who know how to use it."

"The Mordant brings more than chaos."

Her words held the ring of prophecy. She'd always stood closer to the Dark, a fey power wrapped around her like a cloak. Even far from the Dark Isle, she remained the Oracle Priestess. He envied her power. "What do you know? What have you seen?"

"Too much and too little."

A chill passed through him. "As bad as that?"

Her face was grave. "It is not like dealing with mere mortals. He is the oldest Harlequin, the talon of the Dark Lord."

"All the more reason to work together."

She stared at him, her eyes dark and fathomless.

Understanding struck. "You have a plan, you always have a plan." She said nothing but the glint in her eyes gave proof to his words.

Steffan leaned towards her. "I can help you."

Still no answer.

Steffan decided to roll the dice. "You could use me." He waited, balanced on a knife-edge.

"Finally the truth." Her gaze raked across him. "You're cunning, and comely, and still favored by the Dark Lord...and you give great pleasure in bed." Her voice caressed him and he grew hard in spite of himself. "This time we'll do it *my* way." Her eyes gleamed with wicked intentions as she rose from the throne. A slit on her gown revealed a flash of shapely white thigh. She prowled down the dais like a predator, her scent surrounding him in a haze of suggestion. His nostrils flared, breathing deep, sandalwood and something else, something mysterious and wantonly sexy. "I remember that scent." His manhood strained towards her, like iron to a lodestone.

"I wore it on our first night."

His imagination exploded.

"Come." Her voice purred down his spine as she led him to a side door. Sundered by her scent, by every curvaceous detail, he followed, his gaze drinking her in, imbibing her like a heady wine. Graceful and evocative and curvaceous, she led him on a shimmering tease down the long hallway. Enamored by the view, he grew engorged by every sultry detail. Torchlight flickered across silky skin as she slowly shed her gown, leaving a diaphanous trail. Steffan walked as if in a trance. He tripped and nearly fell. And then he noticed the smooth marble floor had given way to rough-cut stone. Stairs descended down. For half a heartbeat Steffan wondered if she led him to the dungeons, but then he caught a whiff of her scent and he did not care.

A guard raced to open a bronze door.

He followed her into the moonlight, a spray of stars overhead. Chilly night air rushed to embrace him, but it did nothing to cool his ardor. They stood in a rocky grotto, cave walls bathed by moonlight. Steam rose from a bubbling hot spring, a cauldron of frothing water, releasing a faint scent of brimstone.

"You're going to like this."

He had no doubt.

She began to undress him, her hands making every movement a caress. She found the knife at his back and the one in his boot but it only seemed to amuse her. For a while, she lingered over his belt, slowly drawing out the leather, and then he stood naked in the moonlight, blowing streams of mist into the chill night air like a beast on the verge of a rampage.

"Not yet." Her whisper restrained him.

His nostrils flared, a stallion chasing a mare in heat.

She reached for an amber bottle, pouring a libation of oil on his chest. Slippery and smooth and smelling of herbs, it released an inner heat. Her hands followed the oil, igniting every part of him. A torture of touch, her fingers trailed down and around, clutching him tight.

Breathing like a bull in rut, he struggled to maintain control. "I can't wait."

"If you want it, you must swear."

This was madness. "Swear what?"

Her lips cascaded down his chest. "You know." Her fingers did something unmentionable. He strained with need, bucking against her hold. Fingernails raking against tender flesh, she constrained him, driving him to a frenzy. It was too much to bear. "I swear!"

"Do it now."

He ripped the last vestige of silk from her shoulders and then lifted her up, her legs wrapping around his oil-soaked hips. And then he took her, like a stallion mounting the moon. Over and over again, he screamed his lust into the night, staking his claim to her. And when he was finally sated, his whole body quivering with ecstasy, he carried her to the lip of the frothing spring. Still inside of her, he tumbled them into the water.

Heat embraced him. The deep-seated heat soothed his every muscle. Separated by the fall, Steffan floated to the frothing surface. Lying on his back, he stared upward, entranced at the stars. He felt as if he floated in a dream. "What have you done to me?"

A throaty laugh was the only reply. And then she was next to him, her hands finding all the right places. "Let me show you what it's like in water." He turned to embrace her and nothing else mattered.

33

Liandra

Sunlight streamed through the stained-glass windows bestowing a flush of colors on the marble gods. Liandra found the princess grieving in the royal chapel. Pale in a gown of dark velvet, Princess Jemma knelt before the statue of winged Marut, the goddess of justice. Her hands clasped, her head bowed, her shoulders hunched, every line of her body bespoke prayer alloyed with grief. Dismissing her guards at the door, the queen crossed the checkered floor, a soft rustle of emerald silks. "We grieve for your loss."

Startled, Princess Jemma looked up. Tears glistened in her eyes. "A messenger came today...my mother..." her voice broke. She struggled to swallow a sob.

Such courage, such beauty, Liandra ached to see the pain etched on the young woman's face. "Sometimes grief has to be shared in order to be endured. Come and sit with us."

Wiping her tears, the princess rose, following the queen to the royal pew. Elaborately embroidered pillows softened the oaken bench. The two women sat side by side beneath the soaring vault. Pierced by sunbeams, the stained glass windows illumed the chapel with dazzling colors. Ruby reds, sapphire blues and emerald greens, the jewel-box colors painted the stone-carved lacework with vibrant hues. A delicate confection of polished stonework melded with light, so beautiful it soothed the soul. Staring at the soaring ceiling, Liandra imbibed the chapel's peace. "My mother died in childbed, giving birth to my stillborn brother. I barely remember her...but I grieved hard for my father."

The princess shook her head in bitter denial. "My mother wished ill on no one. She did not deserve to die..." her voice cracked with grief.

"She must have been a marvelous woman."

"She found pleasure in the smallest things. A colorful seashell washed on the beach, a sea eagle's feather found on the rampart, a rainbow at sunrise, she found joy in them all, yet she was always the queen, and always...our mother." Stories poured out. For more than two turns of the hourglass, the princess shared memories large and small. Liandra listened to the emotions laced beneath the words. By the time the sun dipped towards a russet sunset, the princess's sharp grief had bled to a bearable sorrow.

Falling silent, the princess cast a grateful glance toward the queen. "Thank you."

"You are most welcome, my dear." The queen swallowed her own emotion. "We wished for you to be our own dear daughter-in-law."

"I know. In many ways, I wished for it too. But Jordan will make your son very happy and she will be a fine queen."

"And what of you?"

The princess stilled. "The murder of the Royal Is was terrible...but mother's loss will break my father's heart."

The queen waited.

"Father will pass the crown." The words were spoken with sadness underscored by cold conviction.

"Will you reach for it? Will you dare to try for the seaside crown?"

"Reach for it, no, though I dearly want it." The princess shook her head. "No, the seaside crown must be freely given. The king and council will decide what is best for the kingdom. It is our way."

Such a worthy woman to wear a crown, "They could not choose better."

"Thank you, but we shall see. The council chooses the heir best fit to serve the times. Dark times are upon us."

"Just so." The queen studied her apprentice. "So you won't return to Navarre?"

"Not unless bidden."

"We are pleased to have you by our side." The queen had to ask. "Having lost the Rose Crown, can you be content with the crown of Navarre?"

"*Yes!*" A spark gleamed in the princess's eyes. "It's the challenge, you see. Lanverness is so well run, the treasury full, prosperity shared among the people," the princess shrugged, her cheeks blushing, "the next queen will feel like a caretaker!"

Liandra was smitten by the compliment.

"In Navarre, I'll have the chance to build something fresh, to steer the kingdom in a new direction." She flashed a competitive smile towards the queen. "A chance to grow Navarre till it rivals the prosperity of mighty Lanverness!"

A knowing smile flashed between the two women. The queen well understood the deep-seated need to grow a kingdom, to spread prosperity, to make an indelible difference. The princess truly was the daughter of her heart. "We shall welcome Navarre's prosperity. All of Erdhe will be richer for it."

The two women sat in companionable silence, sharing dreams as grand as the chapel's soaring stonework. The sunset deepened to a crimson glow, painting the chapel the color of dried blood. Queen Liandra shuddered at the ill-omen, her mind turning from dreams to threats. "Darkness reaches for Erdhe."

The princess's voice dropped to a grim hush. "I know."

"All of our dreams will be for naught if the shadows are not defeated."

The princess had no reply.

Liandra stared aloft at the delicate confection of lace-work stone, the soaring vault imbued with an airy grace, now drenched in bloody twilight. "In such a chapel, one almost expects the gods to care."

"Do you think they listen?"

"They must, for evil is real, and without their help, our chances are bleak...yet we've always felt the gods help those who help themselves. We dare not sit idle."

Mired in worry, the two women watched the fading light. Twilight colors dimmed, quenching to darkness, but once the sun set, the candlelight flickered and glowed. Pinpricks of light that had seemed insubstantial in the day held the darkness at bay. *Candles of light,* if enough people held the light in their hearts then perhaps darkness could be defeated by mere mortals. *Strength in many,* Liandra held to the slender thought, for she knew dire darkness threatened all of Erdhe.

34

Steffan

Steffan woke naked and sticky, groaning as the morning's dim light pierced the shutters. Rolling over, he kicked an empty wine goblet from the bed. His hand groped beneath silken covers, finding nothing but a tangle of sheets. *Another empty bed.* Steffan cursed the dark-haired Priestess. His manhood stood rampant, eager for another tumble, yet he had nothing but his own hand for satisfaction, a dull choice compared to the dark-haired vixen. Memories of the night assailed his mind, her scent lingering on his skin. His ache grew to a throb. Just thinking about the woman made him hungry, but no matter how hard he rode her through the night, the mornings were always the same. He always woke alone. The empty bed mocked him; the Priestess took this business of ruling far more seriously than any woman should.

Frustrated, he rolled from bed and made a quick toilet, splashing cold water from the basin across his arms and chest. Steffan shivered, the water chilly enough to dampen even his ardor, such a waste. Ransacking a chest, he pulled on leather riding pants and knee-high boots, a warm jerkin of the finest crushed velvet and then twirled his black cloak around his shoulders. Almost as an afterthought, he buckled his sword belt at his waist. A princely gift from the Priestess, he'd come to favor the sword, a fine rapier with a jewel-encrusted hilt, the weapon of a lord. Making a quick rake through his raven-dark hair, he strode from their chambers, descending the tower stairs two at a time.

His boot heels rang with authority against the cultured stone. Servants in the purple and gold livery of the moon bowed at his passing. He snagged a goblet of wine from a servant's tray. "Where is my lady?"

"I believe the queen is in the audience chamber, my lord."

The *queen,* the title alone was enough to sour his stomach. Steffan quaffed the wine in one long draught, taking the edge off his thirst. "Of course she is." He tossed the empty goblet upon the tray and continued down the hallway. Rounding the corner, he found a pair of soldiers guarding the jeweled butterfly doors, but instead of snapping a salute, their halberds crossed with a clash.

Steffan gave them a venomous stare. "Announce me."

The guard on the left fidgeted but the one on the right looked resolute. "The queen gave strict orders, my lord."

"What orders?" His voice was a dangerous growl.

"Orders that the Lord Steffan was not to be admitted."

Steffan drilled him with his stare but the guard did not flinch. "You dare refuse your lord?" He twisted the words like a dagger, but the guard remained statue-still. Steffan glowered, wondering if the man's stiff loyalty had been bought between bedroom sheets. He wouldn't put it past her. Anger spiked through him, but arguing would only diminish his standing. "No matter." He turned on his heels, his black cape flaring behind him, and strode toward the outer doors. "Tell the *queen,* I've gone riding."

At least the outer guards had sense enough to rush and open the doors in his path, a sop to his pride. Ignoring the guards' salutes, he strode from the keep into the brisk morning air. Rain spattered his face, the sky laden with dark clouds, another gloomy day. He crossed the courtyard and entered the stables. "Saddle my horse and be quick about it." A stable hand leaped to obey, entering the stall of his black gelding. "Not the black, I'll take the red."

"Yes, m'lord." Samuel threw him a reproachful look before slipping into the red's stall. The stallion bellowed. Iron-shod hooves thundered against the doors hard enough to split skulls. The stable lad yelped and cursed but eventually got the roan saddled. Eighteen hands high and trained for war, the roan had a demon's temper, but Steffan enjoyed the challenge. Accepting a leg up, he vaulted into the saddle. A flick of the reins and the roan burst into a full gallop. They thundered out of the stables and into the yard. Guards scrambled, scattering to avoid the stallion's hooves. Steffan charged the outer gates like a demon loosed from hell. At the last moment, the gates swung wide and they sped into the countryside. Steffan laughed, feeling an oppressive weight slough from his shoulders. He reveled in the keep's luxuries, but he could not abide the woman's cloying airs. Putting spurs to his mount, he rode cross-country.

Escaping the keep's shadow, he galloped through the surrounding woodlands and orchards, everything cloaked in the budding green of spring. Rain beat against his face, but he did not care. Riding low in the saddle, he let the stallion have its head, the countryside becoming a green blur. He pressed for more speed. The Priestess was a boon in the bedroom but a bitch in the council chambers. This business of ruling had gone to her head, and now she barred him from the audience hall. *Him,* the Lord Steffan Raven, the true ruler of Coronth, the general of a holy war, a leader of men, yet what had *she* done besides spread her legs? Fury pulsed through him, it wasn't right for a man to be set below a woman; it destroyed the natural order of things.

Lightning flashed overhead releasing a cold torrent of rain.

Suddenly drenched, the storm quenched Steffan's rage. Mopping the wet hair from his eyes, he slowed his stallion to a walk. Old-growth trees crowded close to the trail. He'd ridden far, farther than usual. A chill of foreboding shivered down his back, perhaps he should have brought his guard. His stallion snorted and reared, nearly throwing him. Regaining his balance, Steffan settled his mount, "It's just rain," but he wondered if he spoke the truth. Lightning forked overhead, adding a threat to the forest gloom. And then he saw them. Armed men blocked the trail. Filthy and unshaven, bits of red hidden amongst homespun brown, they looked like a rough lot. Deserters most likely or soldiers turned brigands. Steffan stole a glance behind and found a dozen more sealing his retreat. He swore under his breath, his hand stealing to his sword.

"No need for that, my Lord Raven."

The title alone was enough to give him pause. "Who dares bar my way?"

"A bishop seeking a lord."

Steffan hesitated, sensing a trap of a different sort. "The religion of the Flame is banned by the Lady of the Moon."

"And such a sin it is. That's why we've come seeking a *lord* instead of *queen.*"

Cautiously interested, Steffan pressed for more. "Does this bishop have a name?"

"Bishop Tilden of the fourth brigade."

The name sparked a memory, a dangerous man and a dangerous claim, for only the most fanatical of bishops served with the Flame Army. "The name is familiar, but as I recall the bishop was plump of face and wore finer robes."

The man shrugged. "Hard times make hard men."

Steffan crossed stares with the cleric, matching memories to the face, finding enough details to be satisfied. "What do you want?"

"A lord who knows the worth of good men."

"You mean a lord who pays?"

"You were always quick, Lord Raven." The cleric cracked a hungry smile. "Preferably in gold."

"And in return?"

"Sixty sharp swords at your beck and call, ready to do any service. And I do mean *any* service, m'lord."

He liked the suggestion, a band of secret swords at his beck and call, a hidden edge to counter the arrogance of the Priestess. "Why not offer your swords to the queen? Her gold is as good as mine."

The cleric hawked and spat. "The witch has a way of looking inside of a man. She won't take priests, and never a bishop."

Even better, Steffan suppressed a grin. "And how will I reach you?"

"You like to ride in the mornings. Wear a red cloak and one of us will find you along the way."

"And if I can't leave the keep?"

The cleric grinned. "We've got a few mice tucked within Silverspire's walls. Get word to one of them and your whispers will be heard."

Steffan waited but no names were forthcoming. Making his decision, he pulled a purse from his belt and tossed it to the cleric.

The bishop made an easy grab, the purse hitting his hand with the resounding chink of heavy coin. Tugging on the drawstrings, he poured gold upon his palm. More than one brigand gasped at the sight. With practiced ease, the bishop vanished the coins beneath his cloak. "At your service, my Lord Raven."

"I left that title at the gates of Pellanor."

"Another thrice-damned queen," the bishop spat. "We've all got pasts that are better buried."

"And the mice?"

"A stable hand named Samuel, a scullery lad named Hinton, and a pot boy named Gill."

Where there were three mice there were bound to be more. Steffan knew the stable lad. "You're using children?"

"Sharp ears and sharp eyes, the boys all served as acolytes to the Flame." The cleric sneered, "Your witch delves men but she can't be bothered checking the children."

So she isn't perfect, the words gave hope to his plans. "So we have a deal?"

The cleric gave him a half bow, "We do, my lord." The bishop gestured and the brigands melted back into the forest.

Steffan set spurs to his stallion, his mind ablaze. His luck had not deserted him. He'd gained unexpected allies, a hidden dagger at his beck and call. Steffan laughed, feeling the Dark Lord's guiding hand return to his shoulder. Plans churned in his mind, the Priestess would ignore him at her peril. The Lord Raven was back in the game, and this time the prize would be his. Grinning, he turned for the keep, urging his horse to a gallop. "One lifetime is not enough!"

35

The Priestess

The Priestess sat upon a throne gained neither by marriage nor inheritance but by the dint of her own hand. Having carved a kingdom from the corner of Coronth, she raised her moon banner above a royal keep and set a crown upon her head, yet despite her triumph not a single monarchy acknowledged her court...till now. When the messengers first brought word, she'd scoffed at the notion; a doomed kingdom extending a hand of friendship to the Oracle Priestess, but then curiosity got the better of her. Uncertain times made for uncertain bedfellows. She decided to answer the letter. Promising safe passage, she instructed the emissaries to arrive in the early morning, the better to shield them from Steffan's prying eyes.

As the hour for the audience dawned, her thoughts spun with possibilities. This meeting could lead to so much more than mere talk. The possibilities were delicious, ransom, seduction, subversion, entrapment, or even a secret alliance. The Priestess considered them all. Much would depend on the emissary and his message. Keeping the possibilities in mind, the Priestess took pains to set the stage. After much thought, she selected a samite sheath of dusky purple, so dark it was nearly midnight, and a necklace of moonstones clasped in silver to dangle amongst her cleavage. Glamorous as a dark jewel, the Priestess took a seat upon the silver throne. Her battle commander, General Tarmin, a burly, bearded warrior clad in the purple surcoat of the moon, stood three steps below the dais, his hand on his sword hilt, a possessive glint in his dark eyes.

Rain drummed against the mullioned windows. Somewhere down the hall a slow leak dripped onto the marble floor. Such an irritating sound, it soured her mood, as if one loose shingle could belie the opulence of her captured court. She considered summoning her minstrel to obscure the annoyance, but bards had loose tongues and music would diminish the occasion. The Priestess speared a guard with her glare. "Put a bucket under it."

The guard sputtered, "A bucket?"

Irritation rode her voice, "Use your helm." *If not your head.*

With a sheepish nod, the guard sped to obey, but it did little to solve the problem. The wet drip changed to a metallic ping, more annoying than the first, but there was nothing to be done about it. Smoothing her face, the Priestess nodded to her commander. General Tarmin relayed her order, "Admit the envoys."

Guards in purple rushed to open the butterfly doors. Five men strode into the hall, spurs jangling, their hands hovering over empty scabbards, proving they were seasoned warriors instead of diplomats, men accustomed to saddles and swords, yet they showed the good sense to eschew their queen's colors. Instead of emerald green they wore common leathers and darker colors implying a rare blend of caution and shrewdness. She wondered if the choice best reflected the men or their queen.

The Priestess fingered her moonstone necklace, a flash of jewels bedazzling her cleavage. For more than three moonturns a queen's crown had sat upon her brow, yet the first sovereign to recognize her royal claim was another woman. The Oracle's Eye allowed her to spy on many in the Rose Court but never the Spider Queen herself. Curiosity sharpened her interest. She studied the envoys for hints of their queen.

Reaching her dais, the five men offered courtly bows, not deep enough to be fawning, nor shallow enough to be insulting. The Priestess parried their courtliness with a sultry smile. "Welcome to the realm of the moon."

Three of the envoys stood slack-jawed, captured by her allure. Heat reddened their faces, their stares lost in her cleavage, but the oldest among them merely smiled, drawing her interest. A hawk-faced man with iron-gray hair and sharp eyes, he gave her a respectful nod. "I bring greetings and well wishes from Queen Liandra of Lanverness to Queen Selene of the moon court. Her majesty is pleased to see a queen arise from the ashes of Coronth."

Details often made the man; the speaker wore an elaborately tooled sword belt and a gold ring upon his right hand, both signs of wealth...or royal favor. The Priestess made her voice a caress, "And your name?"

"Lord Highgate, Master Archivist and councilor to the queen."

She'd scried the dark-souled members of the Rose Court, yet his face remained unfamiliar. *An honest councilor, a true rarity in war-torn times.* "An archivist, someone who deals in musty tomes? You don't look the type."

"I'll take that as a compliment."

"But why choose an archivist as a councilor...or an envoy?"

"My queen loves to read," he gave her a sharp smile, "and history matters."

"Does it?" She leaned back in the throne. "The Flame war is still raw upon the land yet your queen dares send a high councilor?"

"Precisely because of that war. My queen desires to know her nearest neighbors, especially one who arises from the ashes of a false religion. Like a comet, you've appeared from nowhere to claim a throne."

His choice of words struck her as prophetic; how little he understood what the red comet presaged. "Silvery words, so you're a diplomat, not a spy?"

"Is there a difference?"

Amused, she rewarded him with a throaty laugh. "An honest courtier, how rare." She measured him with her stare. "When you return to Pellanor, what will you report to your queen?"

"Too soon to tell."

"First impressions?" She leaned back in the silvery throne, arching her back to flaunt her cleavage.

His gaze raked across all that was offered and then returned to her face. "Glamour enough to steal a man's soul...and the skill to use it."

Her voice was a silky purr. "Honest *and* insightful, how refreshing." Enjoying the verbal joust, she gave him a smoky gaze. "And how will I use it?"

"Madam, that is the question." He gestured and one of his companions stepped forward bearing a bundle wrapped in a shimmering cloth of gold. "Please accept this gift as a token of friendship from my queen."

General Tarmin inspected the bundle and then offered it to the Priestess.

Her fingers assessed the cloth, finding its weight of the highest quality. Inside, she discovered a vellum scroll rolled on a spindle of carved ivory. The spindle was exquisite, the ends carved into delicate rosebuds, a not-too-subtle reminder of the gift giver. Unrolling the vellum, she half expected a letter or a treaty but instead her gaze was captured by the brilliance of an illuminated manuscript. Gold and jewel-toned inks swirled across the page, the capital letters adorned with castles and crowns. The vellum was new, so the work was a copy, but the scroll was a masterpiece nonetheless. Intricate calligraphy bedazzled with adornment, she read the title, "*Emrath's Fall*." She gave him a puzzled stare. "Your queen sends a fable?"

"Is it a fable? Or a history?"

"Anything from before the War of Wizards is at best a fable. Myths grow on histories like moss to the trees." She fingered the vellum, considering the scroll. "An odd gift. The craftsmanship is peerless, but I must confess the intent is puzzling."

"Perhaps we can all learn from history."

"Such an odd message. Is your queen always such a riddle?"

"*Women* are riddles, although some are wiser than others, especially my queen."

She heard honest admiration in his voice, and for half a heartbeat she envied the Spider Queen. Somewhere down the hall, the leak dripped into the soldier's helm like the pluck of a badly tuned harp. Annoyed, she set the scroll aside. "Tell me of your queen."

"Queen Liandra hopes that the rose and the moon will be more compatible than the flame."

"So she seeks peace rather than conquest?"

"Always."

The Priestess gave a throaty laugh. "Doubtful. The Spider Queen is not as benign as you would have us believe. She conquers by the coin rather than the sword."

He gave her a rueful smile, as if she'd scored a touch. "Swords destroy while coins build. Good trade is beneficial to both parties."

"Now you speak like a merchant instead of a diplomat."

"Is there a difference?"

She liked his wry wit, an interesting reflection on his queen. "Tell me of the woman beneath the rose crown."

"The two are ever the same. Queen Liandra is first, last, and always, the queen."

Such a stalwart reply, such a ready and flattering defense, yet she wondered. Seeking to unsettle him, she slowly licked her lips and then undressed him with her gaze. Her stare lingered on his codpiece and then flicked to his face, an invitation and a dare. His eyes widened, a hint of wry amusement curving his mouth, but then he gave her a knowing smile. Like a knight errant entering the lists, he dipped his head towards her. "And *I* serve only my queen."

His voice was laced with deep undertones over iron conviction. His resolve surprised her while stoking her own desire. "Are you sure?"

"Certain."

"Pity."

He gave her a courtly bow.

Such a comely counselor, a heady mixture of mature experience, sharp wit, and fierce loyalty, the Priestess found herself aroused. Iron-gray hair and a time-chiseled face yet he stood like a man accustomed to the sword. A purr of desire built in her throat. She considered capturing him, holding him for ransom while she pitted his convictions against her considerable charms. She considered it, but then discarded the idea...at least for now. "We accept your queen's gift and consent to peace between our kingdoms."

"A wise choice." He bowed again, deeper this time. "But my queen hoped for an alliance as well as peace."

"One does not propose marriage on the first tryst."

"One might if haste is a necessity." His gaze turned serious. "You know the Mordant has taken Raven Pass."

She stilled to hear his name spoken aloud, answering with the barest of nods.

"A military alliance would serve both our kingdoms."

"Perhaps, yet we are reluctant to tie the knot."

A scowl flitted across his face. "Where will you stand if the north comes crashing down?"

"That remains to be seen."

"What remains to be seen? The coming of the north, or your choice on where to stand?"

"Both." She tired of the verbal sparring. "You've served your queen well and gained a peace between us. Let that be enough for now." She extended her ringed hand. "You may take your leave of us."

Climbing the dais, he kept his gaze locked on hers. Taking her proffered hand, he bowed, bestowing a soft but courtly kiss, his gaze fixed on her face. Beneath his gentle touch, she felt his swordsman's calluses, proof he was much more than just a spry wit. She gave him a suggestive smile, imagining his callused hands on her bodice. Leaning forward, she ensnared him with her scent, honeysuckle and nightshade mingled with pure allure. She watched his nostrils flair, his gaze delving her bosom. He breathed deep, clearly tempted by her trap.

He stepped back, his face firm. "Beauty to rival the moon...yet I serve but one queen."

Surprise slapped her. She struggled not to gape, knowing no mere mortal could resist the full brunt of her charms lest they were a full-cut eunuch...or deeply smitten by true love. Understanding struck like sharp dagger. The Priestess found herself envying the Spider Queen.

He retreated down the dais, never turning his back on her.

Such a pity, "Perhaps we shall meet again?"

"If my queen wills it."

His steadfast loyalty was growing irksome. The Priestess suppressed a sudden desire to hurt him out of pure spite. "We wish you a safe journey."

"Please consider my words and the gift of my queen."

She nodded, waving dismissal.

The envoys bowed and then turned with military precision. She watched them stride the length of the marble hall, broad shoulders and a flutter of dark cloaks. The butterfly doors closed behind them, morning light filtering through the bejeweled glass casting a rainbow of colors on the white marble floor. For the longest time she sat upon the silver throne, considering the man, the message, and the rival queen behind them, an intriguing conundrum. The longer she sat, the more her anger built. Sorely tempted to send a squad of soldiers to capture him, she imagined the outcome. Chained and bound, she'd have her way with him, pitting her charms against his resolve, a delightful challenge. "General Tarmin."

He snapped to attention. "Yes, my queen."

The command quivered on the tip of her tongue, but instead, she stayed the order, making a rare sacrifice to the god of Eros. Dismissing the general with a wave, she whispered the words, "I send him back to you," as if the love god and the Spider Queen both listened.

Her gaze dropped to the scroll in her lap. *A gift from a queen*, she fingered the vellum, wondering if the Spider Queen was as formidable as her counselor. Perhaps the gift held a deeper insight. The Priestess unrolled the scroll. The calligraphy was a masterwork, gold script embellished with jewel-bright illuminations, but the tale was an odd choice, a fable from before the War of Wizards. The story told of a sorcerous queen tricked into causing great destruction. *A woman scorned, a woman duped by her lover, everything lost in the conflict,* the Priestess wondered at the message beneath the words. She scanned the script till her gaze broke upon a name like a wave shattering upon a rocky shore. Misspelled, yet close enough to hint at the truth, she read the name aloud.

"The Lord Mordranth."

The name alone sounded like a doom. The Priestess considered the message buried beneath the words. *So the Spider Queen knows!* Or perhaps she merely guessed. A lucky guess...or perhaps a shrewd insight...or worse yet, perhaps the Kiralynn monks meddled. Her mind shuddered at the thought. Either way, the game was growing complicated. Opportunities were bred by complications...and so were the risks of mistakes. The Priestess could not afford a mistake. She'd grown accustomed to wearing a crown, but with the Mordant threatening the southern kingdoms, her hold on Rhune was precarious at best. Plots within plots, she'd have to tread carefully, weaving her way through a maze of risks to grow her own power. *One lifetime was not enough;* she felt the prize within her reach. She'd play the Great Dark Game and make her own bid for immortality.

36

The Mordant

Men and horses died for the sake of speed but it mattered not to the Mordant. Intent on the Great Dark Dance, he drove his men hard, galloping through Radagar's sleep-shrouded countryside. On the night of the waning crescent, they reached the appointed farmstead near the border of Lanverness. Armed men in dark hoods glided out of the woods to block the road, crossbows held at the ready. "This way is closed."

The Mordant breathed deep, catching the scent of Darkness in their souls. "Not to me." His stare pierced the leader's gaze. "Darkness knows its own. Kneel to your lord, Garver." Raising his staff, he loosed a bolt of pain as proof of his presence.

With a muffled gasp, the leader fell to his knees. "We've awaited your coming, dread lord." The others made hasty bows, their crossbows pointed to the ground.

"Is everything ready?"

"Just as you ordered."

"And the chests?"

"Safe and unlocked."

"Good, lead the way."

A runner was sent ahead while the guards slipped back into the woods to seal the road. The Mordant urged his sweat-streaked stallion to a trot. Garver, a former captain of the Dark Citadel, led his lord down a rutted road. The road curved through a copse of alders, emerging into a muddy yard. The farmstead had seen better days, a sagging row of huts and a dilapidated barn on one side, a thatched farmhouse and a weed-choked garden on the other, but the farmstead was far from abandoned. The muddy yard swarmed with men in dark leathers.

Garver yelled, *"Attention!"*

The command struck like a lash. The men scrambled to form into ranks, six rows of ten with a troop of a dozen duegar standing to the side. Dressed in a hodge-podge of leathers and armor they gave the appearance of a mercenary band, yet their weapons were of the finest make, and so was their discipline, a strange mixture of menace and restraint. Standing rigid at attention, they leaned forward, their hands gripping their weapons like abused mastiffs straining for the order to kill. The Mordant suppressed a smile; such was the legacy of service in the Dark Citadel.

A tall blond-haired officer with a nasty scar marking the left side of his face approached. "My Lord, the Eighth Fist of the Citadel is eager to serve."

The Mordant nodded. "And the chests?"

"Secured in the barn, awaiting your orders."

Dismounting, the Mordant tossed the reins to the major. "And my women?"

"Awaiting you in the farmhouse."

He gave the major a piercing stare. "Borgan is acting as my seneschal; he has the keys to the lesser chests."

A sneer flickered across the major's face. "A bishop! Let me serve you instead."

The reaction was not unexpected. His dark priests rarely mixed well with the army. Like a poisonous slime coating a sword, both were deadly in their own way, yet each was full of enmity for the other. But in this case, the Mordant needed them to work together. He gave the major a hard stare, a hint of menace in his voice. "Every man has his purpose, bishops and warriors, you *all* serve."

Major Tarq took a step backwards, his fist pressed to his chest. "Yours to command."

"It is time to put off your leathers. Borgan will open the chests and then inspect your men. Listen well, for he's been schooled in the details for deception. Be warned that no detail is too small. Be ready to ride at first light."

The major snapped a rigid salute. "Yes, my lord," but the Mordant had already turned, striding towards the mud-daubed farmhouse. His assassins ringed the hovel, stunted men clad in black leathers, a baldric of daggers marking their rank. Small in stature yet muscled in build, each had gained uncanny abilities. Annealed by hardship and depravation, the dross of the Dark Citadel had been forged into his most fanatical killers, his personal bodyguard, his assassins of the ninth rank. At his approach, the nearest leaped to open the door.

The Mordant ducked beneath the lintel, his eyes adjusting to the gloom. Lavender and pine smoke struggled to mask the mildewed stench of poverty. A rustle of bright silk met his gaze. His three women melted to the floor in obeisance, a blonde, a brunette, and a redhead, chosen as much for their stunning beauty as for their unswerving obedience. Crimson, the redhead, stretched a pale hand towards him, caressing his boot. "We've missed you, my lord."

Ignoring the women, his gaze sought the dark shadow standing next to the blazing hearth. Corlin, one of his master assassins, answered his unspoken question. "All is in order. The food and wine both served from your personal stores."

The Mordant surveyed the room, thick carpets covered a hard-packed dirt floor, fresh silk sheets on the pallet that served as a bed, fragrant steam rising from a cast-iron tub set before a roaring fire. "It will do. See to your men. The women will attend me."

Smooth as a shadow, the assassin slipped from the room, closing the door behind him.

"Attend me."

His women rose, surrounding him with soft touches. They stripped him of his travel-stained clothes, a trail of kisses running down his naked chest. He endured their caresses, letting his need build, and then he had his way with them, indulging his every desire. Finally sated, he sank into the heated tub, sipping wine while his women washed him with rosewater. Rising from the tub, he stood before the fire while his women toweled him dry. Replete and drowsy with warmth, the Mordant slept on silken sheets.

Light filtered through the chinks in the mud-daubed farmhouse. He woke rampant with appetite. Potency, like youth, was a fleeting gift, meant to be indulged and savored, but after a thousand years his tastes had grown complex. His three lovelies knew just how to please. The Mordant took his fill and then he supped on dried figs and sweetmeats. Having sated both his appetites, the Mordant stood naked before the blazing fire, his arms stretched wide. "Time to change colors."

His women opened the cedar chest, pulling sumptuous clothing from within.

Like a bird molting from winter's drabness, the Mordant spurned his dark colors. Putting off the black, his women clothed him in rich fabrics of velvets and silks, purples trimmed with gold, the raiment of a powerful prince. It seemed gaudy after his blacks, but at least the Empire of Ur had a worthy symbol, the Great Wyrm, a golden dragon eating its own tail, the circular symbol emblazoned across his chest. An ancient symbol, he wondered if the Urians even remembered the deeper meaning. *The eater of worlds, the destroyer of life*, a fitting symbol for the long-awaited endgame of this great Dark Dance. Amused, the Mordant flexed his muscles, satisfied with the fit.

His women hastened to finish their work. Crimson fastened a shimmering cloth-of-gold cape at his shoulders while Amber buckled a jeweled sword at his waist. Sable knelt before him, offering him a pillow strewn with jewelry. Magnificent rings fashioned from gold, beset with emeralds, onyx and amethyst, elaborate dragons eating their own tails. Pretty baubles yet their true worth lay hidden in the details. Focus-stones endowed with ancient magics were wrought into the rings, a collection gathered over many lifetimes. Jewels glittered on each finger, power hidden beneath wealth's facade.

"My lord, you look magnificent." Crimson held a mirror aloft and the Mordant studied the transformation. Tall and blond, his beard neatly trimmed, a young princeling stared back at him, his face open and honest, just a hint of arrogance in his stance. The monk's body served him well. Armored with lies and deception, the Mordant stood gird for battle. Satisfied, he strode from the farmhouse.

"*Attention!*"

Instead of a band of mercenaries, a royal guard snapped to attention in the drizzling rain. Bedecked in purple and gold, his men stood in perfect formation, purple banners fluttering from their spear tips. Even the horses were curried and their tack polished bright, a proper escort for a powerful prince. Major Tarq offered the Mordant a crisp salute, while Bishop Borgan scurried to serve, the plump cleric dressed in the silken robes of a seneschal. "Everything is as you ordered, my prince."

The oily-tongued cleric even got the Mordant's stolen title correct. Such attention to self-preservation was ever the hallmark of a good bishop. "And the chests?"

The cleric gestured and a pair of soldiers rushed to open the barn doors, revealing a wagon pulled by a team of white oxen, piled high with ironbound chests. The driver cracked the whip and the oxen lumbered into motion, plowing deep ruts in the mud. The wagon would blunt his speed but the chests were a necessary part of the deception. "Good. My horse."

Two soldiers emerged from the barn leading a magnificent white stallion, his mane braided with gold bells, a bejeweled saddle on his back. One soldier held the reins while the other dropped to his hands and knees in the mud. The Mordant stepped onto the soldier's back and swung into the saddle. Accepting the reins, he surveyed his escort.

The farmhouse door opened and soldiers emerged carrying his women across the muddy yard. Swathed in sumptuous traveling robes, they wore thick veils lest their beauty be sullied by the gaze of commoners. Soldiers settled the three women atop caparisoned palfreys. They rode sidesaddle in the center of the troop, princely jewels of another sort.

Impatient to be gone, the Mordant issued a terse command. "Burn it."

Torches were lit and thrown into each of the buildings. Weathered wood crackled like dry tinder, the fire licking skyward. The Mordant set his spurs to his horse, leaving flames billowing behind him. He'd changed his colors. Bedecked in deception, the oldest harlequin rode for the heart of Lanverness. It was time to break a queen.

37

Liandra

The queen swept into the council chambers, a rustle of amber silk and a dazzling flash of royal jewels. Her loyal lords leaped to their feet, bowing toward her. Winnowed by war, her small council had shrunk, shorn of traitors and the faint of heart. In the queen's eyes, their stalwart qualities far exceeded their lack of numbers.

Liandra took a seat on the oak-carved throne at the table's head. In Prince Stewart's absence, Major Ranoth, her military advisor sat on her left. Master Raddock, her deputy shadowmaster, sat on her right while Lord Highgate was away in the north. Liandra offered a smile to Princess Jemma, relieved to see that grief's harsh yoke was lessened to a bearable sorrow. As a staunch ally and the senior emissary of Navarre, the princess was a most welcome addition to the queen's council. At the far end of the table sat Lord Cenric, looking dashing and wildly exotic with his golden cat-eyes and his shimmering cloak of peacock feathers. Lord Cenric was rarely in Pellanor, but when he was, Liandra welcomed the cat-eyed lord to her council, hoping to bind him close as a trusted ally. Liandra smiled at the feral lord and received his usual stiff-necked nod in reply.

Her gaze circled the table, noting the harried looks on her councilors' faces. Lord Sheldon, Lord Saddler, Lord Rickman, her newly appointed treasurer, Lord Canning, and her new scribe, Lord Grange completed her small council. All of them were overworked, taxed by the need to recover from a war barely won, while preparing for the next. Hard times made for hard tasks. "We will start with the war."

Major Ranoth unrolled a map across the oak table. Brightly painted, the velum portrayed a detailed rendering of cities, castles, forests and rivers stretching from the Delta to the Dragon Spines. A carved wooden knight painted emerald green served as a marker representing the Rose Army. "At last report, the Rose Army is located here, just southeast of Balor. Aside from minor skirmishes, they've met with little resistance. So far the greatest challenge is finding food. The collapse of the Flame plunged the countryside into chaos. Food and fodder are both scarce. We've ordered supplies brought up from Kardiff."

Lord Saddler asked, "What of Balor?"

Master Raddock answered, "Our reports indicate a divided city besieging itself. The last bastion of the Flame priests seeks to rise from their own ashes using their people as tinder. Balor is a war-torn charnel house."

Lord Saddler looked to the queen. "What of the refugees that we sent back to fight the Flame?"

The queen felt the question's sting, a bitter barb to swallow. "War makes hard choices. We can finish the Flame or we can drive north to deter the Mordant, but we cannot do both. The refugees knew the risks." Her voice carried an ominous tone. "We have chosen to confront the greater evil. For the sake of Erdhe someone must." Her gaze circled the table and found no protests. Only Princess Jemma looked away, her face pale, a reminder that her brother, Prince Justin, led the refugees in Balor.

The queen addressed the princess. "What of Navarre?"

The princess answered, her face composed. "The king has called the banners, summoning archers from every village and hamlet. Combined with the army and the guards, we hope to raise a force of four thousand, more than half of them skilled archers."

Major Ranoth bowed towards the princess. "So many archers will make a formidable force. When will they march?"

"Within the fortnight. They'll march north and join the Rose Army at the Snowmelt River." The princess added a tight smile. "My sister will lead them."

Liandra stared, ambushed by the sally. "*Our* daughter-in-law?"

"Yes."

Outrage strangled the queen. *By the Nine Hells, we need a daughter-in-law who rules from a throne and births heirs, not one who fights with a sword.* Liandra struggled to contain her thoughts. Bridling her anger, cold calculation took over. The true weight of her son's decision hit hard, like a lethal sword thrust to the abdomen. "It seems our only heir and our only daughter-in-law both ride to the same battle." Her words carried a sepulcher doom. "Lanverness risks all in this war."

She watched the others blanch as the risk hit home.

Dead silence reigned for a hundred heartbeats.

Lord Rickman was the first to rally. "Majesty, perhaps you could..."

The queen forestalled him with a cold glare. "*Our* son and *his* children will wear the Rose Crown after us. We shall not sully the Tandroth line by choosing some distant eighth cousin from the distaff side."

Her councilors flinched from her gaze.

"The matter is closed."

Anxious 'ayes' circled the table, but more than a few lacked conviction.

The queen let her councilors stew, feeling her displeasure. After a sufficient silence, Liandra turned her attention to the cat-eyed lord. "Lord Cenric, will your people join this war?"

"The Treespeaker is aware."

It was not an answer. Liandra waited but no more was said. The queen fought the urge to pry a response from the feral lord. The cat-eyed archers had proved a boon, saving her city and her crown, but their pride was notoriously prickly. Deciding she dared not risk their ire, at least not at the council table, the queen turned her gaze to Major Ranoth. "And the enemy, where are they?"

"To the best of our knowledge, they continue to hold Raven Pass."

"They're *holding* it, not advancing?"

The major nodded. "So our scouts indicate."

"Why?"

"Only the Mordant knows."

The mere mention of his name cast a chill upon the chamber.

The queen rallied her councilors. "The longer they sit in Raven Pass, the longer we have to prepare. Time is a gift we'll not waste." She turned to Lord Saddler. "How goes the wall." She'd learned the value of stout walls from the Flame War, ordering better battlements built around her capital city.

"Every stonemason and bricklayer within a hundred leagues has been hired. They work night and day to raise battlements on the cobbled buildings and erect new gates. We've made good progress on the northern section...but it is ugly."

"War is an ugly business. Finish the wall, for we fear we shall have need of it." The queen's gaze turned to Lord Sheldon. "Our city teems with refugees. Too many farmers cower in Pellanor, seeking the illusion of safety. We need them to return to the land."

The lord nodded. "My constables patrol the main roadways, hunting bandits, deserters and pockets of enemy soldiers. We hang them as fast as we catch them. The crossroad trees groan under the weight of the dead. My constables feed the crows and ravens, making the countryside safe, but the people are reluctant to believe."

"Then they must be persuaded."

Lord Sheldon shrugged. "How do we make them leave?"

The queen considered the problem. "People respond to a carrot or a stick. In this case, we shall use a mild switch." She gestured to her royal scribe. "Issue a royal proclamation levying a tax on all inns, hostels and wayhouses within the great city of Pellanor."

"A bed tax?"

"No, a head tax."

Some of her councilors groaned in protest, most notably those who invested in inns, but the queen raised a hand forestalling their argument. "Taxes serve to fill the royal coffers, but they also influence behavior, as most sane people try to avoid them. In this case, we need the people to leave Pellanor and return to the land. A head tax will encourage that. This tax will be enacted immediately, a twenty percent charge added to the price of a room. Let it also be written that this tax shall be revoked on the first day of summer of this very same year. We do not enact this tax for benefit of the royal coffers, nor is it meant as punishment; rather it is intended as a mild goad to get our people back on the land. The spring harvest must be planted and the livestock must be husbanded or all of Lanverness will suffer. So let it be written into law."

Her scribe's quill scratched across parchment.

The queen's gaze circled the table. "Any questions, comments, complaints?" When no issues were raised, she stood. "Then this council is dismissed." Liandra extended her ringed hand for her lords to take their leave, but she kept her gaze on Lord Cenric. Before the feral lord could slink away, she said, "Lord Cenric, will you walk with us?"

Turning from the door, he nodded toward her. "As you wish."

Dismissing the others, she offered the cat-eyed lord her arm. He took it, leading her out through the doorway. Courtiers pounced like a pack of hungry dogs, but she waved them away. He led her through the marble corridors, a pair of royal guards following at a discreet distance.

"We wonder how your people fare in Onet Forest?"

"Many great-grandfather trees rule the forest and clean streams tumble down from the Southern Mountains, a good place for my people to settle."

"And Crown Hill?"

"The Flame invaders despoiled many trees, but under our protection the forest will thrive again."

"And how do you find Pellanor?"

He flashed a pointed grin her way. "The stench is appalling but your markets are fascinating. My people have rarely tasted the pleasures and pitfalls of a stone city."

"We trust your people feel welcome."

He gave her a solemn nod. "Some are still unsettled by our eyes, but my people are more welcome in Pellanor than anywhere else in Erdhe...but you did not cull me from the herd to speak of my people."

"True." The queen stopped, staring up at him, a dashing figure in his peacock cloak. "We wanted to ask you about the war. Will you fight?"

"We are here. Our bows will help protect Pellanor and its queen." He nodded to her, a courtly gesture.

"And what of the battle in the north?"

"The Treespeaker will decide."

Always the same answer, "Yes, but when will she decide and what will her decision be?"

"I do not pretend to know the Treespeaker's mind...but this Darkness is also our enemy."

"So you'll fight?"

For the longest time, he did not answer. His voice dropped to a reluctant whisper. "We are fewer in number than you think...but do not underestimate the Treespeaker."

She stared at him, trying to fathom his golden gaze, but his cat-eyes proved inscrutable. Realizing she'd get nothing more, the queen said, "We would hear more of your Treespeaker."

Rapid footsteps approached. Liandra turned to find Lady Sarah rushing towards her. Her haste sent a warning to the queen. Turning back to Lord Cenric, she said, "It seems the duties of a queen come calling. We hope to speak with you another time."

His gaze flicked between the two women. "I ride for Onet Forest on the morrow. We can speak more on my return." Turning with a cat's grace, he stalked the marble hallway with a brisk stride, his peacock cloak shimmering in the afternoon light, an exotic wild-lands prince in her cultured court.

Lady Sarah's gaze followed the archer's broad shoulders like a bee stuck to honey.

The queen sidled close. "What is it?"

Flustered, Lady Sarah tore her gaze from the archer. "It's Lord Frederinko, the emissary from Ur."

The emissary of Ur, she'd barely thought of the man with so much else on her plate, yet this sudden reminder seemed like an ill-omen. The queen kept her voice level. "What of him?"

"He haunts the door to your solar, refusing to leave until he's had a private audience."

A private audience, a pity Robert is still in the north. The queen gestured to her two royal guards, putting them on alert with a subtle hand sign.

A shadowman stepped from behind a pillar. "My queen?"

"Find the Knight Protector and bring him to our solar."

Bowing, the shadowman sped away.

Turning to Lady Sarah, the queen said, "Come, let us see what Ur wants."

38

Jordan

The armor was a gift from her father. Supple chainmail polished mirror-bright, a dove-gray surcoat with Navarre's emblem embroidered in rich colors across the chest, and a new shield emblazoned with red and blue checks surmounted by a white sea eagle with wings spread wide. Everything fit perfectly. Jordan belted on her sword of good Castlegard steel and then twirled her checkered cloak around her shoulders, both gifts from Stewart. She stared in the mirror and a warrior maiden stared back. A smile flickered across her face but her eyes remained solemn, her dreams and her destiny entwined.

Taking a last look at her childhood bedroom, she went to bid farewell to the king. She found him in the throne room, sitting alone on the Driftwood throne. Sunlight streamed through the stained glass, casting waves of blue light across the chamber, as if he sat beneath the sea. Grief had aged her father, his blond hair faded to silver-white, his eyes sagging with sadness, yet he sat on the throne with quiet dignity. Jordan ached to see him so. Crossing the lapis floor, she knelt before him. "Father, I ask for your blessing."

A smile creased his face, a glimmer of light in his sea-blue eyes. "My daughter of the sword," standing, he pulled her to her feet and embraced her. "You are a vision!"

"Thank you for the armor."

"Your Wayfaring gift. Your mother embroidered the surcoat herself." His voice turned gruff with emotion.

Jordan struggled to swallow her own pain. Caressing the exquisite embroidery, made dearer by her mother's own hand, she said, "I'll cherish it always. I wish..." her voice broke.

Her father pulled her close. "I know. So do we all." For a hundred heartbeats, he held her close, and then he stepped away, a determined look on his face. "You ride to war...and to glory."

Jordan hugged his words close. To have a father who not only saw her for who she truly was but valued her for it...that was a gift beyond compare. "Thank you, father. I will do my best for Navarre."

"I know you will." He turned and lifted a silver half-helm from the side table. "This is for you." The helm flashed bright in the sunlight, a sea eagle sculpted on the crest, but what caught her gaze was the crown. A delicate gold crown circled the helm, cresting waves interspersed with rosebuds. "I had the crown added at the last minute, rosebuds for Lanverness and waves for Navarre." He offered it to her. "For my warrior daughter who will be the next queen of Lanverness. You make me proud, daughter, so very proud."

"Thank you, father." Cradling the helm in the crook of her arm, she stared at him, struggling to hold back the tears. "Keep safe, father."

"And you."

There was one more thing she needed to say, her words laden with worry. "I've kept watch from the tower tops, hoping to spy Juliana's sails." Jordan fervently prayed she hadn't sent her sister on a death quest. "When Juliana comes, and I pray she comes soon, tell her I'm sorry to have missed her."

"She'll understand."

Jordan gave her father one last kiss and then stepped back. Saluting the king, she walked from the throne room. Down the tower stairs and through the castle hallways, she saw none of it, acutely aware that she was leaving her childhood home behind. A pair of guards rushed to open the outer doors. Jordan strode from shadowed grief into blazing sunshine. Blinking at the brightness, she found the others waiting in the courtyard, her companions from the Southern Mountains. Thaddeus caught her in a bear-hug. "Keep safe, princess."

"And you." Jordan returned his warm embrace and then stepped away, growing weary of goodbyes. "Are you sure you can't?" Having come to rely on the Zwardmaster's friendship and steady wisdom, Jordan knew she'd miss him more than she cared to say.

"Wish that we could, lass, but we serve the Grand Master."

Jordan already knew the answer, but hearing it made her feel even more bereft, as if she'd become insignificant with the loss of her visions.

Thaddeus leaned close, his voice a low rumble. "Don't think that way, lass. You heeded the gods' call and now the future is yours to decide." His voice dropped to a rough whisper. "Your dream is also your destiny, that's a rare thing in this life. Seize it and never let go." Stepping back, he gave her a jaunty smile. "You'll make a difference with your sword."

The swarthy swordmaster had a knack for knowing just what to say. "I'll miss your wise counsel."

He flashed a rogue's smile, but she could tell he was touched. "I know."

"Keep safe."

"And you."

She bid her goodbyes to the rest of the Zward and to the monk, Yarl, and then turned to Rafe. "Are you ready?"

Clad in plain brown leathers, the young monk flashed an eager grin. "I'm ready." Handing her the reins to an eighteen-hand warhorse, Rafe swung into the saddle of a sturdy roan gelding. Jordan settled the crowned helm on her head and vaulted into the saddle. Her dappled stallion pranced beneath her, spirited and proud, his silver-white coat flashing bright as steel in the sunlight. A pair of guards opened the outer gates, admitting a tangy breath of sea air. Saluting her friends, Jordan gave her stallion his head. The dappled silver leaped to a gallop. They burst through the castle gates, clattering down the ramp and onto the causeway. The tide was out, the turquoise sea retreated. Beds of mussels and bright green anemones lay exposed on either side of the long causeway, the glittering gardens of the sea. Like a magical road, the long causeway stood high and dry, threading a straight path from the castle to the shore. Jordan urged her stallion to a full gallop. Flying across the causeway, she escaped the castle's grief. Reveling in the stallion's speed, in the warmth of the sunshine, and the beauty of the turquoise sea, she loosed a joyous laugh, realizing the swordmaster had the truth of it; life was a destiny waiting to be seized.

She reached the end of the causeway, galloping between the sentinel statues, two giant ospreys chiseled from black basalt. Jordan steered her stallion along the north shore, throwing up clods of wet sand. Slowing to a canter, she surveyed the view, storing the details in her memory like a keepsake. To the east, the capital city gleamed white in the sunshine, limestone houses climbing the coastal hills. Shaped like a crescent, the white city embraced the harbor, a jewel of turquoise with Castle Seamount thrust up from a spit of land like a dark sword, straight and proud. The beauty and tranquility pierced Jordan's soul, a city worth fighting for.

Turning away from the sea, she rode towards the tournament field. An army awaited her. Drawn up in ranks, their battle banners rippled in the steady sea breeze. Two thousand well-trained soldiers clad in the blue and red checked tabards of Navarre stood in disciplined columns. Half were pike men, the other half skilled archers. An additional twelve hundred levies swelled the ranks. Clad in leathers and homespun browns, they'd came from villages, towns and farms, answering their king's call. An undisciplined lot, they sprawled across the hillside, looking like a rag-tag crew, but all of them carried longbows. Jordan smiled to see them, knowing their bows would take a fierce bite from any foe.

A cluster of officers rode towards her. Major Colson snapped a smart salute. "The army awaits your orders."

"And the supply train?" A line of wagons clogged the southern road.

"Ready to follow."

Jordan cast one last look toward the sea, hoping for sails on the northern horizon, but the ocean remained stubbornly empty. Her gaze snapped back to her officers. "Then it's time we marched north. Give the orders."

Officers cantered away, bellowing commands. Wailing conch shells echoed against the hillside, prodding the army to motion. Battle banners billowed and snapped in the wind as the army began to move. Marching in unison, the pike men led the way, their twenty foot pikes angled against their shoulders, steel spear tips glistening like a thicket raised to the cloudless sky.

Roused by the sight, Jordan asked her stallion for a rear. Standing in the stirrups, she unsheathed her sword and raised it to the heavens. "For Navarre and the Light!"

"*Navarre and the Light!*" The men roared her war cry.

Sheathing her sword, Jordan cantered the length of the column. Taking her place at the front, she slowed her silver to a brisk walk, the solid tramp of boots following behind. A baritone voice bellowed a sea chantey and the men took up the song, tramping to the lively beat. In high spirits, they marched away from the sea, passing through the city gates. Jordan grinned, feeling the tug of glory. She knew battle was a grim business, full of death and dying, but war offered a noble glory to those who fought for a worthy cause. If Darkness dared to invade, then she yearned to make a difference with her sword...and she'd have Stewart by her side. An irrepressible grin filled her face. *To battle and to glory,* she rode her horse north to war.

39

Liandra

Liandra took the long way, deliberately letting the emissary stew. Delay was a tactic of statecraft the queen had long perfected. When she finally arrived at her solar, Sir Durnheart was already there, standing guard by the doorway. A vision of knightly splendor, his great blue sword reared over his shoulder, his armor burnished bright, he bowed his head towards her. "Majesty."

The emissary from Ur whirled, his anger quickly subsumed beneath a diplomat's smile. Tall and gangly, the emissary towered a full head over Sir Durnheart. Tanned bronze by the southern sun, his dark skin made the silver ring piercing his right nostril all the more startling. A thin chain ran from his nose ring to a silver collar at his neck, marking him as a chained servant of Ur. Clad in long silken robes of brilliant purple trimmed in gold, he bowed towards her, an exotic stork wrapped in bright plumage. "I greet thee in the name of my master, the Twelfth-fold prince of Ur."

"Had we but known of your wish for an audience, we would have been here to welcome you."

"Your majesty is here, now." Flashing an enigmatic smile, the emissary gestured to the shadows. "We bring you a gift from our master." A small man in purple livery stepped forward carrying an ornate box.

Another gift, yet the queen wondered if such lavish gifts implied friendship or a hidden threat. "Your master is generous with his gifts."

"It is our way."

At the queen's gesture, Sir Durnheart opened the door. The queen swept into her solar, leaving the others to follow. A pine-scented fire crackled in the hearth and a bottle of red wine sat breathing on the side table, proving Lady Sarah had set the tableau. The queen took a seat in the throne chair, basking in the fire's warmth. Offering a smile to the emissary, she gestured to the opposite chair. "Please join us."

The chained servant folded his large frame into the straight-backed chair. Beneath his purple cloak, his tanned chest was bare, a wide silver belt cinching a long skirt of pleated white linen. Obviously suited to warmer climes, the queen found his fashion both odd and unsettling. "You're not bothered by the cold of the north?"

"Before one gains the chain of service, one is inured to small discomforts such as heat or cold."

She knew so little of Ur. All of their customs seemed strange and bizarre. "How long have you worn the chain of service?"

"This one has been bound since his thirteenth year." Pride rode his voice, as if it was a great honor. "But I am insignificant compared to the glory of my master, the twelfth-fold prince of Ur." He gestured to his servant. "Please accept this gift in the name of my master."

The servant stepped forward proffering an elaborately carved wooden chest.

The queen gestured to a side table. "Set it here." Placing the box on the table, the servant withdrew. The queen's gaze flicked to Sir Durnheart. Hovering a sword's length away, the knight made a subtle hand sign indicating that he'd already examined the gift and found no threat.

The queen examined the small chest. Elaborately carved from rosewood, the box itself was a masterpiece. Knights and wizards battled dragons and hellish beasts, a carved battle raging across the top. Liandra ran her hands across the exquisite detail, wondering at the message beneath the design. The top hinged on two opposite sides. Opening the lid, she found a chessboard inside. Darkest ebony inlaid with squares of polished abalone shell, the chessboard was stunning. Lifting the board into the firelight, Liandra was ambushed by its rare beauty. The abalone squares rippled with smoky colors, beautiful as muted rainbows, while the ebony anchored the board with a pattern of darkest shadow. Smoky iridescent shell contrasted with ebony's deepest black created a breathtaking effect. Light against Dark, the board shimmered in the firelight as if it held a wizard's enchantment. "We have never seen its like."

The emissary smiled. "My master will be pleased to learn of your pleasure," he gestured to the box, "but more awaits you."

Setting the board aside, the queen looked inside. Nestled in purple velvet sat a chess set unlike any she'd ever seen, one worthy of the magnificent board. The black was carved of ebony, winged dragons for the knights, a bearded wizard for the king, a sultry sorceress for the queen. Twisted gargoyles served as dark pawns. But the queen was drawn to the green figures. Carved of malachite, the green was even more alluring. Armored knights rode rearing stallions, the king and the queen both stately figures, the pawns carved as stalwart foot soldiers with twin roses inlaid in their shields. Liandra reached for a knight, marveling at the detail. Each figure was a hand span tall, exquisitely carved with small sapphires inset for eyes. Cunningly wrought, and weighted on the bottom to keep them from toppling, each piece begged to be played. "Stunning!"

The emissary nodded towards her. "My master also plays chess. Having heard you are a player of some repute, he wishes to meet you across the chessboard."

"Your master is here? In our city?"

"Within a fortnight, he will arrive."

The emissary was full of surprises. "We must prepare a royal welcome, a reception in the grand audience hall, a royal feast, perhaps a dance."

The emissary waved his hand like a fluttering bird. "There is no need. My master wishes to meet the queen who rules before he meets your court and your people." He gestured to the box. "He prefers to begin with a quiet dinner and a game of chess."

Such an odd but interesting request, Liandra felt her curiosity quicken. "Your master intrigues us."

The emissary chuckled. "He intrigues us all." His face sobered. "May I tell him you will accede to his request?"

"We will be delighted to meet him across the chessboard."

"Excellent." The emissary stood. Bowing toward her, he turned to leave.

Startled by his abrupt retreat, the queen said, "Wait."

The emissary turned.

"We wish to offer your master accommodations within our castle."

"There is no need. My master bid me purchase a manse within your fair city. We have been preparing for his arrival."

Feeling off balance, the queen said, "Did you purchase a suitable manse?"

He nodded. "The former owner was a Lord Nealy. The manse has a most impressive wine cellar."

She knew the manse, a pretentious and overly gaudy confection in the heart of the wealthy district. "Is wine important to your master?"

The emissary shrugged. "I live to serve." He bowed again. "I will send word when my master arrives." Gathering his cloak, he strode towards the door, his servant on his heels.

At the queen's gesture, Sir Durnheart followed. She'd given orders for her shadowmen to trail the emissary. The queen intended to keep a closer watch on the servants of Ur.

Lady Sarah emerged from the far room. "Another gift?"

"It seems the prince is full of them."

"What does it mean?"

The queen considered the chessboard. "That he likes chess, that he's wealthy and gives exquisite gifts, that he prefers private meetings to audience halls, in short, it means that the prince is an intriguing mystery, a royal conundrum. And," she fingered a malachite knight, "he knows us too well."

"You're intrigued."

"Intrigued, yes, but leavened with a healthy dose of apprehension."

"Yet you'll play him."

The queen flashed a predatory smile. "Chess is an excellent way to plumb the mind of an opponent, be they friend or foe."

"Which is he?"

"We'll hope for a friend and plan for a foe." Liandra set the chess piece aside. "Bring our jewel box."

Lady Sarah crossed to the far room, returning with the carved box.

The queen fingered the design, depressing the secret lever. A hidden compartment opened. A skeleton key set on a silver chain rested within, the key to Castle Tandroth's hidden passageways. Liandra set the slender chain around her neck, hiding the key within her bodice. "Do you have yours?"

Lady Sarah delved into her bodice, displaying a twin to the queen's key.

Liandra nodded. "Keep it with you always, for we fear Darkness draws near."

40

The Priestess

Haunted by the need to know, the Priestess climbed the tower to her scrying chamber. For nigh on three moonturns, the Mordant had remained hidden from her sight, a dire malevolence cloaked in impenetrable murkiness. Never before had she been so denied. Night after night, the Mordant thwarted her will, defying the power of the Eye. Like a subtle poison, the not-knowing festered in her soul, gnawing at her like an intolerable threat...but no longer. Fresh from sex, the Priestess thrummed with power, determined to unmask the Mordant's secret.

Dark of the moon, a perfect night for scrying. The Priestess shivered in anticipation, the night's silky darkness magnifying her power. Shuttering the windows against the faint starlight, she knelt, settling the great moonstone into the scrying bowl. The water hissed and bubbled, but the power of the Eye prevailed, turning the water to an inky blackness. The scrying bowl presented a mirrored surface...perfect for reflecting Dark deeds.

The Priestess cast her will upon the dark waters. "Show me the Mordant, the oldest of the harlequins." She held her breath, waiting, watching the mirrored surface. For the longest time, she saw nothing. Anxiety clawed at her, surely she would not be denied. The Mordant's absence proved both infuriating and worrisome. Such a Dark power should never be left to roam unobserved, like welcoming an assassin to your bedchamber. Goaded by pride as much as need, she gripped the sides of the scrying bowl, hurling her will upon the Eye. "*Show me the Mordant, the oldest of the harlequins!*" The air sizzled with her command. Like a tether to her soul, power flowed out of her, pouring into the great moonstone.

The moonstone quickened. Images danced across the scrying waters, faint and indistinct, too blurry for detail. Frustrated, she focused her will, demanding clarity. The image sharpened, showing a familiar face. *The Mordant,* so close his bearded face filled the scrying bowl...as if he stared at her! Fierce with power, his gaze pierced hers! Startled, she flinched away, losing her focus.

Water ripples disturbed the bowl, destroying the image.

"By the nine Hells!" The Priestess swore, taking a settling breath, chiding herself for such a foolish reaction. The Eye served *her*, and no one else.

Regaining her composure, she gripped the scrying bowl, willing the water to settle. The ripples died and the mirrored surface returned, dark as sin. The Priestess breathed upon the water. "Show me the Mordant, the oldest of the harlequins."

Power surged through her. Images danced upon the mirrored surface, settling on the face of the Mordant. *Eyes* stared from the scrying bowl, but this time she was prepared. So close, she saw the fierceness of his gaze, and nothing else. The Priestess manipulated the view. Like a hummingbird hovering overhead, she sculled backwards, gaining a wider perspective. Clad in purple robes, the Mordant stood in a farmer's field, the dark earth striped with fresh-plowed furrows. Inscribed across the fresh-turned earth was a huge pentacle, etched deep in the soil, as if drawn by a sword. A pinioned hawk and a bound man writhed within the Dark Lord's symbol. The man fought his bonds, his face contorted in fear. *A sacrifice...or a summoning*...either way it implied a great working. Intrigued, the Priestess crouched over the scrying bowl, mesmerized by the dark possibilities.

The Mordant raised his arms to the night sky. His lips moved, murmuring incantations, but the Priestess heard them not, for the Eye conveyed only images. A swirl of dark clouds obscured the stars, a potent storm brewing overhead. The Mordant stabbed a finger skyward. A pillar of green lightning answered. Forked lightning spiked down, striking the Mordant, bathing him in power. A nimbus of sickly green light cast an otherworldly glow around the Mordant, yet he stood unbowed, crackling with menace. So much raw power, the Priestess cringed at the strength of it. How could he survive it? How could he channel it? How would he wield it? She stared in awe as he harnessed the power. Green lightning spiked from his fingertips while Darkness swirled around him like a cloak, as if he channeled the power of the gods. The Mordant's mouth moved, shouting an incantation. The storm whipped his blond hair around his head like a writhing crown. Power encircled the Mordant like a maelstrom.

The backwash hit the scrying bowl.

Power surged through the silver bowl, a spark of green lightning scorching her fingertips. The Priestess flinched, her hands pinpricked with a thousand stinging nettles, yet she held to the bowl. Fear shuddered through her; she'd never experienced anything like this. A part of her wanted to pull away, to heed the warning, yet she refused to release the bowl. Caught by an insatiable need to know, she crouched low, peering into the scrying waters, determined to learn the Mordant's secrets

The view changed...*of its own accord!*

Like a fish caught on a line, the view was drawn closer, tightening on the Mordant.

Startled, the Priestess struggled to resist. Pouring power into the moonstone, she sought to wrest control of the Eye, yet the view drew ever closer to the Mordant, like driftwood being sucked into a whirlpool.

His face filled the scrying bowl, malevolent and cruel.

The Mordant peered through the waters! He *saw* her! Reversing the power of the Eye, *he stared back at her!* Terror spiked through her. She tried to pull away, but it was as if his gaze seared her soul.

I see you, Whore of Darkness!

Her mind froze, teetering on the edge of terror. Such a thing was impossible...yet his voice boomed through her mind.

Behold my power! Green lightning crackled around the Mordant's face like a spiked crown. *I am the eldest, the Lord of Darkness, the Master of Erdhe. How dare you scry against me!*

Frantic, the Priestess fought to blank the image. She spent her power, yet the Mordant's stare filled the scrying bowl, mockery in his gaze.

I see you, Whore of Darkness. You live to serve! His voice thundered through her mind. *The Great Dark Dance has begun. Come to Pellanor and serve your master!*

She fought to block him out, to push him away, to wrest control of the moonstone.

And then he laughed. *He laughed!* A terrible mocking sound rolled through the scrying bowl, beating against her.

Power flared through the Eye, burning her hands. A scream ripped out of her as she struggled to pull away, but her hands were locked to the bowl, shackled by magic. Steam billowed upward like a breath hissed from hell. The Priestess flinched away. In less than a heartbeat, the water disappeared revealing the great moonstone lying fallow in the scrying bowl...but the Eye no longer glowed. Pale and sickly, the great moonstone looked dead, devoid of power...but then it began to shudder and quake.

It moved like an egg about to give birth.

Unable to flee, unable to look away, the Priestess stared at the moonstone, trapped by fear and trepidation.

The Eye of the Oracle shuddered and shook...and then it *cracked.* The great moonstone sundered into three pieces. A moaning sigh swept through the tower chamber like the release of a long-imprisoned soul.

Horrified, the Priestess stared in shock. A scream rent through her. "*Nooooo!*" She lunged for the gemstone. Cradling the largest piece against her breast, she willed her strength into it. Clutching it close, she strained to sense a glimmer of magic, but the great gem remained dull and lifeless, devoid of power. A terrible keening burst from her. He'd broken the Eye. He'd stolen the best of her powers. She railed against him, cursing his name. Her horror annealed to hatred...but then the gemstone flared with one last flicker of magic...and it tasted of the Mordant. Green lightning bit her hands. Power hammered against her, strong as a battering ram. Punching her in the chest, it hurled her across the room. She hit hard, cracking her head against the stone wall. Stunned and heart sore, the Priestess slumped to the floor, consumed by darkness.

41

Steffan

Steffan woke with a start, a scream ringing in his ears. Slick with sweat, he pushed the nightmare away. Seeking succor, he reached for the Priestess...but the far side of the bed was empty, the covers twisted in torment. *Gone...again,* anger warred with frustration. The dark-damned woman was always slipping away in the dead of the night, always climbing to her chamber in the tower, but she never let him come, and she never answered his questions. His gaze flicked to the window, confirming night still ruled a moonless sky. Leaping from bed, he reached for his pants, deciding to plumb her secretive tower. Steffan was done with riddles.

Barefoot, he padded up the stairs, determined to end this mute stalemate that hung between them. Nearing the top, he heard a woman's wail. Hastening his stride, he reached the door but it was closed. "Cereus!" He pounded on the door, but it was locked. *"Cereus!"*

Nothing but silence for a reply.

He threw his weight against the door, battering it with his shoulder. The stout oak shook against its frame, proving it was latched not locked. Once, twice, three times he rammed the door until it burst open like a startled mouth.

Torchlight poured in from the open door. He found her crumpled against the far wall. So pale...she looked broken. *"No!"* the cry keened out of him. Scooping her into his arms, he cradled her close. So cold, she felt like death. Fear spiked through him. He felt at her neck, desperate for a pulse. *Nothing!* But he refused to believe. Frantic fingers searched finding a faint pulse...so faint, yet she lived. He held her close, ambushed by his own relief. "Don't leave me," he breathed the words into her raven-dark hair, a prayer and a command. So pale, so cold, she lay still as death, her vibrancy snuffed like candle. He ached to see her this way. Gathering her close, Steffan carried her down the long winding stairs to the rear of the keep. Cultured marble turned to rough cut stone beneath his bare feet. He strode through the corridors with grim purpose, the Priestess clutched in his arms.

Startled guards rushed to open the bronze door, admitting a breath of chill night air. He carried her out into the faint starlight, steam billowing from the hot springs like a dragon's breath. Striding to the shallow end, he walked straight into the bubbling cauldron.

Hot water constricted his leather pants, binding him tight, but he cared only for her. Slowly, so slowly, he eased her cold body into the frothing heat. She made no sound, made no response. His heartbeat quickened, beseeching the gods. Cradling her head, he kept her face clear of the water. Steam rose around her, carrying the scent of brimstone. Her long dark hair floated like a nimbus around her pale white face. So beautiful yet she remained so still. *"Live! Breathe!"* He kissed her, forcing his breath into her mouth. Willing her to live, he held her for an eternity.

Her eyes flickered opened.

Relief coursed through him. "Don't leave me." He held her close, feeling the warmth return to her limbs, a touch of pink blooming in her cheeks...but her face remained gaunt, as if she'd been drained of life.

Gasping for breath, she gave him a wanton stare. Her hands clutched at him. "Need you...need you *now!*" Hungry fingers plucked at the binding of his pants. Her mouth closed on his, a desperately deep kiss, as if she meant suck the very essence from his soul.

Her insatiable hunger enflamed his ardor. Steffan shed his leathers like a snake shedding useless skin. Naked, he stood rampant and eager. Standing waist-deep in the frothing water, he pulled her close, the smell of brimstone billowing around them. She straddled him, her long legs wrapping around his waist. Drinking his gaze, she impaled herself upon him. And then he was deep in her, like a sword finding a moist sheath. He groaned in pleasure, grinding deep, wanting more.

She bucked against him, relentless with need. He answered, matching her rhythm. Her back arched, her dark hair flung wild around her face, her eyes closed, her perfect lips puckered in passion. Fingernails raked across his back, urging him on. Her whole body clenched his manhood, sucking him deeper into her womb, like nothing he'd ever felt. An unbearable ecstasy ripped through him. Twice he came, and still she rode him, making him last, keeping him stiff as steel. So powerful, so hard, he felt like a god mounting a goddess. Bellowing his pleasure, he spewed the last of his strength, collapsing backwards into the frothing water.

They separated, floating side by side.

Bubbles frothed around them, releasing the scent of brimstone, the heady scent of Hell.

Drained yet drunk on pleasure, Steffan floated on the water, staring at her, still smitten by the ecstasy. Vitality bloomed in her face, as if she'd come back from the grave, younger and more beautiful, yet her gaze was cold and forbidding. He struggled to understand. "What...was that?"

"Need...and the backwash of magic."

Magic, he mulled her words, *magic not love.* "I heard you scream. I feared you dead."

Something kindled in her gaze. "The Mordant found me."

Steffan sucked a sharp breath. "Here?"

"In the scrying bowl."

Scrying, so that was the source of her power. The woman was a riddle...a dangerous, ravishing riddle. "And?"

"The Mordant summoned me..."

Like a lackey, he read the words in the hatred blazing from her face. "And me?"

Her dark gaze considered him, caressed him, owned him. "Come with me."

Her gaze alone sizzled his soul. His manhood stirred. Having nearly lost her, he'd never let her go. "Yes." He'd chase her to Hell and back if needs be...but whether it was for lust, or love...or power, he did not know. "Where?"

"To Pellanor."

The name stung like a curse. Steffan snarled. "Why?"

"The Mordant is the oldest among us, the most powerful harlequin."

"So?" Steffan felt danger gathering around them, yet the gambler in him could not resist. "We serve only the Dark Lord."

"True, yet the oldest harlequin must be reckoned with. Favored by the Dark Lord, the Mordant is steeped in power." She gave him a sly smile. "Perhaps he grows too powerful. Our god is a jealous god. There is but one power in Hell...and that power does not share."

Steffan looked thoughtful. "So he baits the gods?"

"Perhaps."

"Then why go?"

Her smile deepened, dangerous and deadly. "For vengeance."

Her words quickened in his soul, summoning him to a quest...or laying a geas upon him...either way, vengeance was something he understood. He pulled her close, kissing her long and hard. "For vengeance"...*and for power*, though the second remained unspoken.

Her fingernails raked across his chest, her kisses trailing down his neck igniting a line of fire. A primal need roared through him, lust mixed with love. Steffan wanted this woman...but he also wanted power. In the depths of his soul, he wondered if he could have both.

In the North

42

Katherine

Kath paced the highest ramparts, staring out at the endless white, a gauntlet of killing cold. *Winter subverted to evil, harnessed as a lethal guardian*...only the Mordant could make winter his slave. It explained why the oldest harlequin chose to reside in the far north. Kath shivered at the thought, daunted by the dark logic. The Citadel, like its master, was formidable in more ways than one. Crenellated battlements spiraling to a dizzying height, the dark fortress cast a long shadow across the winter-bound steppes. Conquering the Citadel should have felt triumphant, instead it tasted of ashes, bitter in her mouth, for the Citadel was empty, her true enemy long gone. And the price...she could not think of the price, better to think of her foe. Somewhere in the south, the Mordant worked his will upon Erdhe, yet she was stuck in his fortress, trapped by winter. Without even trying, the Mordant had outmaneuvered her. The realization galled her. Kicking ice from the rampart, she gripped the crystal dagger, feeling like a caged wolf.

It did not help that the others pecked at her with a thousand questions, a thousand decisions that seemed paltry and quarrelsome. A gaggle of painted warriors and citadel citizens lurked on the far side of the rune-carved courtyard, awaiting an audience. They gathered like starving geese, before the impotent sun barely cracked the chilly sky. Kath scowled, sending them a sideways glance meant to discourage. Ripe with petitions and endless problems, they formed a trap of another sort. Death by a thousand details, their problems could wait. Kath turned a resolute stare towards the frozen steppes, obsessed with finding a way south.

A fresh stare speared her.

Kath turned to find Zith waddling towards her. Swathed in so many sheepskins, the monk actually looked fat. She wondered what need had drawn him from his mountain of scrolls. Feeling stubborn, she waited, letting the monk come to her.

His breath puffed into the cold like a bellows. Drawing near, his gaze was full of reproach. "Put your grief aside."

His words hit hard. Kath closed her eyes, as if she could shutter her soul. She'd never spoken of her marriage to Duncan, yet the monk had wise eyes, shrewd eyes.

"You shirk your duties."

His words hit below the belt. "My *duties?*" Her frustration erupted like a lanced boil. "I'm not meant to be here! I need to get south!"

His face softened. "True, for all of Erdhe depends on it."

The weight on her shoulders multiplied.

"You've conquered the north and now you must rule it."

Kath slumped against the rampart. "The painted people can rule. The Citadel is theirs to keep."

"You are their Svala. Till you find a way south, you must rule." Zith gestured towards the petitioners huddled on the far side. "They expect it of you."

Kath felt a second trap closing around her, tight as a noose.

"Your victory of swords will be for naught if you do not change the north."

His comment cut close to the bone, too close. "What do you mean?"

"Taming a city is a thorny problem, so different from conquering it. Instead of slicing the knot with a sword, you must find a way to untangle it, weaving something new from the strands...something different, something better, something stronger." Zith gave her a solemn look. "Power is more than just swords."

Kath had never sought any power save the sword. She fingered her sword hilt, wondering what Queen Liandra would do.

"In the scrolls of history, conquerors come and go, little more than passing plagues...unless they change those they conquer. You cannot stay, for your destiny lies in the south, but you can make a great difference while you are here."

Kath chewed on his words, finding much food for thought.

Zith leaned towards her, his voice dropping to a whisper. "And while you untangle the Citadel's thorny knots, you will learn the ways of your enemy, for this fortress is a reflection of the Mordant's will, his Dark intent."

Learn the ways of your enemy. Kath looked at the Citadel with fresh eyes. She gave the monk a rueful smile, resolved to untangling the knot. "Just so."

Zith gave her a shrewd look. "You are meant to rule."

When she tried to protest, he stilled her with his stare.

"Born in Castlegard, yet you were forbidden the sword. Despite a multitude of obstacles, you learned the way of warrior and now you've conquered the north." His gaze drilled into her. "Born a girl, you were never raised to wear a crown, yet it is in your blood to rule."

A shiver raced down Kath's spine, the spectral finger of an undreamt destiny. *Castlegard,* the very name rang in her soul, yet she shook her head, denying the scant hope. "The maroon will never be ruled by a woman." Bitterness rode her words.

"By your deeds you will be known."

Her frustration boiled over. "None in the south even know of our victory, and worse yet, none will believe it. None save Blaine, and one knight is not enough."

"The future has yet to unfold."

"You speak in riddles."

"Life is a riddle till you put meaning to it." Zith leaned towards her, his face stern. "You must deal with the Citadel. Wits and heart enabled you to win the north, not just your sword." His voice dropped to a harsh whisper. "Rule the same. Grasp your destiny. Dare to rule...and rule well."

She'd never thought to rule, yet she'd always longed to lead...perhaps the two were the same. An immense weight settled on her shoulders. "I will need your advice."

"As long as I live, you shall have it." He gave her a solemn bow.

"Thank you." Kath smothered her rising emotions with a simple question. "And what of you and your scrolls?"

The monk shrugged. "I've mountains to read and little time in which to do it." A troubled look crossed his careworn face. "But a worrisome pattern is emerging. Many of the scrolls deal with soul magic...and mage-stone."

"Mage-stone?" Her thoughts flashed to Castlegard.

Zith nodded. "The Mordant seems obsessed with mage-stone, collecting every scroll and scrap of parchment he can find on the subject."

"To make it?"

"No, to break it."

Fear spiked through her. "Can he?"

"What the Mordant cannot control, he seeks to destroy, but mage-stone has proven impervious through the ages, a secret only the Kiralynn monks could wield."

Zith's words were meant to be reassuring but a nagging doubt plagued her.

"The scrolls make one thing certain. The history of Erdhe is very different when written by the Dark."

Steel laced her voice. "Then we cannot let the Dark write it."

"Just so."

"Keep searching the scrolls, for we'll need every insight and advantage you can glean." Kath gripped the monk's arm, intensity in her touch. "We each fight the Dark in our own way. Perhaps something in the scrolls will lead to the Mordant's undoing." Straightening her shoulders, she crossed the courtyard, determined to untangle the evil of the Citadel and fashion something new.

43

Katherine

Kath trudged across the great rune-carved courtyard, her maroon band at her back. A cold wind battered against her, flaring her maroon cloak and freezing her breath to frost. Winter held the Citadel in thrall. Despite the bitter cold, Kath was determined to hold court beneath the open sky, as if exposure to the sun's light could solve the Citadel's thorny problems.

Talbert and Conit, two badger-faced lads were busy laying out sheepskins and feeding peat to the braziers. Flames crackled and snapped, throwing off a welcome heat. Greeting the two boys, Kath sat cross-legged on a thick sheepskin, setting her back to the black ramparts, a shield against the knife-sharp wind. Pulling a second sheepskin across her shoulders, she sat hunched, hoarding her warmth. Bear sat to her left, Sidhorn on her right, both men looming large as woolly bears. The rest of her maroon band sat in a crescent around the fire. Her painted warriors shunned chairs, preferring to sit on the open ground. Kath supposed it was a malady of cave dwellers, or perhaps a lack of wood, either way, she complied with their custom.

Conit produced a wicker basket stuffed with great wheels of bread almost as large as small shields. Kath tore a large chunk before passing it on. Brown bread laden with nuts and raisins, still warm from the oven, Kath savored the honest fare. Mugs of heated honeyed mead made the rounds, an added warmth to chase away the winter chill. Huddled around the brazier, her maroon band shared bread and mead while talking of small things. Kath savored the companionship of warriors. As they broke their fast, the dawn's light finally cracked the cloud-strewn sky, seagulls wheeling overhead. The tepid sun rose late in the north, as if it feared to show its face.

All too soon, they finished the meal, a signal for the petitioners to start their stormy deluge.

"*Svala, they come.*" Beside her, Bear whispered a warning.

A few started across the courtyard, but then the petitioners hung back as leaders of the painted warriors swaggered through their midst. Mountain lion, eagle, bear, boar, wolf, fox, badger, hawk and owl, a menagerie of proud predators stared from their tattooed faces. Studded with weapons, they wore a haphazard mix of sheepskins, leathers, and dark armor. Captured breastplates, black cloaks, and dark helms inscribed with pentacles proved the painted people survived the steppes as scavengers. But instead of dented heirlooms, they boasted polished armor embellished with gold. As conquerors of the Citadel, they'd gained much to choose from. Bristling with fresh-won weapons, their captured finery suited their fierce pride.

Kath stood, her hand on her sword hilt, studying their faces. All were comrades-in-arms, but a few she also called friend. Royce led the pack, a big lion-faced man with a wild mane of auburn hair. Gold glinted on his breastplate, the captured armor of a dead general. Fanggold's armor was nearly as ornate, a jeweled helm on his head. Aware of her scrutiny, the wolf-faced war leader gave her a savage grin, showing off his captured finery.

"Svala," Royce gave no sign of deference beyond the use of her battle-won title, "we have come to parley with the War Helm."

So it was to be a formal meeting, Kath nodded assent. "The words of warriors are ever welcome. Join my fire."

The others sat, completing the circle around the fire, a clink of armor and weapons.

"Svala," Royce met her stare across the brazier, "you have led us to a great victory."

"A great victory," the others echoed their agreement.

"Long have we lived in the Citadel's shadow, always outnumbered, always harried by dark soldiers, but now we rule the steppes!" Royce thumped his chest and the men rumbled agreement. "We've gained a victory worthy of legends, fame enough for every warrior." The men hurrahed and Royce smiled. "And we've gained a bounty of plunder, new arms and armor for every man."

"And the wine's good too." Fanggold gave a loud burp, a sign of deep satisfaction. "And the women are most willing." He flashed a rogue's grin.

The men laughed, pounding Fanggold on the back, but Royce stilled them with a raised hand. "Plunder and pleasure are a warrior's due, but too much of it will dull the sword and addle the mind." His face turned solemn. "We've gained a victory long dreamt but never believed. Svala, we've come to ask if you still wear the War Helm?"

Kath froze, caught by the weight of the question.

Royce leaned forward, his voice intent. "Will you lead us to war, Svala, or will you put the War Helm aside to rule the Citadel?"

To rule the Citadel, how little they understood. She stared at their tattooed faces, searching for the right words. "We took the Citadel to cripple the Mordant, to rid the north of his shadow. The Citadel belongs to the painted people."

"Huzzah!"

The men cheered their victory, clashing weapons against armor, but she stilled them with a raised hand. "The Citadel was taken not as a spoil of war, but as a second home." She stared at them, conviction in her gaze. "It is yours to rule. My destiny lies in the south."

"The *south!*" Uneasy mutters rumbled through the warriors, "But what of the War Helm?"

Kath sensed her painted warriors were as restless with victory as she was. "The War Helm is still mine."

Their stares fixed on her.

"You've taken the Dark Citadel but not its ruler. The victory is not complete till the Mordant lies dead."

"But the bastard's gone south."

"He fled the citadel, afraid to face our swords."

Kath raised a hand, quelling them. "He marched his army south to attack the southern kingdoms."

Ringol, the fox-faced leader snarled. "The southern kingdoms are naught to us." Many nodded their agreement.

She challenged them with a question. "Do you know why we won?"

Tarmin, the owl-faced warrior was quick to answer, "Bravery."

Another shouted, "Courage."

"Daring."

"The favor of the gods."

Fanggold flashed a toothy grin. "Because we have a bloody lot of sheep and too much audacity!"

The men roared with laughter, comrades-in-arms, reveling in the sweet glow of a victory they'd never dreamt possible.

"All that you say is true, but it is not the reason we won." Kath let them chew on her words, waiting till they leaned forward, hungry for an answer. "We won because the Mordant *disdained* the painted people." She rubbed salt in the wound. "He *scorned* your swords." Venomous looks darted between tattooed faces, but Kath persisted, driving the sword point home. "The Mordant emptied the Citadel of soldiers because he did not see the painted people as a threat. He did not *fear* you."

Anger rumbled among them. "The bastard insults us."

"He belittles our victory."

"He shames our swords."

Ringol thumped his chest. "Yet *we* sleep in *his* city and eat *his* stores while *his* women warm *our* beds."

"It is not enough," Fanggold snarled. "He has no honor."

Angry murmurs swirled through the leaders.

Royce raised a hand to still the others. "Svala, what will you have of us?"

Kath waited till quiet prevailed, and then she unsheathed the crystal dagger, raising it to the heavens. Sunlight glinted on the crystalline blade. "This dagger is meant for the dark heart of the Mordant. I'll not rest till it finds its true sheath."

The men cheered, weapons clashing against bucklers.

"Svala," Royce raised his voice above the din, "give us the chance to make the victory complete. Lead us to war, for we'll follow you to the end!"

The men stood, weapons raised, shouting a great cheer. "*Svala! Svala!*"

Tears crowded her eyes, awestruck that such fierce warriors believed in her when so many others did not...not even her own father. For a handful of heartbeats, she reveled in their acclaim, but then she raised her voice above the tumult. "I see you! I know your true strength, your courage, your unfettered daring! The painted warriors are a force to be reckoned with! You are the sword hidden in the north! The Mordant scorns you at his peril!"

They cheered her words. Others from across the courtyard came to swell the throng.

Someone shouted, "Svala! We'll follow you to the ends of the Erdhe!"

She raised her voice to a shout. "I will find a way to lead you south, for the greatest victory is yet to come. But you must never follow a leader to the end."

They stilled, their stares full of puzzlement.

"Good leaders find a way to new beginnings, not endings. Follow me to a new beginning, to an Erdhe forever free of the Mordant's shadow!"

They cheered her then, drunk on thoughts of victory. She let them celebrate, but when their revelry subsided, she spoke. "Who among you knows a way to cross the steppes in winter?"

"Cross to the south?"

She nodded, holding her breath.

Dark looks passed among them. Finally Royce spoke. "Winter is the season of the caves. To cross the steppes in winter is to court death."

It was just as she thought, trapped in the Citadel while the Mordant worked his will upon the south. A crushing weight pressed against her, yet she faced the leaders with iron resolve. "Those who would follow me south must be prepared to leave at a moment's notice. Each warrior must gather two moonturns worth of rations and must keep his weapons sharp. Any belongings must fit within a single sack. When we leave, we'll travel light and fast."

They nodded their assent.

"And I'll not deprive the north of protection. One in every four warriors must stay behind to guard what we've gained." She spoke over their protests. "Lose the Citadel and our victory is for naught." Kath drilled them with her stare. "Glory resides in holding the north as well as going south. You must decide who will stay and who will go."

Her words raised a whirlwind of arguments. Finally Royce spoke for the others. "It will be as you say, Svala."

They took their leave, warriors planning their next campaign.

She'd given them much to think about, but anxiety rode her shoulders. She'd kept her army, but somehow she had to find a way south. Kath stared at the winter-locked steppes, beseeching the gods for help.

44

General Haith

Screams ripped through the tent, proving the torturers plied their work well, yet the answers he sought were slow in coming. Impatient, the general followed the screams across the sullied field. A pair of guards leaped to hold the canvas flap aside. General Haith strode from winter directly into hell. The sudden heat was striking, oppressive with the stink of voided bowels and heated metal, fear ripe with the scent of blood, smells he'd long learned to endure in the service of the Mordant.

The torturer snapped to attention, a pair of bloody tongs in his gloved fist, but the prisoner had fallen insensate. Naked and spread-eagled, the knight was strapped upright to a metal frame, the torturer's brutal work written upon his flesh.

"Rouse him."

"Yes, m'lord." The torturer doused a bucket of dirty water over the prisoner's head.

The knight sputtered, licking his bloody lips. One eye was swollen shut but the other roved the tent, fixing on the general. His body stiffened, his nostrils flaring in fear.

"Yes, you recognize my armor if not my face." He'd taken to wearing the breastplate of the Skeleton King, a formidable armor steeped in fear. "The time has come for answers."

"Told you...what I know."

"Not enough, not nearly enough." The general inspected the table laden with torture devices, pincers, saws, screws, brands, knives, a pear of anguish, and a particularly nasty corkscrew. "So far, you've only felt the torturer's kiss, enough pain to hurt but nothing dismembered. Speak now and you'll avoid this sordid nastiness, gaining a soldier's quick death."

"Death? That's all you offer?"

"You'll beg for it before Bruthus is done."

The knight sagged upon the rack. "I know."

"Then tell me what I want to know. Where is the main camp?"

"Always moving, the marshal...keeps us moving."

The octagon king was dead, he'd seen the traitor knight strike the killing blow, but this marshal was proving a capable leader, as elusive as a winter fox. "If you're always moving, how do you get your supplies?"

"Scouts."

"What else?"

The knight scowled. "Axe cuts on the trees, marks the trail."

Axe marks, an ingenious but infuriating solution. If he sent his men looking for axe marks on trees he'd lose them to the wooded wilderness. The Dragon Spine Mountains were proving a tangled fortress of trails and crags. His force had the superior numbers yet he could not bring them to bear for the killing blow. "I need more than that, or I cannot spare you."

The knight stiffened. "Nothing else to tell."

"Is your honor worth the pain?"

The knight said nothing, but fear quaked across his face.

"Honor is a ruse. A hollow coin paid to dupes. Don't die a dupe."

"Damn you to hell!"

The general chuckled. "How little you understand. Hell is coming to Erdhe, and I shall sit among the ruling lords." His voice turned hard. "So will you serve or be damned by your silence?"

The knight remained mute, sweat erupting on his skin.

"So be it." The general flicked a glance to the torturer. "Ply your trade without constraints." The screams started before he even stepped from the tent. The general crossed the muddied field to the command pavilion. Guards leaped to hold the canvas aside as he strode into luxury. Thick wool carpets cushioned his boots, braziers giving off a welcoming heat scented with cedar chips...but he could still hear the screams.

His officers snapped to attention, standing around a table strewn with brightly colored maps.

General Marris said, "What word?"

"None yet, but it won't be long." Striding to the map table, General Haith accepted a goblet of mulled wine.

General Marris scowled. "We've had so few prisoners to work with."

"A poor excuse," yet it was the truth. The octagon tended to take their wounded with them...or give them the mercy stroke. He stared down at the map, a warren of mountains guarded by stone keeps. "What word from Dymtower and Cragnoth Keep?"

General Marris answered, "Empty. Ransacked of men, weapons, and food."

General Haith nodded. "Why guard the back door when the main gate's been breached? I'll wager the other keeps are the same," he traced a finger west, along the mountains to the inked image of a great castle shaped like an octagon, "except for Castlegard. They must be getting supplies from Castlegard."

"Will you order a siege?"

"We haven't the time. We need to trap them in the mountains and finish it." His gaze snapped to Centurion Kirkbee. "What word from the Taal cadre?"

"Nothing yet, but if the octagon takes the bait, the Taals will smash them."

Traps within traps, yet so far, the prey proved elusive. His gaze sought Centurion Erlint. "What of the farms and holdfasts?"

"We've sent patrols ranging along the Snowmelt, seeking their holdfasts. Farms and villages are stripped of supplies and their livestock slaughtered for food. I've ordered the men and children crucified, while the women are brought back as spoils of war." The centurion flashed a lurid grin. "Our soldiers have been most appreciative."

The general nodded. "Yes, the men must have their spoils, but I half expected the knights to come to the villagers' aid."

"No sign of them, my lord...but a few of the holdfasts were empty, as if they'd been warned."

"And their supplies?"

"Gone."

The general glowered. "You disappoint me, Erlint."

The centurion stood braced at attention.

"Perhaps I should have you crucified as an example to my officers."

Sweat beaded on the centurion's face but he had the good sense not to beg. Perhaps Erlint was worth keeping, something to consider.

A gruesome scream pierced the pavilion, halting the discussion.

"Perhaps the answers I need will finally be forthcoming." General Haith sipped his mulled wine, a flavorful vintage from the dead king's stores.

As if summoned, the master torturer appeared at the pavilion's entrance. Gore stained his leather apron. "My Lord, I have your answer."

"Come."

Bruthus took a single step into the pavilion and then stopped, as if he knew his reek was offensive. "My lord, the knight spoke the truth when he said the marshal keeps them moving, changing camps every third night...but he neglected to speak of the gathering place."

His interest spiked. "What gathering place?"

"A place to gather patrols, scouts, and stragglers with the main force."

"And where is this place?"

"At the dark of the moon, they're to meet at the Stone Hand."

"Well done." Dismissing the torturer, he turned to the maps. "Where is this Stone Hand?"

"Here, my Lord." Centurion Kirkbee pointed to a balding mountain overlooking Raven Pass.

"So close?" The general's voice purred with satisfaction.

"It's been used before as a campsite, but it was deserted when we found it, nothing but trampled snow, horse dung, and cold campfires."

"Why is it called Stonehand?"

The centurion hesitated. "At the crest, there's a mage-stone statue, a giant stone hand inscribed with a Seeing Eye."

"The meddling monks." He made the words a curse. His hand sought the amulet hidden beneath his armor, a key to wealth and power. "By war's end, both the Octagon and the Seeing Eye will be eradicated from Erdhe."

"The Mordant's will be done." His officers intoned their assent.

General Marris said, "Three days till the dark of the moon. Will you take them with a direct assault or an ambush?"

"An ambush, the Lord Mordant ordered a quiet annihilation." His gaze settled on the centurion. "Kirkbee, take a cadre of Taals around to the back side of the mountain. You will be the hammer to our anvil."

Kirkbee saluted, fist to his breastplate. "As you command."

"Come the dark of the moon, the Octagon will be finished. See to the details and make it so." He dismissed his officers. Saluting, they took their leave, while he remained staring at the map. The Mordant had crafted a convoluted plan to shatter Erdhe and bring age-old enemies to their knees, but the timing was delicate. Soon he'd ride south to face a far more lucrative foe. By the time this war was finished, he expected to be a king in his own right, a vassal sovereign serving his lord. The general stretched his gauntleted hand across the map, casting a grasping shadow across Erdhe. "The Dark Lord's will be done."

45

Katherine

Word of her court had leaped like lightning through the Citadel. Petitioners appeared before the crack of dawn, braving the frigid cold for a chance to beg boons. Kath crossed the rune-carved courtyard, feeling the incessant peck of their stares, but their endless demands would have to wait.

Conit and Talbert scrambled to lay out sheepskins and stoke the braziers for heat. Kath sat cross-legged with her back to the dark rampart. The morning meal with her maroon band had become a welcome habit. Giant wheels of fresh-baked bread were shared, sometimes laced with raisins, dried apples, crushed nuts, or other treasures from the royal kitchens. Kath tore off a warm chunk, delighted to discover cinnamon swirling through the tasty loaf. Pots of honey for dipping along with mugs of heated mead were passed. Her painted warriors enjoyed the simple fare, sharing jests and tales of daring. All too soon the last crumb was consumed and the mugs drained. Kath gestured to Sidhorn and the big warrior stood to turn the massive sand glass. Cast in solid gold, with dragons entwining the handles, the great glass held blood-red sand brought from some nameless shore. Seeking a way to limit the onslaught, Kath had ordered the great glass brought out to the courtyard. The glass held enough sand in each turn to measure a session of three hours, the limit of her patience for dealing with petitioners.

The turning of the great sand glass released the deluge of petitioners.

Surging across the courtyard, they all spoke at once, uttering a babble of demands.

Her maroon band moved to impose order, reforming the line.

One at a time the petitioners stepped before Kath to state their case. Some wore silken finery while others came clad in a mismatch of scavenged clothing. Kath listened to them all, regardless of wealth or tier. The deluge of petitions ran the gamut from petty quarrels, to petitions for favors, to appeals for the restoration of 'stolen' property, to grim accusations of rape, murder, and collusion with priests. The rogue priests remained a thorny problem. Kath passed any informants to Blaine and his band, but it shocked her to hear how some citizens secretly succored the priests. She'd hoped the citizens of the Citadel would renounce the Mordant, choosing a new way of life, but evil had a way of infesting souls. Many who'd prospered under the pentacle preferred the old ways, choosing bribery and backstabbing to honest labor. Some made it a game to deceive her. At first, many got the better of her, but Kath soon learned that the most corrupt were also the most skilled liars. Lies became the telltale sign of a deeper evil. Once their lies were ferreted out, Kath overturned her decisions, invoking harsh penalties, yet still they tried. Sometimes she despaired, wondering if the Citadel could truly be saved.

A fat merchant bowed low, launching into a tale of stolen goods.

Listening to the endless drone, Kath strove to sort the truth from the fawning tangle of deception. A disturbance snared her attention. The line of petitioners parted, revealing a delegation of raven-faced healers. Led by Thera, they strode towards her, beaks and feathers boldly tattooed across their faces.

The fat merchant fell silent, relinquishing his place with a grudging bow.

Kath flashed a smile towards Thera. "Welcome to my fire."

The healers stood in a crescent before the brazier. Most wore sheepskin cloaks and leather breeches, herb pouches dangling from their belts, long knives belted to their sides.

Kath met Thera's dark gaze, worried by the healer's grave demeanor. "How do the wounded fare?"

"We do what we can. But the healing is slow, too slow." Concern weighed her voice. "Wounds that should heal continue to fester and fevers linger refusing to quench. It is almost as if something thwarts our lore."

The courtyard quaked, as if the demons locked in the depths bragged of their prowess.

Kath cast a sharp glance towards Thera. "You feel it too."

Thera nodded. "All the healers sense it, like a foul curse infesting the Citadel."

Merrick, a tall gangly healer who served as Thera's second, sketched the sign of warding. "This place is unclean; we should never have come here."

Thera stilled him with a glance, her gaze returning to Kath. "We've come to ask the Svala for the captured horses."

"*No!*" Blaine's protest cut sharp as his sword. "Those horses are our best chance to reach the south!"

Kath silenced him with a stern look, yet his words fell like stones on her shoulders. In truth, the horses were her best means to get south, but Danya and Zith would never survive the distance, and none of her painted warriors could ride. And then there was the winter. The god-cursed steppes were most treacherous in winter, a frozen killing field, winter's cruel anvil. The horses were not the answer, yet she saw no other way.

Thera pressed her appeal. "With horse drawn travois we can move the wounded back to the home caves, giving them a better chance to heal."

Blaine loosed an angry snarl. "We *need* those horses."

Furious, Kath rounded on him. "Winter trumps the horses." *And the thrice-damned cold shows no sign of abating.*

"So you'll just sit here, waiting till the spring thaw? By then there will be nothing left to save!"

Kath gaped at Blaine, outraged by his words. Recovering, she met his anger with a flinty stare. "And if we don't help the wounded, how will the gods judge us?"

This time Blaine looked away.

Sighing, Kath sent a silent appeal to Valin. Turning to Thera, she said, "Take the horses and anything else you need."

Blaine turned his back to her, radiating anger, but Thera gave her a knowing nod, as if she understood the cost of her request. "The Svala is worthy of the War Helm."

The healers stood to leave, but Kath stayed them with a question. "What of Danya?"

Thera's face softened. "Danya's sleep is a matter of magic, not healing. The wolf-girl pays a price for her power. Only time will tell."

Kath nodded, knowing the answer but needing to ask.

"Neven and his pack have claimed Danya for their own. They take good care of her."

"I thought as much, but it helps to hear you say it."

"The wolf-girl will wake in due time." Thera gathered her healers, retreating across the vast circular courtyard.

Kath watched them leave, troubled by their message, more proof that evil was real. Staring across the rune-carved courtyard, she wondered if the fortress-city could ever be cleansed. Her hand sought the crystal dagger. She'd taken the Mordant's stronghold but she'd meant to take his life. Rage warred with frustration; she could not afford to be trapped in the north, yet she saw no way south.

The fat merchant resumed his place, bemoaning the loss of stolen goods and ruined property.

Such a petty problem, Kath found it hard to concentrate, yet she forced herself to listen.

The sound of a horn shivered through the frozen air.

The mournful wail sounded...like a call to battle.

Kath sprang to her feet, her hand on her sword hilt. "Did you hear that?"

The horn sounded again, a blaring challenge.

Kath leaped atop the nearest rampart, gazing down on the Citadel's gates and out across the endless expanse, but the vast snowbound steppes remained bleak and cold, unsullied by the tread of friend or foe.

The horn sounded again, impatient to be noticed.

Grenfir joined her on the rampart. The owl-faced warrior gasped, pointing towards the wind-swept sea. "A ship!"

Kath saw it then, a single ship scudding across the white-waved ocean. *The sea,* she'd never considered escape by sea. Kath's heart thundered, "Whose ship? Friend or foe?" She stared at the ship, searching for a sigil.

Blaine joined her on the rampart. "There!"

The ship changed course, the front sail billowing taut with the wind, its colors bright against the slate-gray ocean. Red and blue checks emblazoned with a soaring osprey, a proud sigil unlooked for in the bitter north. Kath grinned in wild relief, feeling the succor of the gods. "Valin hasn't abandoned us!" She thumped Blaine on the shoulder. "Hope comes on southern sails! *Navarre!* A ship from *Navarre!*"

46

The Knight Marshal

The knight marshal crossed the slaughter field, holding his horse to a walk. A putrid stench rose from the gore. *Sixty ogres slain by one squire,* it was a prodigious feat, nigh on impossible, the stuff of ancient legends. Surveying the carnage, the marshal had no doubt that Baldwin had saved the maroon...yet the field held a dark warning. *Not just slain but slaughtered.* Entrails and innards smeared the sullied snow, raising a puking stench. Severed limbs and cleaved heads sat stacked in a grisly pyramid, blood and gore painting gruesome spatters upon the trampled snow. Even the ravens shunned the dead, as if the corpses were tainted. He'd fought on many battlefields, but never in his long years of service had he seen one like this, as if the lords of Hell had come calling. *Not just slain, not just slaughtered...but butchered.* The marshal shivered at the thought, making the hand sign against evil.

Reaching the far side, he turned for one last look. His gaze sought Sir Abrax lying wrapped in his maroon cloak. A good friend and a stalwart champion felled by the king's squire, a tragedy cloaked in arcane treachery. It hurt to leave his friend lying upon the bloody field, but the maroon could neither spare the time nor the strength to raise a cairn over every dead hero. The marshal saluted his friend, his fist thumping his armored breastplate. "By Valin, you shall be remembered."

Turning his horse away, he led the long line of maroon knights back into the woods. Time was against them. Despite his mount's weariness, he urged his warhorse to a trot, desperate for distance. The maroon needed to escape before the circling ravens enticed the enemy.

Sunlight quenched to crimson, setting the mountain peaks aglow. In the waning light, he followed a faint trail around the backside of the mountain. The ice-encrusted Dragon Spines loomed in every direction. Fierce and jagged, the jumbled mountains had proved a boon, hiding the maroon in a labyrinth of trails and valleys, a bulwark against the enemy...but the mountains also took their toll. Cold and bleak and desolate, he'd lost too many men to frostbite and hunger. He longed for a warm bed snug behind stout walls, a pine log fire crackling in the hearth, a goblet of mulled wine in his hand...the marshal shook himself awake. Straightening in the saddle, he lifted his visor exposing his face to the wind's biting-cold slap, yet he could not banish the nagging aches pervading his battered body. Everything hurt. A deep bone-weariness bludgeoned him, slumping his shoulders. Too many battles in too short a time, he was getting too old for this.

Wield me!

The marshal startled alert.

Wield me!

An insidious voice hissed in his mind. A cold certainty gripped him, *the dark sword!* Bundled in furs and tied to his cantle, he wasn't even touching the dark-damned blade, yet it preyed on his mind like a curse. Desperate to snuff the voice, he built a mental wall, images of stone and mortar, yet still the vile whisper invaded.

Wield me now!

He felt like vomiting.

Wield me and victory shall be yours!

"No!"

"No...nooo...noooo!" The marshal's shout echoed against the mountaintops.

A thunder of hooves galloped from behind. Lothar pulled rein on his left, Sir Rannock on his right. Weapons bared, they scanned the forest. "What is it?"

Chagrined, the marshal muttered, "Nothing." Regaining his composure, he made his voice firm. "Stand down."

Sir Rannock saluted, but Lothar threw a skeptical look his way.

His friend saw too much, but thankfully he kept his questions for another time.

Shrugging his shoulders, Lothar sheathed his battleaxe. "We're all war weary, flinching at shadows." He flicked a glance towards the darkening sky. "Nearly the dark of the moon."

"Just so. Time to make for Stonehand."

"How many do you think we'll gather?"

"That's the question, isn't it?" Since the bitter loss at Raven Pass, Stonehand had become the maroon's secret gathering place. On every dark of the moon, the war host returned to the great mage-stone statue, a chance to gather lost scouts and missing patrols, to gain supplies from Castlegard and to bolster the strength of the maroon. His men needed food and rest, but most of all they needed reinforcements.

The marshal turned to stare at his friend, the truth bitter upon his lips. "However many come, it will not be enough. Not nearly enough." The marshal spurred his horse to a canter, but he could not escape the dark whispers slithering through his mind.

47

Katherine

Kath stood atop the rampart watching the ship, but instead of turning towards the Citadel, the brightly checkered sails changed course. The ship zigzagged back and forth across the bay, as if taunting the Citadel.

Beside her, Blaine said, "What are they doing?"

Kath studied the ship, noting the way it kept a wary distance. With fresh eyes, she stared down at the Citadel. The fearsome fortress overshadowed the bay, tiers of crenellated battlements studded with trebuchets and catapults. The Mordant's black and gold banners were long gone, cut loose to ride the wind, but nothing replaced them. Kath had no banner and neither did the painted people. The Mordant's Citadel was conquered, yet from a distance it looked the same, a forbidding fortress of dark stone bristling with menace. "They're testing the Citadel."

"What?"

"They're hoping for friends but they fear a foe." Unclasping her cloak, Kath pressed the maroon wool into Grenfir's hands. "Take this and wave it upon the ramparts. We need to signal the ship."

"Yes, Svala." Grenfir leaped to the battlement, waving Kath's maroon cloak high above his head like a battle banner.

"Blaine, your cloak! Give it to Tangor."

The badger-faced warrior joined Grenfir on the battlement. Yelling and jumping, they waved the cloaks, desperate to be seen.

Kath stared at the ship, willing it closer, yet it stubbornly veered back and forth, scudding across the bay at a wary distance. "It's not enough." She pounded the dark rampart with her fist. "They don't see our cloaks...or they don't trust them." A sudden fear gripped her, knowing she dared not let this one hope pass by. Somehow she needed to lure the ship to shore, yet it held its position, sailing a trebuchet's throw from the dark coastline. *A trebuchet's throw,* the idea teased her mind. Kath peered over the rampart to the tier below. Satisfied, she turned back to the others, her voice ringing with command. "Grenfir and Tangor keep waving those cloaks like your lives depend on it." Kath's gaze found the two badger-faced boys. "Talbert and Conit run and get fresh baskets of bread and bring them to that trebuchet." She pointed to the tier below. "And be quick about it. Run as if your lives depend on it!"

The two boys set off at a hard run.

"The rest of you come with me." Leaping from the rampart, Kath raced across the courtyard, scattering petitioners like wolves through a sheep herd. Blaine and her maroon band pounded at her heels, a jangle of arms and armor. They burst through the ruined gate, following the curving street down and around into the lower tier. People turned and stared, some shouting questions, but Kath never slowed. She led them to the west side, to the first trebuchet overlooking the ocean. "This will do."

Her painted warriors gathered around.

"Do any of you know how this works?"

Blank stares answered her. Kath realized it was a silly question, but she had to try. "Fine, we'll just have to figure it out." She'd watched trebuchets hurl rocks from Castlegard's walls, but she'd never done it herself, and this trebuchet seemed different, bigger and far more intimidating. Crouched like a wooden dragon upon the rampart, the trebuchet had a long arm angled skyward. A leather sling on a rope dangled from the top. The sixty-foot arm was attached to a heavy tripod frame linked to a massive counterweight. Within the frame sat a large caged wheel, like the wheel of a millhouse turned on its side. "First we have to lower the arm." She considered the contraption. "Bear and Sidhorn, stand in the wheel and start walking."

Questioning looks flashed her way, but both warriors obeyed. Gingerly climbing into the wheel, the big men began to walk. Surprise lit their faces when the wheel began to turn.

"That's it! Keep walking." The massive contraption creaked and groaned. Shards of ice rained down as the great wooden beast came to life. The levered arm descended while the heavy counterweight slowly rose. Kath studied the trebuchet, knowing she was missing something. Twice she circled the huge contraption. "There has to be a pin somewhere."

Fanggold searched the far side, hefting a thick iron rod secured to a length of rope. "Is this it, Svala?"

The rod looked like a giant's knitting needle. "Yes!" She took the pin, watching as the great arm sank lower. When it reached the base, she rammed the pin into the aligning holes to lock the arm. "Stop walking and get out!" Sidhorn and Bear scrambled from the great wheel.

The two badger-faced lads appeared. Red-faced and puffing plumes of mist, they carried baskets laden with great wheels of bread.

"Talbert! Load a round of bread into the sling."

"The bread, Svala?"

"Just do it!"

The boy scurried to obey.

"Everyone step back."

The trebuchet sat coiled with tension, like a deadly dragon poised to strike. She'd heard terrible stories of trebuchets flying apart, killing everyone who stood near. Stepping as far away as possible, Kath whispered a fervent prayer to Valin and then she yanked the rope on the restraining pin. The iron pin pulled free.

For half a heartbeat, the trebuchet shuddered...then the great counterweight came whomping down with a bone-jarring thud. The long arm swooped upward with a raptor's speed. The counterweight struck bottom, stopping the arm at the top of its arc. Yanked by the arm, the sling cracked like a whip, swinging upward with lightning speed, hurling the wheel of bread out across the ocean.

Gaping at the trebuchet's fearsome strength, Kath rushed to the rampart with the others.

Holding her breath, she watched the great bread wheel tumble out across the sea. It stuck the gray waves with a splash, disappearing into the depths. The others cheered but Kath knew they'd only half succeeded. She stared at the ocean, gauging the distance between the bread's splash and the sailing ship. "Again! We need to do it again!"

48

Juliana

The *Sea Sprite* sailed off the charts into rumor-drenched seas. Juliana had never sailed this far north. No ship from Navarre ever did, for the north held no profit, only terrible risks and a creeping dread. The risks came in many forms, from tricky currents and dangerous shoals to raging tempests and savage MerChanter raiders. The creeping dread came from ancient legend and whispered lore. Sailors deep in their cups spoke of a cursed sea roiling with monster kraken, deadly whirlpools, and a ghost fleet that lurked in a living mist. Juliana paid scant attention to the rum-soaked tales, but all sailors were superstitious, including hers. With each passing league, she felt the tension tighten like a slip knot. Good luck charms appeared, dangling from the mastheads. Sailors saved a portion of their meal as offerings to the sea god. Crewmen who should be sleeping crowded the foredeck, red-rimmed eyes scanning for threats, real and imagined.

"Bring her two points to larboard and hold her steady."

"Aye, captain."

Chartless, she followed the coastline north. Black basalt cliffs towered three hundred feet above the crashing waves, as if some giant had used a sword to sunder the land from the sea. The black cliffs formed a formidable rampart. If wind and wave turned against her, she'd find no succor on the harsh coast. To the north and the west, a vast endless ocean stretched to infinity, a slate-gray sea furrowed with white-toothed waves, cold and forbidding. And to the south, on the distant horizon, always staying just within sight, the sails of the merchant fleet billowed bright like a glimpse of home. Juliana measured the leagues with a single glance. The distance was the price she paid to bring the others north. Despite the king's seal, the captains balked at the strange orders, insisting the risk was too great. So the *Sea Sprite* took the lead, the tip of the spear, the bait in the trap, forging a path into the bitter north. If evil befell her ship, the others would turn and run, hence the tension clawing at her shoulders.

"*Ware to larboard!*" The lookout called a warning from the crow's nest.

At first, she saw nothing, an endless expanse of waves, but then she noticed it. A dark shadow inked the depths, a leviathan of the deep, thrice the length of the *Sea Sprite*...heading straight for her ship.

"*Captain?*"

Changing course might bait the beast's attention, so she made her voice stone-certain. "Steady as she goes. It will pass." Gripping the railing, she watched the leviathan, willing it to keep to the depths.

The massive shadow loomed close. Sailors rushed the rails, staring down. A few reached for fishing gaffs, mere pinpricks against the great beast.

"*Nearly upon us!*" the lookout called.

The great shadow approached at a frightening speed, faster than any sailing ship. Juliana braced for impact, her feet spread wide, her face a stony mask. Wood creaked and sails snapped while heartbeats hammered. Time seemed to slow, an eternity of waiting...and then the shadow passed beneath, cruising the briny depths without a care for the surface. Sailors cheered and clapped, dancing a jig.

Juliana smiled, the only sign of her relief.

Marcus cast her a questioning glance. "How did you know?"

"Captain's intuition."

He tugged on his seashell earring, respect gleaming in his blue-eyed stare. "May the captain's intuition ever be true."

"Just so."

The wind shifted slightly, adding speed to their sails. Empty of cargo, the *Sea Sprite* skimmed across the white-topped waves. Checking the lines, Juliana ordered full canvas pressing for more speed.

They sailed north into frigid waters, ice riming the sheets and slicking the decks, making the footing treacherous. Darkness held sway for the better part of each day, eldritch lights dancing in the sky like a spectral warning. Fierce storms blew out of the north. Gales battered her ship, hurling stinging ice at her crew. The *Sea Sprite* pitched and rolled over mountainous waves. The northern ocean proved forbidding as any bard's tale, cold and dark and treacherous. Her sailors turned surly, reading dire omens in every luff of sail, every seagull's cry, yet she ruled her ship with an iron will, pressing to the very edge of the world.

In the privacy of her cabin, Juliana fortified her will with the message scrolls from home, her fingers tracing the wax seals. Sitting by the lantern light, she read and reread them, searching for surety beneath the strange orders. Jordan's letter read like a bard's tale, a saga of treachery and poison and god-given visions. She'd never thought of her swordish sister as a seer, yet she put her faith in the words. Drawing a sealskin cloak across her shoulders, she returned to the windswept deck, yearning for an end to the voyage.

On a cold bleak morning, the coastline changed. The dark cliffs fell away, revealing an entrance to a bay. Hope quickened within her. "This must be it!"

Marcus joined her on the aft deck. "Orders, captain?"

"We'll dare the bay."

He gave her a hard stare. "And if we don't find the cursed citadel?"

"We'll find it."

"Captain's intuition?"

She shook her head, knowing he deserved the truth. "More like desperate need." Her ship and crew were both pushed near the breaking point. They needed to reach their goal and make a run for the south. "Take us in."

Marcus roared the orders. "Hard to starboard!"

Sailors scurried up the rigging, trimming sails as the *Sea Sprite* heaved to the starboard side.

Juliana cast a glance behind. The fleet followed, keeping their distance, their numbers diminished by two. Two ships lost to wind or wave or some other calamity, she shuddered at the loss, praying the voyage was worth the price.

The *Sea Sprite* tacked to starboard, riding the swells toward the bay. Jagged spires of dark rock thrust from the sea like a monster baring needle-sharp teeth. At their tips, the spires narrowed to a sharp sword-width, but at their barnacle-encrusted base, the spires were wide enough to hide a ship...or two. "Tell the lookouts to keep sharp."

"Aye, captain."

A flock of seagulls gave escort, screaming a mournful cry. The *Sea Sprite* passed between the spires. Juliana tensed, fearing an ambush, but the sea remained empty of enemies. Overhead the sails fluttered and sagged, caught in the spire's wind-shadow. The *Sprite's* speed slowly bled away, but her impetus carried them forward into the bay. Escaping the spire's shadow, the wind billowed the mainsail, snapping it full, and the *Sea Sprite* leaped forward, slicing the waves.

The entranceway opened into a vast bowl-shaped bay. Towering basalt cliffs ringed the bay like fortress walls. Stark and imposing, the sheer cliffs implied a cold threat instead of safe harbor, as if the land repulsed the sea and those that sailed upon it.

Beside her Marcus growled. "I don't like it. This bay has a foul feel about it."

"More proof we've sailed to the right place."

He sucked air through the gap in his front teeth. "The Mordant's lair."

"Just so." She stood on the aft deck, scrying the wave patterns and the subtle sea colors, the only clues to the bay's depths. "Steady as she goes." She kept her ship on a straight course, plying a path toward the bay's heart.

"*Ware the castle!*" The lookout sang a warning, pointing toward the northeast.

Juliana shivered when she saw it, making the hand sign against evil. A massive fortress reared above the sea cliffs, dark and grim and potent with brutal power. She'd dreamt of the Mordant's castle at journey's end, but this dark monstrosity exceeded all her nightmares. Massive in scale, the fortress loomed over the bay like an armored fist, reeking of menace. Tiers of crenellated battlements spiraled upward like a stone beehive. Studded with catapults and trebuchets, the walls bristled with threat. She half expected to see winged monsters perched on the ramparts, waiting to attack her ship.

"*Captain?*"

Startled from her thoughts, she cast a wary glance at her first mate. "What do you think?"

He scowled. "Too many catapults. One hit and we're holed."

"Just so."

He tugged on his earring, a nervous gesture. "There's no banners on the walls. How do we tell if the dark-damned fortress is held by friend of foe?"

A chill shivered down her spine. She'd expected bright pennants to flutter from the ramparts, proof the citadel was defeated. Instead she saw nothing but dark battlements studded with catapults, a fortress gird for war.

"Friend or foe?"

After such a long voyage, Juliana knew what her answer had to be, but it sat in her stomach like bilge water. "We tempt them."

"What?"

"We sail within range of their war engines and tempt them to attack."

He stared at her, his voice dropping to a low growl. "A tricky gambit. Is it worth the risk?"

"We've come this far, we have to know."

"And if they attack?"

She swallowed hard. "We turn sail and run for home."

He held her gaze. "Seems a risky ploy."

"It's all we have."

He gave her a grim nod. "Dance with the devil, and pray like hell he doesn't catch us."

"Just so." She gave the order. "Helmsman hold steady. Let's give them a chance to see our colors."

"Aye, captain."

She felt the tension ripple through her crew. Sailors climbed the rigging and clung to the railing. Every spare hand manned the rails, watching the fortress. Seagulls screamed overhead as the canvas sails snapped taut, but not a word was spoken. The *Sea Sprite* speared a path across the bay, closing on the grim fortress.

Juliana watched the ramparts, set to flinch at the first sign of attack. With every passing ship-length she felt the menace grow. Fear tightened like a serpent coiling in her stomach, yet she held to the course. A sunbeam pierced the clouds illuminating the mainsail, a checkered pattern of blue and red emblazoned with a white osprey, the proud sigil of Navarre.

"They should see us now, captain."

"Aye, there's no mistaking our colors. Sound the conch just to be sure."

A seaman raised the great conch shell to his lips. The mournful wail rang out across the bay like a challenge. Once, twice, the conch sounded, yet there was no answer from the fortress. The dark castle loomed large, yet the war engines remained dormant. Juliana judged the distance with a critical eye. Close enough to taunt yet far enough to run. "Hard to port! Let's set a sharp tack and run before their walls."

Sailors leaped to obey, climbing the rigging to set the sails. Canvass snapped to the new heading and the *Sea Sprite* hauled to port, throwing up a cold spray. They ran beneath the dark walls, tacking back and forth, like a plump pigeon baiting a hawk.

Details became clear; a long stairway chiseled in the cliffs ran from the fortress down to the sea. A battlement protruded from the cliff's base, a single catapult guarding the stone dock, yet she saw no sign of soldiers. If the fortress feared the sea, they did not show it.

Five times they traversed the width of the bay, flaunting their colors, yet the fortress remained quiet, a dark riddle wrapped in threat.

Marcus leaned close. "Do you think it's a trap?"

"A strange sort of trap...unless they mean to lure us to the dock to board us."

Marcus tugged his earring. "Not what I'd expect from the Mordant."

"Nor I." She flicked a glance toward the helmsman. "Hold her steady." She turned back to Marcus. "We're not done tempting fate. One way or another, we need an answer. Take her closer by another two ship lengths."

The *Sea Sprite* edged closer to the great fortress, tacking back and forth beneath the battlements.

Juliana stood on the aft deck, her gaze scanning the tiered catapults, every one a threat to her ship.

Something splashed white in the slate-gray sea. "Lookout report!"

Wren leaned from the crow's nest, pointing to larboard. "Something hit over there, captain, a splash like a large seabird."

She scanned the wave tops but saw no bird rising from the foam.

"Captain, another one!" One of the deck hands pointed.

She gripped the railing, scanning the sea, but saw nothing.

The lookout sang out, *"Ware the castle, one of the war engines is loosing stone!"*

Her gaze snapped to the fortress. She saw it then, near the top tier, the mighty arm of a catapult snapping forward. Something tumbled through the sky, smaller than she expected. It struck with a white splash, closer to her ship than she liked...yet the splash was small. *A single splash, a single catapult,* why use only one war engine when the fortress was ringed with them? If this truly was an attack, the sea should be frothing with water spouts, her ship imperiled by a bombardment of death. "This makes no sense."

"Captain?"

Hearing the urgency in her first mate's voice, she issued the order. "Hard to port!"

The helmsman put the rudder hard over as sailors scrambled to trim the sails. Another splash hit closer to her ship. The *Sea Sprite* heeled hard to port, the deck slanting at a steep angle. Juliana gripped the railing, willing speed to her ship.

Splat! Something struck the deck.

Juliana cringed, expecting death screams and cracking timbers...but the *Sea Sprite* sailed on. Puzzled, she leaped from the aft deck, needing to know. Seamen clustered in a knot at middeck. Jango turned, a startled look on his tattooed face. "Captain, you'll not be believin' this."

They opened a path for her, and she saw what had hit her ship...*a giant wheel of brown bread splattered on her deck like a pancake!* She struggled not to gape.

Jango offered her a torn hunk, a smile on his swarthy face. "Brown bread, stuffed with nuts and raisins...and it's still warm from the oven!"

She took the offering, sniffed it, and then dared a bite...warm and nutty and rich with raisins.

Marcus appeared at her side. "Captain? What does it mean?"

Juliana grinned. "Unless this is poisoned, it means a warm welcome."

All around her, crewmen cheered.

"Marcus you have the helm, take us in!"

The *Sea Sprite* turned for the coast, heading for the stone dock beneath the dark fortress. Juliana watched from the foredeck, a swell of pride in her crew. They'd made their way north, forging a path through treacherous seas and daring the Mordant's fortress. *Bread from catapults,* she smiled at the strange greeting. Against all the odds, her sister's words had proved true.

49

Katherine

"*A hit!*" Kath and the others rushed to the ramparts, staring down at the ship. Gripping the battlement, she prayed for the message to be clear. "Come on...turn, turn...*trust us!*" Tilting at a drunken angle, the ship began to turn. For a handful of heartbeats, it danced upon the waves, as if balanced on the knife-edge of indecision. Kath held her breath, willing the ship to turn. The wind caught the sails, billowing the red and blue checks. The ship righted and leaped forward, plowing a course straight for the citadel.

"We did it!" Kath grinned with excitement.

Her maroon band cheered a mighty bellow.

Blaine gripped her arm, pointing west. "*Look!*"

Kath stared beyond the ship. Sails filled the bay's mouth, too many to count...all of them bearing Navarre's colors. "The ships of Navarre have come north!" Tears glistened in Kath's eyes, sundered by the unexpected miracle.

"You did it! You found a way south!" Blaine swept her into his arms, planting a kiss on her lips.

Shocked, she stiffened at the ambushed intimacy, but Blaine did not seem to notice.

Setting her back on her feet, he turned and cheered with the others.

Kath backed away, needing to gain some distance. She ran into Bear, a wall of muscled armor at her back.

"Svala, are you well?"

His question brought her back to the moment. *The ships of Navarre had come north* and nothing else mattered. "We need to greet them, lest they change their minds." She returned to the rampart, peering over the edge, craning to see a way down.

Fanggold said, "This way, Svala."

Abandoning the trebuchet, she followed the wolf-faced warrior down and around the Citadel's spiral streets. Blaine and thirty warriors ran behind, sounding like a legion pounding at her back. They raced down through the tiers, garnering sharp looks and questioning stares, but they did not slow. The citadel's immense size took its toll. Puffing like bellows blowing frozen plumes into the cold morning air, they reached the bottom tiers. Slick with sweat, Kath counted the gates. By the time they reached the ninth tier, a sharp ache pierced her side. Kath slowed, too winded to speak.

A pair of painted warriors saw her and leaped to open the north gate.

Gasping for breath, Kath ran through the last gate. A bone-chilling wind struck from the west, icy fingers piercing wool and leather and flesh. Beyond the dark ramparts, the cold seemed twice as killing. Shivering, Kath tugged on a pair of gauntlets lined with wool. "Which...way?"

Fanggold gestured to a cobbled pathway leading toward the sea.

The pathway led straight over a sheer basalt cliff. Kath staggered to a stop, staring down. Giant stairs were carved from the cliff, wide enough for six men abreast, but there was no railing, a deadly drop to the crashing waves far below. Snow encrusted the stairs, adding to the peril. Stone gargoyles crouched at the outer edge of every tenth step. Cloaked in ice, they glared at the sea like demonic sentinels keeping watch.

Staying close to the cliff side, Kath dared the stairs, trailing one gloved hand along the dark rock. Seagulls roiled overhead, their startled cries calling a warning. Her boots slid on ice. She clung to the cliff, regaining her balance. Bear grabbed her arm, holding her till she regained her footing.

The stairs seemed to go on forever. Kath wondered how many men had died carving them from the sheer cliff, more proof of the Mordant's cruel power. Nearing the bottom, she felt the rock shudder beneath her boots, assaulted by the sea's strength. Massive waves pounded the shore like thunder. Kath winced at the sea's ferocity, so different when viewed from the cliff tops. She'd learned to swim in the placid waters of Castlegard's moat, but this ocean seemed like a thing alive, like a wild beast pummeling the shore. Kath marveled that anyone dared to sail the sea. A huge wave pounded the lower steps, throwing up a veil of salt spray. Slick with sea-slime, the lower stairs grew treacherous.

Bear took her arm. "Careful, Svala."

They reached the bottom and found a round battlement carved from the dark cliff, icicles clinging to the ramparts like monstrous teeth. A salt-encrusted catapult kept watch, a smaller set of stairs leading down to a dock. Built of dark stone, the dock jutted from the cliffs at a sharp angle, angry waves battering the far side. The salty breath of the sea hung heavy in the air.

Kath took the stairs down to the dock...and skidded to a stop.

The ship was there, sails furrowed, looming over the dock like a bucking sea monster. Swarthy seamen lined the railings...and all of them held swords.

Kath raised her empty hands, yelling to be heard. "We bid you welcome!" She scanned the sailors, pleased to see a few women among them, but one stood out. The emblem of Navarre embroidered on her leather jerkin, she stood tall and shapely, with bright red hair tied at her nape. Her hand on her long knife, she met Kath's stare.

"In whose name do you welcome us?"

Kath smiled. "In my own! I'm Kath of Castlegard and these are the painted warriors of the far north. Together we've taken the Mordant's Citadel."

Tension bled from the woman's stance. "Then my sister spoke true."

"Your sister?"

"Jordan of Navarre."

Kath pounced on her sword sister's name. "Jordan! Is she well?"

The woman nodded. "She came down from the mountains with visions from the gods."

"Visions?"

"Jordan convinced the king to send the merchant fleet north. She said you'd gained a great victory at the Mordant's Citadel but all would be for naught if you did not find a way south."

"Jordan knows of our victory?" Kath gaped at the revelation, feeling the hand of the gods.

The woman nodded. At a gesture, two seamen lowered a plank. Agile as a squirrel, the woman leaped to the plank and walked it with ease despite the ship's rocking sway.

Kath met her at the base. "You must be Juliana. Jordan spoke of you often."

"Juliana of Navarre, captain of the *Sea Sprite*." She flashed a warm smile and Kath saw the resemblance.

"Then we are well met." They clasped arms like warriors. Kath smiled with relief. "Your coming is a godsend for we do indeed need a way south."

Juliana sobered. "That's why we've come, but the northern seas are perilous, we dare not tarry. We need food and fresh water and then we need to be away. To linger here, is to court death."

A shiver of dread pricked Kath's soul, a warning that time was short. "Come, we'll share meat and mead while your ship is replenished, and then we'll be away. We're anxious to leave the north." Juliana joined her, climbing the great stairs. A gaggle of sailors and painted warriors trailed behind. Hungry for tidings, Kath riddled the captain with questions. "Tell me of the south."

Juliana told a harrowing tale. A vicious holy war had nearly defeated Lanverness while deadly treachery took its toll on Navarre. Poison, war and religion ran amok in the south, yet the captain made no mention of the Mordant. Sifting through the details, Kath listened for all that was not said. She found it hard to believe that the oldest harlequin remained dormant while Darkness stalked every corner of Erdhe. A cold dread grew in her heart. Having seen the Dark Citadel, Kath knew what the Mordant was capable of. Gripping the crystal dagger, she flicked a glance toward the setting comet, fearing the sands of time were nearly run out.

50

The Knight Marshal

A campfire blazed bright at the base of the great stone hand, illuminating the ancient statue. Winter stars wheeled overhead in the cold night sky, distant and indifferent, the slivered moon nearly snuffed to darkness. *Nearly dark,* the marshal used the dark of the moon as a beacon, summoning the scouts and stragglers to Stonehand, a chance to reunite his forces.

Leaning towards the fire's soothing warmth, the marshal soaked up the heat, taking supper with his captains. Firelight flickered across weary faces working hard to chew their meal. The roasted horsemeat was tough and stringy yet it was better fare than anything they'd had in a long while. Second helpings were served and mugs were refilled with mulled wine. Silence reigned yet beneath it the marshal heard a clamor of questions. Just two days ago, they'd witnessed a slaughter-field of ogres and the shattering of a blue steel sword, nightmares a man did not soon forget. Decisions needed to be made, but not this night.

Weary beyond telling, the marshal finished his meal, chewing the gristle till it turned tasteless. Spitting the last of it upon the fire, he savored the smell of sizzling meat, and then levered himself to his feet, suppressing a groan. Bruised and battered, his entire body ached. Feeling the weight of stares, he bid his captains a good night and forced himself to walk without betraying the aching stiffness.

A make-shift camp had sprung up around the great stone hand. Rough structures of branches and canvas and shields crowded the snow, providing meager shelters for his men. At the heart stood three great pavilions brought from Castlegard by the stewards, relics of tournaments past. By rights, the largest should be his alone but the men needed shelter almost as much as they needed food. A pair of guards snapped to attention. Acknowledging their salutes, the marshal ducked beneath the canvas flap, ambushed by the sudden warmth of so many bodies. Stale sweat and woody soot clung to the warmth in a smothering mix. Men slept crowded on the floor, sending up a bevy of snores. A brazier glowed in the center, shadows flickering across the sleeping forms. The marshal stepped between them, making his way to the curtained room at the back. A second pair of guards stood watch, hands on their sword hilts. The marshal met their stares, repeating his orders. "None to pass without my express command."

"Yes, sir!" the guards answered in unison, two of his best.

Twitching the canvas curtain aside, he entered his private quarters. His worried gaze sought the bundled sword lying on the floor, relieved to find it untouched. The cursed sword belonged in a locked chest, or better yet, drowned in the deepest lake, but that was a problem for another day.

Desperate for sleep, the marshal stumbled past the armor stand to the pallet piled high with furs. His squire had been busy, his polished armor gleaming upon the stand like a champion awaiting battle. A pity his aching body did not polish nearly as well. Feeling bruised and dented, he sank down upon the bed, too weary to even undress. "Martyn attend me!"

He heard a rustle outside the canvas walls and then a towheaded lad appeared at the canvas flap. "Yes, my lord?"

"My boots."

His squire knelt, easing the boots from his feet. Nimble fingers worked to remove the marshal's surcoat and padded jerkin. At the tender age of eight, the flaxen-haired lad was way too young to wield a sword but his gaze betrayed his dreams, always returning to the bundled sword. "Is it true what they say, my lord? Is it really Boric's blade?"

Lightning-quick, the marshal reared up. "You're not to touch it!" Grabbing the boy's shoulders, he shook him to emphasize his words. "Do you understand?"

His squire stared white-eyed like a startled colt.

"You're *never* to touch it!"

"Yes, m'lord."

He released the boy and his squire stumbled backwards, his face claimed by shock more than fear. The marshal eased back on his pallet, pulling the furs across his aching body. "It killed Baldwin."

"The king's squire?"

"Yes."

"Just because he touched it?"

In many ways, it was the truth. "Yes."

Martyn swallowed, his face going solemn. "Then I swear not to touch it."

"Good. I'll hold you to your word. Now get to your bed, I won't be needing you till morning."

"Yes, my lord." The lad disappeared beyond the canvas curtain, leaving the marshal finally alone. His gaze roved to the bundled sword, a promise and a threat. Even wrapped in furs, its siren's call whispered through his mind, offering a promise of glorious victory. "Lies, you spew lies." Turning away, he made the hand sign against evil while pulling the fur coverlet over his head. Weary and aching, he sought sleep, but images of the slaughtered ogres haunted his mind. Such a powerful weapon, such a deadly trap, he tossed and turned beneath the furs. Exhaustion clung to his body yet his mind refused to rest. Sleep eventually claimed him, but in his dreams he won every battle and the color of his sword was darkest black.

"Have you died and gone to Valin?" The rough voice prodded him almost as much as the smell. *Roast horsemeat*, his stomach growled, rousing him from sleep. The marshal pried his eyes open. "Lothar, this better be important."

"I need your leave to enter." His friend's voice came from beyond the canvas.

"Given."

Lothar ducked inside, juggling two plates heaped with roast horsemeat and biscuits smothered in gravy. "Rumors were starting to circulate that you'd died in your sleep."

The marshal sat up, pulling a padded tunic over his head. "What do you mean?"

"You've slept clear through the day. I've brought your supper."

"What?" The marshal stared at the pavilion's outer walls, shocked to find the canvas reflecting the brazier's light, a telltale sign it was dark outside. "An entire day?"

"Just so." Lothar shoved a plate into his hands. "You clearly needed it. What in the Nine Hells were you thinking when you attacked Baldwin?"

"I wasn't thinking; I was surviving." The marshal rubbed his face, scratching the extra growth of stubble. "I'm getting too old for this."

"Aren't we all? Eat, you'll feel better." Lothar sat cross-legged on the floor, methodically devouring a plate of horsemeat drenched in onion gravy, but his gaze kept stealing to the bundled sword. The marshal knew what was on his friend's mind, but he delayed the subject, talking instead about smaller things. "Have you selected the supply squad?"

"Ready to ride at first light."

"You chose the fresh-made knights?"

Lothar nodded, "Just as you ordered."

"Good, give them a chance to live before battle claims them." Suddenly ravenous, the marshal shoveled a mouthful of horsemeat chased by a bite of biscuit. "And Sir Abrax and Baldwin, I want their names added to the list for the Chronicler."

"Already done. When the squad returns to Castlegard their names will be inked on the Roll of Honor." Lothar stared at him, his voice querulous. "But why Baldwin? He slaughtered three knights and tried to kill you! Why does he deserve to be among the honored dead?"

The marshal snapped with anger. "Because he served the maroon. I should never have burdened a mere squire with that sword." He shook his head, remembering the slaughter field. "Even tainted by the cursed blade, Baldwin gave the Octagon a great victory."

"If you truly honor what he did, then *use* the sword! If a mere squire can kill sixty ogres, what can a champion do?"

"How many patrols have we lost?"

"What?"

"You saw Baldwin's mismatched armor. Who's to say he only fought the black?"

Lothar's eyes widened. "You're clutching at straws."

"Am I? I crossed swords with him. I saw the madness in his eyes."

Stubbornness rode his friend's gaze. "The sword is a god-given gift."

"From which god?"

"With Boric's blade we could turn the tide of war!"

"Boric's blade was sapphire blue, not sin-drenched black!"

Lothar sputtered.

The marshal pressed the attack. "And who will wield it?"

Lothar stared like a man being robbed of a dream.

"Baldwin fought like a demon instead of a man. That sword changed him, corrupted him."

Lothar's voice dropped to a harsh whisper. "We're losing the war."

The truth hurt like a thousand sword cuts. Wounded, he stared at his friend.

Lothar raked a hand through his graying hair. "Yes, we win battles, and your strategies of ambushes have stretched the lives of our men, but we both know we need something more, something to level the numbers and turn the tide. Boric's sword could be the answer."

"No, it's tainted, it's cursed. Whoever wields it will become demon-damned."

Lothar stared at him and then at the bundle-wrapped sword.

A surly stillness settled between them.

Lothar gave him a measuring look. "I will wield it."

"Are you mad?"

"No, listen. I'll go alone, keeping the sword under wraps until I reach the enemy's main camp. Only then will I wield it."

"The sword is cursed. It'll drink your soul."

"How do you know?"

The marshal could not answer, unable to speak of the whispering voice.

Lothar scowled. "Perhaps you're right. Perhaps the dark-damned sword will drink my soul, but not before the enemy is slaughtered and the war won." Lothar gave him a ragged look. "I'd trade my soul to save the maroon."

The marshal sighed. "I know." He shook his head, his voice laden with worry. "You might destroy an army...or you might spawn something worse. You heard Baldwin. With that demon-cursed sword in your hand, you'll yearn for a crown. And then who will stop you?"

His friend met his gaze. "You will."

"What?"

"You slew Baldwin."

The marshal looked away. "A lucky strike."

"No, something more. We all saw it. The black blade shattered the blue steel sword like it was glass, but not your blade." Lothar shook his head, his face glazed with wonder. "Your blade remained whole, an ordinary sword of Castlegard steel. Why?"

The marshal shoved his plate aside, his hunger suddenly fled. "I don't know."

"You know something; I saw it in your face."

His friend knew him too well. Stalling for time, the marshal drew a deep breath. "When the supply squad returns to Castlegard, I want another name added to the Roll of Honor."

Lothar gave him a flinty look. "Who?"

"Sir Tyrone."

Lothar stared at him, as if trying to place the name. "The knight they burned in the signal tower of Cragnoth Keep?"

"Yes."

"Why?"

"It's his sword I'm wielding."

Lothar raised a bushy eyebrow brimming with questions.

The marshal sighed, the words spilling out of him. "I took it from the signal fire atop Cragnoth Keep. Everything else was burnt and blackened but not the sword. I don't even know why I took it. Since then I've often wondered if Sir Tyrone died a hero or a traitor. Now I know."

Lothar's voice turned solemn. "A sword steeped in honor."

The words blazed with truth. "Just so."

Lothar stared at him. "What happened?"

"Something unexpected. Something I've never felt before." The marshal stared at his friend, struggling to find the words. "I was beaten. You saw how Baldwin fought. Lightning-quick, he struck like a demon and I was already spent. Just parrying the black sword was taking a grim toll...and then, when I thought all was lost, strength flowed into me, strength and surety...from Sir Tyrone's sword."

Lothar's gaze went wide.

"Do you believe me?"

"Something damn-sure happened; else you'd have died under the black sword." Lothar's voice dropped to a whisper. "So you think Sir Tyrone's sword is bespelled?"

The marshal shook his head. "I don't know what to think...but it did not feel like that."

"Perhaps his sword is meant to foil the black?"

"No, it felt like something else."

"Tell me."

"It felt like the strength of brotherhood, like succor when it was most needed."

Lothar chewed his mustache. "Magic?"

The marshal shrugged.

"Magic cost us Raven Pass."

"Just so."

"Perhaps only magic will turn the tide?"

"No, I'll not believe it."

Lothar scowled. "We're fighting a war we can't win and suddenly we have two magical swords. The gods must be laughing."

"Or perhaps they've finally lent a hand."

Lothar barked a rude laugh. "If they really want to help, they should just smite the enemy."

"I don't think it works like that."

"More's the pity." Lothar gave him a shrewd look. "The black sword can win this war."

"No."

"One life to save the maroon. I'd count my life well spent."

"That way is damned."

"Think on it." Lothar gathered up the plates and slipped beyond the canvas.

Mired in thought, the marshal tugged on his boots. Swirling his maroon cloak across his shoulders, he shrugged on the harness with Sir Tyrone's great sword. Stepping beyond the canvas curtain, he reaffirmed the guards' strict orders and then left the pavilion. Night shrouded the camp, confirming that he'd slept the day away, yet his muscles still ached. Sighing, the marshal made the rounds, knowing the men needed to see him whole and in command. He stopped often, speaking of battle plans and strategies, doing his best to stoke morale. The men feasted on roast horsemeat and baked onions, a hearty meal but the stringy meat was just another sure sign of defeat, their own dead mounts butchered after the battle. Honor and fortitude were not enough; he needed something to turn the tide of war. His mind turned to the dark sword, though he knew it reeked of evil. A dangerous thought pierced him, wondering if it took evil to defeat evil. Shivering, he pulled his maroon cloak close. Visions of dead ogres haunted his mind. The weight of Sir Tyrone's sword was a comfort across his shoulders, but it could not slay the black sword's temptation. In the back of his mind he could still hear the sword's dark whispers, a siren's song promising sweet victory...if only he dared wield it.

51

Katherine

The Citadel roiled like a kicked anthill, everyone working to hasten the army's departure. Casks of fresh water were filled, rounds of bread were baked and provisions prepared, while bands of warriors said their farewells and boarded the ships. In the midst of the chaos, Kath slipped her guards and stole away. Taking one of the few remaining horses, she rode alone, cantering along the windswept cliffs. Seagulls wheeled overhead, their mournful cries offset by the muffled boom of waves battering the cliffs below. A killing cold snatched at her breath, frosting it to plumes of white. The north was such a desolate and brutal place, it pained her to leave him here.

At the edge of the sea cliff, beyond reach of the Citadel's shadow, the burial mound stood twice the height of a tall man. Weapons and battle banners piled high, a tribute for a fallen hero, yet it did little to salve her heart. Tethering her horse, Kath knelt by the grave. There should have been trees overhead, a great grove of grandfather trees to guard his bones and hum his name for all eternity. Duncan would have wanted that, but none grew north of the Dragon Spines, another reason to curse the north. Kath wondered if the Treespeaker knew. Tugging off her gauntlet, she thrust her hand beneath the snow crust, delving into the fresh-turned soil, as if she could reach him. *"Duncan, my love, my heart, my husband..."* a single tear coursed down her cheek. For the longest time, she knelt by the grave, remembering his smile, his voice, his touch. She yearned for the past; she yearned for a future by his side, anything but this. Memories of her wedding night filled her mind, tenderness and longing overflowing her heart. She swayed, remembering every touch, every kiss. Shadows lengthened and the seagulls screamed a mournful cry, yet she noticed neither.

A sheepskin dropped across her shoulders. Startled, Kath reached for her sword, but her hand was too cold to obey.

"Svala, you will freeze to death." Bear stood behind her, his tattooed face full of concern.

Kath staggered to her feet, suddenly crippled by the biting cold. "I did not hear you." Shivering, she pulled the sheepskin close.

"Your senses yearned for the Otherrealm. But it is not your time to cross over." He tucked the wool blanket around her, rubbing warmth into her arms and hands. "You are needed. You have much to do."

Pins and needles lanced her, a rude return to life. "Yes, the gods must have their due."

"Svala," his voice held a hint of reproach, "this man you loved would not want this. He died a hero. Be joyful in his memory."

"But I ache for him."

"That is fitting, but while your heart will always miss him, you must still drink from the joy of life." Bear gestured to the burial mound. "You must drink for him as well as yourself, else you do him a great disservice."

His words struck like truth, filling a hollow in her heart. "When did you get so wise?"

Bear flushed beet red, his voice turning to a low mumble. "Something the Ancestor told me when my wife died."

She hadn't even known he'd had a wife. Shame and sorrow gripped her in equal measure. Kath felt her face flame red. "I'm sorry."

He shrugged. "It was long ago."

"Did you come to bid farewell to Boar?" A smaller, fresher mound sat beside Duncan's, another bitter loss in the war against the Mordant.

"Svala, I came for you." Bear nodded towards the smaller mound. "Boar is in the Otherrealm, feasting in the hall of heroes." He untethered the horse. "Come, we should return." He gave her a leg up, and then he took the reins, and began leading her back to the Citadel.

"Wait." Kath turned in the saddle. Closing her eyes, she thought of Duncan, whole and unharmed, muscles clad in black leathers, a warm smile on his ruggedly handsome face. Her voice dropped to a soft whisper, pitched to carry to the Otherrealm. "I'll look for you in the Light." She held her breath, listening hard, but the only answer was the booming waves and the seagulls' cries... the sounds of life. Perhaps Bear had the truth of it. Perhaps she needed to live for the both of them. Nodding farewell, Kath turned in the saddle and rode back to life and to duty.

52

Katherine

Voices drifted up from below, feeble as gnats compared to the waves' incessant pounding. Kath leaned on the cliff-top rampart, watching the last of the ships come and go. A captain bellowed orders as men scurried across the sea-drenched dock. Tethered by ropes, the great ship bucked like a wooden beast angry to be loosed. One by one, the merchant ships took turns at the stone dock, loading men and provisions before setting sail for the south. Most were already loaded and gone, their sails billowing in a diagonal line across the storm-tossed bay. She watched as the lead ship entered a haze of iron-gray sleet at the bay's mouth. For a fleeting heartbeat, the ship stood bold against the storm, but then it disappeared, as if swallowed...or fallen from the edge of the world. Kath studied the sea with fresh eyes. Storm and wave, the ocean held a mighty ferocity unlike anything she'd ever experienced. For the thousandth time, she wondered if the sea was the only way south.

"Svala, are you sure about this?" Bear stood behind her, his voice laden with doubt. "Men are not meant to trod the sea."

"The gods heard our need and sent ships north so we could defeat the Mordant. The sooner we reach the south, the better."

"As you say, Svala."

Chainmail tugged at her shoulders, but the added weight felt like a comfort. Kath favored fighting leathers like her lord father, but the treacherous nature of the Citadel had taught her the value of chainmail. With her axes strapped to her back and her sword belted to her side, the added weight felt right. A sixth sense warned her that the dark fortress would not let her leave without a fight. Glaring up at the oppressive battlements, she made the hand sign against evil.

"What is it, Svala?"

"Nothing, we need to be gone." A sack held her few possessions, a small octagonal shield, the War Helm wrapped in a sheepskin cloak, spare clothes...and Duncan's boots. *Duncan*, his name echoed in her soul. She gripped his silver warrior ring worn on a chain around her neck.

A shuffle of many footsteps came from behind. Zith strode towards her, his midnight-blue robes billowing in the wind, his empty left sleeve pinned at the elbow. Eight of her maroon band followed the monk, struggling to carry four massive chests.

Kath gestured to the chests. "Plunder from the citadel?"

Zith gave her a rare smile. "Secrets and power plucked from the Mordant's treasury crypt." His face clouded. "I hope I chose wisely. Without the Quickner, it's impossible to winnow the magical from the mundane."

Kath paled, her hand reaching for her gargoyle. So much had been lost in that bloody cavern; she prayed it wasn't a fatal mistake.

Zith's voice dropped to a conspirator's whisper. "If we can't wield them, at least we can deny them to the Mordant."

"Just so." She watched them pass, struggling to carry the heavy chests down the steep cliff-carved stairs.

Neven came next with four wolf-faced warriors. They bore Danya on a litter, strapped and cocooned in sheepskins. The mountain wolf, Bryx, trotted close by, never far from Danya. Kath stopped them, her gaze fixed on Neven. "Are you sure?"

"We promised, Svala."

Swathed in sheepskins, Danya looked pale yet serene, despite being lost in a magic-induced trance. Kath did not want to risk her friend, but she could not afford to leave her behind. "Look after her. And tell me the moment she wakes."

"As you say, Svala."

Blaine strode towards her, shimmering in his silver surcoat, the hilt of his great blue sword rearing over his shoulder, looking like a hero from the bards' songs. A dark-haired lad walked in Blaine's shadow, wearing a pilfered helmet too big for his head. A short sword belted to his side, the lad struggled to carry a large sack.

Kath gestured to the boy. "Who's this?"

"My squire, Dermit."

She raised an eyebrow, the lad's naked face proving his origins. "A squire from the Dark Citadel?"

"Just so."

She'd taken two squires herself, two badger-faced lads, both orphaned by the fight to capture the Citadel. "Castlegard will forever change if we ever make it home."

"We've a long way to travel ere we worry about that."

"Just so." She noticed Blaine wore chainmail under his surcoat. "So you feel it too?"

Blaine gave her a grim nod. "The dark-cursed fortress makes my shoulder blades itch." He gave her a level stare. "I've seen things here I'd sooner forget, yet the war is far from over."

Kath knew what he meant. She carried nightmares of her own, too many nightmares. "All the more reason we dare not lose."

"Just so." He stayed by her side, staring down at the storm-tossed sea.

The rest of her maroon band straggled from the Citadel. Clad in captured armor burnished bright, their belts and baldrics studded with weapons, they carried sacks bulging with the spoils of war. Kath smiled, certain their sacks held weapons, armor and wool, instead of gold, silver and silk. She liked them all the more for it. "Are you ready to chase the Mordant south?"

"Yes, Svala." Sidhorn gave her a hearty grin. "But you're not to leave just yet."

Her maroon band surrounded her, smiles on their tattooed faces. They were plotting something. Kath gave Sidhorn a narrow gaze. "Why?"

And then she saw the others streaming from the Citadel's north gate, a thousand warriors or more, led by Royce and Thera. The lion-faced war-leader hailed her. "We've come to see you off, Svala."

Royce was solemn but Thera flashed a warm smile. "You wear our War Helm, but we've heard from Sir Blaine that kings in the south fight under banners...yet you have no banner...till now." Thera gestured and a lanky lion-faced lad stepped forward bearing an iron standard. Royce cut the bindings with his sword and a banner unfurled. Twelve feet of maroon silk shimmered in the wind.

Kath stared in surprise. Dyed a deep maroon, the banner was a perfect match for her cloak, yet it differed from any of the Octagon's battle standards. Stitched in bright gold, the banner bore an emblem unique to the north. The detailed embroidery was amazing. Proud and bold and shimmering in gold thread, the War Helm blazed across the banner, a perfect image of the ancient helmet embroidered on the Octagon's maroon.

Thera smiled. "You came from Castlegard and your color is maroon, but you have claimed our War Helm, and we have claimed you. It is fitting that you go south with our war sigil on your standard. May the gods smile on your journey as they smile on your sword."

The lad hefted the standard, waving it in the wind. Silk snapped overhead, a long shimmer of maroon with two spiked tails of gold. *"Svala!"* The shout roared from a thousand voices.

Kath stood humbled by their acclaim. "I'm honored."

And then they knelt, more than a thousand bowing toward her.

"No!" Kath shook her head, her voice raised. "You dared to fight the Darkness and you won! Stand, for you've earned the right as warriors of the Light."

A thousand warriors roared to their feet, their weapons raised in triumph. Someone shouted, "Victory for the Svala!" A multitude of voices echoed the cry, *"Victory for the Svala!"*

Kath bowed toward them, both humbled and proud.

Royce raised his hand, stilling the throng. Turning to Kath, he said, "You wear the War Helm well. May victory ever follow your sword."

Kath clasped arms with the lion-faced leader. "Keep the north safe."

"We will."

She turned to the raven-faced healer. "Thank you for your wisdom."

Thera nodded. "May the blessings of the Ancestor protect you."

"And you." Kath reached for the standard, but Sidhorn stepped forward.

"Allow me, Svala?" The big warrior stood hunched, a sheepish look on his chiseled face.

"It's yours to carry, Sidhorn."

He took the standard, raising it high, his face beaming with pride.

Bear nudged her from behind. "We'd best be going, Svala."

"Just so." Kath took a last look at her friends and then turned her back on the Dark Citadel. She would miss Thera and Royce...but her destiny lay in the south. Halfway down the cliff-carved steps, she blamed the cold wind for her watering eyes. Her cloak billowed by the frigid wind, her maroon banner rippling overhead, Kath made her way down the ice-rimed steps. Gray waves battered the cliff's base, shivering the steps with a relentless pounding. A single ship bucked against the dock, the first to arrive and the last to leave, a red-haired sea nymph with a saucy smile carved on the prow.

"Hurry," a pair of swarthy seamen urged them towards a boarding plank, "the captain wants to be away."

The ship seemed alive, bobbing against the dock.

The plank seemed awfully narrow, bucking up and down, a short drop to the frigid sea.

"Best to do it quick."

Gripping her sack, Kath leaped on the plank and skipped upwards. Near the top, the plank and the ship suddenly dropped, leaving Kath treading air. She toppled forward, nearly falling into the sea. A strong hand grabbed her arm. A burly seaman pulled her over the railing. "Welcome aboard."

The deck rolled beneath her feet. "Is it always like this?"

"Depends on the sea."

Another seaman took her sack. "I'll stow this for you. The captain invites you to the aft deck."

"Aft?"

The seaman cracked a gap-toothed smile, a gold earring dangling from his left ear. "Rear to you landlubbers."

"Thanks." Kath moved away from the plank. Staggered by the ship's bucking motion, she felt awkward as a rum-soaked drunk. Clinging to the railing, she tried to get her bearings. The *Sea Sprite* had three masts tall as fir trees. The sails were furrowed, ropes running like spider webs from the lofty crossbeams to the spindled rails. Pennants snapped overhead, the red and blue checks of Navarre. All around her, the ship bustled with sailors securing ropes and stowing casks and crates. Feeling lost, and more than a little bewildered, Kath climbed the stairs to the rear deck, relieved to find Juliana and her first mate, Marcus, locked in conversation.

Juliana cast a distracted glance her way. "Welcome aboard." She gave Kath an appraising stare. "You'll get your sea legs soon enough, but stow the chainmail. Armor is a death knell at sea."

Kath knew she had much to learn about sea travel, yet she was reluctant to relinquish her armor. "I'll wear it till the Citadel is out of sight."

"As you wish, but keep your feet under you and steer clear of the sea's reach. If a wave claims you, you'll sink like an anchor."

Kath nodded, doubling her grip on the railing.

Blaine, Bear and Sidhorn climbed the stairs to the rear deck. Sidhorn carried her standard, the maroon banner snapping in the wind. The three big men edged towards her, looking bewildered. Bear's deep voice dropped to a low growl. "What should we do, Svala?"

"Stay out of their way and learn how a ship works." Kath studied Juliana, noting the easy way the captain moved about the pitching deck. She supposed it was like riding a horse, something that came easy as breathing once you spent enough days in the saddle.

"Cast off and push her away!" The captain spoke the order and her first mate bellowed her command. A sailor blew three short notes on small whistle. Men leaped to obey, some rushing to the dockside railing while others scampered up the rigging. The ship thrummed like a kicked beehive, every sailor moving to their appointed task. Kath took it all in, impressed by the seamless coordination of so many men doing so many different tasks, like an intricate dance. Ropes were pulled aboard and coiled, while sailors leaned from the railing wielding long hooked spears, pushing the ship from the dock.

"Prepare to make sail!" Juliana's order echoed the ship's length.

Timbers creaked and the *Sea Sprite* drifted away from the stone dock. Overhead, sailors moved out along the narrow crossbeams, risking a deadly fall.

"Make sail!"

Ties were released and great canvas sheets dropped open with a thunderous clap. Red and blue checked, the main sail was emblazoned with the white sea eagle of Navarre, a proud sigil, bold and bright. Sailors shimmied down ropes, landing light-footed on the deck. Canvas flapped overheard, limp and lifeless as a bird's broken wing. Sluggish and slow, the ship ambled away from the cliffs, tossed by the waves.

"Come two points to larboard."

Sails hanging listless from the crossbeams, the ship wallowed in the waves, a disappointing start. Two of her painted warriors raced for the railing, vomiting their last meal into the cold waves, a reluctant offering to the sea god.

Slow and sluggish, the ship eased beyond the cliff's dark shadow. A sudden gust caught the canvas with a hard snap. Sails billowed taut and the ship leaped forward with lively energy, like a hound loosed to the hunt. The *Sea Sprite* scudded across the waves, carefree as her namesake. Kath gripped the railing, feeling the thrum of the ship's timbers. Elated by the windborne speed, she leaned out, salt spray licking her face. *So this is what it is to sail!* The wind whipped her long blond hair loose from its knot. Shaking out her hair, she let it stream behind like a battle banner. Kath reveled in the effortless speed of the ship, in the salty tang of the waves, in the clean smell of the ocean air. She loosed a joyful shout, *"For Honor and the Octagon!"*

A large hand gripped her shoulder. "Careful, Svala." Bear pulled her back, concern in his voice. "Are you sea drunk?"

"Sea drunk?" Puzzled, she looked at the others. Blaine was whey-faced and Sidhorn leaned across the far rail, retching his morning meal. Compared to the others, perhaps she was sea drunk, intoxicated by the effortless speed of wind and wave. Kath flashed a joyous smile. "I'm fine, Bear. Look after the others."

She turned to find Juliana watching her.

"The sea god favors you."

"Is it always like this?"

"We're on a broad reach with a powerful aft wind, our fastest line of sail. It'll get tricky once we leave the bay, especially with the storm brewing ahead." Juliana pointed west, toward the bay's mouth. Black spires thrust up from the roiling sea, guarding the bay's entrance like jagged teeth. Beyond the teeth, a curtain of gray sleet obscured the sea and sky, as if the world came to a sudden end. "I don't like the look of that storm." Juliana prowled her ship, issuing terse orders.

Kath remained on the rear deck. Staring east, she watched as the Dark Citadel grew small. Holding her thumb aloft, she blotted out the fortress, a measure of the distance crossed. Relief washed through her, elated to escape the Mordant's insidious trap. Glancing at Blaine, she saw an echoing smile on his face. "I guess we won't be needing our chainmail!"

Blaine gave her a terse nod and then abruptly gripped the railing. Leaning out, he emptied his stomach into the slate-gray sea.

Kath crossed to the far side, gradually growing accustomed to the rocking motion. Seagulls dipped and screeched overhead, following the ship's wake. Their incessant cries sounded hungry, as if begging for morsels, like pigeons of the sea. Her painted warriors drifted away, some slumping to sit cross-legged on the deck. Gray-faced and miserable, they sought shelter from the wind and waves, but Kath remained standing, one hand gripping the rear railing, thrilled by the feel of the ship.

Under full sail, the *Sea Sprite* skimmed across the waves, cutting a straight path for the mouth of the bay. As the Dark Citadel dwindled to insignificance, the great sea stacks loomed large. Dark spires, jagged as teeth, rose in a grim line cutting across the bay's narrow mouth. Waves beat against the pinnacles, breaking white at their base, a swirl of foam surrounding the sinister rocks.

Kath stared beyond the pinnacles, yearning for her first glimpse of the open ocean.

"*Ship ho!*" The cry rang from the rigging.

Kath felt an electric jolt race through the crew.

Sailors leaped to action. Scurrying up the rigging, several pointed north.

"*Red sails approaching!*"

"*A MerChanter trireme!*"

"*Ware the north!*"

Kath heard fear in their voices.

Juliana snapped a volley of orders. "Release the jib and turn one point to larboard! I want every scrap of speed we can muster! Let's see if we can outrun the bastards!"

Grim-faced sailors scurried to obey.

Kath sidled close to the captain. "An enemy ship?"

Juliana sent her a baleful look. "It seems the north is not yet done with you."

53

The Knight Marshal

Under cloak of darkness, the marshal sought a glimpse of the enemy. Lothar and Sir Rannock rode at his back, but he missed Sir Abrax. His steady strength and the surety of his blue steel sword could not be replaced. A hollow sadness gripped him. The winter war was taking a ferocious toll on the maroon, yet he would not relent. Like a badger locking jaws on a lion's throat, he continued to gnaw and chew, desperate to bring down the larger beast. He wondered if the Octagon stood a chance.

A shooting star blazed a path across the night sky. With the moon nearly dark, the slash of light flashed brilliant as a drawn sword. Such a glorious burst of light, but so brief...as brief as a warrior's life. The marshal shook his head, dismayed by his gloomy thoughts.

They rode along the ridge, the horses picking a path among the winter-bare trees. Fetlock-deep snow crunched beneath hooves, enough to leave tracks without slowing the horses. A scout stepped from behind a cedar. "This way, my lord." Clad in a dark gray cloak, a bow strung over his back, Targin led them towards a rocky spur overlooking Raven Pass. Hobbling the horses, they crept towards the edge.

Campfires crowded the valley below, too many to count. Like a river of fire, the enemy encamped the length of Raven Pass, securing the gateway to the south.

Beside him, Lothar hissed, "By the gods!"

The marshal shared his friend's anguish. For nigh on two turns of the moon, they'd fought the Pentacle, waging a winter war, yet for all their bravery and blood they'd barely culled the horde.

Sir Rannock whispered. "At least we've kept them bottled in the north."

The knight had the truth of it. The horde might have splintered, leaving a smaller force to chase the Octagon, while the rest plundered the south...but it seemed a slim comfort...and an odd strategy. "Come, we've seen their numbers." The marshal turned, leading them back from the edge. Reaching their horses, they mounted as the scout slipped back into the forest. They rode in silence, retracing the trail back along the ridgeline.

Lothar nudged his mount forward, riding beside him. "We should move the camp. Stonehand is too near Raven Pass."

"The scouts say it lies beyond the Pentacle's regular patrols. Far enough to be safe yet close enough to be ignored. They'd never expect us to have so much audacity."

Lothar tugged his mustache. "I don't like it."

"One more night till the dark of the moon. We'll collect our scouts, stragglers and supplies and be off, forging a path deeper into the Spines."

"You saw their numbers," Lothar cast him a sideways glance. "It will take more than steel to win this war."

The black sword again, the marshal bristled. "That way is damned."

"Yet it may be our only hope."

Anger riddled the marshal's words. "I'll not speak of it." Yet in his heart, he feared it was true.

54

Katherine

A ship emerged from behind a sea stack like a lurking marauder. Blood-red sails billowed in the wind, a horned skull emblazoned in black on the canvas. Three rows of oars flashed from the ship's sides. Painted red, the oars knifed the sea with deadly precision, thrusting the ship on a straight path towards the *Sea Sprite*. Kath knew little of ships, yet this one cut the waves like a predator, like a falcon stooping for prey. "An enemy ship?"

Marcus, the first mate, flicked a glance her way. "Aye. The MerChanters are fearsome raiders. They'll take us if they can."

"Take us how?" but Marcus had already turned away, attending to his captain.

Juliana barked a string of orders.

A grim tension thrummed through the crew. Sailors leaped to the rigging, adjusting sails and tugging on lines. A triangular sail burst from the ship's front spar. Canvas-white it puffed with wind, straining at its bindings. The *Sea Sprite* leaped forward like a startled horse, moving from a brisk canter to a spurred gallop.

The deck lurched beneath her boots. Kath clutched the railing, her gaze locked on the enemy. Unlike the *Sea Sprite,* the trireme moved by wind and by oar, a lethal menace plowing the waves.

The enemy's oars flashed bright, doubling their pace. Cleaving the water with frightening speed, the ship leaped forward like a hound slavering for the kill. Indifferent to the wind's direction, the MerChanter knifed through the waves, cutting a straight course for the *Sprite.*

Kath gripped the railing, urging the *Sprite* to speed. "*Faster...faster!*"

The enemy oars maintained their furious pace. Churning the water, they clawed the distance between the two ships, narrowing the gap.

"We're not going to make it." Kath gripped Bear's arm. "Tell the men to prepare for a fight. Have them don arms and armor, ready to rush the top deck."

Bear nodded. "As you say, Svala."

Kath sidled towards Juliana. "Can you evade them?"

The captain gave the barest shake of her head, her gaze fixed on the enemy ship. "This is our best line. If we tack, we'll only bleed speed."

"My warriors are fierce but we're unaccustomed to the sea. We need to know how the enemy fights."

Juliana spared a glance her way. "We can't outrun them, but I know a trick or two."

The captain started to turn away, but Kath gripped her arm. "I can help but I need to know what to expect."

Juliana's gaze raked Kath with a mixture of anger and annoyance. Kath thought the captain might pull away but practicality won out. Her answer was short and clipped. "They'll try to ram us, to hole our ship. They'll use grapples to bind us close and then they'll board. They'll kill us or enslave us and take our cargo, and then they'll leave the *Sprite* to sink to a watery grave."

"But you've got a plan."

Juliana flashed a lethal smile, like a predator about to bite. "I won't let them ram us. When they get close, I'll jibe the ship around, avoiding their ram and smashing them with our starboard side."

Kath interrupted. "Jibe?"

"A sudden wrenching turn, like a violent pivot."

"And starboard?"

"Our right side."

"So our right side will smash into their ship?"

Juliana nodded. "Just before their ram hits." Her face sober. "Then it will come down to knife work, their tridents against our swords."

"A battle of swords, I'll take that bet."

"You've never fought MerChanters. They're fierce fighters. They'll show no quarter."

Kath flashed a feral grin. "Yes, but they're expecting merchant sailors not seasoned warriors."

Juliana looked at her then, as if truly seeing Kath for the first time. "Jordan sent me north for you...but what are you?"

"A woman who wields a sword."

Juliana gave her a piercing stare. "I suspect you're more than that."

Kath shrugged. "I don't like to lose."

An iron determination flooded the captain's voice. "Then help me win this battle else you'll never leave the north."

55

The Knight Marshal

*H*orns *blared in the night, a desperate call to arms.* The marshal leaped awake, reaching for his sword. In the dim brazier-light, the first sword that came to hand was bound in furs. A jolt raced up his arm. *Wield me!*

Repulsed, he flung the cursed sword aside.

Horns blared in warning, summoning the maroon to battle. Beyond the canvas walls, he heard men scrambling for arms and armor.

Lothar and Martyn burst through the curtain into the marshal's sleeping cell. Lothar was already gird for battle, his battleaxe in his gauntleted hand, his silver surcoat gleaming in the dim light. "Scouts discovered a troop of ogres approaching from the east!"

Martyn stirred the brazier to life and began armoring the marshal. "How many?"

"Eighty or more. Hard to tell in the dark."

"*Eighty!*" Visions of the slaughter field assaulted his mind. "Where do they get these beasts?" He shrugged on a gambeson followed by chainmail.

"Valin only knows, but they're coming."

"From the east, you say?"

Lothar nodded. "They're making their way up the backside of Stonehand Mountain."

Martyn strapped on his breastplate and then knelt to buckle his greaves.

"At least we have the high ground...and some time."

Lothar scowled. "Time to flee or time to attack?"

That was the question. "What word from the west?"

"None so far."

"None?" The answer bothered him, a prickling at the back of his neck. "Ogres are attacking from the east, yet there's nothing to the west? This close to Raven Pass that makes no sense." He swirled his maroon cloak across his shoulders. "Either there's nothing there...or our scouts are dead."

"A trap?"

"Eighty ogres attacking at the dark of the moon, sounds like a trap to me." The marshal reached for Sir Tyrone's great sword, shrugging the harness across his shoulders. "They know we're here."

"Betrayed?"

"Or merely discovered."

Lothar scowled. "Fight or flee?"

The marshal moved to the map table. The rugged terrain held answers but the telltale snow remained their enemy. "If we flee they'll only follow, especially if a larger force lurks to the west." He considered his choices. "Our scouts foiled their surprise and we have the high ground, so somehow we have to turn that to our advantage."

Martyn thrust a stale biscuit into the marshal's hand and then began to pack.

"Lothar, I want you to lead the bulk of our forces north along this ridgeline." His finger traced a path along the map. "And then cut down this ravine. Double back around behind the ogres to...this meadow, and I'll meet you there."

Lothar raised a bushy eyebrow. "You'll meet me there?"

"I'll lead a charge of a hundred mounted knights down the Stonehand's backside. With the mountain at our backs, there'll be no stopping us. Our horses will barrel through their lines, our swords cutting like scythes."

"You'll charge *eighty* ogres?"

"They won't be expecting it."

"They bloody well won't."

"Then I take it you like my plan?"

"It's mad...and daring...but the odds could be improved." Lothar stepped close, his voice dropping to a whisper. "Give me the dark sword and *I'll* lead the charge."

"No." The marshal's voice held firm, but his gaze slid away. "We'll kill what we can and then punch through their lines to meet you in the meadow."

A horn sounded beyond the canvas.

"Silence that horn! We've given them enough warning!" Beyond the canvas flap, someone scurried to obey. The marshal turned to Lothar, grasping his arm. "Get the war host away. Save the maroon to fight another day...I'll meet you in the meadow."

"I'll hold you to that." They locked stares and then Lothar hastened away.

"Martyn, take the maps, food and weapons. Leave the rest."

"Yes, lord."

The marshal reached for the black sword. Even through the fur wrappings, he could feel it pulsing with power.

Wield me!

Grinding his teeth against the temptation, he slung the cursed blade across his back and strode beyond the canvas curtain. In the pavilion's heart, knights struggled to don their armor. "I need a hundred mounted knights for a diversionary charge. Who's with me?"

"I'm with you, my lord!"

"And me!"

"Count me in!"

Their rousing response lifted his heart. "Tonight we ride into the teeth of death!"

"For Honor and the Octagon!" They followed him out into the cold night, scrambling for their mounts. The camp swarmed with men preparing for battle. A pair of stewards struggled to bring down the pavilion but the marshal gainsaid them. "Food and weapons only, we haven't time for more."

Sir Rannock appeared leading a string of saddled horses. "Sounds like we've got a fight on our hands."

The marshal swung into the saddle, his ribs still sore from the last battle. "It seems like a never ending fight." He stood in the stirrups, his voice ringing above the tumult. "A hundred knights to me! The rest of you follow Sir Lothar!"

The swirling chaos quickly resolved into order. Lothar got the others moving, a long maroon line riding the ridgeline, while the marshal gathered his vanguard beneath the great Stonehand.

Warhorses stamped and snorted in the cold night air, breathing plumes of frost, eager to be released. On the marshal's command, his vanguard deliberately milled their horses, creating an army of hoof prints, as if a much larger force stood poised to attack. Satisfied with the ruse, the marshal called them to order. Three rows of knights formed below the Stonehand, poised for the charge. The marshal looked left and right, seeing a grim resolve mirrored in their faces. The maroon line readied for battle, knights tightening their armor, weapons whispering from scabbards. For half a heartbeat, the marshal stared aloft, beseeching Valin. Stars glittered overhead, cold and keen as ice-chips in the moonless night, but if the gods cared, he could not tell. Reaching back, he drew Sir Tyrone's sword, five feet of good Castlegard steel gleaming sharp in the night, a welcome weight in his mailed fist. Standing in the stirrups, he raised the sword to the heavens. *"For Honor and the Octagon!"*

"Honor and the Octagon!" More than a hundred voices roared their answer.

The marshal spurred his mount to a gallop, the others following behind. Iron-shod hooves churned the shallow snow, a jangle of arms and armor galloping over the crest. The line of knights plunged downhill into the waiting darkness, the snow muffling their hoofbeats. The balding mountaintop gave way to a thicket of trees, bare branches snatching at maroon cloaks like feeble hands. The marshal shrugged off their touch, barreling through the thicket. His vanguard formed a deadly wedge, like the armored wings of a raptor stooped to the attack. They plummeted down the steep slope, horses snorting with effort, armored knights clanking, both steaming with heat like otherworldly beasts. Leaning forward, the marshal peered between the trees, seeking the enemy, the snowy landscape bright despite the darkened moon. His grip tightened on his sword, battle lust mixed with anxiety. The steep slope pulled them ever downward, adding speed to their charge. Weapons couched, they rode amongst the trees, seeking fodder for their blades.

And then he saw them. Clad in horned helms and thick furs, the ogres lumbered uphill like malformed monsters loosed from hell, huffing and puffing gouts of frost. One stopped to sniff the night, bellowing a howl.

The marshal marked his foe, a towering ogre carrying a massive cudgel. He loosed his warhorse to a full gallop, speed adding weight to the blow. Horse and rider barreled into the beast. His stallion whinnied at the impact, like riding into a stone wall, but then the ogre toppled backward, bowled by the charge. Leaning from the saddle, the marshal struck a two-handed blow. Blood spewed across the snow, hot and foul. He hacked at the beast, desperate to slay it.

"Behind you!"

The marshal whirled, narrowly evading a spiked cudgel. He asked his stallion for a rear, iron-shod hooves lashing at the ogre's ugly head. Grunting from the impact, the ogre backed away. The marshal attacked, slashing at the beast's chest. His blade found flesh, biting deep, but the beast did not die.

The ogre roared, lashing out. A massive fist struck the marshal's chest, punching the air from his lungs. He struggled for breath, bruised by the blow. The second blow punched him from the saddle. The marshal hit the ground hard. Stunned, he sprawled on the trampled snow. His warhorse reared overhead, iron-shod hooves keeping the ogre at bay. Disarmed, his ribs aflame with pain, the marshal floundered for his sword.

Wield me the voice of the dark sword thundered through his mind.

"No!" He glimpsed his sword and lunged for it. Hands locking on the hilt, he came up swinging. His stallion bugled, attacking the ogre's head. The marshal knelt, hacking at the beast's hamstrings.

The ogre fell in a roar.

Iron-shod hooves plunged down, delivering the killing blow.

Spattered with gore, the marshal staggered to his horse. The chaos of battle roared around him. He climbed into the saddle, hewing left and right. Sweat ran in rivulets down his face. Hampered by his helm, he flung it off, needing to see. A nightmare of screams surrounded him. The ogres closed in, smashing with ham-handed fists and massive cudgels. Ducking low, he evaded a spiked club. A knot of four knights formed around the marshal. Surrounded by ogres, they fought back to back, slashing and hacking, desperate to hold the beasts at bay.

Wield me! the dark sword whispered in his mind but the marshal refused. "We need to cut our way out!" Having lost the impetus of their mounted charge, the battle slowed to a slaughter.

Sir Rannock appeared from the left, ramming into an ogre. The big brute went down, pummeled by iron-shod hooves.

An opening appeared. "To me! To me!"

The marshal spurred his horse through the gap. The others followed, fighting through the tangle. Breaking free, they galloped downhill into open ground, gaining a respite. The marshal turned his horse. His stallion stamped and snorted, lathered in sweat. Men and mounts were both spent, yet the battle continued to rage on the mountainside. The sound of clashing steel echoed from above, the shouts of men mixed with the bellow of ogres. The marshal could not abandon his men. He looked at the others. Fourteen knights had won free, all of them battered and bloodied. "We need to break the others loose!"

A charge up hill was usually ill-advised, but he saw no other way.

"Form a line! We'll slam into their rear, create an opening and then turn and ride for the meadow."

Their horses were tired, lathered and blowing, yet they formed a ragged line. The marshal gestured and the knights put spurs to their mounts. The warhorses obeyed, lumbering uphill for one last desperate charge. Armor and weapons clanking, the knights couched their weapons, riding in grim silence, urging their mounts up the steep hillside.

Fortune favored the bold, for the ogres never turned. Consumed by battle lust, they kept at the slaughter.

The ragged line slammed into their rear.

The marshal used the last of his strength to strike a mighty blow.

The ogre dropped like a boulder, opening a path to the trapped knights.

"*To me! To me!*" The marshal shouted above the tumult. Whirling his horse, he slashed left and right, desperate to hold the opening. Amidst the clashing steel, a horse squealed in terrible pain. He turned at the sound, catching a glimpse of ogres mobbing a fallen horse. Locked in a feeding frenzy, they tore hunks of raw flesh from the still-kicking horse, their lantern jaws dripping a disgusting slaver of blood and guts. The marshal pitied the horse, yet it kept the ogres occupied.

"*Rally to me!*" He spurred his stallion into the nearest ogre, attacking the beast with a two-handed stroke. Dark blood spurted from its shoulder, yet the beast roared in defiance. The marshal stabbed his sword into the ogre's gaping mouth. Teeth snapped shut on steel, as if the ogre would eat the blade, but the marshal had rammed his sword deep. Blood gushed from its mouth. Struck dead, the ogre toppled backward, its great weight nearly dragging the marshal from the saddle. Yanking his sword free, he whirled to find another foe. Scanning the battle, he realized his men had opened a narrow corridor to the trapped knights. Standing in the stirrups, he yelled, "*To me! To me!*" The trapped knights responded, charging through the gap, some riding double.

"*Away! Away! Ride for the meadow!*"

As the last knight passed, the marshal put spurs to his mount. Fleeing death, they thundered downhill. He spied a knight afoot, stumbling in the snow. Leaning low in the saddle, the marshal extended his hand. Locking hands with the knight, the marshal swung him over his stallion's withers, grunting at the sharp pain in his shoulder. For three heartbeats, his horse floundered under the added weight, but then the warhorse proved his heart, surging to a desperate gallop. They raced downhill, a ragged ride, beating through naked branches.

Tearing through a dense thicket, they burst into an unsullied meadow.

The marshal slowed his mount, steam rising from his spent stallion.

The rescued knight slid to the ground, sprawling in the snow.

Lathered in sweat, his valiant warhorse lowered his head, sucking air like a bellows about to burst. The marshal slipped from the saddle, staggering when his boots hit the cold hard ground. Ambushed by his own exhaustion, the marshal sank to the snow. Bone-weary, he stared up at the wooded hillside. If the ogres chose to follow, he did not have the strength to fight.

56

Katherine

Kath crouched behind the railing. The great trireme bore down on the *Sea Sprite* like a many-legged beast. A drumbeat boomed across the closing gap, tolling the time. Oars cleaved the frothing waves with determined menace. Striking the water in deadly unison, they flashed blood-red. A brass ram shaped like a saw tooth protruded from the enemy's prow. Jagged and keen, it turned the trireme into a fearsome weapon, like the snout of a monstrous beast. Eyes were painted above the ram, as if the ship could see its prey. Kath's heartbeat thundered. Death rowed towards them with a reaper's speed.

So close, the details became clear. She saw the enemy crowding the deck, thrice the number of her own band. Big swarthy men with dark braided hair and forked beards, they hefted tridents and double-bladed axes. Beneath their horned helms, the raiders looked fierce and eager, but Kath judged their armor to be their weakness. Copper scales sewn onto leather brigandines, a meager defense against sharp steel. Outnumbered and unaccustomed to the sea's bucking motion, her painted warriors desperately needed the slender advantage.

Kath's gaze sought her own men. Blaine, Bear and Sidhorn, crouched by her side, the others spread across the deck. Hiding from the enemy, they kept low. Weapons sheathed, they braced for the collision. Twenty-seven seasoned warriors, they'd fought the Mordant's gore hounds and stormed his Citadel and lived to gain their glory. Mountain lion, eagle, bear, owl, wolf, badger and boar, she claimed them all, fierce fighters and loyal friends, risking their lives on a chancy sea voyage. It seemed the thrice-cursed north would not release them without a blood price. Gripping her gargoyle for luck, Kath whispered a prayer to Valin, *grant us victory...and protect my men.*

Beside her, Blaine hissed, "Look at that thing!"

Oars flashed to a frantic drumbeat, the great trireme bore down on them at a ramming speed. Her gaze fastened on the ram, a jagged saw of hardened brass. So close, it loomed lethal. Kath cringed for the impact, fearing the captain had left it too late.

"Ready about!"

Sailors scurried up the rigging.

"Helm's alee!"

Canvas snapped and timbers creaked. The *Sea Sprite* groaned, heaving violently to the right. Kath gripped her shield and clutched the nearest railing. The deck pitched to a steep angle. Torkin, a wolf-faced warrior, lost his grip, sliding across the deck, headed for the briny deep. Kath lunged for him, her fingertips snagged his, nearly yanking her arm from her shoulder. Refusing to let go, she swung him to the right, aiming for the nearest railing.

The *Sea Sprite* smashed into the trireme, a violent blow. The raider's oars snapped and shattered. Someone shrieked in pain. The two ships hit with a fearsome crunch. Kath was thrown backwards, landing hard, tasting blood in her mouth.

Grappling hooks arced through the air, impaling the *Sea Sprite*.

Kath scrambled to her feet and drew her sword. *"Attack!"* Racing across the deck, she jumped to the railing and leaped the gap. Shield first, she slammed into the enemy's ranks, hitting with her full weight. Beneath her, a sea raider crumpled to the deck. Kath got her sword up and lunged for his throat, a killing strike. Hot blood spurted across her hand. Cut and slash, she fought for space, she fought for her life.

Men screamed and yelled, locked in close quarters. Blood slicked the deck. Kath spun left and then right, evading a battleaxe. The deck rolled beneath her boots, yet she took it in stride. A trident snaked in below her guard, slamming into her side. Her chainmail deflected the triple barbs, but the blow staggered her, knocking her to her knees. A heavy boot stomped on her shield arm, pinning her to the deck. A battleaxe whistled towards her head. Kath wrenched to the right, desperate to twist away, but then Blaine was there, his great blue sword slicing the axe from the arm. Blood spurted across the deck as the maimed MerChanter staggered away.

Released, Kath scrambled to her feet.

Blaine waded into the enemy, bellowing his war cry. *"For the Octagon!"* Sparks flew as steel clashed against steel. His great blue sword cut a swath through the enemy, hewing limbs from bodies and severing heads from shoulders. None could stand in his path. Kath rushed to fight by his side. The deck rocked beneath her boots, making the footing treacherous. A trident slashed towards her face but she parried the strike with her shield. Sidhorn and Bear joined her. They formed a wedge, following Blaine, hewing into the enemy. Stroke and parry, they forced the MerChanters back.

More of her maroon band leaped the gap, adding their swords to the fighting wedge.

The MerChanters bellowed a mighty roar. Surging forward, they fought to reclaim their ship. Packed in the narrow deck, the fighting was fierce. Kath could smell fish oil in the enemy's braided beards. A wild-eyed raider pressed towards her. Kath ducked beneath a vicious slash of his double-bladed axe. Lunging forward, she buried her sword in his armpit. Howling in pain, he crumpled to the deck.

Steel clanged and blood flowed. Corpses became obstacles, tripping the living. The MerChanters fought like fiends. Stabbing low with their barbed tridents, they pressed forward.

Flaming arrows whistled overhead. One stuck the red sails. Canvass ignited with a deadly whoosh, flecks of flame falling to the heaving deck.

The MerChanters howled, redoubling their effort. Jabbing with tridents, they brought their numbers to bear.

Kath slipped on blood, stumbling over a body. She flicked her shield down, protecting her center while her sword stabbed upwards, slicing a MerChanter between the legs. Bright blood spewed across her arm. Screaming, the man crumpled on top of her. A hand grabbed her by the back of her chainmail, hauling her to her feet. Kath turned to strike, but then stayed her sword.

Bear steadied her. *"Take care, Svala!"*

She crouched beside him, taking stock of the battle. The enemy ship was on fire, the great sail flaming overhead, but too many of the MerChanters still lived. Fighting like demons, their eyes' crazed, they attacked with tridents and axes, berserkers forcing her men back. Blaine held the center, his blue sword taking a deadly toll, but the warriors on either side of him retreated under the MerChanters' crazed attack, the wings slowly collapsing under the onslaught. Once the wings collapsed, they'd all die. She had to do something to turn the tide.

Heat beat down at her, singeing her hair. Kath stared aloft at the burning canvas, a great square of flames, and then she noted the wind's direction. Her gaze followed the ropes to the ship's railings. *"Bear!"* She gripped his arm, pointing. "Cut that rope!" She left him, slashing her way to the far side. Reaching the railing, she hacked at the rope, but her sword had little effect, the blade blunted by the battle. Swearing, she sheathed her sword and reached for a throwing axe.

Three sharp whistles came from the *Sea Sprite*, the signal to retreat.

Fear spiked her. *"No! Too soon! Hold the line!"* Kath yelled the command, but some of her painted warriors started to retreat. *"Hold the line!"*

Kath struck at the rope, desperation lending her strength. The axe proved sharp. The rope parted. She stared aloft. The great sail fluttered and fell. Pushed by the wind, it collapsed backwards onto the MerChanters, a fiery shroud straight from hell. Shrieks erupted from the enemy. Flaming figures writhed beneath the burning canvas, horrible screams raking the air.

"Retreat! Retreat!" Kath danced backwards, yelling to her men.

Three urgent whistles came from the *Sea Sprite*.

Her painted warriors began to disengage, rushing for the side railing. Kath waited long enough to see Blaine pull back, his silver surcoat reflecting the flames. Sheathing her axe, Kath jumped on the railing and then leaped across the widening gap. Her jump was short, her fingernails raking the *Sprite's* railing. Strong hands grabbed her. A pair of sailors hauled her aboard. More of her painted warriors made the leap. She watched as Bear and Sidhorn reached the *Sprite*. Torven climbed the railing, a terrible gash on his face. Many bore wounds but they'd live to fight another day.

"Shove off!"

Sailors cut the enemy's grappling hooks.

"No!" Kath pushed her way to the railing, certain there must be others. *"Wait!"* Two more painted warriors reached the *Sea Sprite*. Kath helped pull Torkin aboard. Looking across the widening gap, she saw Blaine on the enemy ship, a wall of flames behind him. Sheathing his blue sword, he leaped for the *Sprite*...but the gap was too wide. Landing on shattered oars, he made a desperate lunge but fell short. Weighed down by his chainmail, the sea sucked him under.

Kath saw the horror on his face. *"No!"*

A sailor with a rope tied round his waist, dove in Blaine's direction. The sea thrashed white, but then a hand emerged clutching the rope. Sailors heaved the line, pulling them both aboard. Shivering and sopping with seawater, Blaine collapsed on the deck, gasping for breath.

Kath sagged in relief.

The distance between the ships widened.

The trireme burned like an inferno. Flaming figures dove from the enemy ship, plunging into the foaming sea. Most sank like rocks but a few heads bobbed among the waves, shouting for help. Dark fins appeared in the churning water. A streamlined shadow cruised beneath the waves, circling the survivors. One man yelled, a single horrid shriek, and then disappeared in a thrash of blood.

Kath gagged. *Men eaten alive,* she'd never seen such a thing. She turned away in horror.

Checkered sails flapped overhead, empty of wind. The *Sea Sprite* slowly turned. The wind caught the sails and the *Sprite* leaped forward.

An ominous shape shadowed the deck. A dark pinnacle loomed overhead. They'd sailed close to a rocky spire, too close. Kath gripped the railing, fearing they'd crash. Juliana shouted orders and sailors scaled the rigging. The ship started to turn but not fast enough. The spire loomed large, a sharp black rock thrust up from the sea like a razor-sharp tooth. Waves battered the base, an angry froth of white. The ship moved closer, like iron drawn to a lodestone, close enough to see orange starfish clutching the dark pinnacle. Kath held her breath, wondering if they'd survived the battle only to be dashed against the rocks.

Sailors rushed the railing wielding long poles with hooked ends.

The deck slowly tilted, sails snapping in the wind.

Sailors leaned out, muscles straining, pushing against the spire with their poles.

The deck tilted higher, rising towards the dark spire, so close Kath could almost touch the rocky menace. Timbers groaned and Kath heard a terrible scraping noise, wood screeching against rock, the death knell of a ship. Clutching her gargoyle, she whispered a fervent prayer to Valin. The rocky spire loomed overhead, sharp and dark and deadly...and then they were past. The wind took the sails and the *Sea Sprite* leaped forward, escaping the bay, escaping the north. The deck settled to level, salt spray licking the far side. Kath released a long-held breath. Gray waves stretched to forever, an endless open ocean.

Kath slumped to the deck. Everything ached, her ribs, her shoulder, her sword arm. Too tired to stand, her gaze swept the deck, taking note of her men. Bloody and battered, they sprawled on the deck, some felled by sleep, while others cleaned their weapons or bound their wounds. A fierce pride flashed through her, *exhausted but victorious, they'd won free of the north.* Kath turned towards Blaine. "Are you hurt?"

"Not a scratch from the raiders but the sea damn near killed me." He shivered, swiping wet hair from his face. "Let's not do that again."

"You should get out of those wet clothes or the cold will finish what the sea started."

Blaine groaned. "Too tired to move."

She flashed a smile. "Get Dermit to help. That's what squires are for."

Overhead, a sailor shouted. *"Sail ho!"*

Kath sat up, peering over the railing, but she saw nothing.

Sailors scrambled across the deck.

"Sail ho! A MerChanter raider!"

Kath leaped to the railing. She saw it then, another blood red sail emerging from behind a distant sea stack. Oars flashing black against the wave-tossed sea, it raced towards them. Kath's heart sank. *Another enemy, another fight,* the north was relentless, demanding their deaths.

57

The Knight Marshal

Sprawled on the snow-crusted ground, the marshal took stock of the others. Twenty-four knights out of more than a hundred, with many of the survivors bearing bloody wounds. The losses staggered him. A litany of names ran through his mind, some of them friends, all of them brothers-in-arms. Yet mingled with the sorrow, he felt a swell of pride. A hundred mounted knights against eighty ogres; it was a feat worthy of legends. Yet how long could the maroon dare such odds?

Battered and sore, the marshal sat sprawled in the snow, not caring if his armor rusted, not caring about the cold, just breathing in and out, grateful to be alive. He stared up at the wooded hillside, listening for the enemy, for the blunder of ogres crashing through the thorny thicket, yet he heard nothing. Not yet. With the horses spent, fleeing wasn't an option. He needed to rally his men to a defensive position, but he could not bestir himself, too exhausted to do anything but live.

Dawn light cracked the sky, a golden glow dispelling the darkness.

He stared at the sky, mesmerized by the beauty of the glow.

"Riders approaching!"

The marshal staggered to his feet. He had no strength left to fight, yet he'd meet his fate standing with a sword in his hands. Leaning on his sword, he stared across the meadow, waiting for succor or death.

Wield me!

So tempting, but for the hundredth time, he ignored the cursed sword strapped to his back.

A line of mounted knights galloped into the clearing...all of them wore maroon.

Tension bled from the marshal's shoulders. It took all of his strength just to remain standing.

Lothar found him. "Too tough to kill?"

"Just so."

Lothar slid from his horse and the two friends clasped arms. "You had the truth of it."

"What?"

"Bartlet stayed behind, shinnied up a cedar tree. It was a trap. A host of black-cloaked soldiers came charging up the east side of Stonehand. A few tracked us along the ridgeline and fell to our archers, but most followed you down the west side, playing the hammer to the ogres' anvil."

"They wagered we'd fight rather than flee."

"Just so." Lothar's gaze roved the survivors. "I count twenty-three."

"Twenty-four."

"A stiff price."

The marshal did not answer.

Lothar leaned close. "Did you wield it?"

"No."

"Why not?" Lothar gave him a sharp look.

The marshal's voice dropped to a harsh whisper. "You don't know this sword the way I do. It begs to be wielded, as if it thirsts for blood." Shuddering, he made the hand sign against evil. "It whispers like teeth gnawing at my mind." He shook his head. "The sword is cursed."

Lothar stared at him. "But how many knights might have been spared?"

And that was the question. The same awful damning question he'd been asking himself since they'd reached the meadow. "That way is cursed."

"Even if it brings us victory?"

The marshal scowled.

Lothar stepped close. "I'll wield it if you won't."

"We'll talk no more of this."

His friend gave him a measured look. "We'd best be going. If we linger, they're sure to find us."

"Tell the others to mount up." The marshal swung into the saddle, the cursed sword bound in furs and strapped to his back, a nagging whisper clawing at his mind.

58

Katherine

The MerChanter raider cleaved the sea, rowing on a killing path towards the *Sea Sprite*...but this time they had more warning. Kath measured the distance, wondering if it was enough. Hovering near the captain, she asked the fateful question, "Can you outrun them?"

"If the gods owe you any favors, ask now." Juliana snapped orders while sailors scuttled to obey. The *Sea Sprite* jigged left and then right, tacking across the ocean like a frightened hen evading an eagle's talons. The vast open ocean proved a wild place compared to the placid bay. Massive gray waves rolled in from the deep, tossing the ship between watery hills and deep troughs. Kath's warriors turned wretched. Clinging to the railings, they spewed their guts to the sea. Kath pitied them, but she could do nothing to ease their suffering. Remaining by the captain, she clutched the railing and stared at the sea. The *Sea Sprite* slid down a slate-gray wave into a deep gully, massive walls of water on either side. Kath feared the walls would collapse, crushing the *Sprite*, but the plucky ship gained speed, always climbing the next wave. At every peak, Kath looked back, praying for empty seas...but always the MerChanter followed like a hound locked on their scent.

For nigh on half the day, they sailed south on a zigzag path, following the dark coastline, but the MerChanter raider held to the hunt. Dark oars slashed the slate-gray sea in deadly unison, the red-hulled raider churning towards them, slowly eating the distance.

Tension gnawed at Kath. "If we keep on like this, they'll catch us."

"I know." The captain stared aloft, a calculating look on her face. "Time to roll the dice. Hard to starboard."

Marcus repeated the order in a loud bellow. "Hard to starboard!"

Sailors climbed the rigging, tending the sails. The *Sea Sprite* swung hard to the right, heading due west into the ocean deep. Salt spray licked the prow as they beat into a massive wave.

Beside her, Juliana said, "Now would be a good time for the god's favor."

Kath clung to the railing, the wind whipping her hair. "Why?"

"An old sea captain's rumor says that MerChanter raiders never sail beyond sight of the coastline. I've never had reason to test it. Pray that it's true."

The *Sea Sprite* leaped forward like a startled horse, beating a path through ferocious waves. Kath gripped the railing, watching for the enemy ship, praying for it to cling to the coast. For the longest time, she saw nothing but waves...but then she spied the red hull. The MerChanter had turned to the west, black sails straining overhead, chasing the *Sprite* towards the briny deep. "*Damn.*" Kath cursed their ill-luck.

Juliana said, "It's not over yet. They can still see the coast."

Kath stayed with the captain, keeping watch on the enemy. It seemed they sailed for an eternity, pressing deeper into the mountainous sea. Towering waves battered the ship like a mighty hand swatting a fly. Her painted warriors flopped on the deck like dead fish, pale and empty. Sailors moved among them, offering flagons of water. Kath widened her stance, riding the waves, like balancing on a bucking horse. She fixed her gaze on the distant coast, the last glimpse of land. The dark horizon dwindled, shrinking to nothing, as if swallowed by the sea.

Beside her, Juliana muttered, "Now we'll learn the truth of the rumor."

Nothing but waves in every direction, Kath swallowed, gripped by a primal fear. Her knuckles strained white on the ship's railing. Beyond sight of land, the sea stretched to forever, vast and cold and hostile, every rolling wave filled with deadly menace.

Juliana sidled close. "You feel it, don't you?"

Her mouth suddenly dry, Kath could only nod.

"Many a captain will not sail beyond the sight of land. Pray that the MerChanters feel it too."

Kath prayed to Valin like she'd never prayed before, wondering if the warrior god could hear her amidst the pounding waves.

The sun began to set, turning the ocean to a violent crimson...as if they sailed into nightmares. Making the hand sign against evil, Kath scanned the waves for the enemy ship. And then she saw them. The dark sails had shrunk small...but they never vanished. "Will they turn back?"

Juliana shook her head, her face grim. "They should have turned long ago." Her voice dropped to a harsh rasp. "They've got our blood scent. They won't stop without a fight."

"Damn," Battered by the sea, Kath knew her warriors were in no fit state to fight. "We can't fight them, not here, not now. What can you do?"

"Outrun them...or evade them."

"Evade them?"

"When the sun sets, there'll be naught but a thin crescent moon. With luck, the clouds will shutter the moonlight and then we'll turn and race for the south. Under cover of darkness we'll duck between the waves, trying to evade them. With a favorable wind and a lot of luck, we might lose them."

Kath stared at the captain. "So it comes down to luck?"

"Luck and boldness and the wind's favor."

She did not like the odds. "We haven't had much luck in the north. I'd rather trust to wits and steel."

"It may come to that." Juliana studied the rigging, taking stock of her ship. "At least this strong westerly has outrun their oars. We've bought some time."

"How much?"

"A day. Less if the wind dies, more if we evade them." Juliana gave her a grim look. "Best if you and your men get below. You'll need food and rest."

Kath heard the warning beneath the words. "Just so." Taking leave of the captain, she made the rounds, careful not to be ambushed by a rogue wave. Salt spray leaped the railings, stinging with numbing cold. Crouched on the deck, she spoke to each of her men, checking their spirits and their wounds, advising them to go below deck, to get dry and stay warm. Despite the rolling waves, she urged them to eat and to rest, for tomorrow their swords might be needed. Wretched with seasickness, yet they gave her dogged smiles. "We'll keep our swords sharp, Svala."

The trust in their faces touched her heart, untarnished despite the sea's ill treatment. A fierce pride leavened with duty swelled through her. Kath felt the burden to protect them...but the sea was a battleground she did not understand. "Come, we need to get below."

Making her way to the ship's center, Kath pried open the main hatch and descended the rope ladder. Warmth embraced her, the warmth of too many bodies laden with the scent of fear and piss and seasickness. She nearly gagged on the stench.

Lanterns swung from the ceiling beams, swaying with the ship's motion. The swinging light somehow made the swaying worse, multiplying the effect. Kath swallowed, forcing down the taste of bile.

Hammocks crowded the hold, strung at different heights, crisscrossing the space like canvas cocoons. Many were filled, more than a few men moaning with seasickness. Across the hold, she saw Blaine peeling off his soaked surcoat, Dermit lending a hand. At least the knight had the good sense to get dry. Kath searched for Zith and found the monk sleeping fitfully, his face as pale as curdled whey.

"Let him sleep, Svala." Seffer looked at her, one of the wolf-faced warriors in Neven's pack. "The sea's taken a hard toll on the monk."

"And you?"

He shrugged, feigning indifference despite looking green beneath his wolf tattoo. "I'll live."

"And Danya?"

"Still sleeps." He gestured across the hold.

Neven sat with his back against the ship's curved hull, surrounded by a nest of bedrolls, Danya's head cradled in his lap. Kath crossed towards him, ducking beneath hammocks. Bryx raised his shaggy head, looked at her, and then slumped back to the deck. The wolf looked miserable, like most of the men in the hold. "How is she?"

Neven stroked Danya's hair. "Still asleep, still peaceful, as if she hasn't a care."

Kath regretted bringing her friend south, but at least she was spared the sea's malady. "Perhaps you should have stayed in the Citadel."

Neven gave her a level stare. "We gave our word, Svala."

She nodded, wondering if Danya's magic would work at sea. Angered by the thought, Kath rebuked herself, dismissing the idea as unworthy. Danya paid a steep price for their victory at the Dark Citadel. "There's another raider chasing us. The captain will try to lose them in the dark. If it comes to another fight, we'll need every sword."

"The wolf band will fight with the maroon."

"My thanks." She looked at Danya. "Keep her safe."

"Always."

Kath worked her way through the hold, passing word of the MerChanter ship. Towards the rear, she found her two badger-faced squires, Talbert and Conit. Both looked bright-faced and alert, as if their youth protected them from the rollicking sea.

"Svala, we saved a hammock for you!"

Kath was not used to having one squire, let alone two, but the orphan lads had insisted on following her south. Sitting perched on the swaying hammock, she tried to look solemn as they tugged off her boots and eased her throwing axes from her shoulders. Conit thrust a bowl into her hands filled with dried meat and biscuits while Talbert offered her a wineskin. She took the wine, savoring the rich taste, a fine vintage from the Mordant's personal stock. Kath wasn't hungry, but she forced the food down while listening to the two boys chatter about battles and victories.

"We haven't escaped the north."

Conit looked at her. "The Svala will find a way."

Such confidence. "If a battle comes, I want you two to stay in the hold."

Both lads looked indignant. "But Svala, we can fight!"

"I know you can fight. I want you two to help protect Danya. Her magic is important."

The lads looked at each other, as if weighing her order, and then they gave her a solemn nod. "We can do that."

"Good. Now get some rest." Swinging her legs into the hammock, she pulled up a wool blanket and curled on her side, swaying back and forth to the ship's motion. Rocking like a cradle, the hammock should have been soothing, but sleep eluded her. In her mind's eye, Kath refought the sea battle, recalling every warrior lost. Seven dead and twelve wounded, she shuddered at the loss of friends and comrades. Her painted warriors had gained a hard-fought victory...but her men had taken a mauling...and that was before the wretched seasickness claimed them. They weren't fit to fight. The knowledge haunted her. Despite their stalwart courage, they'd lose without some clear advantage. Ships were so confining, an island surrounded by wind and wave. Kath tossed and turned, desperately seeking a solution. Exhaustion finally claimed her. She fell asleep...and woke to nightmares.

59

General Haith

General Haith urged his horse to a canter. Lifting his helm's visor, he enjoyed the brisk winter wind whipping against his face. The horses needed exercise, but in truth, the general wanted to view the enemy's camp for himself. Sometimes the smallest details carried the most potent insights. Farther up the trail the gore hounds howled, their twisted cries echoing against the mountaintops. He'd sent a vanguard ahead, a formidable force to sweep the forest. All reports indicated the enemy was long gone, fled the trap, leaving less than a hundred dead. Heads would roll for this failure, but first he'd view the camp and gauge the details for himself.

His escort followed the trail upwards, riding through a thicket of aspen before reaching the balding mountaintop. General Haith slowed his stallion to a walk. Blackened fire rings and hovels built of cedar branches littered the mountaintop, proof of an army camp hastily abandoned. *Hovels built of branches;* the enemy did not even have tents for their men yet they persisted in fighting. The Octagon displayed an uncommon tenacity. The general might have admired his foe...if he hadn't been ordered to annihilate them. Near the crest sat three maroon pavilions, one of them leaning like a drunkard. *So the officers had a modicum of luxury,* but now even that was abandoned.

And then he saw it, the true reason he'd come. A great mage-stone hand towered at the mountain's crest, a relic of a bygone age. He'd seen mage-stone before, but only from a great distance. Curiosity pulled him forward. Riding straight to the hand, he dismounted, flinging his reins to a waiting centurion. More than a thousand years old, yet the sculpted stone showed no sign of weathering, no sign of age. Smooth and unblemished, the mage-stone statue stood thrice the height of a tall man, the pale-gray stone glistening in the waning light. The Seeing Eye chiseled in its palm looked crisp and clear as if it was made yesterday, a stone sentinel watching from the mountaintop, undaunted by the centuries. Forever polished to a gleam, he saw his reflection in the great Eye. *Mage-stone, a wonder of a lost age,* he tugged off his gauntlet, setting his bare hand against the smooth stone. *What tales could you tell? What ageless wonders await me in the monastery?*

"Beware, my lord!" Trantor, his personal snargon waddled towards him. Pointed teeth bared, the swarthy duegar stood no higher than the general's belt. "I don't like the smell of that."

The general stepped back, fighting the urge to wipe his hand on his surcoat. He watched as the duegar sniffed the stone hand, his nostrils spread wide like a hound on the scent.

"Magic, very old magic." The duegar circled the hand, sniffing deeply but never touching. "Magic bound to the stone, bound to its making."

The general tugged on his gauntlet. "Can it be wielded? Is it a threat?"

The duegar shook his shaggy head. "The spark is set deep. The hand slumbers...waiting."

"Waiting for what?"

Trantor shrugged. "Who knows? A dead wizard? A live enemy?" The duegar must have felt the general's anger, for he stepped away and bowed low, wiping the sarcasm from his voice. "No way to tell, my lord. But have a care, the ancient wizards were tricky."

That at least was true. Covering his unease, the general snapped an order. "Sniff the camp. I doubt the knights have any magic, but I'll have it searched anyway."

"Yes, my lord." The duegar bowed and began to turn away.

"And Trantor?"

"Yes, my lord." A quaver rode the snargon's voice.

"Take care, lest you lose my favor."

The duegar made a deep bow and scurried away.

"General Haith!" A cadre of centurions approached, a string of prisoners bound between them. Chained and shackled, the prisoners were forced to their knees. Bruised and battered, their faces showed evidence of a lost fight...or abuse by their guards, yet the general recognized most of them.

"You failed me. Worse yet, you failed the Lord Mordant."

The sudden stink of hot urine filled the air.

Kirkbee tried to stand. "My lord, the scouts misread the signs!"

The general flicked a glance and a centurion struck Kirkbee from behind, hammering the prisoner to his knees.

"I expect success from my officers. When you serve Darkness you succeed or you pay. Now it is time to pay." He studied their faces, fascinated by the way men met their doom. Some wept, others cowered, but two held his gaze, pale-faced but stoic. The general decided to be merciful. "Spare these two. Disembowel the others and feed them to the gore hounds."

"*No!*" Kirkbee writhed against his bonds. "*No, I beg you!*"

The general smothered a smile. "Order the men from their cadres to watch so their deaths will be a lesson to all." His smile deepened. "Start with Kirkbee."

Kirkbee groveled on the snow-trampled ground.

The centurions saluted, dragging the doomed men away.

Guards released the shackles from the two spared men. Dropping to their knees, they crawled towards the general. Prostrating themselves, they kissed his boots.

The general indulged them for a few moments and then sent them away with orders to join his personal guard. Mercy shown at the right moment had a way of engendering a fierce loyalty.

"My lord General!" Trantor returned, waddling with his stunted gait. "I've found the stink of potent magic."

The discovery ambushed him. "Where?" So far the knights had displayed a shocking lack of magic. The snargon's discovery was as surprising as it was disquieting.

"This way, my lord."

The snargon led him to the largest pavilion, the one that tilted like a sloppy drunk. Ducking through the canvas flap, the general was assaulted by the lingering stench of too many unwashed bodies. *So the commander shared his pavilion with his unwashed men, how noble, how ridiculous.* The general's lips curled in disdain. Power and luxury went hand in hand; to give up one was to abdicate the other. Little wonder the knights were losing.

The snargon waddled to a curtained chamber in the rear corner. "We found it here, my lord."

The general ducked into the curtained alcove. A small, cramped space, yet it held a few humble comforts. An empty armor stand, a low pallet for a bed, a plank table, an abandoned goblet...all spoke of an officer's quarters...not a knight commander's, yet it was the only luxury in the camp. "Where?"

The snargon squatted by the pallet. His head bent to the ground, he sniffed deeply like a bloodhound on the scent. "Here, my lord." The ugly little duegar closed his eyes, his face suffuse with delight as if sniffing ambrosia. "Dark magic, powerfully Dark magic."

"*Dark* magic? But where would the knights get...?" And then the general understood. He bit back his question, a smile twisting his face.

The Dark Sword, so the Mordant's trap had snared its prey. At least in this, his lord would be pleased. "Well done, Trantor." The general turned, issuing orders. "Burn it. I want everything burned, a beacon of futility for the enemy." He strode from the pavilion and swung into the saddle, an escort of sharp-faced centurions forming around him. Turning his stallion, the general took a last look at the pitiful pavilion and the ancient mage-stone hand. His curiosity satisfied, he turned away, secure in the knowledge that he served the winning side. The Lord Mordant cast a long and fearsome shadow. All of his enemies would die screaming.

60

Katherine

Kath startled awake. *Something was wrong.* She reached for her sword and nearly flipped from the hammock. Clinging to the canvas, she took stock of her surroundings. The others slept, lying in their canvas cocoons, soft snores echoing through the hold, but the ship did not creak, and the hammocks did not sway.

The hammocks did not sway, a premonition of dread slithered down her spine. Kath rolled from the hammock and tugged on her boots. Shrugging on her throwing axes, she threaded her way through the hammocks and scrambled up the rope ladder. Cold sea air poured through the hatch, easing the warm stink of the hold. Kath winced at the bright sunlight, proof she'd slept through the night and into the day. Emerging on deck, she half expected the ship to be deserted, but it was not. Sailors lined the railing, staring out to sea, keeping a tense vigil.

Kath climbed from the hold into a startling silence.

Gone was the billowing wind and frothing whitecaps, replaced by an eerie stillness. Instead of mountainous waves, the slate-gray sea lay smooth and flat, unnaturally calm, as glassy as a mirror. Kath stared slack-jawed. It seemed impossible, as if some ancient wizard had ensorcelled the sea, taming the ocean's wild ways...or the *Sprite* had sailed off the world's edge straight into a nightmare.

Flat as a millpond, the ocean stretched to infinity.

A chill gripped her, so bone-numbing cold it seemed otherworldly. Shivering, Kath said, "What is this?"

No one spoke. No one made a sound. Even the seagulls were gone, as if they'd abandoned the ship. Overhead the sails hung limp and lifeless. The *Sea Sprite* sat still as death, marooned upon a listless sea.

Unnerved, Kath made her way to the rear deck.

Juliana stood at the ship's wheel. Clad in the same clothing as yesterday, her face looked haggard, her red hair tugged from its binding making a ragged halo. She gave Kath a hollow-eyed stare. "We're clapped in irons."

The phrase meant nothing, but the captain's grim tone said it all. "And the enemy?"

Juliana shrugged. "We fled south under the crescent moon...till the winds died. Now all we can do is wait."

"Wait?"

"For the winds to speed us home...or the enemy to find us."

Worry riddled the captain's voice. Kath turned her gaze to the listless sea. "Is this natural? Or some arcane spell?"

"A spell?"

"By the MerChanters, to trap us."

Juliana's gaze widened, ambushed by the question. "If they have that kind of power, I've never heard of it." She gave Kath a harrowing look. "Pray that you're wrong...although the lack of wind clearly favors the trireme." Her gaze scanned the dead calm sea. "Sometimes this happens, the wind dies and the sea calms...but it is rare, very rare."

"There must be something we can do?"

"Pray."

Kath shook her head, frustration lacing her voice. "The gods help those who help themselves." She stared out at the glassy sea. "How long will this last?"

"Only the gods know."

Kath studied the mirror-flat ocean, so unnatural, so eerie. It seemed such an ill turn of luck...but this was the north...where Darkness held sway. She shivered making the hand sign against evil. Kath prowled the ship, staring at the sea from every angle. Not a breath of wind rippled the ocean. The strange calm was unnerving. At least the glass-flat sea would give her men a chance to recover from the wretched sickness. Returning to the rear deck, Kath stood by the captain. "What will happen if the enemy finds us?"

"That depends."

"On what?"

"The wind. Without wind, we have but two choices. Fight or surrender."

"*Surrender?*" Kath was shocked to hear the word.

"It is said that if you fight the MerChanters and lose, then they'll slay everyone onboard, but if you surrender, they'll keep those fit to serve as slaves." Juliana gave her a bitter grin. "Live to fight another day."

*Those fit to serve...*the words echoed in Kath's mind, a death knell for Danya and Zith. A chill raced down her spine. She hadn't brought her friends south just die beneath a MerChanter's trident.

"Of course, it's only a rumor." Juliana shrugged. "Rumors about the MerChanters hugging the coastline were clearly wrong. Few who meet the sea raiders live to speak of it."

Surrender was unthinkable...but without an advantage, her men would lose a straight-up fight. *A straight-up fight,* the thought sparked an idea. "How many archers onboard?"

Juliana cracked a wan smile. "Born and bred in Navarre, most of us are archers, middling at best, but archers nonetheless." Her smile fled. "But we've only three bows among us."

Kath's voice strangled on the number. "Only *three?*"

Juliana shrugged. "We're merchants not warriors."

The answer stunned Kath. A dozen bows might have turned the tide of battle. Desperate for a solution, she prowled the deck and then searched the all the holds, poking in every nook and cranny, seeking an advantage. Such a small ship, surrounded by an endless ocean...it seemed like a trap waiting to snap shut. The crew knew it. Brittle and on edge, they jumped at the slightest sound.

"*Ship ho!*"

The warning sang from the crow's nest.

Kath raced to the railing, praying for a friend, fearing a foe.

Juliana pointed toward the northeast. "There!"

"*Ware the northeast!*"

In the distance, a red hull glided towards them, black oars beating the mirror-flat sea. Time had run out.

61

The Knight Marshal

The maroon won another hard-fought battle, but it did not feel like a victory. Corpses littered the ground; so many the trampled snow ran red with blood. The knight marshal stood upon the slaughter field, leaning on a bloody sword. His gaze scanned the battleground, taking the reaper's tally. For every four dead, three wore black cloaks, proving the prowess of the maroon. But what did prowess matter against an endless horde? So many battles, so many dead...the losses kept mounting. The truth stared him in the face, the bitter, harsh truth. All the valor in the world could not change the outcome. If the Octagon kept fighting this way there'd be nothing left save cripples and lads too young to shave. The marshal shuddered at the thought. He'd not do that to the maroon. He'd not let the Octagon be whittled away to nothing. Not on his watch.

Sheathing Sir Tyrone's great sword, the marshal trudged a path among the dead.

Wield me!

Strapped to his back, the dark sword whispered its siren's song. The marshal grimaced, fighting the sword's temptation.

Crows cawed from the winter-bare trees, awaiting their feast. The marshal crossed the field, studying the dead, looking for friends, looking for the living. Lothar sat on the far side, cradling his battleaxe, a wicked cut bleeding above his left eye. The marshal suppressed a grin. "You still alive?"

Lothar shrugged. "Just another scar to impress the ladies."

His friend's jest could not leaven the truth. "We lost too many."

"I know."

"We can't keep fighting like this."

Lothar gave him a solemn nod. "I know." His voice dropped to a harsh whisper. "I'll wield it if you won't."

The marshal scowled. "If anyone pays the price, it'll be me."

"Are you sure there's a price?"

"I'm sure."

Snowmelt dripped from the trees, ten thousand teardrops raining down, as if the forest wept. Like harp strings plucked in mourning, the sorrowful sound echoed in the marshal's soul. "Winter is fleeing. Soon we'll be wallowing in mud instead of snow."

Lothar shrugged. "Not as cold but just as miserable."

He offered his friend a hand, tugging him to his feet. "We'd best see to the wounded."

Lothar grunted in agreement, his face set in a grimace. Dealing the mercy stroke was a terrible task, but they both knew it had to be done. Together they walked the field, checking the wounded. Those too far gone to save were given a clean stroke. Better a quick knife from a brother-knight than a tortured death in the enemy's hands. The maroon left no wounded upon the battlefield.

"Water...give me water."

They followed the weak croak to a mound of dead. Pulling black-cloaked corpses away, they found a friend sprawled at the bottom. Sir Towlin lay on his back, a gray-haired veteran leaking blood from half a dozen wounds. The worst was a gaping axe cut at his side, dark blood pooling in the melting snow.

The marshal knelt. Gently lifting his friend's head, he held the water skin to the knight's pale lips.

Sir Towlin sucked on the water till he turned his head away. "Wish it was...brandy."

The marshal forced a smile. "You deserve brandy. You fought valiantly."

"Slipped in the damn snow...lucky axe stroke...but I took his damn head." Blood bubbled at the side of his mouth. "Hurt like hell at first...doesn't hurt anymore."

The marshal held his friend, knowing death hovered near. "Your deeds will be remembered."

Something quickened in the knight's eyes. "Will they?" His gaze locked on the marshal like a drowning man clinging to a rope. "Will they remember? Will anyone...live to tell the tale?"

The question pierced the marshal like a fatal sword stroke, sealing his decision. "Yes." The single word held the heavy weight of a dire promise.

"Good." The knight closed his eyes...and died.

The marshal gently lowered his friend to the ground. Whispering a prayer to Valin, he closed his friend's eyes for the last time, placing a sword in the dead man's hands. "Valin keep you."

A scout's warning whistled through the forest.

Lothar hissed, "From the south!"

The marshal stood. Fearing an ambush, he scanned the battlefield, but the alpine meadow offered nowhere to hide and it was too late to run. Bellowing a desperate order, he unsheathed his sword. "Form a shield wall!" Plucking a maroon shield from a corpse, he ran to join the others. A hundred knights, many of them wounded, answered the marshal's call. Staggering to the battlefield's heart, they formed a crescent. Shields overlapping, they faced south, presenting a defensive barrier. Weapons held at the ready, they crouched behind the shield wall, braced for another dance with death.

Three short whistles followed by one long, the marshal sagged with relief. The scout signaled friends approached.

The knights lowered their shields, more than a few slumping to the ground. The marshal took a deep breath. Flicking a glance towards Lothar, he stepped forward to meet the others.

Hoof beats approached from the south. A tattered maroon banner topped the rise, followed by two hundred mounted knights. The lead knight raised a bloody morning star in salute. His shield battered and his horse lathered, Sir Rannock pulled his mount to a halt. "Found the bastards just where you said they'd be. We took them from behind and rode them into the ground." He flashed a deadly smile. "There won't be any ambushes today."

The marshal nodded. "Losses?"

"Twelve dead."

The marshal added them to the grim tally. "We're moving camp to Twin Boulders. We'll meet you there."

Crows cawed from the trees, dark wings launching towards the battlefield.

The marshal glared at the telltale birds. "To linger here is to invite the enemy."

Sir Rannock saluted. "We'll meet you at the boulders." He turned his mount and the others followed him west.

Squires trudged up the far hill bringing the horses.

"Mount up! We ride for Twin Boulders." The marshal swung into the saddle, suppressing a groan. Everything ached, his sword arm, his back, his bruised ribs, but he'd lived to fight another day, while so many others remained upon the battlefield, food for crows. His gaze swept the meadow. Nothing moved save the hungry birds. Too many dead, the truth plagued him. In the back of his mind, the dark sword whispered its temptation, *Wield me!* This time, the marshal chose to answer. "*Yes.*" Asking for a trot, he turned his horse to the west.

62

Juliana

Black oars cleaved the sea, striking ripples in a listless ocean. Juliana watched the enemy approach, a scar upon the ocean. The red-hulled trireme cruised south with menacing speed, a predator chasing a blood scent. For half a day, her crew watched them draw closer, stalking her ship, relentless and implacable. Waiting seemed like a torture, yet now that the enemy drew near, she wished for more time. So close, Juliana could see the raiders crowding the trireme's deck. Their fish-scaled armor gleamed bright as a coppery sunset. Gripping tridents and axes, their eager grins flashed in their bearded faces, keen for a fight.

Death rowed towards her ship, death or enslavement, a grim choice for a captain.

Juliana stood upon the rear deck, gauging the distance. A faint breeze had sprung up, gently rippling the sails. The *Sea Sprite* meandered south, but it was too little too late, as if the gods mocked her crew's entreaties, but it gave her a chance to maneuver.

"Turn to starboard and hold her steady."

Marcus bellowed the order. *"Turn to starboard and hold her steady."*

Sailors tense with the long wait, leaped to answer the call. The *Sea Sprite* gently swung to starboard, presenting her broadside to the raider, like a deer offering her throat to a wolf.

Beside her, Marcus fretted. "Are you sure about this?"

Keeping her voice to a whisper, she answered, "I'm sure of nothing." Louder, she said. "Furl sails."

"Furl sails!"

The checkered sails were furled, another sign of surrender. The *Sea Sprite* sat dead in the water, her wings furled, a plump pigeon awaiting capture.

Juliana swallowed hard, tasting bile in her mouth. Keeping her face stone-still, she watched as the trireme approached. Smooth as silk, the enemy ship banked to starboard, the red hull pulling alongside the *Sprite*. Their port-side oars were shipped, retracting into the hull like a crab pulling its legs into the shell. Grappling hooks sprang from the enemy vessel, piercing the *Sprite's* deck. Bound together in a death grip, the two hulls touched with a dull thud.

Enemy raiders leaped aboard her ship. Big swarthy men with braided beards, they wielded tridents and battleaxes, their scaled copper armor gleaming in the afternoon light. Brandishing their weapons, they scowled at her crew. "Kneel and live or fight and die!"

Her crew retreated like sheep before wolves...but they did not kneel.

One of the MerChanters barked a rude laugh. "*Kneel* or I'll have southern blood on me trident!"

Juliana rushed to the railing. "We surrender!" The words tasted foul in her mouth, but she had to protect her crew.

"A *wench!*" The warrior licked his lips, giving her a lecherous stare. "I claim the wench as my spoils!"

Juliana swallowed her revulsion, refusing to be quelled by his lewd stare.

"Stand down, Balthar." A MerChanter with a weathered face and gray streaking his dark hair sauntered aboard her ship. Gold coins braided his tri-forked beard, a cutlass and three daggers thrust through his belt, all of them gleaming with jewels and polished gold. "Or are you challenging me for the captain's share?"

If plunder was a mark of rank, then Juliana guessed this was their captain.

The burly warrior scowled. "No challenge from me, my lord, just a request for sloppy seconds!"

The others roared with vulgar laughter, crude and coarse, like jackals at a feast.

Bile resurged into Juliana's mouth, but she forced it back down.

The MerChanter lord quieted his men with a stern look. "Put the captives on their knees."

The MerChanters stepped towards her crew, menacing their weapons.

"*Kneel!*" Juliana barked the command, willing her crew to obey.

Sullen, her men dropped to their knees, laying daggers and long knives on the deck.

The MerChanter lord speared her with his stare. "And who are you, that men obey you?"

Juliana steadied her voice, mustering all of her bravado. "The captain of this ship."

"The *captain!*" The lord spat the words while quirking a lewd smile. "A *wench* for a *captain?* You land-peoples keep such strange ways. Little wonder you surrendered." The lord grinned, showing a rich gleam of gold-capped teeth. "I've never tupped a captain before." His voice turned to a hungry growl. "Come here, wench."

Beside her, Marcus reached for his long knife, but she stilled him with a glare.

Taking a steadying breath, Juliana sauntered down the stairs to the middeck. She kept her face stone-still despite her galloping heartbeat. A gauntlet of stares feasted on her. It felt like a gang rape, yet she refused to flinch. At the base of the stairs, the MerChanters parted before her. Grinning like drooling hounds, they opened a path to their lord. Juliana looked neither left nor right, keeping her gaze fixed on the sea lord.

"*Captain, don't!*" Soothby, her second mate, snatched up his long knife and lunged at the lord.

Snake-fast, the lord sidestepped the long knife, plunging a jeweled dagger into Soothby's throat. Impaled, the sailor stood transfixed, his eyes widening in shock, blood frothing at his throat. His long knife clattered useless to the deck. Soothby stopped twitching. Sliding from the gilded blade, he slumped dead beside his knife, spewing blood upon the *Sprite's* deck like a libation.

The lord cleaned his jeweled dagger. "A jealous lover?"

Juliana struggled to appear indifferent.

The lord's dark gaze roved across her, lingering on her curves. "A comely wench, a fitting spoil for a MerChanter Sea Lord."

Under his raking gaze, Juliana felt like a whore put to auction.

Stepping toward her, he leaned close, so close she could smell the fish oil slicking his braided beard.

His gaze delved her breasts.

Repulsed, Juliana struggled not to flinch. "We surrender...so you'll let us live?" A quaver laced her question. Juliana swallowed, uncertain if it was deliberate or fake.

The captain leered at her. "Those who serve, live." His right hand mauled her breast. "A comely lass like you can best serve with your legs spread."

She leaped backwards, her hands clenched.

"A feisty one." He grinned. "I like a little fight in my captives."

Two MerChanter warriors moved behind her, blocking her retreat.

"Best if you're disarmed." The captain plucked her long knife from its scabbard, letting the blade clatter to the deck.

Juliana felt naked without the knife, yet she forced herself to meet his gaze, putting a plea in her voice. "In my cabin?"

"*In your cabin!*" He roared with cruel delight. "Or perhaps I'll take you here, spread across your own deck?"

She gave him a brazen look. "I know how to please."

"Do you now?" A sharp gleam filled his dark eyes.

From the hungry tone of his voice, she could tell the hook was set.

63

The Knight Marshal

The Dark Sword preyed on the marshal's mind, clawing at his will, tempting him with promises of victory. He knew the sword was cursed, knew it would most likely eat his soul, but he saw no other way to save the maroon.

At dawn's first light, the marshal slipped from camp like a thief. Seeking solitude, he rode north, gaining some distance from the others. His horse picked a path through a forest of aspen mixed with ash and dusky cedar. Slanting sunlight speared the towering trees, the first hint of green coloring their branches. Birdsong greeted the sun, a half-forgotten melody so different from the bitter clash of steel. The marshal slowed his horse to a walk, letting the unexpected peace soothe his troubled soul.

Wield me!

The dark-damned sword intruded, denying him a moment's respite. Urging his horse to a canter, he rode till he found a mountain meadow large enough to be devoid of shadows. Securing his horse, he shrugged the harness of his great sword from his shoulders, *Sir Tyrone's sword*. For a dozen heartbeats he held the scabbarded blade in his hands. A true sword of the maroon, it had saved his life in many battles. He recalled the strange impulse to claim the sword from the knight's funeral pyre, like a boon from the gods. Unsheathing, the sword, he raised it to the heavens, saluting the Light. *"For Honor and the Octagon!"* His battle cry went unanswered, nothing but startled birds winging towards the morning sky.

Perhaps he should have left Sir Tyrone's sword with Lothar, but that would have meant relying on the dark blade for protection, and he wasn't ready for that. Somehow, in the depths of his soul, the marshal felt the dark sword should only be taken up as a deliberate choice, wielded for the right reasons. He wondered if it would make a difference. Perhaps he deluded himself, a desperate man grasping at straws. Fastening Sir Tyrone's scabbarded sword to the back of his saddle, the marshal turned and strode to the meadow's heart.

In the clear light of day, beyond reach of any shadows, he knelt, laying the bundled sword on the ground. A quick slash of the bindings and the furs and cloaks came unwrapped. The dark sword gleamed deadly in the morning sun, steel so black it seemed to drink the sunlight. Repulsed by the dark-damned steel, yet his gaze drank in the details. Coiled dragons entwined the cross hilt, the pommel fashioned into an octagon. Orrin Surehammer's maker's mark etched deep on the blade, as clear as when it was first forged. The sword was a masterpiece, forged to be wielded by heroes. *Boric's sword,* the first blue steel blade...corrupted to Darkness. Anger blazed through him. The sword was a trap, a taunt...yet a part of him longed to wield it. *A mere squire slayed sixty ogres, what could a sworn knight do?* Yet Baldwin had changed, paying a steep price for the sword. He stared at the dark blade, a promise and a threat. For the sake of the Octagon, he'd take the risk. "Valin help me."

He reached for the sword, grasping the hilt.

Pain flared through his gauntlets, a crippling cold. He hurled the blade from his hands.

It landed in the shadows.

He glared at the sword, realizing the dark blade was going to make him work for it. The marshal strode towards the blade, lying at the edge of the meadow. Naked branches cast shadows like grasping hands reaching for the sword. The marshal reached for the blade and then stopped short. The cursed blade was touched by shadow. Refusing to start in darkness, he levered his boot under the blade and flipped it towards the meadow's sunlit heart. He kicked it with his boot till it fell in sunshine, a dark slash across the snow-patched ground.

Once more, he reached for the hilt. Pain lanced his hand, a searing cold, but this time he was ready for it. "By Valin, you will serve me." He tightened his grip, enduring the biting agony. So cold, he half expected to see ice forming on his gauntlet. Gritting his teeth, he endured the agony, fearing his hand would blister and blacken to frostbite. Just when he reached his limit, the pain receded and strength flowed through him. The marshal gasped in surprise. Strength roared up his sword arm pouring into him...and with it came a heady elation, like a warrior's flush of victory after a hard-fought battle.

Grasping the sword with two hands, he claimed it for his own.

Raising the blade to the heavens, he swung it in the classical forms. *Slash of the eagle*, the diagonal cut flowed into *strike of the snake*. The marshal danced the steel, stepping through the forms.

Perfectly balanced, the dark sword cleaved the air with a deadly whistle. An extension of his will, it felt right in his hands. Laughing, he marveled at the five-foot blade. Light enough to be wielded with one hand, the dark sword blurred through each stroke, keening for souls. Twisting and turning, the marshal worked the forms, finding joy in the ancient patterns. A sense of jubilation roared through him. *He was the knight marshal of the Octagon and this was his sword!* Slash and cut, he ended with *strike of the dragon.*

The world came back in a rush. Sunlight warmed his face. He noticed the shadows had lengthened, nearly reaching his boots. He wondered how long he'd danced the forms...yet he was not tired. *He was not tired!* The marshal took stock of his body, realizing his shoulder no longer ached...and neither did his knee. He stared at the dark sword, *a boon from the gods.*

Laughter roared out of him...but then he caught himself, wondering if he was drunk...drunk on dark steel. The marshal sobered, but the feeling of elation did not leave. "You serve *me* now." The sword's strange whispers had fallen silent, as if the blade acquiesced...or bided its time, but the marshal put the grim warning from his mind.

Keeping the sword in his fist, he strode toward his horse. It was time to find the others. It was time to turn the tide of war.

64

Katherine

Dangling from a knotted rope, Kath hung from the side of the *Sea Sprite*. She'd needed a place to hide her warriors, but the open deck was too exposed. With the sea tamed to a dead-calm, she dared to hide her men on the outside of the hull. Twenty-two painted warriors dangled from knotted ropes, waiting for the order to attack.

Kath tightened her grip. Blind to what was happening on the deck; she listened to the sounds of the ship.

The cold gray sea lapped gently at the hull below, indifferent to their plight.

Overhead, sailors climbed the rigging to furl the sails, sending a signal of surrender.

Kath felt a dull thump shudder through the hull, as if the *Sea Sprite* was repulsed by the raider's lethal touch...and then she heard the grim thunk of grappling hooks. Sweat trickled down her back despite the biting cold. Kath smeared her doeskin boots against the *Sprite's* outer hull, seeking a better perch, fighting to ease the strain in her arms. Looking left and right, she nodded at Blaine and Sidhorn, giving them a reassuring smile...but lower down the rope, she caught the look of terror on Tangar's face. The hawk-faced warrior had lost his grip. Slowly sliding down the rope, he struggled for a better hold, but the rope slipped between his gloved hands.

None of her painted warriors could swim. Kath reached for him, but he was too far.

Her own grip slipped.

Tightening her hold, she watched in horror, unable to save him. Tangar fought to regain his grip, but the weight of arms and armor slowly dragged him down. Kath held his gaze, trying to leach the terror from his eyes. She heard his muffled gasp as the cold water lapped around him, slowly swallowing him whole. The hawk-faced warrior held her stare, even as the sea reached his chin. Flashing a fierce grin, full of defiance, he slipped below the sea without a sound, not even a splash to mark his passing.

Such bravery, Kath closed her eyes, stunned and angered by the loss. *By Valin, your courage shall not be forgotten.*

Kath's hand slipped.

Tightening her grip, she stared aloft, anxious for the signal to attack.

65

Juliana

The MerChanter captain flashed a lusty grin. "And where might your cabin be?"

Juliana gestured to the door tucked next to the aft stairs. "There, next to the stairs."

His gaze followed her gesture. "Good enough." He grabbed her arm as he snapped commands. "Balthar, fit the prisoners with shackles and chain them below. Gallwax, plumb the hold for treasure. Corway, secure the ship while I have my way with the strumpet."

"Aye, Lord." His men scrambled to obey, scattering across the deck.

"Come here, wench." The captain pulled her close, his breath stinking of sour ale. "I expect a rollicking good time," his gaze turned deadly, "or I'll turn you over to my crew for sport." His tongue licked the side of her face. Repulsed, Juliana squirmed away, but she did not get far. His fist clamped tight on her arm, pulling her close. "You'll do more than squirm when I take you." Laughing, he tugged her toward her cabin. As he reached for the latch, Juliana dove to the side.

The door slammed opened.

A snarling mountain wolf burst from the cabin. Loosing a primal howl, Bryx attacked. Teeth slavering, the wolf lunged for the lord, clamping his jaws on the MerChanter's throat. Blood sprayed across the deck. Bryx snarled, smothering the lord's nerve-shattering scream with a vicious growl.

The MerChanter warriors cringed backwards, stunned by the wolf, as if some monster summoned from lore had appeared aboard the ship.

Teeth bared and hackles raised, the big mountain wolf straddled the lord, shaking the corpse like a rag doll. Blood spatters rained across the raiders.

Chaos erupted across the deck.

66

Katherine

At the sound of the wolf's howl, Kath scrambled up the rope. She reached the railing in time to see Bryx straddle a MerChanter, his teeth savaging the man's throat to bloody shreds. The other MerChanters stood frozen, staring slack-jawed at the blood-spattered wolf as if he were a demon summoned from the netherworld.

Fierce and savage and totally unexpected, the huge mountain wolf evoked a primal fear, providing the perfect distraction.

Vaulting the railing, Kath leaped lightly to the deck, her sword whispering from its scabbard. Blaine was on her left, Bear on her right. She tugged her octagonal shield from her back, settling it on her left arm. All along the length of the *Sprite,* painted warriors climbed the railing as silent as death. Weapons bared, they fell on the MerChanters.

Kath's sword slid beneath the brigantine armor, deep into a MerChanter's back.

The man's dying shriek roused his comrades to battle.

Snarling in rage, the MerChanters erupted in motion. Whirling, they brought their tridents to bear. Steel clanged against steel as the ship's deck became a battlefield. Arrows thunked down from above, skewering the raiders. Sailors snatched up their long knives, lunging at the enemy. Bryx loosed a chilling howl, adding to the chaos.

Blaine waded into the fray, cleaving bearded heads with a single stroke of his sapphire blade. *"For Castlegard!"* The MerChanters fell back under the knight's fierce onslaught. Kath fought on Blaine's right, taking a hard stroke to her shield. Forming a wedge with Bear and Sidhorn, they battled their way into the heart of the enemy. Kath spied Juliana fending off a MerChanter with only her long knife. Juliana ducked a blow to the head, but lost her footing, slipping beneath the MerChanter's battleaxe. Kath leaped forward, intercepting the axe with her shield. The bone-jarring blow drove Kath to her knees. Gritting her teeth against the pain, she lunged upwards with her sword, taking the raider in the groin. He loosed a bloodcurdling scream, collapsing to the deck. Kath leaped aside, shielding Juliana. "Are you hurt?"

"No." Juliana scrambled to her feet, her face pale, her long knife clutched in her fist.

"*The oil!*" Kath hissed the command. "We've got to cripple the trireme and then get the *Sprite* away!"

Nodding, Juliana scrambled up the stairs to the aft deck while Kath battled her way toward the far railing. Stroke and parry, she fought her way forward but it was like swimming against a deadly current. The fighting grew fiercest near the railing, a thicket of clashing steel as MerChanters leaped from the trireme to the *Sprite's* deck, howling for vengeance.

Bear and Sidhorn cleaved a path to her side. Together they fought their way to the first cask. Hidden in the *Sprite's* hold, Kath had found three casks of lamp oil crucial to her plan. Sheathing her sword, she quickly freed the cork. Sidhorn heaved the cask to his shoulder with a grunt and then hurled it onto the trireme's deck. The cask hit hard. Cracking, it spurted a pale puddle of oil.

A trident snaked towards Kath's head. She ducked, avoiding the blow. Unsheathing her sword, she lunged forward but her blade skittered on scaled armor. Unharmed, the burly warrior grinned down at her. "*A wench!*" A lewd smile curdled his ugly face, gold coins winking in his beard. Anger blazed through Kath. She punched him in the gut with her shield and then slashed upward, opening a second smile in his bearded throat. "*Pig!*" She spat the word as he toppled over the railing.

A second MerChanter loomed over Kath, but an arrow took him in the shoulder before he could strike. Slipping past the wounded raider, Kath fought towards the second cask, but Grenfir was already there. The owl-faced warrior heaved the cask onto the trireme and then disappeared as the battle closed around him. Beyond him, the fighting was so thick she could not see the third flask. *Two will have to be enough.*

An arrow thunked from above, narrowly missing her head. Blood slicked the deck, making the footing treacherous. "*For Castlegard!*" She charged into the fray, hacking left and right.

Flaming arrows streaked overhead like sizzling comets. Kath grinned, praying Juliana's aim struck true.

Bryx appeared at her side, darting in to hamstring a MerChanter. As the warrior's leg crumpled, Kath slashed her sword across the raider's throat. Cut and parry, she fought to hold her position near the railing.

Flames erupted on the trireme, licking skyward with a billow of dark smoke.

"*Cut the grapples!*" Kath yelled the command. She hacked at the nearest grapple, the pronged hooks sunk deep in the *Sprite's* deck. On the third stroke, the rope sliced through, slithering over the side. Kath moved along the railing, slicing grapples while Bear and Sidhorn fought to shield her from the raiders.

Flames billowed on the trireme.

Wild-eyed MerChanters rushed the railing, leaping aboard the *Sprite*. They fought like fiends, wielding battleaxes and tridents with terrible effect. Caught in onslaught, Grenfir and Tomlin were cut down before Kath could reach their side. Howling for their loss, Kath pressed forward, attacking the nearest MerChanter, seeking vengeance with her sword. The *Sprite* ran slick with the blood of both sides.

From the aft deck, Juliana bellowed a command, "*Release the sails!*"

Overhead, the checkered sails dropped open like a thunderclap.

"*Hard to port!*"

The *Sprite* was slow and sluggish as a rheumy old man. The checkered sails gave a feeble flutter...but then the *Sprite* began to slowly turn. A slight breeze puffed the canvas, tugging the *Sprite* towards the south...but the trireme stayed locked with her prey, snagged by grapples. Kath stared in horror as the burning trireme lurched towards the *Sprite,* the two ships bound at the prow.

Flames spread along the trireme, turning the ship into an inferno. Kath cringed from the heat, fearing for the *Sprite*.

"*Cut the grapples at the prow!*" Kath screamed the command, but her voice was swallowed by the din of battle. "*Sidhorn, Bear, with me!*" Painted warriors formed a wedge around her. Fighting with grim ferocity, they battled a path towards the last grapples. Flames roared on the trireme, spilling a terrible heat onto the *Sprite*, like hell come calling. Kath reached the nearest grapple and began hacking at the rope, desperate to sever the two ships.

67

The Knight Marshal

The marshal spurred his horse to a hard gallop, the dark sword clutched in his mailed fist. Thundering down the mountainside, he wove a path through the trees. Spying an obstacle, he veered towards it, urging his stallion over the fallen log. They took the jump at a flying gallop, clearing the log with room to spare. Standing in the stirrups, he loosed a triumphant shout. Flushed with exhilaration, he scanned the forest for a foe, keen for a true test of the dark sword...and then he remembered.

He slowed his horse to a trot, shaking his head at the reckless ride. Lifting the dark sword, he glared at the midnight blade. "You are not the master. I am," But the blade did not reply.

Angling his horse toward the northwest, he eventually found the path. By mid-day, he reached the Broken Keep. An ancient ruin, little more than a circle of timeworn stones, the broken tower served as a landmark in the forest wilderness. Slowing his horse to a walk, he rode to the hill's crest. Dark stones crowned the hilltop like broken teeth, the remnant of another age. Spying a gleam of armor, the marshal fought the urge to attack. Rounding the tumbled tower, he found Lothar sitting upon a toppled stone, basking in the sunshine.

Lothar glanced his way, but otherwise he remained relaxed, his hands empty of weapons. "So you've claimed the sword."

"I have." The marshal lifted the sword, a flash of darkness in the sunlight. "And it is like no other I've ever held."

"Yet you remembered."

The truth came hard to his lips. "Just." The marshal dismounted, standing over his friend.

"You should have let me bear it."

The black sword came up, the tip aimed at Lothar's heart, but the knight-captain remained statue-still. By dint of will, the marshal lowered the dark sword, his voice a low growl. "Mine to wield."

Lothar gave him a measured look. "Yes, it's done. And now you're keen to wet the blade."

The marshal grinned.

"Brannock's found a patrol for you. Forty soldiers with two ogres among them."

Only forty, he quelled his disappointment. "A fair test of the blade."

Lothar scowled, "Sounds like a death-wish to me."

"I have to know."

"And the other sword?"

The marshal gave him a puzzled look.

Lothar gestured to the marshal's saddle. "Sir Tyrone's sword."

Disdain flashed across his face. "A mere pig-sticker compared to the dark blade." Slashing the bindings, he threw the scabbarded sword toward the knight. "Yours to wield."

Lothar caught it. "I'll keep it safe for you."

"I've no need of it."

"All the same."

"Forty, you say, and two ogres?"

Lothar nodded.

The marshal swung back into the saddle...but something gnawed at his mind. The words struggled to his lips. "Watch over the maroon."

Lothar nodded.

Their stares locked, a friendship remembered, so many years of duty and honor and battles well fought.

Wield me! The marshal shook his head, trying to keep his mind clear. "You'd best point me towards that patrol."

"Brannock will lead you."

A brown-clad scout ghosted out of the trees. Saluting, he kept his distance, standing on the edge of the ruins, a longbow in his fist.

A single archer, not much of a threat, the marshal silently soothed the dark sword. Turning his horse towards the scout, he said, "Lead the way."

The scout set off at a loping run. The marshal followed at a steady trot. They plunged down the hillside, forded a swiftly flowing stream and then turned towards the southwest. Brannock led him to a cliff overlooking a valley. Crouched on the rocky outcrop, the scout pointed below. The marshal nudged his horse forward. Peering over the edge, he saw the dark-cloaked patrol toiling up the mountain path. *Forty with two ogres,* the marshal grinned, eager to wet his sword.

Leaving the scout behind, he forged a path along the ridgeline, gaining a lead on the enemy below. Satisfied with his position, he put spurs to his horse and galloped down the steep hillside. Branches beat against his chainmail, as if to hold him back. Putting spurs to his mount, he bulled through the low scrub, emerging at the crest of the trail. The marshal slowed his horse to a stop. Bred for battle, his warhorse stamped and snorted, pawing at the dark earth. "Soon," he soothed the horse as much as himself. Taking a position in the center of the trail, the marshal blocked the way forward, the dark sword gleaming wicked-keen in his gauntleted fist.

He heard them before he saw them, the tramp of heavy boots, the clangor of armor, and the harsh breath of men climbing a steep rise. The first foe came into sight, a plumed helmet over dark armor, the black shield inscribed with a golden pentacle. The leader saw him and paused, a startled look on his face.

The marshal raised the black sword in salute.

The black-cloaked leader hesitated, reaching for his sword.

"Prepare to die!" The marshal charged. His warhorse rammed into the leader, forcing him backwards into the others. Leaning from the saddle, the marshal swung the dark sword like a scythe. With a single stroke, he took the man's head. The headless body took one last lurching step before crumpling to the ground. Head and helm bounced down the trail, a fitting herald.

Exhilaration roared through the marshal. *"Fight me!"* He galloped into the enemy, hewing left and right. His progress slowed as the weight of numbers pressed against him. Frustrated, he leaped from his horse, the better to slay them. Surrounded by enemies, the battle became a blur. Slash and turn, he moved through the forms, killing and evading. The dark sword thrummed in his hands, power flowing through him like a heady elixir. He dealt death like a god. The battle slowed, as if his foes fought in rusted armor. So slow, the marshal anticipated their every move. Strike and evade, he cut a path through their numbers.

An ogre approached, towering over him. The malformed beast wielded a spiked war club with deadly force, rending the earth with each blow...but to the marshal's one-eyed stare its movements appeared dull and slow, as if the beast swam through molasses. Avoiding a head-high swing of the war club, the marshal glided within the ogre's reach, slicing an arm from the shoulder. Blood gushed and the beast roared, the war club falling useless to the ground. Another cut and the marshal took its ugly head.

Raising the black sword in triumph, he felt invincible, he felt like a god. *"Fight me!"* The challenge roared out of him. Spying the second ogre, the marshal cut a path towards the hulking brute. The dark sword moved in a blur, slicing through flesh and bone and sinew. The ogre charged, smashing his war club in a head-high swing. Ducking low, the marshal slipped inside to hamstring the beast. The ogre toppled forward, crashing to the ground like a felled tree. The marshal leaped atop the beast's back. With both hands, he drove the dark sword down, plunging through armor and bone. Heart's blood fountained up. Wrenching the dark sword loose, he roared his prowess. *"Fight me!"*

A space opened around him, nothing but the dead and dying. The remaining soldiers cringed away. Dropping their weapons, they fell to their knees, begging for mercy.

"Spare us!"

"We yield!"

"Mercy!"

"No!" Anger roared through him. He craved blood not meek surrender. *"Fight me!"*

Enraged, he attacked, slicing at heads and hands, forcing the kneelers to reach for their swords. A few picked up their weapons, offering a feeble defense, but others simply cowered, covering their heads with their hands. Consumed with battle lust, the marshal slew them all, the kneelers and the sword wielders, hewing left and right, striking till there were no more to kill.

He staggered to a stop.

The trail was littered in corpses, heads and limbs, butchered and hacked, all dead save him. Surrounded by death, the marshal realized he was not even winded. Unscratched, unharmed, unscathed, he felt invincible. Elation thrummed through him. Victory was his. He raised the dark sword to the heavens. "I am a god!" His shout echoed against the mountains, a challenge hurled to all of Erdhe. *"I am the god of war!"*

68

Katherine

Kath cut the last grapple, willing the *Sprite* to separate from the trireme. A blistering heat beat against her, the crackling flames too near the ship. Checkered sails rippled overhead, stirred by a faint breeze, a mere tease of wind. The *Sprite* began to drift south, opening a small sliver of sea, but it was not enough. Sparks erupted from the trireme, releasing a belch of dark smoke. The MerChanter ship burned with infernal heat. They needed distance or both ships would be lost.

A trident thrust towards her face. Kath ducked, lurching backwards. Regaining her balance, she slashed at the MerChanter, but the looming enemy had the advantage of reach. Reeking of fish oil and sweaty leather, he barked a berserker's mad laugh, attacking with wild abandon. Towering over her, he stabbed at her with his trident, the triple barbs flashing orange in the flickering flames. Kath hacked at the deadly prongs, deflecting the blow. Stroke and parry she beat him back.

A sharp pain pierced her chest. Transfixed, Kath crumpled to the deck, her sword slipping from her hand. Her vision wavered, shuttering to darkness. The world flickered and blurred as if it was about to unravel. Something was wrong, terribly wrong.

Steel clanged in front of her face.

The song of swords snapped the spell.

Shrugging off the pain, Kath startled alert.

A trident speared towards her.

She flinched backwards.

A sword blocked the trident. Torkin grinned at her. "Just paying my debt, Svala." The wolf-faced warrior forced the MerChanter back with a vicious slash.

While the two men grappled, Kath scrambled for her sword. She rubbed her aching chest, but found no wound, no sign of blood. Befuddled, she swallowed her uncertainty and sprang to battle.

Fighting beside Torkin, she lunged towards the MerChanter, seeking a chink in his armor. Her sword slid beneath a bronze scale, piercing his side. Jerking away, he snarled, jabbing at her with his trident. Blood blossomed on his armor, yet still he fought. Enraged, he hurled his trident at her. She dodged the barbs, but was yanked backward, strangled by her cloak. A glance behind showed the trident pinned her cloak to the railing. Steel whistled towards her head. Trapped, she raised her shield blocking the blow. The battleaxe struck an arm-numbing blow. Wood splintered into a hundred shards. Deflected by her shattered shield, the axe shaved past her, narrowly missing her shoulder. Hurling the useless shieldstrap at her enemy's eyes, Kath drew a dagger from her belt. Pinned against the railing, she snarled up at the MerChanter, a sword in one hand, a dagger in the other, a poor match against a battleaxe.

The half-moon blade flashed sinister, reflecting the flames.

Kath braced for the blow.

A sword skewered the MerChanter from behind, the blade erupting from his gut. Surprise flashed across his bearded face as the light died from his eyes.

Bear shoved the corpse from his sword and then reached for the trident pinning her to the railing. Tugging the prongs loose, he hurled the forked weapon into the sea. "Are you well, Svala?"

"Well enough."

Canvas snapped and timbers creaked. The *Sea Sprite* began to move, slowly pulling away from the flaming trireme.

Across the deck, the wolf howled, a feral call to battle.

As the two ships separated, Kath hoped the MerChanters would surrender, but instead of yielding, they fought with desperate ferocity. Steel clashed and blood flowed. Corpses from both sides littered the deck. Standing shoulder to shoulder with Bear and Sidhorn, she cleaved a path into the enemy...and then she found herself facing Blaine. Kath lowered her sword. "Is it done?"

"Near enough." He gave her a weary grin, blood dripping from his sapphire sword.

The sounds of battle fell silent, replaced by the moans of the wounded.

Kath looked around her, finding too many friends among the dead and dying.

Blaine grinned. "Another victory."

Kath felt no elation. "Give the dead to the sea and tend to the wounded."

Suddenly too tired to stand, she crumpled to the deck. Everything ached, her arms most of all. Too tired to think, too weary to move, she stared out to sea. As if by magic, waves appeared, breaking the wind's stalemate, bringing the ocean to life. The *Sea Sprite* gained speed, scudding south. Across the widening distance, the trireme collapsed in hellish flames, a pillar of dark smoke marring the sky.

A shadow blocked the sun.

Kath looked up to see Juliana watching her.

"You'd best get that armor off."

Kath shook her head. "I'd rather sink like a rock than be eaten alive."

"Sometimes the sea offers hard choices." Juliana nodded, respect in her voice. "Your battle plan turned the tide."

"Your flaming arrows helped."

Juliana smiled. "A skill from my childhood." Her face sobered. "You saved my life...and the lives of my crew."

"If you hadn't come north, you wouldn't have been in danger."

"Perhaps not...or perhaps the danger would have found us anyway. Darkness looms close these days." Her voice dropped to a pensive whisper. "My sister sent me north for a reason." Her gaze narrowed. "What are you?"

Kath shrugged. "Someone who does not give up."

"No, you're more than that." Conviction laced the captain's voice. "You're a force to be reckoned with."

Kath studied the captain's face, the details so similar to her sword sister's despite the bright red hair. "Can you get us to Navarre?"

"The sea can be fickle. Storms, leviathans of the deep...and MerChanter raiders, there's always a challenge, but the gods willing, we'll make it home."

"I'll hold you to that, and the gods as well." Weary to the bone, Kath slumped to the deck. Befuddled by the sharp pain that had pierced her chest, she tugged aside her chainmail and gambeson, straining to see. Beneath her armor, she found no sign of a wound...but her skin tinged red in the shape of her gargoyle. *Her gargoyle.* An icy fear shivered through her. Something was wrong, very wrong. Making a quick check of the crystal dagger, she gripped Duncan's warrior ring and stared west, her gaze seeking the red comet. It was still there, hanging a thumb's width above the horizon, a mocking goad writ upon the sky, a reminder that time was running out. Somewhere in the south, the Mordant schemed, planting deceits and twisting souls, plotting the Battle Immortal...but the oldest harlequin was not the only threat. Kath rubbed her chest, grimacing at the strange warning, as if

Hell had opened all its gates, disgorging countless nightmares. More than one kind of evil stalked Erdhe. While she sought to escape the north, Darkness was winning. Darkness was laughing.

Epilogue

Wagons trundled across the snow-patched greensward bearing their bitter burden. Horns blared from the outriders, giving the 'all clear' signal. A trumpeter stationed upon the gatehouse barbican answered, welcoming the wounded home with a single mournful note. The silvery sound shivered across Castlegard, piercing the early morning mist.

Quintus rushed to the gatehouse, his dun-colored cloak pulled close against the gray drizzle. Out of breath, the pudgy healer scrambled atop a mounting block, the better to take the grim tally.

The great drawbridge descended, thudding across the castle's slate-gray moat. Soldiers moved to the second set of winches. Metal clanked as the great portcullis slowly rose. Sharp-toothed with fierce spikes, the metal grate clattered open like a hungry mouth. Fully raised, the sharp incisors disappeared into the barbican's mitered stone; proof the castle hid half its menace.

The first wagon drew near the drawbridge. Steam rose from the drays' broad backs, their muscled flanks streaked with sweat, their feathered hooves drumming a steady rhythm on the sturdy planking. The massive drays plodded across the drawbridge, gentle giants drawing their burden beneath the portcullis and through the tunneled passageway.

From the vantage of the mounting block, Quintus peered into each wagon as it passed, making a quick assessment of the wounded. His heart sank. Too many were in dire need of his help.

As the last wagon rolled past, he leaped from the mounting block to catch the wagon's tailboard, struggling to pull himself over the rim. Hands hauled him into the wagon bed. The wounded made space for him. Some muttered greetings, looking at him with hope-filled eyes, while others had the glazed look of the nearly dead. He moved among them, tightening bandages and sniffing wounds for signs of rot.

The wagons threaded their way through the castle's labyrinth of defenses, plodding between the outer walls raised by the sweat of ordinary stonemasons and the soaring inner walls of mage-stone raised by the wizards of a distant age. Shadows fell across the wagons, everything dwarfed by the majesty of the inner walls.

The wagoner clucked to his drays, urging them to a faster pace. Nearly home, the massive horses surged to an eager trot. They reached the second portcullis, the entrance to the inner castle, but the wagoner took too sharp a turn. The rear axle caught on the mage-stone gateway. Metal scraped against stone, both refusing to give. Heads bowed, the mighty drays surged forward like horses yoked to the plow. Wedged against mage-stone, the wagon tilted at a precarious angle. Quintus feared the wagon would tip...but then something gave way. Abruptly dropping to level, the wagon trundled through the gate.

A cold dread shivered down the healer's back. Needing to know, he leaped from the wagon and scurried back beneath the portcullis. Low on the mage-stone wall, he found something impossible. He gaped to see it. The wagon's metal axle had clipped the mage-stone...and left a scar.

Dear Reader,

Thank you for following Kath, Liandra and Blaine, through the kingdoms of Erdhe. Their adventures continue in the sixth book of the saga, The Prince Deceiver. More excitement awaits, so I hope you will read on.

I'd love to know what you think of my books and what you'd like me to write next (The Silk & Steel Saga is finished!). So tell me what you liked, loved and even what you hated. You can contact me at k_azinge@hotmail.com or on Facebook at Karen Azinger.

I'd love to hear from you.

And now I have a favor to ask. Readers have the power to make a book or a saga successful. The fate of The Silk & Steel Saga rests in your hands. Please support my books by posting a review on Amazon or Goodreads or any other social network. Even a one sentence review matters. I'd love to see my books on the silver screen, but that will only happen if you show the world you care. Thanks for your time and your support, I write for you. For Honor and the Octagon!

APPENDIX

CASTLEGARD

Three hundred years after the War of Wizards decimated the kingdoms of Erdhe, a group of knights banded together to protect the southern kingdoms from the ravages of the north. They claimed Castlegard, the great mage-stone castle left empty after the War of Wizards, as the seat of their power. Adopting the shape of the great castle as their symbol, they became known as the Octagon Knights.

To bolster their cause, the knights were ceded land running along the length of the Dragon Spine Mountains. Stretching from Castlegard all the way to the Western Ocean, this land became known as the Domain. A series of castles, keeps, and walls were built along the Dragon Spines, allowing the knights to control the mountain passes and deny access to the southern kingdoms. The Domain also includes the only iron ore mine in all of Erdhe to yield blue ore, the rare ore required to forge the knights' fabled blue steel swords.

As a sworn brotherhood of elite knights, the candidates forsake their lineage and their past when they win their maroon cloaks. Their symbol is a maroon octagon emblazoned on a silver shield.

KING URSUS ANVRIL, King of Castlegard and the Knights of the Octagon, Lord of the Domain, bearer of a great blue sword named *Honor's Edge*.

>-his wife, **QUEEN PHYLA**, died giving birth to their only daughter
>-their children:
>**PRINCE ULRICH**, First-born son of the king, a sworn knight of the maroon, former commander of the wall at Raven Pass, bearer of a great blue sword named *Mordbane*
>**PRINCE GRIFFIN**, Second-born son of the king, a sworn knight of the maroon, former commander of Dymtower

PRINCE GODFREY, Third-born son of the king, a sworn knight of the maroon, former commander of Shieldhold

PRINCE TRISTAN, Fourth-born son of the king, a sworn knight of the maroon, slain while leading a patrol into the steppes

PRINCE LIONEL, Fifth-born son of the king, a sworn knight of the maroon, former commander of Cragnoth Keep

PRINCESS KATHERINE, Sixth child of the king, also known as the Imp or Little Sister or Kath. As a female, the Octagon symbol of Castlegard is forbidden to her. Instead she uses the Anvril's ancient heraldic symbol of a red hawk attacking with talons outstretched on a field of white. The wielder of the crystal dagger, Kath travels into the far north with a small band of companions, seeking to slay the Mordant. After being tested in a trial by combat, Kath is hailed as the **Svala,** the war leader of the Painted People.

KATH'S COMPANIONS

DUNCAN TRELOCH - a master archer

SIR BLAINE - a knight of the Octagon who wields a blue steel great sword named *Stonecutter* by the Painted People

SIR TYRONE - a veteran knight of the Octagon with skin the color of ebony, often referred to as the 'black knight', a hero slain at the battle of Cragnoth Keep

ZITH - a master monk of the Kiralynn Order, father of Bryce

DANYA - a young woman who sought sanctuary in the Kiralynn Monastery with her mountain wolf, **BRYX,** she is called a 'Beastmaster' by the monks and a 'Beastspeaker' by the Painted People. She is locked in a healing coma after expending her magic to help take the Dark Citadel.

ARMY OF THE OCTAGON KNIGHTS

SIR OSBOURNE, The Knight Marshal of the Octagon, right hand of the King, a one-eyed man with a scar-crossed face, he wields a saber as his weapon of first choice, but then takes up

Sir Tyrone's great sword from the signal tower of Cragnoth Keep.

SIR LOTHAR, knight-captain of the Salt Tower, wields a battleaxe, close friend to the knight marshal

SIR ABRAX, knight of the maroon, champion of the sword, guard to King Ursus, he wields a blue steel sword named *Protector*

SIR RANNOCK, knight of the maroon, champion of the morning star

SIR BLAZE, knight of the maroon, champion of the mace

SIR BORIS, knight-captain of Holdfast Keep

SIR VARLIN, knight-captain of Dymntower

SIR KRISMIR, knight-captain of Shieldhold

SIR KILGAR, knight-captain of Cragnoth Keep

SIR DALT, knight-captain of Ice Tower

SIR GRAVIS, knight-captain of Sword Keep

SIR ODIS, knight of the maroon, champion of the lance

SIR ADLEMAR, knight of the maroon, champion of the claymore, wields a blue steel claymore named *Stalwart*

SIR TRASK, knight of the maroon, champion of the battleaxe, assigned to Cragnoth Keep as a punishment posting, slain at the battle of Cragnoth Keep

SIR TYRONE, knight of the maroon with skin the color of ebony, often referred to as the 'black knight', a companion to Princess Katherine, he was slain at the battle of Cragnoth Keep

SIR RAYMOND, branded as an unmade-knight of the Octagon, exiled from the Domain of Castlegard on penalty of death, sworn to serve the Mordant

SIR BROCK, wounded knight

SIR KEIFER, wounded knight

SIR ZAKERY, maroon knight

SIR TRADON, maroon knight

SIR MALVOY, a fresh-sworn knight of the maroon

SIR DEVLAN, a fresh-sworn knight of the maroon, died of battle wounds

SIR SPARLIN, maroon knight died of battle wounds

SIR CORBIN, a slain knight of the maroon

SIR TANCIL, a slain knight of the maroon

SIR MARIN, a knight of the maroon
SIR AMBROSE, a knight of the maroon
SIR WINTON, a knight of the maroon
SIR VARDINE, a knight of the maroon
SIR MELLOT, a knight of the maroon
SIR TOWLIN, a slain knight of the maroon
HADRIAN, master archer of the maroon, slain at Raven Pass
BENFORD, master archer of the maroon
BALDWIN, senior squire of the maroon, squire to King Ursus
MARTYN, squire to the knight marshal
TARGIN, a scout of the maroon
BARTLET, a scout of the maroon
BRANNOCK, master scout of the maroon
ORRIN SUREHAMMER, legendary Master Swordsmith of the maroon, first forger of blue steel blades, some believe he forged magical abilities into his blue steel blades making them destine for the hands of heroes
OTTO, the current Master Swordsmith of Castlegard's forge, responsible for the forging of all blue steel weapons
QUINTUS, the master healer of Castlegard

THE DARK CITADEL

The Dark Citadel is a forbidding fortress-city in the far north. Perched atop three-hundred-foot cliffs that overlook the Western Ocean, it is built upon a huge monolithic boulder. The tiered city has nine layers spiraling upward around the central stone monolith. Each layer holds a distinct class of people, with the poorest at the bottom and the palace of the Mordant at the summit. The stone monolith contains steps leading down to a cave, the ancient source of Dark power.

The Mordant's domain also includes the steppes, a vast sea of grass that serves as a desolate greensward for the Dark Citadel, a barren killing field that becomes the anvil of winter. The northern steppes are divided from the south by a dark wall studded with ten Gargoyle Gates.

The domain also includes the Pit, a massive crater with near vertical glass-sheer walls. Slaves live within the Pit, toiling within the Mordant's iron mines. Female slaves are forced to serve as whores for the Mordant's army. Residual magic in the Pit results in the massive abnormalities of newborns. Two new sub-races have been born and bred in the Pit: the Taals, an ogre-like sub-race with massive strength and limited intellect, and the Duegar, also called the Hounds of the Mordant, dwarves with the ability to scent magic.

The symbol of the Dark Citadel is a gold pentacle emblazoned on a field of black. The Darkflamme is the Mordant's personal battle banner, twelve feet of black silk ending in two silken tails of bright red flecked with gold, creating the illusion of darkness on fire

THE MORDANT- With over a thousand years of life, he is the oldest of the harlequins, the god-king of the north, the ruler of the Dark Citadel. He wields the Staff of Pain, an iron scepter with a red crystal focus inset at the top.
>   -his officers and priests:
>   **HIGH PRIEST GAVIS-** High Priest of the Pentacle, Keeper of the Trials of Return, the ruler of the Dark Citadel in the absence of the Mordant

DERMIT, an orphan lad of the middle tiers, his brother is taken as an acolyte to the priests

MARA- a serving girl assigned to the upper mines of the Pit, the niece of Honorable Elswin, later assigned as a seller of dung patties

BRUCE TRAGGER, a prisoner of the iron mine in the Pit, turned traitor to the rebellion

THE MORDANT'S COMPANIONS

DOLF, a master assassin of the Ninth Rank, posing as a manservant to the Mordant

BISHOP BORGAN, a bishop of the Pentacle serving as the seneschal to the Mordant

HOLDOR, a master assassin of the Ninth Rank

CAPTAIN GARVER, a guard captain from the Dark Citadel sent south to serve the Mordant

MAJOR TARQ, commander of the Eighth Fist, a cadre of elite guards from the Dark Citadel, sent south to serve the Mordant

CORLIN, a master assassin of the Ninth Rank

CRIMSON, a concubine from the Dark Citadel

AMBER, a concubine from the Dark Citadel

SABLE, a concubine from the Dark Citadel

ARMY OF THE PENTACLE

GENERAL HAITH- High General of the Army of the Pentacle, witness to the beheading of the Mordant in his prior life

GENERAL MARRIS- General of the Army of the Pentacle

TRANTOR, a snargon of the duegars, serves General Haith as his personal snargon (magic-sniffing duegar)

MAJOR RUGGAR, military aide to General Haith

VOLTRAN, chief handler of the gore hounds

CAPTAIN LYNDON, captain of the pentacle

CAPTAIN CROWLEY, captain of the pentacle

BRUTHUS, Master Torturer
CENTURION KIRKBEE, a centurion of the pentacle
CENTURION ERLINT, a centurion of the pentacle

THE PAINTED PEOPLE

An ancient people, forgotten by most of Erdhe, the Painted Warriors are the descendents of escaped slaves and runaway soldiers. Living in the shadow of the Dark Citadel, the Painted People have forged a fiercely independent warrior culture that spans a thousand years. Outnumbered and poorly equipped, they strike back at the Pentacle in lightning raids across the steppes, reaping steel and armor from their enemies. They make their home in a secret labyrinth of caves hidden in the Ghost Hills. Deeply spiritual, they invoke the power of nature by tattooing their faces with the images of beasts and birds, a spiritual melding of man and animal. Divided into dens depending on their tattoos, they are guided by the Ancestor, a shaman of mystical memories, and led by a Council of Leaders made up of representatives from all the dens. A secret and forgotten people, few in the southern kingdoms have ever heard of them.

THE ANCESTOR- Also known as the Keeper of Memories, the Old One. The Ancestor is always a woman, following a matriarchal line of mystical seers that stretches back for nearly a thousand years. As the spiritual leader of the painted people she is respected and revered but she does not rule as a queen. Instead she serves as a guide to the council of leaders.

VALDUR- a Taishan of the mountain lions, lost on a vision-hunter on a quest in the southern steppes. Attacked and left for dead by soldiers of the Pentacle, a patrol of Octagon knights found him and took him to Castlegard where he died in Kath's arms.

THE SVALA - After being tested in a trial by combat, **Kath of Castlegard** is hailed as the Svala, the long foretold war leader of the Painted People.

ROYCE- warrior leader of the mountain lions, leader of the Council

THERA- leader of the ravens, master healer

BRANT- leader of the boars

FANGGOLD- warrior leader of the wolves

RINGOL, warrior leader of the foxes

MERRICK, a raven-faced healer, second to Thera

CORWIN, painted warrior, hunts with Blaine
TOMKIN, painted warrior, hunts with Blaine

THE MAROON BAND

A brotherhood of painted warriors who claim the honor of protecting the Svala. Survivors of the original eighty warriors who witnessed Kath's trial at the Gargoyle Gates and then formed the vanguard for the attack on the Dark Citadel, they call themselves the Maroon Band. Their symbol is a tattered strip of maroon cloak tied to their right bicep. Their strips of maroon come from the extra length of Kath's maroon cloak, given to her by Blaine after the battle with the hellhounds. Led by Bear and Boar, they have become the personal guard to the Svala.

BEAR- a bear-faced warrior assigned to guard Kath, he refuses to reveal his true name, adopts the name of Bear and becomes Kath's personal guard and friend, wields a sword
BOAR- a boar-faced warrior assigned to Kath, refuses to reveal his true name, adopts the name of Boar and becomes Kath's personal guard and friend, wields a mace
TORVEN- eagle-faced warrior patrol leader
SIDHORN, eagle-faced warrior
TINGOLD- a wolf-faced scout, hunts with Blaine
GRENFIR- an owl-faced warrior
RUTHGAR - boar-faced warrior, hunts with Blaine
TANGOR- a hawk-faced warrior
PREN, a bear-faced warrior
CLEMIT- a wolf-faced warrior
VIN- an eagle-faced warrior
TARLY- a boar-faced warrior
BRIN- a wolf-faced warrior
BRINGOLD- fox-faced warrior
GRIFF, lion-faced warrior
TANGOR, a badger-faced warrior
TORKIN, a wolf-faced warrior
TANGAR, a hawk-faced warrior

TOMLIN, a wolf-faced warrior
TALBERT, a badger-faced lad, son of a maroon band warrior who died taking the Dark Citadel, he becomes a squire to Kath, adopted by the maroon band
CONIT, a badger-faced lad, son of a maroon band warrior who died taking the Dark Citadel, he becomes a squire to Kath, adopted by the maroon band

THE WOLF BAND

A band of wolf-faced warriors who have formed a den and are sworn to protect Danya.

NEVEN- the leader of the wolf band, a wolf-faced warrior hand-fasted to Danya.
BALTHUS- wolf-faced warrior

The MERCHANTERS

An ancient seafaring people, the MerChanters are the scourge of the oceans, born and bred upon the high seas. The self-styled Sea Lords claim no land as their own. Nomadic raiders, they rove the oceans in their great triremes, pillaging the coastal kingdoms for food, women and plunder. Their absolute leader is the Miral. Their weapon of choice is the trident. The MerChanters have a long-standing alliance with the Mordant. Little is known about the MerChanters other than rumors steeped in terror.

THE MIRAL - Absolute ruler of the MerChanters
LORD ASKAL - A MerChanter Sea Lord, captain of the *Dark Fin*
TORMUND - First Mate of the *Dark Fin*
BALTHAR- a MerChanter raider aboard the *Shark*
GALLWAX - a MerChanter raider, First Mate aboard the *Shark*
CORWAY- a MerChanter raider aboard the *Shark*

NAVARRE

The youngest kingdom of Erdhe, Navarre was founded less than four hundred years ago by a daring adventurer, Alaric Navarre, who rescued the youngest daughter of the king of Coronth from a band of sea pirates infesting the Orcnoth Islands. Gaining the king's confidence, and his daughter's hand in marriage, Alaric earned a freehold of land running along the Western Ocean where he later established his kingdom. His domain includes the Orcnoth Islands.

While defeating the nest of pirates, Alaric discovered a long-forgotten focus. The magic of the focus renders the royal house very fecund, enabling the queens to bear six to ten children in a single pregnancy. After using the magic, both the king and the queen become sterile. The focus is the secret strength of the royal house of Navarre, the bedrock for the succession to the throne. Alaric abandoned the convention of primogeniture, declaring that all of the tuplets have an equal chance to the throne. He instituted the practice of Wayfaring, a type of fostering where the heirs develop their greatest interests, striving to become excellent at a skill, a knowledge, or a trade, so that they can bring this knowledge back to Navarre and thus enrich the kingdom. After the Wayfaring, the King, together with the royal council, chooses the successor to the throne based on the talents, skills, and temperament that best fit the needs of the kingdom at the time. Navarre is well known for its uncommonly wise rulers…but with every great boon there is also a cost, the hidden focus brings with it the Curse of the Vowels.

The symbol of Navarre is a white osprey soaring on a checkered field of red and blue. The seat of their power is Castle Seamount, perched on a rocky outcrop on the edge of the Western Ocean. Navarre has always had close ties to the sea.

KING IVOR NAVARRE, the ninth ruler of the kingdom of Navarre
    -his siblings:

PRINCE IRWIN, died of poison, believed to be a victim of the Curse of the Vowels

PRINCESS INGRID, fell from the rigging of a ship and died, believed to be a victim of the Curse of the Vowels

PRINCESS IRIS, accused of murdering her two siblings, exiled to the Orcnoth Islands, she murdered her guards and then disappeared

PRINCE ISADOR, Commander of the Army of Navarre, advisor to the king, nearly fell victim to the Curse of the Vowels

PRINCESS IGRAINE, Counselor to the king, court historian, tutor to the Royal Js

PRINCE IAN, Royal Bowyer, advisor to the king

PRINCESS IVY, Captain of a royal merchant vessel of Navarre

-his wife, **QUEEN MEGAN**, a princess of Tubor
-their children known as the Royal Js:

PRINCESS JEMMA, Wayfaring with the Queen of Lanverness to learn the way of multiplying coins

PRINCE JUSTIN, Wayfaring to become a bard, he receives permission from the King and Council to travel to Coronth to try and overthrow the Pontifax, also known as the Dark Harper

PRINCESS JORDAN, Wayfaring with the Kiralynn monks to learn the art of war, felled by the treachery of the Mordant she is healed by the monk's magic, sword sister to Kath of Castlegard

PRINCE JARED, Wayfaring with the Octagon Knights to learn the way of the sword

PRINCESS JULIANA, Wayfaring with Navarre's merchant fleet to learn the way of the sea, merchant captain of the *Sea Sprite*

PRINCE JAMES, Wayfaring in Tubor to learn to become a vintner

PRINCE JAYSON, Wayfaring in the Delta to learn the secrets of a new water wheel

his retainers:

MARY, Prince Ian's wife

GARTH, Princess Ivy's husband
SIR LEON, an older knight, serves the queen on market days
MATILDA, a wise woman, an herbalist, a midwife, and a fortuneteller, a friend to Queen Megan
MASTER SIMMONS, the royal healer

CREW OF THE *SEA SPRITE*

JULIANA, Princess of Navarre, a Royal J, captain of the *Sea Sprite*
MARCUS, First Mate
SOOTHBY, Second Mate
WREN, lookout
JANGO, a sailor

THE ARMY OF NAVARRE

MAJOR COLSON, veteran major of the Army of Navarre
RAFE, a monk of the Kiralynn Order, a friend and advisor to Princess Jordan

LANVERNESS

Lanverness is an old kingdom, steeped in tradition, often relying on its wealth of natural resources and the shrewdness of its rulers to grow in prosperity and influence. Never fecund, the royal line of Lanverness has been forced to branch out several times over the centuries. The Rose Throne is currently held by the Tandroths. The Tandroths nearly lost the throne when the last king of Lanverness, King Leonid, failed to produce a male heir. The king survived a revolt and forced his noblemen to accept his only daughter, Liandra, as the heir to the Rose Throne on the condition that she marry a peer of the realm. Liandra is the only queen to rule a kingdom of Erdhe. Under Queen Liandra's stewardship, Lanverness has become the wealthiest kingdom in all of Erdhe.

The symbol of Lanverness is two white roses crossed on a field of emerald green. The seat of their power is Castle Tandroth, rising from the heart of Pellanor, the capital city.

QUEEN LIANDRA TANDROTH, ruler of the Rose Throne, also known as the White Rose of Lanverness, also known as the Spider Queen

-her husband, **PRINCE-CONSORT DONALD TERREL**, chosen from among the noble families of Lanverness, Lord Terrel was raised up to be the Prince-Consort to the queen on condition that he forsake his name and his lineage. He died in a hunting accident shortly after the birth of his second son. The heraldry of house Terrel is a red unicorn rearing on a field of green.
-their children:
PRINCE STEWART, heir to the Rose Throne, promoted to general of the Rose Army, wields a blue steel sword
PRINCE DANLY, spare heir to the Rose Throne, a condemned traitor
PRINCESS ASELYNN, died at birth
UNNAMED PRINCESS, died at premature birth, some consider it murder by poison

-her councilors:

> **LORD ROBERT HIGHGATE**, the Master Archivist, the
> queen's shadowmaster, right hand to the queen
>
> **MASTER RADDOCK,** deputy shadowmaster serving the
> queen, was once a condemned thief, rescued from the dungeons
> by the Master Archivist
>
> **SIR DURNHEART,** the Knight Protector, raised to a knight
> after the Red Horn rebellion, wields a blue steel sword named
> *Loyalty*
>
> **LORD TURNER**, a former member of the queen's council,
> boiled alive for treason, a harlequin of the Dark Lord
>
> **LORD SHELDON**, the Lord Sheriff, leader of the constable
> force of Lanverness
>
> **MAJOR RANOTH,** promoted after the rebellion, he serves as
> a military advisor to the queen
>
> **LORD SADDLER,** a goldsmith raised to a lord after the
> rebellion, the Master of Coin on the queen's council
>
> **LORD RICKMAN**, the Lord of Mines, responsible for the
> ruby, emerald and iron ore mines of Lanverness
>
> **LORD CENRIC,** a cat-eyed archer, he sits on the queen's
> council when he is in Pellanor, leader of Clan Hemlock, his
> loyalty is to the Treespeaker and the Deep Green, he wears a
> cloak of peacock feathers
>
> **LORD CANNING,** newly appointed Treasurer
>
> **LORD GRANGE,** newly appointed Royal Scribe
>
> **PRINCESS JEMMA,** princess of Navarre, a Royal J,
> wayfaring with the queen to learn the way of multiplying coins,
> sits on the queen's council as the representative from Navarre

-her ladies-in-waiting:

> **LADY SARAH JAMESON,** a distant cousin of the queen,
> principal lady-in-waiting to the queen
>
> **LADY MARTHA,** a lady-in-waiting to the queen
>
> **LADY AMY,** the youngest of the queen's ladies-in-waiting
>
> **LADY LINDSEY,** a lady-in-waiting to the queen

-other members of the court:

> **SIR CARDEMIR,** fifth son of the Duke of Graymaris, the seahorse knight, sent by the queen as an emissary to the Kiralynn monks, murdered by the Mordant's treachery
>
> **FREDERINKO,** an emissary from the Empire of Ur, a chained servant of the twelfth-fold prince of Ur, come to the Rose Court bearing gifts, sent to prepare for the prince's arrival
>
> **MASTER FINTAN,** an emissary from the Kiralynn Monks to the Rose Court, mysteriously murdered in the queen's castle
>
> **CAPTAIN BLACKMON,** captain of the queen's guards
>
> **HEALER CRANDOR,** a master healer of the Rose Court
>
> **LORD NEALY,** once a lord on the queen's council, he fell from favor and was banished from the queen's presence, owns a wealthy mansion in Pellanor

THE ROSE ARMY

PRINCE STEWART, heir to the Rose Throne, General of the Rose Army, wields a blue steel sword

-his officers and soldiers:

> **LORD DANE,** eldest son of the Duke of Kardiff, fostered to the Rose Court at a young age, a sword brother to Prince Stewart, second in command of the Rose Army, the symbol of the Dukes of Kardiff is a rearing griffin
>
> **KELSO,** serves as one of Prince Stewart's commanders
>
> **MATHIS,** serves as one of Prince Stewart's commanders
>
> **MAJOR BATTON,** a commander of the Rose Army
>
> **OWEN,** a soldier captured by the Flame, becomes a royal guard to Prince Stewart
>
> **CROCKER,** a scout captured by the Flame, becomes a royal guard to Prince Stewart
>
> **CRISPIN,** a soldier captured by the Flame, becomes a royal guard to Prince Stewart

LINGARD

Lingard is a fortress citadel, the second greatest fortress in Lanverness. The heraldic seat of the Rognalds, staunch supporters and loyal lords serving Queen Liandra. Their symbol is an iron fist on a field of yellow-gold.

BARON ROGNALD, a peer of the realm of Lanverness, a friend and staunch supporter of Queen Liandra, the ruler of Lingard, he is slain by treachery
-his officers, soldiers, and servants:

> **LORD RONALD ROGNALD,** eldest son of Baron Rognald, commander of the south gate of Lingard, heir to Lingard, becomes Baron Rognald on his father's death
> **CAPTAIN LEONARD VENGAR,** captain of the guard for Lingard
> **DASCHEL**, seneschal to Baron Rognald
> **KURT,** a soldier sworn to the baron, friend of Vengar
> **SANDRA,** a whore in Lingard, friend of Vengar

THE ORACLE PRIESTESS

Hidden in depths of the Great Southern Swamps, the Isle of the Oracle is an ancient wellspring of Darkness, a place of power where the Dark Lord reaches through the Veil to touch his dedicates. The Isle is currently ruled by a Priestess endowed with special gifts from the Dark Lord. At times of great prophecy, the Dark Lord releases his priest or priestess into the kingdoms of Erdhe to work his will.

THE PRIESTESS, the ruler of the Isle of the Oracle, the priestess to the sacred well, wielder of the Eye of the Oracle. She rarely uses her true name, but often goes by the name of Lady Cereus, a name given to her by Prince Razzur. Beyond the Oracle Isle, she takes the phases of the moon as her symbol, gold on a field of purple. After the collapse of the Flame religion, she claims the southwest corner of Coronth for her queendom, establishing a capital in the ancient city of Rhune. She assumes the name of Queen Selene, the Lady of the Moon. Silverspire is her castle.

-her servants and soldiers:

> **GENERAL TARMIN,** a major of the Flame Army, sworn to the service of the Priestess and promoted to the general of her army, he commands her forces in Rhune, a lover to the Priestess
>
> **LORD STEFFAN,** formerly the Lord Raven of Coronth, goes by the title of the Lord of Darkmoor, a dedicate to the Dark Lord, lover to the Priestess
>
> **BRAXUS,** a captain serving the Priestess, a lover to the Priestess
>
> **HUGO,** captain of the guards, a lover to the Priestess
>
> **LYDIA,** dark-haired handmaiden to the Priestess
>
> **TARA,** blond-haired handmaiden to the Priestess
>
> **MARIO,** a minstrel serving the Priestess
>
> **SAMUEL,** a stable hand serving in Silverspire
>
> **BISHOP TILDEN,** a fugitive, formerly a bishop of the Flame in the fourth brigade of the Flame Army
>
> **HINTON,** a scullery lad in Silverspire
>
> **GILL,** a pot boy in Silverspire

THE DEEP GREEN

The Deep Green is an ancient power reborn from the ashes of the War of Wizards. Rising from the ruins of a great city, the forest grows with frightening speed. Trees at the heart of the forest are giants, growing to more than thrice the height of normal trees, while the dense tangle of underbrush forms a nearly impenetrable barrier. The forest protects its own, a race of people with golden cat-eyes. Calling themselves the Children of the Green, the cat-eyed people live within the boundaries of the forest in a confederation of clans under the leadership of the Treespeaker.

Outside of the forest, the cat-eyed people are shunned as evil abominations, said to be born from the perverse mating of man with animals. The cat-eyed people are persecuted across the kingdoms of Erdhe, and often put to death by the 'white-eyes'.

THE TREESPEAKER, as old as the forest, she is a seer, a witch, the embodiment of the power of the Green. As the leader of the clans, she wears a cloak of snow-white swan feathers.
-her clan leaders:

>**CENRIC**, leader of Clan Hemlock, he wears a cloak of peacock feathers

>**AGATHA**, leader of Clan Aspen, she wears a cloak of blue jay feathers. She leads a faction that opposes dealings with the white-eyes

>**BRAN**, leader of Clan Ash, he wears a cloak of raven feathers

>**CAMILA**, leader of Clan Maple, she wears a cloak of orange kestrel feathers and is a member of the faction that opposes dealings with the white-eyes

>**DEREK**, leader of Clan Redwood, he wears a cloak of red woodpecker feathers and is a member of the faction that opposes dealing with the white-eyes

>**CONRAD**, leader of Clan Spruce, he wears a cloak of brown thrush feathers

>**LANA**, leader of Clan Oak, she wears a cloak of golden finch feathers

-her people:

JORAH SILVENWOOD, a ranger of Clan Cedar, killed in the Mordant's fire

RONAH, a ranger of Clan Hemlock

JENKS, a patrol leader of Clan Hemlock

MARTYN, an attendant to the Treespeaker

ALWIN, a ranger of Clan Hemlock

CORONTH

The kingdom of Coronth was long ruled by one of the oldest royal families in Erdhe. Tracing their lineage back to before the War of Wizards, the Manfreds struggled to maintain their kingdom despite the aftermath of chaos and famine caused by the magical war. Their descendents ruled in an unbroken line for over a thousand years until a preacher of the Flame God brought a new religion to the capital city of Balor. Enthralling the crowds with the miracle of the Test of Faith, the Pontifax gained a rabid following. In less than a year, the new religion consumed the kingdom, making the Pontifax more powerful than the king. Ruling from the pulpit, the Pontifax declared that only a true believer of the Flame God could wear the crown of Coronth, forcing the king, his wife, and all of his children to submit to the Test of Faith. When the searing flames consumed the royal house, the Pontifax became the spiritual and secular ruler of Coronth.

The symbol of house Manfred was a golden lion rearing on a field of blue. The new symbol of Coronth is a golden flame on field of red, the symbol of the Flame God. The seat of power is the capital city of Balor.

THE PONTIFAX, the supreme spiritual and secular ruler of Coronth, also known as the Enlightened One, he died in a public Test of Faith, his ill-timed death spewed a ripple of chaos through all of Coronth -his priests and counselors:

> **THE KEEPER OF THE FLAME,** Senior priest of the Flame, leader of the Confessors of the Flame, he becomes the ruler of Coronth and the leader of the faith after the death of the Pontifax, he remains in Balor
>
> **LORD STEFFAN RAVEN,** Counselor to the Pontifax, the leader of the Army of the Flame, his personal symbol is a black raven on a blood-red field, fleeing from his defeat in Pellanor, he goes by the name of Steffan of Darkmoor.

RADAGAR

Over five hundred years ago, fierce warriors from a distant desert kingdom followed the caravan route north and invaded Erdhe, carving out a vast new kingdom named Radagar. The proud conquerors maintained their desert culture, with the king and the royal houses taking many wives. The harems spawned an abundance of royal princes, all competing for the Cobra Throne. Treachery and poison became the tools of succession. Over time, the royal in-fighting caused the once great kingdom to dwindle in size and stature. The kingdom is now a shadow of its former size and strength. Radagar is known as a purveyor of mercenaries, poisons, and aphrodisiacs.

The symbol of Radagar is a red coiled cobra on a field of pea-green. Their seat of power is the capital city of Salmythra. The king of Radagar is known as the ruler of the Cobra Throne.

KING RAZZUR, the king of Radagar, the ruler of the Cobra Throne, he attained the throne by assassinating his half-brother, King Cyrus. A proud descendent of desert-born conquerors, he is the leader of House Razzur, his personal symbol is a black scorpion on a sky-blue field. As king, his royal symbol becomes a red coiled cobra on a field of pea green.
-his lords:
>> **GENERAL XANOS,** general of Radagar's mercenary army
>> **HAMID,** seneschal to King Razzur

THE KIRALYNN MONKS

Founded over two thousand years ago by a group of scholars, knights, and wizards, the Kiralynn Order has always presented an enigmatic face to the world, a face that is open yet closed. One hundred years before the start of the War of Wizards the monks withdrew from the southern kingdoms, retreating to their monastery hidden deep in the Southern Mountains. As if erased from the minds of men, the monastery's location disappeared from the maps of Erdhe. The memory of the Kiralynn monks has slowly faded, becoming little more than legend and myth. Yet select rulers of the southern kingdoms still receive scrolls sealed with the symbol of the Order. History has proven that these scrolls contain an uncanny prescience. Kings ignore the advice of the Order at their own peril.

The symbol of the Kiralynn monks is a Seeing Eye in the palm of an Open Hand. Their seat of power is their mountain monastery. The motto of the Order is "Seek Knowledge, Protect Knowledge, Share Knowledge".

THE GRAND MASTER, the leader of the Kiralynn Order, his/her identity is a closely guarded secret
-monks and initiates of the Order:
> **MASTER RIZEL**, a Master of the Order
> **MASTER GARTH**, a Master Healer of the Order
> **BRYCE**, an initiate of the Order, he studied to take his vows to become a monk and a healer but was subsumed by the Mordant's Awakening, becoming a prisoner in his own mind
> **MASTER AEROTH**, an ambassador monk sent to the kingdoms of Erdhe
> **MASTER ZITH**, a Master of the Order, accompanies Kath as one of her companions, he is the father of Bryce, he lost his left forearm in the battle with the gore hounds
> **RAFE,** a sworn monk of the Order, he has worn the blue for five years, sent with Princess Jordan of Navarre
> **MASTER YARL,** a master of the Order, an expert with a quarterstaff, sent with Princess Jordan of Navarre

MISTRESS ELLIS, a master of the Order

MISTRESS LENORE, a master of the Order

GILBERT, a monk of the Order serving as a hidden Wanderer in Pellanor

ASTER, a monk of the Order serving as a hidden Wanderer in Pellanor

MASTER FINTAN, an emissary from the Kiralynn Monks sent to the Rose Court, mysteriously murdered in the queen's castle

MASTER NUMAR, a master of the Order serving as a hidden Wanderer in Pellanor, posing as an apothecary

THE ZWARD

The Zward are sons and daughters of Kiralynn monks who choose to serve by the sword instead of the scroll. An ancient and secret order, they serve the will of the Grand Master. Their symbol is a small silver ring emblazoned with a fist holding an upright sword.

THADDEUS TOKHEART, also known as Thad, a captain of the Zward

DONAL, a sworn member of the Zward

BENJIN, a sworn member of the Zward

MARCUS, a sworn member of the Zward

The Front Cover artwork was done by the Australian artist, Greg Bridges. Greg's artwork has appeared on the book covers of many well-known fantasy authors. Thanks to Greg for the front cover, the spine, and the fabulous rendering of the Dark Sword. To see more of his art or to contact Greg, visit his website at http://www.gregbridges.com/

The Maps and the Back Cover artwork were done by a graphic artist from Oregon, Peggy Lowe. Her illustration of the two maps helps to bring the kingdoms of Erdhe to life and her portrayal of Stonehand conveys the wonder and mystery of mage-stone. Peggy can be contacted at her e-mail address, peggy@portfoliooregon.com

ACKNOWLEDGEMENTS

My dream of an epic fantasy continues, and like all my other books, it takes a lot of people to make this saga come true. First and foremost, to my husband Rick, who is always keen for the next adventure and always believes no matter the odds. To my best friend and sword sister, Danae Powers, who listened from the very first chapter. To my alpha and beta readers who continue to cheer for my books, Mike, Nick, Bill, Peggy, Diane, Bob, Mary, Christine, Ruthie and Gina, your enthusiasm means so much to me. To Greg Bridges for the totally awesome front cover and the book spine. To Peggy Lowe, graphic artist extraordinaire, for the back cover, the two maps and the logo, well done! To all of my readers around the world who are eagerly following the saga, I write for you. And to my mom, for everything, I so hope you know.

Other books by Karen L Azinger

Hungry to learn more about the kingdoms of Erdhe? Then consider reading my short story collection, *The Assassin's Tear*. The first story, *Prophecy's Twist*, explores the start of the War of Wizards, and the second signature story, *The Assassin's Tear*, explores the Dark Citadel from the perspective of a young thief.

The Assassin's Tear- Explore the medieval kingdoms of Erdhe, raid the tomb of the first emperor of China, survive an apocalyptic event Down Under, time travel to learn the secret of a famous scientist, and unravel the enigma of Dark Space in this collection of fantasy and science fiction tales from the author of *The Silk & Steel Saga*.

Power Writing: Make Your Genre Fiction Soar! - Fans of *The Silk & Steel Saga* will peek behind the curtain, gaining insights into the author's imaginings. Revisit the wonders of Erdhe with the author as your tour guide. Writers will learn how to color outside the lines and write bold genre fiction that will enthrall your readers and make your stories soar. *Power Writing* provides insights into many unique topics rarely discussed by other writing books. You'll find tips on writing magic, fortune telling, making maps and writing great battle scenes. Learn how to spice it up with romantic subplots and how to write with iconic images and tropes. Examples are drawn from genre masterworks like Tolkien's *Lord of the Rings*, Martin's *Game of Thrones*, Herbert's *Dune*, Rowling's *Harry Potter,* and the author's own *Silk & Steel Saga*, as well as examples from silver screen blockbusters like *Star Wars, Star Trek, Braveheart* and *Gladiator*.

ABOUT THE AUTHOR

KAREN L. AZINGER has always loved fantasy fiction, and always hoped that someday she could give back to the genre a little of the joy that reading has always given her. Twelve years ago on a hike in the Columbia River Gorge she realized she had enough original ideas to finally write an epic fantasy. She started writing and never stopped. *The Steel Queen* was her first book, born from that hike in the gorge. Before writing, Karen spent over twenty years as an international business strategist, eventually becoming a vice-president for one of the world's largest natural resource companies. She's worked on developing the first gem-quality diamond mine in Canada's arctic, on coal seam gas power projects in Australia, and on petroleum projects around the world. Having lived in Australia for eight years she considers it to be her second home. She's also lived in Canada and spent a lot of time in the Canadian arctic. She lives with her husband in Portland Oregon, in a house perched on the edge of the forest. Her seven book epic fantasy, *The Silk & Steel Saga,* is finished! This saga includes: *The Steel Queen, The Flame Priest, The Skeleton King, The Poison Priestess, The Knight Marshal, The Prince Deceiver,* and *The Battle Immortal.* Karen also published a collection of short stories, *The Assassin's Tear,* including two stories set in the kingdoms of Erdhe. She also published a book on writing, *Power Writing: Make Your Genre Fiction Soar!* You can learn more at her website, www.karenlazinger.com or at her Facebook page for The Steel Queen.